## THE MUSIC
## OF THE SPHERES . . .

From far-distant stars to alternate worlds, from our own possible futures right here on Earth to the artificial environment of a space station, there are some things which will always be part of the human experience, and music—the universal language—is very definitely one of them. So let twenty of today's finest composers of captivating tales take you on an unforgettable tour of the soon-to-be-discovered universe with such memorable stories as:

**"Bluesberry Jam"**—He'd lived in the traffic jam since he was a young child. Now he wrote and sang the songs of the road—while he waited with thousands of others for the jam to end—hoping that if he found the right song he would finally be free. . . .

**"To Drive the Cold Winter Away"**—Lythande, minstrel and mage, could not abide the frozen silence of a town where music had been banned. But what price would she pay for violating the Duke's edict?

**"Space Station Annie"**—For years she'd been the hottest singer to hit the starways. But now time was passing her by, and others were claiming the spotlight. Was there any place in the universe where a girl like Annie could get a second chance?

# SPACE OPERA

# More Imagination-Gripping Anthologies Brought to You by DAW

FUTURE NET *Edited by Martin H. Greenberg and Larry Segriff.* Such top visionaries as Gregory Benford, Josepha Sherman, Mickey Zucker Reichert, Daniel Ransom, Jody Lynn Nye, and Jane Lindskold explore the possibilities and promises, perils and challenges that await us in our virtual tomorrow. From a chat room romance gone awry ... to an alien monitoring the Net as an advance scout for interstellar invasion ... to a grief-stricken man given the chance to access life after death, here are sixteen original tales that you must read before you venture online again.

IT CAME FROM THE DRIVE-IN *Edited by Norman Partridge and Martin H. Greenberg.* Science fiction, horror, and the truly unbelievable—it's all here in an original collection that captures that almost-gone and highly romanticized era—the Age of the Drive-In Movie. Return now to that amazing time with such remarkable tales as: "The Blood on Satan's Harley," "The Thing From Lover's Lane," "Plan 10 From Inner Space," " '59 Frankenstein," and 14 other imagination-grabbing mini-sagas.

WHITE HOUSE HORRORS *Edited by Martin H. Greenberg.* Brian Hodge, Max Allan Collins and Barbara Collins, Graham Masterton, Bill Crider, Billie Sue Mosiman, Edward Lee, and their fellow wordsmiths reveal sixteen unforgettable stories of destiny and death, of the eerie and the inexplicable, of the might have been or the might yet happen—from Thomas Jefferson's use of a writing machine with a mind of its own ... to a voodoo-fueled attempt to seize control of Abraham Lincoln ... to Harry Truman's confrontation with a 150-year-old ghost ... to a president determined to mastermind his own exit from office.

# space
# opera

### EDITED BY
## Anne McCaffrey
## and
## Elizabeth Ann Scarborough

## DAW BOOKS, INC.
### DONALD A. WOLLHEIM, FOUNDER
375 Hudson Street. New York, NY 10014

### ELIZABETH R. WOLLHEIM
### SHEILA E. GILBERT
### PUBLISHERS

First Printing, December 1996

1  2  3  4  5  6  7  8  9

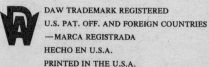

DAW TRADEMARK REGISTERED
U.S. PAT. OFF. AND FOREIGN COUNTRIES
—MARCA REGISTRADA
HECHO EN U.S.A.
PRINTED IN THE U.S.A.

# CONTENTS

# INTRODUCTION

When Anne McCaffrey and I were asked to edit an anthology together, our mutual interest in music was a logical choice of theme. Since several other music anthologies were in the works at the time, we were able to narrow it a bit more—to vocal music, an ongoing thread in the stories we both write.

The types of vocal music are somewhat different, although they overlap. My interest is primarily in folk songs—my first novel, *Song of Sorcery,* had at its core the ballad of the Gypsy Rover or the Gypsy Davey, as well as the story of the Brown Girl and those of Fair Ellen and Sweet William. I wrote the whole series, *The Songkiller Saga,* about other folk ballads and their importance in our cultures. So when the opportunity came to write my own story for an anthology I edited, I naturally chose "my" song, "Scarborough Fair," a derivative of one of the oldest folk ballads on record, for my theme. I even visited the town of Scarborough in England to get the setting straight.

But my own story was only part of the fun of doing this for me. I had the opportunity to work not only with Anne, but with other writers whose work I have long admired, such as Peter Beagle—who did his first anthologized story for us simply because of his own love for music—and Gene Wolfe, whose "Bluesberry Jam" goes through my head every time I'm in a bad traffic gridlock. Marion Zimmer Bradley, Alan Dean Foster, and two of Anne's other collaborators—Margaret Ball and Jody Lynn Nye—also had fascinating stories about the songs they love. Josepha Sherman and Elisabeth Waters contributed the sort of operatic tales that are more in Anne McCaffrey's area of expertise than mine, but are still purely enjoyable as stories, taking the opera back to its original roots in folklore and myth, embellished with a twist or two.

It's also a pleasure to introduce several writers who will either be totally new to readers—such as my friend Paula Lalish, a harper whose amusing story is her first mass-market sale—or more familiar as musicians than as writers. Leslie Fish has long been known in science fiction circles for her witty, gritty songwriting, as has Cynthia Mc Quillin, but each of them bring new facets of song and story to the anthology. Others, like Robin Wayne Bailey and Suzette Haden Elgin, are well known and enjoyed both as writers and filk/folk musicians.

All in all, it added up to the kind of creative cross-germination that I hope readers will find as stimulating as Anne and I did. I will now turn the introducing business over to Herself, the author whose singing pocket dragons, crystal singers, Harper Hall, operatic spaceships, and of course, the latchkey singers of our collaborative arctic planet Petaybee, are widely known and loved. Take it away, Anne. . . .

My involvement with music has been long-term—I could always sing louder than anyone else in the school choir, and the church ones which I joined wherever we were. I was a choir singer for eighteen years. My solo bits were always the descant because I could be heard above full organ, a seventy-member choir, and trumpets. My party pieces in those days were "The Shape of Love" and "In Questo Reggio" (which is a lot more difficult to sing than "Nessun Dorma"). Like Killashandra, my voice had a burr around G and F, but I could hit a fine E above high C that wasn't half bad—and nearly get down as low as C below middle C. So there was quite a range.

In Stuart Hall, where I spent a year and learned how to study, I was the Major General in the *Pirates of Penzance* spring show. I still remember all those words! At college I tended to the dramatic and comedic and once spent half of

Act II holding up the scenery in *The Importance of Being Earnest.*

When I was out in the wicked world working, I met Wilbur Evans and his wife, Susanna Foster, she of the brilliant coloratura voice (*Phantom of the Opera* with Claude Rains). They were to be lead singers at the first Lambertville Music Circus in New Jersey. I came along as script-rewriter, cook, and supporting actress. I even got my name in *Variety,* the one and only time, for my part as Margot, the Innkeeper, in *The Vagabond King.* I had a small part in the next week's *Bittersweet,* but after that, I had had my vacation and went back to work, going down to Lambertville for the weekends, to cook and help with the next week's rescripting. I had great respect for Wib's talents as director, singer, and actor, and plenty of admiration for Susanna, who never could understand why the pretty heroines said such daft things all the time. But I liked the weekly paycheck: so why did I end up as a writer who gets paid twice a year? Never mind.

I also met my husband that summer of 1949—and our special music was John Gay's *Beggar's Opera,* complete with the 78rpm (anyone out there remember them?) recording of Michael Wilding playing the part of Captain Macheath. I've still a great fondness for John Gay and all that beautiful music.

When my husband was transferred to Wilmington, Delaware, I joined some of the amateur groups that flourished at Breck's Mill. I worked in costumes, stage managing, as a singer, and also as stage director, ending, as I'm fond of saying, that phase of my career by stage directing Carl Orff's *Ludus de Nato Infanto Mirificus* with Clarence Snyder, the innovative organist of Greenville, Delaware. I enjoyed stage direction of opera, and produced *The Devil and Daniel Webster, Kiss Me Kate, Down in the Valley,* and I sang Queen Agravaine in *Once Upon A Mattress.*

But my favorite role, and one I did sixty-five times over several years was that of the Old Lady in Bernstein's first *Candide.* Wilmington had many well-trained singers to call on, people like myself, with talent but a preference for a reliable paycheck so the climate for such amateur productions was excellent and the productions scarcely "amateurish."

In 1965, we left Wilmington for Long Island. I did one more show, the Eve Arden character in *Babes in the Woods*—mainly because I could hold the B-flat in "Johnny One-Note" for the required thirteen measures. I still sang in choir but that was my last show. Here in Ireland I have the wrong accent.

One has to keep a voice going, as they say, and while my chest voice is still decent, I don't do the higher registers anymore.

As you may know, I've used that musical background in any number of my novels and stories. So I was glad to help Annie Scarborough edit *Space Opera* . . . for all those grand days, and the smell of Max Factor pancake and the applause and the sheer fun of it all.

# BLUESBERRY JAM
## by Gene Wolfe

Gene Wolfe was trained as a mechanical engineer. He practiced that profession for seventeen years, and was an editor on the staff of an engineering magazine for another eleven years; he left the position in 1984 to write full-time. He is the author of *The Fifth Head of Cerberus; Peace, Shadow and Claw;* and other books, including *Castle of Days,* which contains a good deal of advice on writing. He has won two Nebulas, two World Fantasy Awards, the British Science Fiction Award, and various other awards—most recently the Deathrealm Award for horror. He lives in Illinois with his wife, Rosemary.*

Sitting on the hood and thrumming the strings of his chevycap, Aldo watched the sun rise over the black semi in the slow lane. The question, Aldo told himself, wasn't when Mar' would come back. The question was, was there any particular weather that would be better for looking for a new song? Winter would be good. Folks sang more then. They'd feel sorry, too, and let you set in their cars to hear you, like they maybe wouldn't now. Rain would be good, too. Rain made you feel blue, and it was feeling blue that brought the best songs.

It wasn't that he made his songs up, not really. That was what people figured, and was why he could when they couldn't. Thinking made the songchopper go off and leave you to work out whatever was troubling you, like anybody would. What you did (this was the best) was scooch up on the hood and lean back with your back up against the windshield so the songchopper, the little sun-colored chopper that nobody ever saw, could see you weren't doing nothing and fly up behind and throw down a song to your ear. A new song.

*This way,* Aldo thought, scooching up on flaking steel still cold with night. He leaned back, eyes half closed.

> *"Yeller sun risin', climbin' up the sky,*
> *Sure to be a hot one, me-oh-my!*
> *Yeller sun, yeller sun, bring her back,*
> *Make her to lie in my Cadillac."*

He spaced out the final notes of the refrain, trying to make them sound as lost and lonely as he had felt since Ma'am pined, but only half succeeding. It was a good song, but not a new song; he had done it almost a year ago, when Mar' had been gone only half a day.

The airman was coming down the lane with his little putt-putting motor and his tire gauge. "How do," Aldo called. The airman and the other choppermen wouldn't hardly ever tell you their names.

"Howdy, Aldo," the airman answered. "How's your tires?" The airman always said that.

"Might have a look at the left front," Aldo replied; today he added, "I'd 'preciate it. Goin' to be gone a li'l."

Stooping to check the left rear of the Ryder in front of Aldo's Caddy, the airman glanced up in some surprise. "You takin' off, Aldo?"

He shook his head. "Just walkin' on down a ways, Airman. Maybe you and me could walk along together a while?"

The airman straightened up. "I go slow. Got to, to check the ones that look soft."

Aldo nodded, and his fingers found the strings of his chevycap.

> *"Airman, airman, stop at every wheel,*
> *Slow down, airman, let me get my meal,*

*Chowchopper's hummin', chopper wind's a-blowin',*
*Got to grab my supper, 'fore you get a-goin'.*

*"Yeller sun risin', climbin' up the sky,*
*Sure to be a hot one, me-oh-my!*
*Yeller sun, yeller sun, bring Mar' back,*
*Make her a bed in my Cadillac."*

"You certainly can play that thing," the airman said, and Aldo grinned.

*"Fast-lane gals, come kick at the moon,*
*Rattle your spoons, dance to my tunes!*
*Fast-lane gals are the best for a fling,*
*Don't want no ring, don't mind a thing!"*

His fingers tap-tappity-tapped the chevycap, as well as strumming the strings, so that it seemed for a moment he had three arms at least.

"I can't wait for you to go," the airman said, smiling, "but maybe you could catch up to me." He stooped to put his gauge on Aldo's right front.

"I'll go now," Aldo told him. "Soon's you do." He had not known that, not certain sure, until he said it; but it was true: he was ready.

"She is a mite soft." The airman put his hose on the valve, and the putt-putting of his little motor slowed and deepened.

"You think that gasman might come any time soon?"

The airman shook his head.

"I wouldn't want to miss if he did, that's all."

The airman straightened up again. "if you freewayers didn't run your engines so you could listen to your radios, you'd always have plenty of gas."

"I don't," Aldo said truthfully.

"Well, a lot do. Sometimes I can hear them switchin' off as I go down the lane."

"Sure. But we got to run—" He had said *we*. He counted the days since Ma'am had driven out of the jam. Thirty-three. Maybe thirty-four.

"Come along if you're comin'," the airman told him.

It was slow work, and there was no way Aldo could make it go faster, nothing he could do beyond cheering the way with a song. Sometimes he sang without playing; more often he played without singing, listening to the silver notes lose themselves in the hot morning sunlight. These were good strings, these new ones he had untwisted from the hood-release cable of the empty Toyota.

"How far you been this way, Aldo?" the airman wanted to know.

"Down to the Junction." It was a lie. He had been to within sight of the Junction, that was all.

The slatternly woman whose tires the airman was checking said, "I been past the Junction, just about to the Spaghetti Bowl."

Aldo stopped strumming. "I never heard tell. What's that?"

"I won't tell you," the woman said. "What do I need for you to call me a liar? You born in the jam?"

Aldo shook his head.

"Yes, you was!"

"I was three," Aldo explained. "I was ridin' with Ma'am."

"Who's that?"

Aldo looked up-lane in the direction of his Caddy. There were cars, trucks, and station wagons as far as he could see, but not one he recognized. He and the airman had come farther than he thought—that was easy to do. "Ma'am's my ma," he said. "Everybody 'round where we live, they called her Ma'am. She drove out 'bout this time last month. Little more, now."

"I'm sorry to hear," the slatternly woman said.

The airman straightened up, hooking the nozzle of his air hose to the side of the handcart that held the airtank and the putt-putting motor. "You get a bodybag for her, Aldo?"

"Yes, sir, Airman," Aldo said truthfully.

"Give her to the deathchopper for sanitary disposal?"

"Yes, sir," Aldo lied; he had put her in the trunk, which was what most people did—laid them in the trunk or in the back of the black semi in the slow lane. The black semi had been empty once; it was nearly a quarter full of bodybags now, and there were two or three who weren't in bags and lent the black semi a scent putrid yet almost sweet, a smell that became an overpowering stench when the big doors in back opened for somebody else.

Rapidly, as if she sensed the need for a change of topic, the slatternly woman said, "My son, he's born right here in our Tornado, an' he's 'bout as tall as you."

"There's lots taller than me," Aldo conceded. He pointed to a crack in the concrete. "You see that? That's grass, that green stuff there."

"Sure, I know."

Aldo nodded. "You would, 'course. Well, so would I, an' I do. I remember a whole lane that was all over grass, an' soft. I remember runnin' on it with some kind of a animal that was white an' brown."

"A dog?" the slatternly woman hazarded.

"I don't know. Might of been."

The woman nodded to herself. "What you doin' down this way? Takin' off?"

Aldo shook his head.

"They don't like it if you do. That airman, he'll tell."

The airman, who had moved beyond the slatternly woman's Tornado by this time, looked back at them. "That's what you think. I don't give a shit, Aldo. You're a nice boy, an' if you want to risk it, you do it. I won't tell anybody."

"I'm not," Aldo repeated.

"Usually," the woman said, "when somebody like you comes by, they're lookin' for somebody."

Aldo shook his head.

"Lookin' for a gal, most often." When Aldo said nothing, the slatternly woman added, "Don't people I don't know come by often, but when they do an' it's somebody 'bout your age, Aldo, they're lookin' for a gal."

"I'm not," he told her, "but I'll take one if you got one. Where she be?"

The slatternly woman laughed. "Not so long back I'd of said me, Aldo. What is it? What you lookin' for?"

Aldo hesitated. He was by nature candid, yet he hated to expose himself to mockery. "You goin' to laugh?"

"Not if it's not no joke."

"I'm lookin' for a song."

"Uh-huh." The slatternly woman chewed her lip. "You lose one? How you lose a song?"

"Forget, I guess. But I didn't." Aldo leaned against the side of her gray Tornado and ran his fingers over the strings of his chevycap. "I can remember every song that I ever heard. Ma'am used to say some's good at one thing an' some at another. Only I've seen some that wasn't good for nothin'."

The slatternly woman nodded her agreement.

"Me, I got somethin' I'm good at." The chevycap trilled happy laughter. "I'm good at this. I want a new song, though. I'm tired of the old ones."

"You the one that the chopper's lookin' for?"

Aldo froze. "Don't think so. The chowchopper?"

The slatternly woman laughed again. "Chowchopper don't look for nobody. We look for it."

"Used to look for Ma'am," Aldo declared, " 'cause she'd help. Tell who was sick, an' not to give to them that'd lined up twice. But don't look for me, now Ma'am's drove out."

"This was 'nother," the slatternly woman explained. "I never hardly seen it before. Not to talk to, anyhow. Yeller, it was, got Number Three an' TV on the side, all blue."

Aldo opened his mouth to speak, then closed it again. He had imagined a small chopper, so tiny that nobody could see it, but yellow as the sun. Songs had to come from somewhere, and it seemed to him that his own came from a place outside himself, brought to him by this song-chopper. Then, too, Mar'd gone off lookin' for a chopper that was—

"They was lookin' for somebody," the slatternly woman repeated. "Can you play that thing? Let's hear you."

Aldo nodded. "What kind you like?"

The slatternly woman hesitated, and something sly crept into her expression. "You're not lookin' for a gal, you said."

"For a song. A new one. I told you."

"But you know lots?"

"More'n most."

"You'll play whatever kind I want?"

Aldo considered. "If you'll tell me 'bout the song-chopper after."

Her eyes widened. "How you know they want to know 'bout songs an' stuff? I guess you been talkin' to folks."

"I mean the yeller chopper with the blue on. Song just sort of slipped out. What kind you want?"

"One 'bout a boy lookin' for a gal that he loves, a quiet one so we don't wake folks up. There's lots of those. You got to know one."

He nodded slowly. "Twenty, maybe. Maybe more. You'll tell me 'bout this yeller chopper after?"

She nodded, too.

"All you know?"

She raised her right hand. "As I hope out."

"All right, then," Aldo said, and woke his chevycap.

*"When I was a young man, 'bout seventeen,*
*I loved a li'l gal that they called Mary Dean.*
*Her hair was the brightest for six lanes 'round,*
*Her mouth was the sweetest a man ever found,*
*When late at night on the roof we'd lie,*
*Watchin' the dark clouds hurryin' by."*

The slatternly woman nodded. "I know this one."

"I didn't say it was no new song," Aldo told her, "only I was the first to sing it."

*"I loved her more than a man ought to love,*
*But she's gone up to the clouds above.*
*Now late at night when the clouds roll by,*
*I hear Mary callin', up there in the sky.*

*"We'd lie on the roof an' we'd look at the stars.*
*She called them the headlights of all God's cars,*
*Jammed up in Heaven where the dark clouds fly,*
*An' those was God's choppers, hurryin' by.*
*Someday, she'd say, the Blood of the Lamb*
*In them Heavenly tanks goin' to bust this jam.*

*"I loved her more than a man ought to love,*
*But she's gone up to the clouds above,*
*Now late at night when the clouds roll by,*
*I hear Mary callin', up there in the sky."*

The slatternly woman said, "I think there's more."

"Sure." Wishing he could wipe his eyes, Aldo plucked the last, plaintive note. "Only I doubt you want to hear it all."

"Besides," the woman continued argumentatively, "it's not 'bout no boy lookin' for his gal. Mary's dead."

Aldo shook his head.

"You're not lookin' for a gal. That's what you say."

"For a song, a new song. You were goin' to tell me 'bout that chopper an' the Spaghetti Bowl, too, only you never did."

Not to be gainsaid, the slatternly woman insisted, "You're lookin' for some gal. What's her name?"

"Mar'."

"She's not dead?"

"No," Aldo said. " 'Least I hope not. She's gone's all. Up that other way. That's why I'm walkin' this way, downjam."

"I don't figure I ought mess in this," the woman decided after a moment's thought. "I don't figure I can help none, an' I might hurt."

Relieved, Aldo nodded.

"That yeller chopper's mixed in, too. I could tell from how you looked. It come down lookin' for people, an' maybe it found some. That's all I know for sure anyhow."

She looked at Aldo as if she expected him to be angry, and he said, "All right."

"You must of rid through the Spaghetti Bowl when you was little. You don't remember nothin'?"

"Don't know, 'cause I don't know what 'tis. Maybe if I was to see it, I'd remember."

"Jam up on top of jam, heaped over jam." The woman made gestures, one hand flat above the other.

"You mean up in the sky where the choppers are?" Aldo was incredulous.

"That's right."

His fingers sought for the strings of his chevycap again. "Only a man can't go up there, can he? That jam's up there on top of this one, ain't it? A man couldn't get up to it."

"Sure you could. It leads on 'round."

He was not certain that he understood her, but he felt his resolution strengthen in a way that surprised him. "I'm goin' there." He ceased to lean on her car and took the first two steps of many, calling over his shoulder politely, "Thanks for tellin' me."

"Wait up!"The slatternly woman hurried after him. "I can tell you somethin' more that's worth knowin'."

Aldo stopped.

"You look over yonder in number two lane. See that orangy truck?"

"Behind the big camper?"

"That's the one. Don't pay any mind to that. Keep your eyes goin' on past," the woman pointed, "till you see— get up on our Tornado. Go 'head. You can't see it from here."

Aldo pulled off his shoes, laid his chevycap on the filthy concrete beside them, and vaulted up, helped by an easy toehold on the sill of the rear window.

"Now look on past that one you seen before. Way past, near to the h'rizon. Way on past's another orangy truck, real high. Higher than anythin' 'round there."

"I got it," Aldo called down.

"Well, you get up on that, an' you can see the Spaghetti Bowl for yourself. Look real careful then, an' don't get to thinkin' your eyes is playin' tricks."

\* \* \*

Aldo quizzed the airman when he caught up to him. "You know 'bout the Spaghetti Bowl, Airman? That lady was tellin' me 'bout it."

"I used to have that route." The airman fingered his gauge, eyeing a tire that appeared a little soft.

"You did? Where's there's jam up in the air?"

The airman chuckled. "They go over the edge up there. Know what I mean, Aldo? Over the side, an' it falls down on the ones underneath a lot. Lots of fightin' there."

"You don't go there no more, though? Go with your air, I mean."

The airman shook his head, and Aldo hurried on.

The sun was four fingers above the slow lane now, and the jam was awakening, roused by its brightening light. Small and soiled children emerged from doors, windows, and even sunroofs, shooed like so many sparrows by mothers determined to dust and tidy while the good weather lasted. Small dogs who had crept under their owners' cars to take refuge from the heat emerged to yawn, stretch, and attend to various strategically located tires in a way markedly different from the airman's, and to bark at Aldo. Sleepy men turned out with the children frowned, fingering knives ground from the leaf springs, and reached back into their cars for tire irons they thrust into their belts or slapped against their palms.

"I don't want your women," Aldo sang, "I don't want your chow. For I am but a stranger, passin' your car now. Smile at a stranger, let him walk past you. Then there'll be no danger when you go walkin', too."

A few of the men actually did smile.

*"I be from the center—Aldo is my name.*
*Never walked for hatin', never walked for shame.*
*Walkin' now for learnin', walkin' for a song,*
*Playin' to the people, as I walk along."*

It was not a new song, but it *was* a new verse; Aldo was seized by a premonition that he would find his new song in the Spaghetti Bowl. A splendid new song, and perhaps something else, something still more splendid,

too. What was it the slatternly woman had said about the
yellow-and-blue chopper? That it was looking for somebody? It sounded like it might be the one Mar' had gone
looking for; and although she had gone the other way and
he would be double danged if he'd go looking for her, she
might turn around and come back if she heard that the
chopper was in back of her.

*"I don't want your women, I don't want your chow.*
*For I am but a stranger, passin' your car now.*
*Smile at a stranger, let him go past you,*
*Then there'll be no danger when you go walkin', too.*

*"Once I seen a stranger, let him pass on through.*
*Once I seen a stranger. Maybe that was you?*
*Once I seen a stranger, give him my best smile,*
*Son, he says, I'm weary. I've walked many a mile."*

"I don't want your women, I don't want your
chow. . . ."
Aldo stopped playing to shade his eyes against the sun,
wondering if he could see the high orange truck from the
ground here. A man said, "Chowchopper ain't stopped for
us in two days." It was a conventional lie.
"Comin' now," Aldo told him, and pointed. Looking
for the distant truck, he had caught sight of the chowchopper, a minute speck of white and red, gleaming in the
level sunshine.
"Got to see where it goes." The man clutched Aldo's
arm. "Don't see why they don't always go to the same
place." He shaded his eyes, too. "Then we'd know, be all
ready."
"They used to, Ma'am said, only there was some that
killed for the cars close to there."
The man was gone, dashing down the lane. Another,
running too, pushed Aldo aside.
Aldo shook his head. When the chowchoppers had
always come at the same time to the same place, Ma'am
had explained, everyone gathered there in advance. There
had been frantic fights, not between a few men but

between hundreds; and in the end the strong had eaten twice, and the weak had not eaten at all.

Aldo had been too young to remember. Now, as he strolled along, keeping well to one side to give the runners room, he wondered whether it had really been worse than this. Wouldn't it be better to have chowmen with carts of chow walk down the lanes as the airmen and the gasmen did? They could leave, say, three chows at each car.

The runners were mostly women and children now, boys and young gals sprinting faster than most men, and women carrying babies and clutching the hands of toddlers, too wise to run.

"Down by that bus with the dog on it," a woman told him.

Aldo nodded, smiling. "That where it come last time?"

"Three times ago. Bus's due again." She picked up her child and hurried on.

The chowmen with carts would be mobbed and robbed, Aldo decided. Perhaps that had been tried already; if it had been, a day or two had probably been enough to show it didn't work. This way was the best after all.

He stood on the high fender of a tow truck to look ahead. Most of the runners were converging on two identical dark green delivery trucks in the slow lane. That was where the chopper had come last, most likely. Women and children, with a few gals and elderly men, were assembling at the bus with the dog picture.

As he watched, the chowchopper flew past the green trucks, the men who had waited there running behind and waving. Soon it had passed the dog bus too, so low it seemed like it had to stop any minute. Chopper wind whipped his long hair like a gale as the chopper appeared to settle—not quite landing, because there wasn't room for that—between a red Horizon and a LeBaron convertible with the top gone.

Aldo stood back, watching the chows handed out, each in its own crispy crackerbox. His mouth watered.

"Ain't you goin' to get in line?" a gal nearly as pretty as Mar' inquired.

"I'm not from 'round here," he explained. "I'll go the last."

She winked at him, then ran up the line to a tall young man with bumper-wide shoulders; there was a rumble of protest as the tall young man made room for her, a rumble he silenced with a glance.

Aldo got in line, too, standing at the end behind a girl child who did not quite come up to his waist. "We won't get nothin' back here," the girl child informed him. "Hardly ever do."

He grinned at her. "I'm not real hungry. You get one, maybe you could give me your box?"

"No," she said firmly; and then, "Prob'ly I won't neither. I hardly ever. Ma gives me some of hers, sometimes."

"That's good."

A policeman came down the line, his chow tucked under his arm and a waterbottle in his hand. He wore slopchopper clothes like everyone else's, but the badge on his shirt and the gun at his waist marked him.

He stopped beside Aldo. "Not from 'round here, are you?"

"No, sir."

"Passin' through?"

"Yes, sir. I'll be gone 'fore the next one comes."

When the policeman seemed not quite satisfied, Aldo added, "I went past your car real early. I figured it'd be better not to waken you."

"Next time you wake me up," the policeman said.

"Yes, sir."

"An' don't you give no trouble here."

"No, sir."

"You be gone next time I see you."

The girl child tittered, but Aldo said politely, "Yes, sir. I sure will be."

When the policeman himself was gone, the girl child said, "He don't have no more bullets."

"I figured." Aldo called to mind what Ma'am had always said. "He tries, though." For a few seconds he debated the best way to explain that order was better, and that those who tried to keep order deserved respect and cooperation even if they had no bullets, or had never had any.

He crouched and held out his chevycap so the girl child could see it, then ran his hand across the strings. "That's music. Hear?"

"It's pretty," she said.

"See here?" He displayed his callused fingers. "These right here tells each string what to play. If they was to get cut off, the strings'd still be there," he sounded one with his thumb, "an' they could talk, but they couldn't play no music."

"You could with that one." Interested, she touched his thumb.

"It'd be a long time till it learned the work. See now—"

There was a disturbance in the line ahead of them, angry yells and an unmistakable sound.

"I got to go," Aldo said, and stood up; he was running before the final word. Not once but twice he had clumsily, foolishly, dropped his chevycap. The sound it had made when it struck the concrete was engraved on his memory, and through the tumult coming from the front of the line he had heard that sound.

The new player was down. Aldo threw himself on top of him, sheltering him with his own body. A kick struck his ribs, another his right cheekbone, but the shouting men were crowded too closely to swing their feet effectively. A gal's voice called, "Don't get him. He didn't do nothin'."

Aldo clutched his chevycap to his chest as a kick landed on his shoulder.

A man's voice shouted, "That's enough! Hold on!" And abruptly it was over. Strong hands grasped Aldo and lifted him to his feet. "This a friend of yours?"

Aldo managed to nod. "He sure is." He was looking around for the new player's chevycap; it was so strangely shaped that he nearly missed it, almost like Ma'am's plug-in.

"How come you was back at the end, an' not him?"

"I guess he didn't know," Aldo said. "I ought to of told him."

"You." The wide-shouldered young man nudged the new player with his foot. "Get up."

The new player rose, his face streaked with sweat and dirt. Aldo handed him his strangely shaped chevycap.

"You get back there to the end," the wide-shouldered young man said. "You eat after us. All of us."

"Come on," Aldo led the new player away. "You made it out of a muffler, didn't you? I never seen one like that."

The new player nodded, slinging his chevycap behind his back on a thin strap. "A replacement muffler, from one of the muffler shops, and about a foot of tailpipe. Good replacement mufflers are better than the original equipment kind." He was older than Aldo, who found it hard to guess just how old.

"You cut those fancy holes with a li'l file? There's a man by us had a file. He let me to use it one time."

The new player nodded. "You've got to hollow them out, extract the parts used to muffle the sound of the engine. The S-shaped holes are helpful then, and afterward they let the sound come in and go out."

"It get busted? I'd like to hear it." They had reached the end of the line.

"I'd be happy to play it for you," the new player said, "I owe you a great deal more than that." He offered his hand. "I'm Tim Benson."

Aldo shook it. "Aldo Berry." He hesitated, then grinned. "We both of us play, an' we both got names with a *B*."

The stranger smiled, unslung his chevycap, and said, "You get in front, Aldo. You were here before, and you're hungrier than I am, I'm sure."

The girl child looked back at them pessimistically. "You won't neither one get nothin'. Me neither."

"What's your name?" Tim asked. "You know ours, if you were listening. I'm Tim and he's Aldo. Who are you?"

"B'neice."

Tim stooped to bring their eyes to a level. "How old are you, B'neice?"

The girl child stamped. "Ber-nice!"

Tim straightened up. "Older than you should be at your age, I imagine. Well, Bernice, you may not get any food, but I can give you a song."

His fingers stroked the strings of his strangely shaped chevycap, educing tears of gold that left Aldo breathless.

> *"The minstrel boy to the war is gone,*
> *In the ranks of death you'll find him;*
> *His father's sword he has girded on,*
> *And his wild harp slung behind him.*
> *Land of Song! said the warrior bard,*
> *Though all the world betrays thee,*
> *One sword at least thy rights shall guard,*
> *One faithful harp shall praise thee. . . ."*

As the final notes died, it seemed to Aldo that somehow all the people had been snatched away, leaving him alone with a new song more beautiful than he had ever believed a song could be. The steady *whick-whick-whick* of the chopper blades sounded like the beating of a giant's heart.

At last he managed to say, "You got to learn me."

"No, you have to teach me, Aldo. You have to teach me to be as brave as you are. You play and sing yourself, don't you? You implied a moment ago that you did."

Men eating from crackerboxes were crowding around. One handed Aldo a strip of cold bacon, and he stuffed it into his mouth, nodding.

"May I try your instrument? You may try mine, of course, if you like."

Mutely, still chewing, Aldo handed over his chevycap and received Tim's strangely shaped one.

Tim touched Aldo's strings, a sound like the laughter of the moon. "One's a trifle off, I think." A glance was enough for him to understand the way in which Aldo's strings were held and adjusted, and he tightened one. The broad-shouldered young man who had rescued them gave him a pecan Danish, which he gave to Bernice.

Again Aldo's strings sounded, yearning tones telling of unsullied valleys down which rivers rushed shouting to the sea.

*"Oh, Shenando' I long to hear you.*
*Away, you rolling river.*
*Oh, Shenando' I long to hear you.*
*Away, I'm bound away,*
*Across the wide Missouri.*
*Oh, Shenando' I love your daughter.*
*Roll away, you rolling river.*
*Oh, Shenando' I'm bound to leave her.*
*Away, I'm bound away,*
*Across the wide Missouri!"*

There was a short silence after the last muted chord, then wild cheering.

"That's just like me!" Aldo felt overwhelmed by a rush of ideas. "Me walkin' on. I'm goin' to the Spaghetti Bowl, but I'll stay right here with you, Tim, or go back even, if you'll try to learn me."

Tim shook his head and stepped away, smiling and accepting the praise of those he pushed to one side. "If you're going to the Spaghetti Bowl, Aldo, then I'm going to the Spaghetti Bowl, too; and I'll try to teach you, if you'll teach me."

When they had passed the green delivery trucks and were practically alone, Aldo said, "You didn't get nothin'. I saw somebody gifted you with a roll, but you give it to that li'l Bernice girl."

"I wasn't really hungry," Tim explained, "and she was." He was studying Aldo's chevycap.

"If you wasn't hungry, why'd you get in the line an' get beat up like that?"

For a dozen strides, Tim was silent. At last he said, "I didn't know—didn't know they would beat me as they did, when they realized I was a stranger. I want to be one of you for as long as I can, to eat and sleep and work like you, while I play and sing. I saw men forming a line, so I

joined it. I have a great deal to learn here, I know, and I
hope that you'll teach me."

"I got a crackerbox." Aldo held it up. "Somebody
gifted me with it when we were leavin'. It's empty, but
the cracker's good. You want to try some?"

"A small piece, perhaps. Thank you, Aldo."

From the lid, Aldo snapped a fragment half the size of
his hand, then broke off another for himself, which he
munched as he watched Tim nibble at his. "Don't bite
down hard, 'less you got good teeth."

"I understand. It's best to let one's saliva soften it first,
I suppose."

"Or water, if you got a bottle." Aldo took a deep breath.
"There's the offroad way an' then the freeway, Tim.
We're the freewayers, but you're a offroader, ain't you? I
won't tell."

"An outsider? Yes, I am. It's obvious, I suppose."

Aldo chewed and swallowed. "You got clothes like us,
though."

"I suppose I do." Tim glanced down at his dirty white
shirt and ragged trousers. "Where do you get them, by the
way? I've been wondering about that, as well as hundreds
of other things."

"The slopchopper brings them. It don't come down an'
pass out like the chowchopper does, though. Just goes low
an' slow, while the chopper men throw out."

"Warm clothing for winter, I imagine and cooler
clothes—like these—in summer."

Aldo nodded. "Shoes're hardest, shoes an' boots.
There's never enough for everybody."

"Yet you're wearing out yours by walking to this
Spaghetti Bowl, whatever it is."

"It's where the jam goes up in the air, bendin' 'round
over itself. That's what I heard. I never been there. Well, I
guess I was, once, only I was real little."

"Before all these cars and trucks stopped."

"That's it, back 'fore the jam. An' my shoes. . . ." Aldo
fell silent, and to cover his embarrassment took another
bite of crackerbox.

"What about them, Aldo?"

"You know, I guess."

Tim shook his head. "I know very little, believe me. I didn't even know that the jam, as you call it, existed, until I found myself in it."

"They're offroad shoes, used to be. They was about like this when I got them, not much better."

"Someone gave them to you?"

"The slopchopper, like I said. You ever see one like that before?" Aldo pointed at a hot-pink car with a dragon pictured on its side, with huge rear wheels and small front ones far out in front of its engine.

"Yes, as a matter of fact, I have." Tim nibbled again at his crackerbox. "The clothing is not new when you receive it. That's what you're trying to tell me, isn't it, Aldo?"

"It's your clothes," Aldo confided miserably, "offroader clothes. You turn them in, Ma'am said, to churches an' things, an' they pick them up an' put them in the slopchopper, an' then throw them down for us."

When Tim did not speak, Aldo added, "Ma'am was my ma."

"I see."

"Can I tell you 'bout her? You might make a song 'bout her, an' it'd make her proud if she knew."

"I don't believe I can make songs," Tim said.

Stunned, Aldo could only stare.

"Do you do that? Compose your own songs?"

Aldo nodded. "That's why I'm goin' to the Spaghetti Bowl. I'll get a new one there, but I can't say how I know it. I just do. The songs you sang back there where the chowchopper was—didn't you make them up?"

"They are old songs, both of them. Very old. I—all my life I have listened to folk songs, mostly on tapes and compact discs. There were years, decades actually, in which it was my sole pleasure. I have tried, once or twice, to make such songs myself, but every attempt has been a ludicrous failure." He handed Aldo's chevycap to him. "Sing me one of your songs, please, Aldo. A song you made yourself."

Aldo passed the strangely-shaped chevycap back to

Tim, together with what remained of the crackerbox, then
cradled his own rounded and familiar chevycap in his
arms, delighting in the feel of it.

> *"In all this jam, there's none like Ma'am,*
> *For playin' nor for singin'.*
> *She drove the land, her an' her band,*
> *And set the big rooms ringin'.*
> *Her face you'd see on your TV,*
> *'Most any day you played it,*
> *She'd like to gone, with me, her son,*
> *But this here jam's delayed it.*
> *Now here we stay, an' pray each day,*
> *That them that tried to get her,*
> *Will try ag'in, helped by the win',*
> *Or best in stormin' weather.*

"It's not a very good song," Aldo apologized when he
had finished, "an' that's all the farther I ever got with it,
an' now she's drove out."

Tim looked at him quizzically.

"Dead, it means."

"I understand. You loved her very much, didn't you?"

"Sure I did. It's not no disgrace for a man to love his
ma, is it?"

"I'm certain it isn't." Tim's fingers touched the strings
of his chevycap. "I still think about mine at times. Not as
often as I should, I'm afraid."

"You talked 'bout folksingers."

Tim nodded.

"That's what I am, Ma'am said. But Ma'am was
Country an' Western. She's real big, or was, an' when the
jam hit, a whole lot of offroaders come here tryin' to get
her out, only they dropped gas on them."

" 'Now here we stay, an' pray each day, that them that
tried to get her, will try again, helped by the wind, or best
in stormin' weather,' " Tim quoted.

"That's it. She always said if it'd been rainin' hard or
the wind blowin', they'd have got her out. Then she'd of
hired somebody to stay with her car an' move it when the

jam broke. Back in them times, they thought it was goin' to. The airmen an' so on, they still talk like that."

"But you don't believe it. After seeing the condition many of these cars are in, neither do I."

"Thing is," unconsciously, Aldo let his voice drop. "Now there's a chopper comin' around takin' people out." He cleared his throat. "That's what some say. I ain't sayin' it's true, and I don't believe it myself. This gal that I know, Mar's her name, she went off lookin' for it."

"But not you. You didn't go."

Aldo hesitated, biting his lip. At last he said. "Nope, I didn't. Chopper must of brought you, Tim. Was that the same one?"

"I have no way of knowing."

"I guess not. Mar', she wanted us to. Wanted us to go off lookin' for it together, like. I said she'd get herself killed. I said, you wait here, an' I'll go look, if you're so certain sure of this new chopper that didn't nobody saw."

Tim pointed. "What's that up there, Aldo?"

"I don't see nothin'. I said I'll go, Mar'. You stay here safe. Only she thought I wouldn't look, not hard. Just go up a ways an' come on back. She waited till I was asleep. I doubt—"

Something had seized Aldo by the throat, choking him. "I doubt she got far, but I hope she did."

Tim did not reply, studying a dot that Aldo could see now as well as he.

"Only I'm not lookin' for her. She's got to learn, I guess." He sighed. "I'm going this other way, and maybe— That's a yeller chopper, ain't it?"

"Yellow with blue or black lettering on the side," Tim confirmed. "I can't quite make out the lettering."

"Looking for somebody, a lady I met said." Aldo stood straight again, peering into the sun's glare. "Askin' after them, I reckon. I never did see one so little as that."

"Four persons," Tim told him. "Three passengers, and no cargo to speak of. I've ridden in similar helicopters."

"There's a pull-off over there!" Now it was Aldo's turn to point. "It's fixin' to set down there sure. Come on,

Tim!" He ran, and arrived in time to watch the yellow chopper land.

A slender gal in tight-fitting blue clothing of a design Aldo had never seen before stepped from the chopper, followed by a sulky-looking man with a black box on his shoulder. The black box ended with a headlight, and when he and the gal had gotten out from under the chopper blade, he aimed that part at Aldo and the other freewayers who had gathered at the sound of the chopper.

The gal said something Aldo could not hear, then shouted back toward the chopper, "Phil, you're going to have to turn that thing off." She held something in her hand that brought tears to Aldo's eyes; he pushed through the crowd to look at it.

"Hello!" the gal said, and this time her voice was as loud as the choppermen's, when they talked down from their choppers. "I'm from WWBB. Many of you listen to our radio affiliate on your car radios, I know, and they used to get calls from you on your cell phones."

The crowd stirred.

"I'm from the television station. You older folks must remember television."

As loudly as he could, Aldo said, "I got a TV in the back of our car. Still works, too."

"Wonderful! You haven't forgotten us."

Tim rejoined Aldo, and Aldo confided, "Ma'am had a thing like what she's talkin' into, only there wasn't nowhere to plug it in. I put it in her one hand and her plug-in chevycap in the other when I laid her in the bag. Her gee-tar's what she called that plug-in chevycap."

"So if there's anyone here like that, I hope that he or she will step forward," the gal was saying. "Any of you that exemplify the burgeoning culture of the traffic jam."

No one moved.

"In compliance with our agreement with the Department of Transportation, we will have to bring you back here *when your engagement is finished.*" She gave heavy emphasis to the final words. "Meanwhile—and it may be for quite a while—you'll be treated royally. The Consort-Hilton's a wonderful hotel, and you'll get new clothes and wonderful meals. You'll earn a great deal of money, also, and be able to buy things to take back with you, for yourself and your friends."

A voice from the crowd called, "There's somebody back at the chowchopper that sings real good!"

"That's you," Aldo told Tim happily, but Tim did not appear to hear him.

The gal was approaching them. "What's that you've got? Our other crew discovered a girl last night who had something like that."

It was a moment before Aldo realized she was addressing him. He held up his chevycap for her to see. "Was her name Mar'?"

"Marta? No, I don't think so. Mary something." The gal turned to the man holding the black box. "Do you remember her last name, Don?"

The man holding the black box shook his head.

"Do you play that?" the gal asked Aldo. "And sing?"

Shyly Aldo nodded.

"Then you've got to play and sing for us." Smiling, the gal caught his arm. "Don's camera will let the brass back in our building see and hear you."

"Tim's better," Aldo told her.

"Fine, we'll hear Tim by-and-by. But right now we want to hear you. Sing something about the traffic jam."

Aldo's fingers brushed his strings, trying to find which one Tim had tightened; the whole chevycap sounded better than it had, he decided, though he could not be sure which had changed. "You want me to commence?"

"Any time that you're ready," the gal told him. "Don't be nervous."

He grinned at her. "Playin' an' singin's the only time I ain't never."

> *"Choppergal, choppergal, dressed so fine,*
> *Got a gal already, an' that gal's mine.*
> *Your chopper's still hummin', chopper wind's a blowin',*
> *Got to grab a seat in back, 'fore you get a-goin'.*

*"Yeller sun risin', climbin' up the sky,*
*Sure to be a hot one, me-oh-my!*
*Yeller chopper hummin', take me with you,*
*Got to kiss my Mar' again, 'fore the day's through.*

*"Yeller chopper hummin', take me out this jam,*
*Good-bye Cadillac! So long, Ma'am!*
*Sure to make you proud, Ma'am, sure to marry Mar'.*
*Goin' to be what you were, goin' to be a star.*

*Yeller sun risin'—"*

The gal motioned him to silence as the crowd applauded. "That's enough, I think. That was . . . ?"

"Aldo Berry," Aldo said. The crowd clapped again.

"And you, sir. What's your name?"

Two men were pushing Tim forward. "Tim Benson," he said.

"Will you play for us, Tim? We'd like to hear you."

Tim shook his head; Aldo said, "Go 'head, Tim." Then to the gal, "He's so fine! Wait till you hear."

Tim got his strangely shaped chevycap positioned, one hand on the tailpipe, the other on the strings.

*"My gentle harp, once more I waken*
*The sweetness of thy slumbering strain,*
*In tears our last farewell was taken,*
*And now in tears we meet again. . . ."*

It seemed to Aldo a very long time before the listeners, including the gal, began to clap. After a moment he joined them, and was still clapping some minutes afterward, when the others had stopped.

"That was—was just so wonderful, Tim," the gal said, "but won't you play something about this mess? This traffic jam that's kept so many of you here so long? That's what they want to hear at our building."

Tim looked at her, then at Aldo, and at last back to her. "I'd like to go with you. That's been my dream, to sing folk music and be a star, as Aldo said." He spoke so softly that even Aldo, standing beside him, could scarcely hear the words. "But I don't know any. Only one, actually."

"Then sing that."

"It's Aldo's. May I, Aldo?"

"Sure thing. You go 'head, Tim." Aldo tried to smile, and discovered to his own surprise that the smile was real.

It was his tune, the tune he had found three years ago, long before Ma'am pined. Yet it was changed, the way that people were supposed to change up in Heaven, no longer half serious and half funny, but as lonesome and lovely as a bird overhead—a swift and solitary bird that flew over the jam, looked down at the cars, and was gone.

> *"In all this jam, there's none like Ma'am,*
> *For playin' or for singin' . . ."*

It was over before it had begun, or so it seemed, and the cheers of the crowd were still echoing from the cars and trucks of the jam and the concrete sides of the bleak buildings beyond the safety wall when the chopper lifted, bearing Tim away.

Waving, Aldo withdrew into the cramped files of the stationary vehicles, knowing that no one had so much as noticed that he had left. "Goin' to that Spaghetti Bowl anyhow," he said under his breath, "and I best be movin', be somewhere else when the chowchopper comes back."

All through the long, hot afternoon he threaded his way between motionless automobiles, as he had been doing all his life, until at last, with evening closing in, he realized that there were fewer than a dozen separating him from a towering orange semi. Studying it, he could not be certain that it was the one the slatternly woman had pointed out that morning; but he would not go much farther that day, and there seemed to be no harm in looking, in trying to see the Spaghetti Bowl today before the last light faded.

From the front bumper, he was able to scramble up onto the hood without much trouble; but the high cab was surmounted by a varashield nearly as tall as itself, which was bound to prove difficult. Standing at one side of the hood with his left foot where the vanished windshield should have been, clinging to the mirror mount, he found a secure purchase for his right foot on the top of the door and swung himself out.

The melody of the song he called *In All This Jam* played itself in his mind. He hummed it under his breath when he had scrambled onto the rusting top of the cab—not his tune, but the melody as Tim had played it, powerful and haunting.

Aldo got to his feet (very much crowded and obstructed by the varashield), and put one hand on top of it and the other on top of the huge semitrailer. How had Tim made it to sound like that? Aldo sought to fathom Tim's technique as he swung himself up, catching his heel on the top of the semitrailer and rolling over onto it.

The light was fading fast, but the haze that had obscured the jam that morning had dissipated. Peering downjam, his eyes traced its dwindling ribbon back toward the loftiest buildings, until it was visible largely as a streak of night among the brightly lit office towers.

Below him an engine started, coughed, and died.

Somebody tryin' to charge up, he told himself, so he can listen to that radio.

A cool breeze caressed his sweating cheek, very welcome after the afternoon's heat. Briefly he wondered whether the people down on the roadway could feel it. If they did, there had to be hundreds of hundreds as grateful as he was, which was nice to think about. He tried to picture them, the thread of freewayers strung over a thousand miles.

The office towers, he noticed, were rendered visible only by their lights now, outlined against a sky much darker than that above his head. A jagged spark divided it as he watched; he held his breath, counting to thirteen before the rumble of the thunder reached him.

His chevycap was on the roadway, safely hidden, he hoped, behind the right front wheel. He looked down, but there was no one groping there. He would have to get it and find somebody with a not-too-crowded car who would let him inside before the rain came, let him sleep inside in return for his songs.

"Better than's on them radios," Aldo muttered under his breath, and knew that he spoke the truth—and that the new song, still small and weak, was already scratching at the doors of his mind. Tim was on the little yellow song-chopper, that was certain sure, because just by the scratchings Aldo could tell that it was not just a new song but a new kind of a song, not like any he had ever heard or sung. Tired though he was, he felt himself standing taller from the thrill of it.

Still a long way off, but nearer—much nearer—than it had been the first time, lightning split the sullen sky beyond the city. For a fraction of a second Aldo saw, as though in a dream, nightmare lanes of cars and vans and trucks looped and swirled like the yarn of a raveled sweater, trucks and vans and cars hanging in the air, an impossible creation that appeared to mount up and up without limit.

He leaped from the top of the semitrailer then, hitting the concrete with the first big drops, his feet together, rolling as he fell.

Half a minute more and he was up again, with his chevycap in his hand and his hair streaming, his chevycap singing of wind and rain and lightning, and of a fury that had scarcely begun.

> *"Big storm a-risin', a-risin', a-risin',*
> *Big storm a-risin', the risin' of the free!*
> *Clear to the h'rizon, the h'rizon, the h'rizon,*
> *We're the freewayers, an' we'll be free!"*

Rhythmically, compellingly, Aldo's chevycap snarled like an angry cat, a fighting tomcat driven to the last extremity and furious for war.

> *"Blood on the roadway, blood on the wall,*
> *Blood on our irons, our knives an' all,*
> *Waitin' since the jam began, s'posed to be a day,*

*S'posed to be a month, a year.*
*Someone's got to pay!"*

As he began the chorus again, he heard a new voice
that sounded as loud and as angry as the thunder singing
with him.

Before the chorus was over, a third voice, and a fourth,
had joined theirs.

*Back in the summer of '94 a whole hash of police agen-*
*cies stopped a bus on the road between Chicago and Mil-*
*waukee, convinced that there was a murderer on it, and*
*incidentally stopped all traffic both ways on a heavily*
*traveled eight-lane highway. The driver and some passen-*
*gers got out, and for hours and hours after that, the cops*
*deployed snipers, yelled through bullhorns, and jumped*
*up and down. The media (who covered this four ways*
*from breakfast) felt sure that they were in contact with*
*this guy, presumably by radio or cell phone, and that he*
*had hostages. As darkness closed in, and people stuck in*
*this incredible traffic jam began to crash through*
*farmers' fences, the SWAT team rushed the bus. There*
*was nobody inside, and as it turned out the driver and*
passengers had been telling the cops that.

*I wrote an account of all this to my friend Todd*
*Compton, and he suggested I write a story about a traffic*
*jam that hadn't moved an inch in years. I know Todd's a*
*lot smarter than I am, and I'd just done a story called*
*"Flash Company" based on folk music and wanted to do*
*another in which my hero could write his own music and*
*lyrics.*

# TO DRIVE THE COLD WINTER AWAY

## by Marion Zimmer Bradley

Marion Zimmer Bradley was born in Albany, NY in 1930, and sold her first story to *Fantastic/ Amazing Stories* in 1949. Her novel about the women of Arthurian legend, entitled *The Mists of Avalon,* was a national bestseller, remaining on the New York Times bestseller list for four months. She is also known for her novels and anthologies about Darkover. Currently living in Berkeley, California, she has completed two prequels to *Mists of Avalon—The Forest House* and *Forest of Avalon*—and edits *Marion Zimmer Bradley's FANTASY Magazine,* as well as the yearly anthology *Sword and Sorceress.*

It was very dark, and needles of sleet pierced the grayish-black sky as the mercenary-magician Lythande fought to find a path through the freezing cold. The only light was that fitful radiance which came from the snow itself, and, at a distance, there was a faint glimmer as if a single candle sent a stray gleam of light.

*Hell, the abode of lost souls—if there is one,* Lythande thought, *must be very like this: silent, cold, and dark.*

The minstrel struggled through the dark silence toward the faraway light, carrying a lute in an ornately decorated woolen case, hoping that the damp cold would not damage it. It seemed that the idea of song—the very idea of sound itself—had died out in the cold silence.

The single candle shone through the encompassing dark

like a metaphor for Light against Darkness; a symbol of the great struggle of humankind. The night seemed to grow even more still as Lythande struggled up the stone, snow-covered steps outside the inn.

The minstrel thrust open the door, entering the common room with footsteps which sounded loud against the silence. Indoors it was nearly as cold as outside. A fitful and inadequate fire barely revealed the faces of the few scattered men and women in the gloom, seated around the pitiful hearth. Lythande shut the door quickly to keep any more of the already-diminished heat from escaping, then stepped into the room itself, shaking snow off the cloak that hung down over the minstrel's shoulders. A man in an innkeeper's leather apron turned to look at Lythande.

"Here, you don't want to bring that lute in here," he said glumly. "Our Duke's forbidden music in this town."

"Forbidden music?" Lythande had never heard of such a thing. "Then how are minstrels to get their living?"

It was a ridiculous interdiction, and Lythande knew it when the innkeeper said morosely, "T'Duke says it would be better if none of 'em got a living a'tall; rogues and vagabonds all of 'em, he says."

This was a reason to cause alarm to Lythande, for, because the laws of the Adepts of the Blue Star—the magical order to which Lythande belonged—forbade her to be known as a woman, she traveled in disguise as a man, and a minstrel-mage. As a minstrel, she earned her coin, for magic never put beans on the table. Still, she did no harm to anyone who did not justly earn it.

"Now I resent that," Lythande said. "For, while I am a vagabond and wanderer, no man can call me a rogue. Nor any woman either."

"And why are you a wanderer, when even a fool would be at home?" asked the glum innkeeper. "In weather like this, a man should stay by his own fire, and not steal the warmth from another's."

"But alas, I have neither home nor fire," Lythande said, "nor beasts nor child nor wife. And I wander because it is a *geas* laid on me: that I roam the world till the Last Day shall come, the great battle of Good against Evil and

Chaos. I am sworn to fight against Evil, and I must say your Duke's ban on music strikes me as great evil. For what save music distinguishes man from beast? The birds may sing better, but they have no lore of ballads. Any dog may bark louder, but none of their noises sings, or makes sense. And, but for music, what is it that distinguishes the work of man from that of any beast? What else is there that men can do, that some beast cannot do better?"

"Why, you argue as good at t'Duke's preacher," said the innkeeper without much interest.

"Give me a pot of beer," Lythande said wearily, not willing to continue the dispute. She felt that whatever was said or not said, she had won her argument and defended her way of life. That was enough.

"No beer in this town," said the innkeeper. "Duke says wine is a great evil, and beer worse. Ain't there no men in your town beat their wives and children when they been drinking?"

Once again, Lythande had never heard such a thing. "You might as well say that my lute should be outlawed, because I could use it to beat someone over the head till he is dead. Some men use knives to kill. By that logic, if you call it so, should I tear my meat with my teeth like a dog? Because some men are beasts, should all men suffer, and none use reason?" The innkeeper was looking blank, so Lythande abandoned the argument. "Coffee, then?"

"No coffee, neither," said the innkeeper. "Coffee contains wicked stimulants."

"Whatever folk drink in your town against bad weather, then," said Lythande, sick of the argument and only wanting to be warm. The innkeeper set before her a cup of steaming straw-colored fluid.

"Herb tea. 'S good for you; contains none o' them wicked stimulants," the innkeeper remarked. Lythande, touching the colorless stuff to her lips, could well believe it. It tasted almost as flavorless as it looked.

At least it was warm. Not very, but since Lythande could not drink it, due to another restriction imposed by her Order, she could at least enjoy what little warmth the vapors gave off. She made no comment on that, however, lest they should suddenly decide that warmth was evil, too, because it was so much sought after.

"A bowl of soup then, served in your warmest bed-chamber," Lythande commanded. "And a fire, if that is possible," she added wryly.

A maid conducted her to a cheerless bedroom, but at least a small fire was burning, though fitfully. Lythande sat down by the fire, wondering what would happen. The maid went to fetch the soup, and Lythande remained by the sluggishly burning fire, and thought about the ban on music in this town. She had never heard of anything like it in all her long travels.

"But is it laid on me that, because I think the ban on music is evil, I must be required to fight it?" she wondered. By the peculiar laws of magic, the very fact that she could formulate the question probably did mean just that.

But how, then, was she to fight it? Had she done enough by protesting it? No, for the ban still existed. She groaned, knowing that she must do something more.

But what? This, at least, Lythande knew she need not concern herself about. The answer would soon appear in her life, probably causing her great trouble and discomfort. Lythande resolved to sleep while she could. If the answer—and, thus, the problem—was to come to her, it would come, but there was nothing she could do to bring it nearer or to delay it. Like curses, most blessings came home to roost eventually.

The maid arrived, gave Lythande a small bowl of thin and not-too-tasty soup, then scurried back downstairs—most likely to huddle near her tiny fire with the rest of the miserable folk. Lythande ate only a few spoonfuls before rolling herself in the clammy blankets, and, after a while, she fell asleep.

When she woke, the pale light in the room told her it was still snowing. She thought it was late in the year for that; spring should have come at least ten days ago.

Surely the ban on music could not delay the coming of spring! Or could it? The very fact that she could put the question that way, meant it was very probable that the ban on music—and the ban on joy in men's hearts, which was what the ban on music was really all about—was something she might well be expected to remedy.

Lythande rose, and looked out of the window so that she could see what there was to be seen. Only a dreary gray landscape greeted her eyes, a hard pelting of snow piling up into drifts like a great bowl of whipped cream. She smiled at the innocence of the simile and drew on her boots, wrapping herself in the mage-robe which had dried overnight. The tight windows reduced the noise of the storm to a faint distant roaring; the snowdrifts seemed to move soundlessly, a curious effect. Lythande unslung her lute from her shoulder, and, hoping to raise her own spirits before facing the hostility downstairs, began to play a song of many years ago, unheard since she was young. It had been the first song she had learned to play as a young girl, many years before the Blue Star was inscribed between her brows. At that time her name had still been—

She slammed the thought shut, unwilling to let the forgotten name cross the barrier of her memory for the first time in—how many years? Could music then comfort her for the loss of a woman's name and identity, when nothing else in all these years had done so? Perhaps not; but if there ever had been such a possibility, music was perhaps the only thing she could think of that could have done so.

As the last notes of the song died into silence, Lythande prepared once again to take up the burden of her minstrel's identity and of this town. A random glance out the window showed her that the hard-driving snow had died down and its hiss was replaced by a dull roaring of the wind. Dim stretches of damp dismal-looking browned grass just turning green showed through the soggy-looking runnels of melted snow.

*So—what is this?* she thought. *Has music's power already shown itself? Is the answer coming, after all, as I knew it would?* She grimaced, reminding herself that with the answer came the problem. Then she hoisted the rewrapped lute, and went down the inn stairs. In the common room, many of the people were staring out into the gray and silver lines of rain, their eyes wide with amazement, making tiny noises of wonderment. As the gloomy innkeeper of last night set a cup of the colorless herb tea before her, he actually smiled, dispelling some of his ever-present gloominess.

"The bread this morning is fresh-baked," he said, and as she lifted the tea to her lips, she caught a whiff of cinnamon. The bread—which she could smell in the kitchen—did, indeed, smell fresh . . . as well as wonderfully delicious. The innkeeper continued, saying, "Would you like some, minstrel?"

"I would indeed," Lythande said, with heartfelt thankfulness. For the first time in perhaps a century, she resented the prohibition on eating or drinking in the sight of any man or woman who was not also a Pilgrim of the Blue Star; yet another law laid down by her Order in a struggle to make them more enigmatic than they already were.

The innkeeper said, in a soft, conspirator's voice, "I heard you playin' that there lute upstairs! That ain't allowed, minstrel. Like I told you, t'Duke won't have it in this town. . . ."

Lythande ignored him, her mouth watering at the smell of bread. It smelled so good, she wished she dared to snatch a bite, but she had not tried to break her *geas* in many years and did not know what would happen if she did.

She decided not to think about it, looking out the window instead. The view encouraged her to come back to the innkeeper, and to say, "You can see the results of my playing; should I not go on?"

The innkeeper guffawed. "Looks like there's been a spring thaw, that's all," he said, then eyed her strangely. "You trying to tell me you did that, minstrel?"

"Not I," Lythande replied. "But the power of music."

He looked at her dubiously. Quietly, deliberately, Lythande stripped off her lute's casing. Lythande's eyes stayed on the innkeeper, and, when he did nothing, she turned her gaze defiantly back onto the room—steadily filling up with travelers—and then brought the lute to her fingers and began to play again, a slow chord progression.

No one protested, instead staring at her, a few daring to nod in time to her music. Not even the morose innkeeper stopped her; but something suspiciously like a smile cracked the frozen dignity of his face.

"I'll get you some o' that bread," was all he said, and withdrew from the room.

He was back moments later with a carved wooden tray piled with rolls. Lythande stopped strumming and reached for a roll, when a voice near the door to the inn said, "T'Duke wants t'see you."

Lythande turned to see a slouched, morose-looking man standing in the doorway, a sour look on his face. "And what does the Duke have to say?" she asked.

The man pulled a long face and said gloomily, "Well, I don' know what t'Duke'll say," and glared at Lythande.

The innkeeper set down the tray and said, "I'll tell you what t'Duke'll say! He'll say this minstrel here is under arrest for playin' inside his jurisdiction." He gestured toward the outside, where a little more of the snow had melted, revealing more of the withered grass. "Well if what t'Duke has to say matters so much, Giles, let 'im come himself an' stop this freeze! Or do you want to try it?"

The man the innkeeper had called Giles made an even sourer face; if that were possible. "Not my job," he replied. "All'n I have to say is t'Duke wantsta see t'minstrel, an' if he won't come, I'm to tell you t'Duke will be sure to get him there in his own way."

The innkeeper sighed and laid the hot fresh bread atop Lythande's pack, saying, "If I were you, sir, I wouldn't resist. T'Duke's men are strong, and they've got swords thicker than any lute. Here—" He handed her a few rolls "—take 'em with you, an' eat it on the road, minstrel. But like I said, best not to thwart t'Duke when he wants to see you."

Lythande nodded, rewrapping her lute. Then, taking the bread with a grateful smile, she stood, following Giles out the door.

*It would seem,* she thought as she stepped outside and looked at the small wall of men that waited for her, *that the Duke wasted no time in risking my resistance.* She sighed as the men—armed with shields, spears, and swords—filed around her and escorted her up to the Duke's home.

As far as royal buildings went, she observed as she marched beneath the portcullis, it was nothing impressive; in her travels, she had seen nicer. It looked damp, all gray stone and chalky mortar, hardly suited for the winter's cold.

They walked through two sets of doors, and then she—and her assembled escorts—were in a long, gloomy hall. Of a sudden, she was frightened, her spirit pressed down by the cold and the silence and the gray. Her hand clenched tightly around the wrapped neck of her lute—was it her fate to die for her art? The urge to break and run almost consumed her—but before the assembled men, all she could do was walk, outwardly calm, into the long hall.

Giles turned to her and gestured toward a stairwell set into a far wall, winding into darkness, saying, "Straight up the stairs, an' to the left."

Lythande nodded, stepping past him and toward the shadowy opening. She climbed the stairs, assuming an air of bravado which she put on at the thought of facing the Duke. A set of doors awaited her at the top, and she knocked faintly on the door to the left, as she had been instructed.

"If he who knocks is the minstrel, enter," came a bass voice from within.

Lythande opened the door and walked into the room, squinting into the fitful firelight, burning on the hearth and casting precious little radiance. A woman, pale and careworn but richly dressed, bent over a cradle from which came a thin and fretful whimpering cry. Across from her, also bent over the cradle, was a tall, old man. The Duke, Lythande supposed, for he wore a narrow coronet and his robe was of a crimson so rich it approached purple.

The Adept bowed slightly and said, "Lythande, minstrel and magician, salutes you, my Lord Duke."

The Duke, for it was none other, said, with his face screwed into a worried frown, "I will not deceive you, minstrel; I do not like music and have forbidden it in this town; but I also have eyes and ears, and I am not a stupid man." His eyes went toward a window that overlooked the small town. "I have seen from here the ring of thaw that has appeared around the inn since you arrived, and my men have told me of the magic you have wrought with your playing." The next words seemed to come out of his mouth reluctantly, and caused great surprise in Lythande, "My only son and heir has lain here all week, suffering and wasting as if he were under a curse, and I have asked you to come to beg you to play for my poor child. For the first time in a fortnight he ceased to cry and fell quietly asleep this morning, when you played your lute and stopped the snow. Will you—" He swallowed. "Will you play again? If not for me, then for my son?"

Lythande gestured to the Duke to move to the side, then stepped forward and bent to look at the baby, loosening and then taking off his warm wrappings. The Duchess cried out faintly in protest, but Lythande said, "From the look of his skin, I would say he suffers from the liver sickness. Do you see how yellow he is? The cure is to let him lie naked."

"You mean—unclothed—?" interrupted the Duchess, her mouth slightly open, aghast. Lythande looked up at her, then looked closer, and saw where the woman's skin was covered with an angry red rash, except where it was hidden by her rich clothing. "Will he not sunburn?" Her hand flew to her slightly exposed bosom, lightly touching her own doubtlessly burned skin.

Lythande shook her head. "He will not; it is the sun's light alone that will cure his illness." She nodded toward the Duchess. "If the sun makes you thus ill, madam, let some other take him out into the sun for twenty minutes every day, and, sooner than you think, he will be running out into the sun on his own."

"That is," said the Duke with a mild note of humor in

his voice, "when he is grown to the age where he can walk on his own."

Lythande smiled and turned to look at him, unwrapping her lute. "Indeed, sir." She touched her fingers to the strings to make sure they were in tune.

"So simple a thing as sunlight?" the Duchess said, frowning. "He needs no spells or magic?"

Lythande shook her head. "None, Lady; the only cure he needs is the good sunlight."

As if on cue, the baby began to whimper again, causing a look of pain to cross his mother's face; Lythande smiled briefly and began to play her lute.

The whimpering died to nothing, but Lythande hardly noticed as she lost herself to the time and movement of her songs. She had not played twenty minutes when a loud cracking sound could be heard, startling all in the room.

"What was that?" Lythande asked sharply, not stopping in her playing as the Duke ran to the window, flinging it open.

"Look!" he cried, pointing. "The river to the east of town—it is thawing!" He turned to her. "Minstrel, you are truly amazing!"

The Duchess smiled, still bent close to her cradle, her eyes glowing warmly. "Well, hark to this, my love. The river is loud and our son is silent for once!" she said, amazed. "You must give the minstrel a rich present indeed for all that he has done!"

The Duke looked hard at Lythande, all joy hidden from his face once more, and asked warily, "What reward will you ask, Sir Magician? You have made my Lady very happy. Is it gold you wish?"

Lythande only smiled. "Sire, although gold is fine, it is not what I want. What I ask of you is a favor—that you take back your interdiction against music in this town."

The Duke scowled, and Lythande said quickly, "There are rogues enough, my Lord, and banning music will not stop them from earning their living. I, a stranger, a *minstrel*, cured your son, and have saved your people from an eternity of winter. Please, leave the minstrels to their peace; unless they break some other law, of course!"

"Well, I don't know. . . ." He sighed reluctantly. "Is it—is it truly that you want?" Lythande nodded. The Duke looked at the baby kicking lustily and gurgling in the sunlight, and past that, to the window. Then he spread his hands and said, "Well, then, let it be so."

Lythande smiled and ceased her playing, her job done. She wrapped her lute, stood, and patted the baby's cheek.

The Duchess smiled at her. "My mother, when I was a child, gave me a gift of a harp. It has sat, dusty in the cellar for many years . . . perhaps I should take the time now to learn how to play it?"

The mage nodded. "Perhaps you should," she replied. "I'm sure your son will appreciate it, he seems to love music well. Perhaps he, too, shall become a musician when he grows older."

"Heaven forbid," the Duke muttered, but his wife smiled.

Outside the Duke's home, Lythande made her way toward the inn to pay her respects to the innkeeper. He smiled as she entered, and seated her at a table. The common room was empty of people, for they were all outside, wondering at the stray spikes of green that were poking their way through the soggy lawn.

As she took out some coins, he shook his head. "You've done more than your share. No, sir, I won't take your money—no indeed. A glass of wine before you leave us? You're more than worth it to see folk lookin' so happy all round."

"I thought you said that wine was a great evil?"

The innkeeper turned red and coughed. "Well, sir, it ain't evil if I ain't drinking it, now, is it? And it ain't evil to have around. And—ah—"

Lythande could tell that he was reaching for an excuse for admitting to having bootleg spirits. She nodded. "Wine is not quite my style," she said, cutting him off. "Do you have any beer?"

He beamed, nodded, and came back presently with a

pot of beer. Lythande put her slim fingers around the rough ceramic and then, softly, began to sing:

> *"Surely the time of singing has come*
> *The voices of birds and springing of grass*
> *With every living thing rejoicing;*
> *Loving and nesting*
> *Robins springing and warbling everywhere*
> *Yes, everywhere around us,*
> *Birds are singing, and waters flowing*
> *And the first blossoms of the spring*
> *Aye, the first promises of summer,*
> *Can be seen."*

Beyond the window, the dead gray of the sky had begun to show stretches of blue, strewn with puffy clouds, and on the wide lawns pale and delicate flower buds were replacing the hills of snow. From somewhere beyond the window came the delicate sound of a little pipe. The travelers—even the innkeeper—were all outside by now, reveling in the spring morning.

Since she was now alone in the room, Lythande drained the mug, and left the cup of herb tea he had also set before her when he served the beer. She thought the stuff might make a good eyewash—from its smell, that was about all it was good for.

And Lythande sang again:

> *"Birdsong drenches the land;*
> *The birds, every one, are building nests;*
> *Even the worms from their holes*
> *Seeks each one his mate."*

From the corner of her eye, Lythande saw a pair of rabbits enjoying themselves in the way rabbits always did. Quietly, still singing, she went out of the inn, and down the steps. Far away, the shepherd's pipe was still playing, taking up the music where she had left it off. And, even farther off against the hills, less clear than the music, she could see where two shadows blurred into one, in time to their own music.

When she was out of sight of the inn and the seemingly universal rejoicing, she began the last verse of her song:

*"Yes, all things seek a mate,*
*And only I languish in loneliness . . ."*

Well, she had restored joy and song to the blighted people there; wasn't that supposed to be the next best thing to a love of one's own? Lythande turned her back on the village and, unobserved, bit into her bread. Continuing up the road, she took note where patches of snow still lingered, slowly melting under the warmth of the sunlight. She blinked, and that same sunlight refracted her world back at her through a rainbow of tears, as she remembered past love songs and past loves, all gone or dead now.

She looked up and squinted toward the sun, a star that glowed by itself, shedding warmth on others, asking for none in return.

*Yes . . . I, like every star, am alone.*

*But,* she thought, *there is still beer and hot bread. And the spring has come.*

And that thought, she mused, just might be enough to get her through the summer.

Enough, even, to drive her own cold winter away.

*When I was asked to write a story involving music for this anthology, my character Lythande, being a superb musician with magical talent, was a natural choice for a protagonist. The title comes from a folk song, although I have used it a bit more literally than the song did. I have often wished that winter could be driven away by a song.*

# THE LAST SONG OF
# SIRIT BYAR

## by Peter S. Beagle

Peter Beagle is fifty-seven years old, a child of
the Bronx who now resides in Davis, California.
He is the author of five novels, the most recent
being *The Unicorn Sonata,* as well as four nonfiction books and the libretto for the opera *The
Midnight Angel.* "Sirit Byar" set him happily off
on a series of novellas, all set in the world of
*The Innkeeper's Song,* which will be published
in book form in 1997.

*How* much? *How* much to set down one miserable tale
that will cost your chicken wrist an hour's effort at the
very most? Well, by the stinking armpits of all the gods, if
I'd known there was that much profit in sitting in the
marketplace scribbling other people's lives and feelings
on bits of hide, I'd have spent some rainy afternoon
learning to read and write myself. Twelve coppers, we'll
call it. *Twelve,* and I'll throw in a sweetener, because I'm
a civilized woman under the grease and the hair. I
promise not to break your nose, though it's a great temptation to teach you not to take advantage of strangers,
even when they look like what I look like and speak your
crackjaw tongue so outlandishly that you'd mimic me to
my hog face if you dared. But no, no, sit back down, fair's
fair, a bargain's a bargain. No broken nose. *Sit.*

Now. I want you to write this story, not for my
benefit—am I likely to forget the only bloody man who
ever meant more than a curse and a fart to me?—but for
your own, and for those who yet sing the songs of Sirit
Byar. Ah, *that* caught your ear, didn't it? Yes, yes, Sirit

Byar, that one, the same who sang a king to ruin with a single mocking tune, and then charmed his way out of prison by singing ballads of brave lovers to the hangman's deaf-mute daughter. Sirit Byar, "the white *sheknath*," as they called him out of his hearing—the big, limping, white-haired man who could get four voices going on that antiquated eighteen-course *kiit* other men could hardly lift, let alone get so much as a jangle out of it. Sirit Byar. Sirit Byar, who could turn arrows with his music, call rock-*targs* to carry him over mountain rivers, make whiskery old generals dance like children. All trash, that, all marsh-goat shit, like every single other story they tell about him. Write this down. Are you writing?

Thirty years, more, he's been gone, and you'd think it a hundred listening to the shitwits who get his songs all wrong and pass them on to fools who never heard the man play. The *tales,* the things he's supposed to have said, the gods and heroes they tell you he sang for—believe it, he'd piss himself with laughing to hear such solemn dribble. And then he'd look at me and maybe I'd just catch the twitch at the right corner of his mouth, under the wine-stained white mustache, and he'd say in that barbarous south-coast accent he never lost, "What am I always telling you, big girl? Never bet on anything except human stupidity." And he'd have limped on.

I knew Sirit Byar from when I was eleven years old until his death, when I was just past seventeen. No, he didn't die in my arms—what are you, a bloody bard as well as a mincing scribbler? Yes, I *know* no one ever learned what became of him—I'll get to that part when I bloody well get to it. Don't gape at me like that or I'll pull your poxy ears off and send them to your mother, whatever kennel she's in. *Write*—we'll be all day at this if you keep on stopping to gape. Gods, what a town—back-country cousin-marriers, the lot of them. Just like home.

My name is Mircha Del. I was born around Davlo, that's maybe a hundred miles southwest of Fors na'Shachim. My father was a mountain farmer, clawing a little life from stone and sand, like everybody in this

midden-heap. My mother had the good sense to run off as
soon as she could after I was born. Never met her, don't
even know if she's alive or dead. My father used to say
she was beautiful, but all you have to do is look at me for
the facts of that. Probably the only woman he could get to
live with him, up there in those starvation hills, and even
she couldn't stand it for long. No need to put all that in—
this isn't about her, or about him either. Now he *did* die in
my arms, by the way, if that interests you. Only time I can
remember holding him.

At the age of eleven, I had my full growth, and I looked
just as hulking as I do now. My father once said I was
meant for a man, which may be so, though I'd not have
been any less ugly with balls and a beard. That's as may
be, leave that out, too. What matters is that I already had a
man's strength, or near enough—enough anyway to get a
crop in our scabby ground and to break a team of
Karakosk horses—you know, those big ones? the ones
they raise on meat broth?—to do our plowing. And when
our neighbor's idiot son—yes, a real idiot, who else
would have been my playmate even when I was little?—
got himself pinned under a fallen tree, they sent for me to
lift it off him. He died anyway, mind you, but people took
to calling me "the Davlo *sheknath*" for a while. I told Sirit
Byar about that once, the likeness in our nicknames, and
he just snorted. He said, "You hated it." I nodded. Sirit
Byar said, "Me, too, always have," so maybe there was
our real likeness. It made me feel better anyway.

Well, so. There used to be a tavern just outside Davlo,
called the Miller's Joy. It's long gone now, but back then
it was as lively a pothouse as you could find, with gaming
most nights, and usually a proper brawl after, and every
kind of entertainment from gamecocks to *shukri*-fighting,
to real Leishai dancers, and sometimes even one of those
rock-munching strongmen from down south. My father
spent most of his evenings there, and many of his mornings as he got older, so I grew in the habit of walking
down to Davlo to fetch him home—carry him, more times
than not. And all that's the long way of telling you how I
met Sirit Byar.

It happened that I tramped into the Miller's Joy one night to find my father—purely raging I was, too, because our lone miserable *rishu* was due to calve, and he'd sworn to be home this one night anyway. I delivered the calf myself, no trouble, but there could have been, and now I meant to scorch him for it before all his tavern mates. I could hear their racket a street away, and him bellowing and laughing in the middle of it. Wouldn't have been the first time I snatched him off a table and out the door for the cold walk home. Grateful he was for it most times, I think—it told him that someone yet cared where he was, and maybe it passed for love, how should I know? He was lonely with my mother gone, and too poor for drink and the whores both, so he made do with me yelling at him.

But that night there was another sound coming from the old den, and it stopped me in the street. First the fierce thump of a *kiit* strung with more and heavier courses than the usual, and then the voice, that voice—that harsh, hoarse, tender southern voice, always a breath behind the beat, that voice singing that first song, the first one I ever heard:

> *"Face it,*
> *if you'd known what you know today,*
> *you'd have done the same stupid fucking thing*
> *anyway . . ."*

Yes, you know it, don't you, even in my croak? Me, I didn't even know what I was hearing—I'd never heard anything like that music before, never heard a bard in my life. Bards don't come to Davlo. There's nothing for even a carnival jingler in Davlo, never mind someone like Sirit Byar. But there he was.

He looked up when I pushed the door open. There was a whole sprawl of drunken dirt farmers between us—a few listening to him where he sat cross-legged on a table with the *kiit* in his lap, most guzzling red ale and bawling their own personal songs—but Sirit Byar saw me. He looked straight across them to where I stood in the doorway: eleven years old, the size of a haywagon and twice as ugly, and mucky as the floor of that taproom besides. He didn't smile or nod or anything, but just for a moment, playing a quick twirl on the *kiit* between verses, he said through the noise, "There you are, big girl." As though he'd been waiting. And then he went back to his song.

> *"Face it,*
> *if she'd been fool enough to stay,*
> *you'd be the same mean, stupid bastard*
> *anyway . . ."*

There was one man crying, doubled over his table, thumping his head on it and wailing louder than Sirit Byar was singing. And there was a miner from Grebak, just sitting silent, hands clasped together, pulling and squeezing at the big scabby knuckles. As for my father and the rest, it was drinking and fighting and puking all over their friends, like any other night at the Miller's Joy. The landlord was half-drunk himself, and he kept trying to throw out little Desh Jakani, the farrier, only he wouldn't go. The three barmaids were all making their own arrangements with anyone who could still stand up and looked likely to have two coppers left in his purse at closing time. But Sirit Byar kept looking at me through the noise and the stink and the flickering haze, and he sang:

> *"Face it,*
> *if we all woke up gods one day,*
> *we'd still treat each other like garbage*
> *anyway . . ."*

What did he look like? Well, the size of him was what I mostly saw that first night. Really big men are rare still in those Davlo hills—the diet doesn't breed them, not enough meat, and the country just hammers them low— and Sirit Byar was the biggest man I'd seen in my life. But I'm not talking about high or wide—get *this* down now—I'm talking about size. There was a color to him, even with his white hair and faded fisherman's tunic and trews; there was a purpose about him as he sat there singing that made everything and everyone in that roaring tavern small and dim and faraway, that's what I remember. And all he was, really, was a shaggy, rough-voiced old man—fifty anyway, surely—who sang dirty songs and called me "big girl." In a way, that's all he ever was.

The songs weren't *all* dirty, and they weren't all sad and mean, like that "Face It" one. That first night he sang "Grandmother's Ghost," which is just silly and funny, and he sang "The Sand Castles"—you know it?—and "The Ballad of Sailor Lal," which got even those drunken farmers thumping the tables and yelling out the chorus. And there was a song about a man who married the Fox in the Moon—that's still my favorite, though he never sang it much. I forgot about my father, I even forgot to sit down. I just stood in the doorway with my mouth hanging open while Sirit Byar sang to me.

He really could set four voices against each other on that battered old *kiit,* that's no legend. Mostly for show, that was, for a finish—what I liked best was when he'd sing a line in one rhythm and the *kiit* would answer him back in another, and you couldn't believe they'd come out together at the end, even when you knew they would. Six years traveling with him, and I never got tired of hearing him do that thing with the rhythms.

The trouble started with "The Good Folk." It always did, I learned that in a hurry. That bloody song can stir things up even today, insulting everybody from great lords to shopkeepers, priests to bailiffs to the Queen's police; but back then, when it was new, back then you couldn't get halfway through it without starting a riot. I don't *think* Sirit Byar yet understood that, all those years ago in the Miller's Joy. Maybe he did. It'd have been just like him.

Anyway, he didn't get anything like halfway through "The Good Folk," not that night. As I recall it, he'd just sailed into the third stanza—no, no, it would have been the second, the one about the priests and what they do on the altars when everyone's gone home—when the man

who'd been crying so loudly stood up, wiped his eyes,
and knocked Sirit Byar clean off the table. Never saw the
blow coming, no chance to ward it off—even so, he
curled himself around the *kiit* as he fell, to keep it safe.
The crying man went right at him, fists and feet, and he
couldn't do much fighting back, not and protect the *kiit*.
Then Ko what's-his-name got into it—he'd jump anybody
when he was down, that one—and then my bloody father,
if you'll believe it, too blind drunk to know what was
going on, just that it looked like fun. He and the crying
man tripped each other up and rolled over Sirit Byar and
right into the legs of the big miner's table, brought the
whole thing down on themselves. Well, the miner, he
started kicking at them with his lumpy boots, and *that* got
Mouli Dja, my father's old drinking partner—"Drooly
Mouli," people used to call him—anyway, that got *him*
jumping in, yelling and swearing and chewing on the
miner's knees. After that, it's not worth talking about,
take my word for it. A little bleeding, a lot of snot, the rest
plain mess. Tavern fights.

I told you I had near to my grown strength at eleven. I
walked forward and yanked my father away from the
crying man with one hand, while I peeled Mouli Dja off
the miner with the other. Today I'd crack their numb-
skulls together and not think twice about it, but I was just
a girl then, so I only dropped them in a corner on top of
each other. Then I went back and started pulling people
off Sirit Byar and stacking them somewhere else. Once I
got them so they'd stay put, it went easier.

He wasn't much hurt. He'd been here before; he knew
how to guard his head and his balls as well as the *kiit*.
Anyway, that many people piling on, nothing serious ever
gets done. Some blood in the white mustache, one eye
closing and blackening. He looked up at me with the other
one and said for the second time, "There you are, big
girl." I held out my hand, but he got up without taking it.

Close to, he had a wild smell—furry, but like live fur,
while it's still on the *shukri* or the *jarilao*. He was built
straight up and down: wide shoulders, thick waist, thick
short legs and neck. A heavy face, but not soft, not sag-

ging—cheekbones you could have built a fence, a house with. Big eyes, set wide apart, half-hidden in the shadows of those cheekbones. Big, quiet eyes, almost black, looking black because of the white hair. He never smiled much, but he usually looked about to.

"Time to go," he said, calm as you please, standing there in the ruins of a table and paying no mind to the people yelling and bleeding and falling over each other all around us. Sirit Byar said, "I was going to spend the night here, but it's too noisy. We'll find a shed or a fold somewhere."

And me? I just said, "I have to get my father home. You go on down the Fors road until you come to the little Azdak shrine, it'll be on the right. I'll meet you there." Sirit Byar nodded and turned away to dig his one sea-bag out from under Dordun the horse-coper, who was being strangled by some total stranger in a yellow hat. Funny, the things you remember. I can still see that hat, and it's been thirty years.

I did carry my father back to our farm—nothing out of the way in that, as I said. But then I had to sit him down on a barrel, bracing him so he wouldn't go all the way over, and tell him that I was leaving with Sirit Byar. And that was hard—first, because he was too drunk and knocked-about to remember who any of us were; and second, because I couldn't have given him any sort of decent reason for becoming the second woman to leave him. He'd never been cruel to me, never used me the way half the farmers we knew used their daughters and laughed about it in the Miller's Joy. He'd never done me any harm except to sire me in that high, cold, lonely, miserable end of the world. And here I was, running away to follow a bard four, five times my age, a man I'd never seen or even heard of before that night. Oh, they'd be baiting him about it forever, Mouli Dja and the rest of his mates.

I don't think I tried to explain anything, finally. I just told him I'd not be helping him with the farming anymore, but that he wouldn't need to worry about feeding me either. He said nothing at all, but only kept blinking

and blinking, trying to make his eyes focus on me. I never
knew if he understood a word. I never knew what he felt
when he woke up the next day and found me gone.

There wasn't much worth taking along. My knife, my
tinderbox, my good cloak. I had to go back for my lucky
foreign coin—see here, this one that's never yet bought
me a drink anywhere I've ever been. My father was
already asleep, slumped on the barrel with his head
against the wall. I put a blanket over him—he could have
them both now—and I left a second time.

The Fors na'Shachim road runs straight the last mile or
so to the Azdak shrine, and I could see Sirit Byar in the
moonlight from a long way off. He wasn't looking around
impatiently for me, but was kneeling before that ugly
little heap of stones with the snaggletoothed Azdak face
scratched into the top one. "Azdak" just means *stranger*
in the tongue I grew up speaking. None of us ever knew
the god's real name, or what he was good for, or who set
up that shrine when my father was a boy. But we left it
where it was, because it's bad luck not to, and some of us
even worshiped it because why not? Our own hill gods
weren't worth shit, that was obvious, or they wouldn't
have been scrabbling to survive in those hills like the rest
of us. There was always the chance that a god who had
journeyed this far might actually know something.

But Sirit Byar wasn't merely offering Azdak a quick
nod and a marketing list. He was on his knees, as I said,
with his big white head on a level with the god's, looking
him in the eyes. His lips were moving, though I couldn't
make out any words. As I reached him he rose silently,
picked up the *kiit* and his sea-bag, and started off down
the Fors road. I ran after him, calling, "My name is
Mircha. Where are we going?"

Sirit Byar didn't even look at me. I asked him, "Why
were you praying like that to Azdak? Is he your people's
god?"

We tramped on a long way before Sirit Byar answered
me. He said, "We know each other. His name is not
Azdak, and I was not praying. We were talking."

"It'll rain before morning," I said. "I can smell it. Where are we going?"

He just grunted, "Lesser Tichni or a hayloft, whichever comes first," and that was all he said until we were bedded down between two old donkeys in an old shed on very old straw. I was burrowing up to one of the beasts, trying to get warm, when Sirit Byar suddenly turned toward me and said, "You will carry the *kiit*. You can do that." And he was sound asleep, that fast. Me, I lay awake the rest of that night, partly because of the cold, but mostly because what I'd done was finally—*finally,* mind you—beginning to sink in. Here I was, already further from home than ever I'd been, lying in moldy straw listening to a strange man snoring beside me. Tell you how ignorant a lump I was back then, I thought snoring was just something my father did, nobody else. I wasn't frightened—I've never been frightened in my life, which is a great pity, by the way—but I was certainly confused, I'll say that. Nothing for it but to lie there and wait for morning, wondering how heavy the *kiit* would be to shoulder all day. It never once occurred to me that I could go home.

The *kiit* turned out to be bloody heavy, strong as I was, and bulky as a plow, which was worse. Those eighteen double courses made it impossible to get a proper grip on the thing—there was no comfortable way to handle it, except to keep shifting it around: now on my back, now hugged into my chest with both arms, now swinging loose in my hand, banging against everything it could reach. I was limping like Sirit Byar himself at the end of our first full day on the road.

So it began. We stopped at the first inn after sunset, and Sirit Byar played and sang for men dirtier and even more ugly-drunk than ever I'd seen in the Miller's Joy. That was a lesson to me, for that lot paid no attention at all to "The Ballad of Sailor Lal," but whooped and cheered wildly for "The Good Folk," and made him sing it twice over so they could learn it themselves. You never know what they'll like or what they'll do, that's the only lesson there is.

Two nights and a ride on a tinker's cart later, we dined and slept in Fors na'Shachim—yes, at the black castle itself, with the Queen's ladies pouring our tea, and the chamber that Sirit Byar always slept in already made up for him. Four of the ladies were told off to bathe me and find me something suitable to wear while the Queen had to look at me. I put up with the bath, but when they wanted to burn my clothes on the spot, I threw one of the ladies across the room, so that took care of that. It quieted the giggling besides. So I've had royalty concerning itself with what nightgown I should wear to bed, which is more than *you've* ever known, for all your reading and writing. They'd probably have bathed you, too.

And two days after that, we were on our way again, me back in the rags I'd practically been born in (they probably burned that borrowed dress and the nightgown), and Sirit Byar wearing what he always wore—they didn't sweeten *him* up to sing for the Queen, I can tell you. But he had gold coins in his pocket, thirty-six new strings on the *kiit,* a silk kerchief Herself had tied around his neck with her own fair hands, and he was limping off to sing his songs in every crossroads town between Fors and Chun for no more than our wretched meals and *dai-*beetle-ridden lodging. I was a silent creature myself in those days, but I had to ask him about that. I said, "She wanted you to stay. They did."

Sirit Byar just grunted. I went on, "You'd be a royal bard—you could have that palace room forever, the rest of your life. All you'd ever have to do is make up songs and sing them for the Queen now and then."

"I do that," Sirit Byar said. "Now and then. Don't dangle the *kiit* that way, it's scraping the road." He watched me as I struggled to balance the filthy thing on my shoulder, and for the first time since we'd met I saw him smile a very little.

"The singing is what matters, big girl," he said. "Not for whom." We walked a way without speaking, and then he continued, "To do what I do, I have to walk the roads. I can't ride. If I ride, the songs don't come. That's the way it is."

"And if you sleep in a bed?" I asked him. "And if you sing for people who aren't drunk and stupid and miserable?" I was eleven, and my feet hurt, and I could surely have done with a few more days in that black castle.

Sirit Byar said, "Give me that," and I handed him the *kiit,* glad to have it off my shoulder for a few minutes. I thought he was going to show me a better way of carrying it, but instead he retuned a few of the new strings—they won't hold their pitch the first day or two, drive you mad—and began to play as we walked. He played a song called "The Juggler."

No, you don't know that one. I've never yet met anyone who did. He hardly ever played it—maybe three times in the six years we were together, but I had it by heart the first time, as I always did with his songs. It's about a boy from a place about as wretched as Davlo, who teaches himself to juggle just because he's bored and lonely. And it turns out that he's good at it, a natural. He juggles everything around him—stones, food, tools, bottles, furniture, whatever's handy. People love him, they come miles to see him juggle, and by and by the King hears about it and wants him to live at the palace and be his personal juggler. But in the song the boy turns him down. He tells the king that once he starts juggling crowns and golden dishes and princesses, he'll never be able to juggle anything else again. He'll forget how it's done, he'll forget why he ever wanted to do it in the first place. So thank you, most honored, most grateful, but no. And it has the same last line at the end of every verse: *"Kings need jugglers, jugglers don't need kings ..."* I can't sing it right, but that's how it went.

He sang it to me, right there, just the two of us walking along the road, and it's likely the most I ever learned about him at one time. Never any need to explain himself, not to me or anyone. I asked him that day if it bothered him when people didn't like his songs. Sirit Byar just shrugged his shoulders as though my question were a fly and he was a horse trying to get rid of it. He said, "That's not my business. The Queen likes them, your father didn't. No business of mine either way."

He really didn't care. Set this down plain, if you botch all the rest, because it's what matters about him. As long as he could make his songs and get along singing them, he simply did not care where he slept, or what he ate, or whom he sang to. I can't tell you how much didn't matter to that man. When he had money, he bought our meals with it, or more strings—that old *kiit* went through them like my father through red ale and black wine—or once in a while a night at an inn, for us to clean ourselves up a bit. When there was no money, there'd be food and lodging just the same, most often no worse. For a man who could go all day saying no more than half a dozen words, he had friends in places where I'd not have thought you could even find an enemy. The beggar woman in Rivni—we always stayed with her, just as regular as we stayed at the black castle, in the abandoned henroost that was her home. The wind-witch in Leishai, where it's a respectable profession, because of the sailors. The two weavers near Sarn—brothers, they were, and part-time body-snatchers besides. That bloody bandit in Cheth na'Deka—though that one always kept him up singing most of the night, demanding first this song, then that. The shipchandler's wife of Arakli.

I'll always wonder about her, the chandler's wife. Her husband had a warehouse down near the river, and she used to let us sleep in it as long as we were careful to leave no least sign that we'd ever been there. She was a plain woman—dark, small, a bit plump, that's all I remember. Nice voice. And what there was between her and Sirit Byar I never knew, except that I got up to piss the one night and heard them outside. *Talking* they were, fool-talking they were, too softly for me to make out a word, sitting by the water, not even touching, with the moon's reflection flowing over their faces and the moon in Sirit Byar's white hair. And I pissed behind the warehouse, and I went back to sleep, and that's all.

We had a sort of regular route, if you want to call it that. Say Fors na'Shachim as a starting point—from there we'd work toward the coast through the Dungaurie Pass, strike Grannach Harbor and begin working north, with

Sirit Byar singing in taverns, kitchens, great halls, and marketplaces in all the port towns as far as Leishai. Ah, the ports. The smell—salt and spice and tar, miles before you could even see the towns. The food waiting for us there in the stalls, on the barrows—fresh, fresh *courel, jeniak, boreen* soup with lots of catwort. Strings of little crackly *jai*-fish, two to a mouthful. And the light on the water, and children splashing in the shadows of the rotting pilings, and folk yelling welcome to their "white *sheknath*" in half a dozen tongues. The feeling that everything was possible, that you could go anywhere in the world from here, except back to Davlo. That was the best, better than the food, better than the smells. That feeling.

No, you'd think so, but he hardly ever sang sea-songs in the port towns. One, two, maybe, like "Captain Shallop and the Merrow" or "Dark Water Down"—otherwise he saved those for inland, where folk dream of far white isles and don't know what a merrow can do to you. In the ports he sang—oh, "Tarquentil's Hat," "The Old Priest and the Old God," "My One Sorrow," "The Ballad of the Captain's Mercy." "The Good Folk." Now *they* always loved "The Good Folk," the ports did, so there you are.

From Bitava we usually headed inland, still angling north, but no farther than Karakosk, ever. I've been told that he sang often in Corcorua; maybe, but not while I was with him. He'd no mind at all to limp across the Barrens, and he disliked most of the high northland anyway for its thin wine and its fat, stingy burghers. So I never saw anything loftier than the Durli Hills in those days, which suited me well enough—I've never been homesick for mountains a day in my life. We'd skirt the Durlis, begin bearing back south around Suk'kai, and fetch up in Fors again by Thieves' Day. A bath and a warm bed then—a few days of singing for the Queen and being made over by her ladies—and start all over again. So it was we lived for six years.

Duties? What were my *duties?* How daintily you do put it, to be sure, chicken-wrist. Well, I carried the *kiit,* and I brewed the tea and cooked our meals, when we had something to cook. A few times, mostly in Leishei, I ran off pickpockets he hadn't seen sliding alongside, and one night I broke the shoulder of a hatchet-swinging Bitava barber who'd taken a real dislike to "The Sand Castles." For the rest, I kept him mostly silent company, talked when he wanted to talk, went 'round with the hat after he sang, and kept an eye out at all times for that wicked west-country liqueur they call Blue Death. Terrible shit, peel your gums right back, but he loved it, and it's hard to find much east of Fors. He drank it like water, whenever he could get it, but I can't remember seeing him drunk. Or maybe I did, maybe I saw him drunk a lot and didn't know it. There were things you never could tell about with Sirit Byar.

Once I asked him, "What would you do if you weren't a bard? If you just suddenly couldn't make up songs anymore?"

I thought I knew him well enough to ask, but he stopped in the road and gaped at me as though he'd never seen me before. That was the only time I ever saw him looking amazed, startled about anything. He mumbled, "You don't know?"

I stared right back at him. I said, "Well, of course I don't know. I don't know a bloody thing about being a bard, not how it *is,* you won't ever talk about that. All I know is what you like to eat, where you like to sit when you sing. Maybe you think that's all a hill girl from Davlo can understand. Maybe it is. You'll never know that either."

Sirit Byar smiled a real smile then, not the almost-smile he wore for everyone always. "Listen to the songs, big girl. It's all in the songs, everything I could tell you." We walked along a way after that, and by and by he said, "A bard always hoards one last song against the day when all the others go. It happens to every one of us, sooner or later—you wake up one morning and it's over, they've left you, they don't need you anymore. No warning. No warning when they flew into you, no warning when they fly away. That's why you always save that last song."

He cleared his throat, spat into the road, rubbed his nose, looked sideways at me. "But you have to be very careful, because a bard's last song has power. You never tell that song, you never sing it anywhere, you keep it for that day when it's the only song left to you. Because a last song is always *answered*." And after that he hardly talked at all for the rest of the day.

He taught me a little about playing the *kiit,* you know. I'm sure he did it just because he'd never found anyone besides him who could even handle the thing. I'm no musician, I can't do what he could do, but I know how he did it. Someday I'd like to show someone how he played, just so it won't die with me. Not that he'd have given one tiny damn, but I do.

Every so often we'd strike a song competition, a battle of bads, especially in the southwest—it's a tradition in that country to set poets a subject and start them out-rhyming one another. Sirit Byar hated those things. He'd avoid even a town where we usually did well if he heard there was a contest going on there. Because once he was recognized, he never had a choice—they'd cancel the whole event if he didn't enter. He always won, but he was always cranky for days afterward. Me, I liked the song tourneys—we ate well those days, and drank better, and some of the townsfolk's celebration of Sirit Byar was for me, too, or anyway it felt so. I was proud as any of the Queen's ladies to walk beside him in the street, holding the *kiit* so people could see the flowers woven in and out between its strings. And whenever Sirit Byar looked down through all the fuss and winked at me, bard to bard almost—well, you imagine how it was, chicken-wrist. You imagine this big freak's insides then.

No. Oh, no. Get *that* out of your head before it ever gets in, if you know what's good for you. I was eleven, lugging that *kiit* for Sirit Byar, and then twelve and thirteen and fourteen, sleeping close for warmth in fields, barns, sheds, whores' cribs, and never in all that time. *Never.* Not once. It wouldn't have occurred to him.

It occurred to me, I'll tell you that. Yes, you can gape now, that's right, I'd be disappointed if you didn't. Listen to me now—I've had three, four times as many men as you've had women, for what that's worth. You think men care about soft skin, perfect teeth, adorable little noses? Not where I've been—not in the mines, not on the flat-boats, the canal scows, not in the traders' caravans slinking through the Northern Barrens. Out there, I even get to say, "No, not now, piss off." Can you imagine *that* at least, chicken-wrist? Try.

I had my first while I was yet on the road with Sirit Byar. Not yet fourteen, me, and sneaking up on myself in every stockpond, every shiny pot, just on the off-hope that something might have changed since the last time. If I'd had a mother . . . aye, well, and what could the most loving mother have told me that the bottom of any kettle couldn't? What could Sirit Byar have said, who never looked in a glass from year's-end to year's-end? I truly doubt he remembered the color of his own eyes. Now me, I couldn't remember not knowing I was ugly enough to turn milk, curdle beer, and mark babies, but it hadn't mattered much at all until that boy at Limsatty Fair.

Ah, gods, that boy at the fair. I can still see him, thirty years gone, when I can't remember who pleased me last week. Pretty as you like, with lavender eyes, skin like brown cambric, bones in his face like kite-ribs. He was selling salt meat, if you'll believe it, and when Sirit Byar and I wandered by, he looked at me for a moment, and looked politely away, so as not to stare. That's when I learned that I had a heart, chicken-wrist, because I felt such a pain in it that I couldn't believe I was still walking along and not falling dead on the spot. We were to make our camp in a field a mile from the fair, and I think I walked backward all the way. Sirit Byar had to grip me by the back of my smock and tow me like a bloody barge.

There was a little creek, and I was supposed to scoop some fish out of it for our dinner. Any hill child can do that, but instead I lay there on my stomach and cried as I've never cried in my life, before or since. I didn't think it was ever going to stop. Leave that out. No. No, keep it in. What do I care?

Sirit Byar had probably been sitting by me for a long time before I felt his hand on my neck. He never touched me, you know, except to help me on the road, or to remind me about holding the damn *kiit* just so. Once, when I was sick with the white-mouth fever, he carried me and the *kiit* both for miles until we found a mad old man who knew what to do. This was different, this was— I don't know, leave it, just leave it. He said, "Here."

He took off the Queen's silken kerchief he always wore around his neck and handed it to me so I could dry my eyes. Then he said, "Give me the *kiit*." I just stared at him, and he had to tell me again. "Give it to me, big girl."

He tuned it so carefully, you'd have thought he was getting ready to play at the black palace once again. Then he set his back against a tree, and began to sing. It wasn't a song I'd ever heard, and it didn't sound like one of his. The rhythm wasn't any I knew, the music was jags and slides and tangles, the words didn't make any sense. I told you, I had all his songs by heart the moment I heard them, but not that song. I do have a bit of it, like this:

> *"If you hear not, hear me never—*
> *if you burn not, freeze forever—*
> *if you hunger not, starve in hell—*
> *if you will not, then you never shall . . ."*

That line kept coming round and round again. *"If you will not, then you never shall."* It was a long song, and there was a thing about it made my skin fit all wrong on me. I lay where I was, sniffling away, while Sirit Byar kept singing, and the sun wandered down into twilight, slow as that song. At last I sat up and wiped my face with the Queen's kerchief, and remembered about our fish. I was moving myself back over to the creek when the music stopped, sudden as a door slam, and I turned and saw the salt-meat boy from the fair.

He was still so beautiful that it hurt to look at him, but something in his face was changed. Some kind of vague, puzzled anger, like someone who hasn't been blind long enough to get used to it. But he walked straight to me, and he took my hands and drew me to my feet, and we stood staring at each other for however long. When he began to lead me away, I turned to look back, but Sirit Byar was gone. I don't know what he had for dinner that night, nor where he slept.

Me, I slept warm on a cold hillside, as they say in the old ballads, and I woke just a minute or two before I should have. The salt-meat boy was up and scurrying into his clothes, and looking down at me with such bewilderment and such contempt—not for me, but for himself—as even I haven't seen again in my life. Then he fled, carrying his boots, and I lay there for a while longer, to give him time. I didn't cry.

Sirit Byar was at the creek, breakfasting on dry bread and cheese and the last of our sour Cape Dylee wine. There was enough laid out for two. Neither of us spoke a word until we were on our way again, bound for Derridow, I think. Finally I said, "The song brought him."

Sirit Byar grunted, looked away, mumbled something. I stopped right there on the road—he actually walked along a few steps before he realized I wasn't with him. I said, "Tell me why you sang that song. Tell me now."

He was a long time answering. We stood there and looked at each other almost the way I'd stood with that salt-meat boy, years and years ago it seemed. Finally Sirit Byar rubbed his hand across his mouth and muttered, "You're my big girl, and you were so sad."

And that was how I knew he liked me, you see. Two, almost three full years carrying his instrument, cooking his meals, grubbing up coins from tavern floors, and he'd never said. He turned right around then and started walking on, as fast as his limp would let him, and I hurried after him with the *kiit* banging the side of my knee. He wouldn't talk for a long time, not until a rainshower came up and we were huddled in the lee of a hayrick, waiting it out. I asked him, "How does it happen? The song making someone come to you."

Sirit Byar said, "Where I come from, there are songs for bringing game to the hunter—fish, birds. I just changed one a little for you."

I started to say, "Please, don't ever do that anymore," but I changed my mind halfway through. Whatever came of it, he gave me what I'd wanted most in all my life till then, and no blame to him if I woke from the dream too soon. So instead I asked, "Can you make other things happen with your songs?"

"Little things," Sirit Byar said. "The great ones who walked the roads before me—Sarani Elsu, K'lanikh-yara—" no, I never heard of them either, chicken-wrist "—*they* could sing changes, *they* could call rivers to them, *they* could call gods, lightning, the dead, not silly lovers." He patted my shoulder clumsily, I remember. He said, "All songs are magic, big girl. Some are more powerful than others, but all songs are always magic, always. You've seen me start our cooking fires in the rain—you remember the time I cured the farmer's dog that had eaten poison. My songs make little magics, that's all. They'll do for me."

Write that down, remember that he said just that. Remember it the next time you hear someone jabbering about Sirit Byar's great powers. *Little magics,* he never claimed anything more than that for himself. He never needed to.

Where was I? The rain let up, and we set out again, and presently Sirit Byar began singing a new song, one he hadn't yet finished, scrawling it in the air with one huge hand as we walked, the way he did. It ran so:

*"Long ago,*
*before there were landlords—*
*long ago,*
*before there were kings,*
*there lived a lady*
*made all out of flowers,*
*made of honey and sunlight*
*and such sweet things . . ."*

Yes, of course you know it, that one got around everywhere—I've heard it as far north as Suk'kai, just last year. He sang it through for me the first time, the two of us shivering there in the rain, and when the sun came out we walked on. Neither of us ever said another word about the salt-meat boy, as often as we came again to Limsatty Fair.

After that, something was a bit different between us. Closer, I don't know—maybe just easier. We talked more, anyway. I told Sirit Byar about the little scrap of a farm where I'd lived, and about how I'd chanced into the Miller's Joy that night, and that I was worried about my father—we hadn't been back to Davlo in three years. I asked after him whenever we met someone who'd passed through there, but for all I knew he might have died the day I left. I'd go days at a time without thinking of him at all, but I dreamed about him more and more.

Sirit Byar spoke sometimes of his south-coast town— not much bigger than Davlo, it sounded—and of his older sister, who raised him after their parents' death. Even now I can't imagine Sirit Byar having a family, having a sister. She set his leg herself when it got crushed between two skiffs and there wasn't even a witchwife for miles. She married there, and was killed in the Fisherman's Rebellion, and he never went back. Did you ever hear anyone sing that song of his, "Thou"? Most people think that song's about one god or another, but it's not, it's for his sister. He told me that.

Bedded down one night in the straw of a byre, with an old *rishu* and her calf for company, I asked him why he'd said that in the Miller's Joy when he first saw me— *"There you are, big girl."* How he knew that I was supposed to go with him and help him and do what he told me—how *I* knew. Sirit Byar was sitting up across from me, fussing over a harmony on the *kiit* that never did satisfy him. He answered without looking up, "He told me. The one your folk call Azdak." I didn't understand him. Sirit Byar said, "When I came to Davlo. I saw him by the road, and we talked. He told me to watch for you."

"Azdak," I said. "Azdak. What would Azdak care about me?"

"He is the god of wanderers," Sirit Byar said. "He knows his own." The *kiit* wouldn't do a thing he wanted that evening, and he finally set it down gently in an empty manger. He went on, "Your Azdak told me you and I had a journey to make together. I didn't know what he meant then."

"Aye, and so we had, sure enough," I said. "Where was the mystery in that?" Sirit Byar laughed. He said, "I don't think Azdak was talking about walking the roads, big girl. Gods likely don't bother much with such things."

"Well, they bloody should," I said, for he'd been limping worse than usual lately, and I'd had a stone bruise on my heel days on end. "He's no more use than our regular gods, if that's all he could tell you."

Sirit Byar shrugged. "I know only what he didn't mean, not what he did. That's how it is with gods." He stretched out on the far side of the *rishu,* wriggling himself down into the straw till all you could see of him was a big nose and a white mustache. He said, "Our real journey is yet to come," and was asleep.

Now whether it was the words or the way he said them that took hold of me, I couldn't tell you, but it was nightmare on nightmare after that—every time the damn *rishu* snuffled in her sleep, another monster turned up in mine. The last one must have been a pure beauty, because I woke up on Sirit Byar's chest, holding him tighter than ever I had the salt-meat boy. That wild, deep-woods smell of his was the most comforting thing in the wide world just then.

Well, there's comfort and comfort. I'll get this part over with quickly—no need to embarrass us both for twelve coppers. He held me for a while, petting my hair as though it might turn in his hand and bite him any minute. Then he started to put me by, gently as he could, but I wouldn't let him. I was saying, "It's dark, it's dark, you won't even see me, just this one time. Please." Like that.

Poor Sirit Byar, hey? The poor man, trying to get this whimpering hulk off him without hurting her brutish feelings. Ah, *that* one you can imagine, I can see it in your little pink eyes. Yes, well, I pushed him back down every time he sat up, and when he said, "Big girl, don't, no, you're too young," I kept on kissing him, saying, "I don't care, I won't tell anybody, please, I won't ever tell." Ah, poor, poor Sirit Byar.

He did the only thing he could do. He shoved me away, hard—big as he was, I was the stronger, but it's amazing what you can do when you're desperate, isn't it?—and jumped to his feet, panting as though we really had been doing it. For a moment he couldn't speak. He was backed into a far corner of the stall; he'd have to bolt past me to get out. I wasn't crying or laughing, or coming at him or anything, just standing there.

"Mircha," he said, and that was the only time but one he ever called me by my name. "Mircha, I can't. There's a lady."

A lady, mind you. Not a plain woman, a lady. "The bloody *hell* there is," I said. I don't think I screamed it, but who remembers? "Three years, almost, never out of each other's sight for ten minutes together, what bloody *lady?*"

"A long time," Sirit Byar said very softly. "A long, long time, big girl." The words were coming out of him one by one, two by two. He said, "I've not seen her since before you were born."

Never mind what I said to him then. If there's little enough in my life that warms me to remember, there's less that truly shames me, except for what I said to Sirit Byar in the next few moments. Just set it down that I asked him what he thought his great love was doing while he was wandering the land being forever faithful to her. Just set that much down—so—and let it alone.

Sirit Byar bore it all, big hands hanging open at his sides, and waited for me to run out of words and wind. Then he said, sounding very tired, "Her name is Jailly Doura. She is mad."

I sat down in the straw. Sirit Byar said, "Jailly Doura. There was a child. Her family married her to a man who took the child gladly, but it died." He swung his head left and right, the way he did sometimes, like an animal that can't find its own way out of a place. "It died," he said, "our child. She has been mad ever since, fifteen years it is. Jailly Doura."

Two *l*s in the name, are you getting it? I said "Crede-vek. That place where the rich people live. We always walk wide of Credevek—you won't pass the city gates, let alone sing there."

"Once," Sirit Byar whispered. Slumped against the wall, gray as our old stone Azdak under the road-brown weathering, he looked like no one I'd ever seen. He said, "I sang once for her in Credevek."

"Once in fifteen years," I said. "We do better than that in Davlo. Well, maybe faithfulness is easier if you don't have to see the person. I wouldn't know." There was a calmness on me, just as new and strange as all those tears I'd shed over the salt-meat boy. I felt very old. I patted the straw beside me and said, "Come and sit. I won't attack you, I promise. Come *on,* then."

Fourteen, and ordering Sirit Byar about like a plow-horse. But he came, and we sat close against each other, because the night had turned wickedly cold. Sirit Byar even laid his arm across my shoulders, and it was all right. Whatever happened, whatever it was took me for a little time, it never happened again. Not with him, not with anybody. I asked, "Did you know there was a baby?"

Sirit Byar nodded. After a while he said, "What could I have done? Her parents would have locked her away for-ever, rather than have her walking the roads with a moneyless, mannerless, south-coast street-singer. And here's a wealthy man waiting to marry her and take her to live in Credevek, and what's a street-singer to do for a gently-bred girl and a child?" He shivered suddenly, hard, I could feel it. He said, "I went away."

"What became of her?" He blinked at me. "I mean, after—afterward? Where is she now, who takes care of her?" In Davlo we had Mother Choy. She took in all our strays—animals, children and the moontouched alike—and if the lot of them lived in rags, on scraps and under rotting thatch, well, they were glad enough to get it. Sirit Byar said, "Jailly Doura's husband is a good man. Another would have sent her away, but she lives with him still, in a house just north of Credevek, and he looks after her himself. I have been to that house."

"Once," I said. Sirit Byar's hand tightened on my shoulder, hard, and his face clenched in the same way. I couldn't tell you which hurt me more. He said, "She would not come into the room. I sang all night for a dark doorway, and I could smell her, feel the air move against me when she moved, but she would not let me see her. I could not bear that. I could not bear to come back again."

I knew there was more. I knew him that well, anyway. Nothing to do but sit there in the stall, with the *rishu* snoring and her calf looking sleepily at us, and the air growing lighter and colder, both. And sure enough, in a year or two Sirit Byar said, "I thought I could make her well. I was so sure."

He wasn't talking to me. I said, "All songs are magic, always. You told me that."

"So they are," Sirit Byar answered. "But my songs are for farmers' dogs, I told you that also. I learned that before you were born, in that house in Credevek." He turned to look at me, and his eyes were as old and weary as any I ever saw. He said, "The great ones, they could have healed her. Sarani Elsu could have brought her back. *I*—" and he just stopped, and his head went down.

I knew there wouldn't be another word this time, no matter how long I waited for it. So after a while I said, "So you tried to sing her madness away, and it didn't work. And you never tried again. Fifteen years."

"Her husband told me not to come back," Sirit Byar mumbled. "I left her worse off than before, what could I say to him? He is a good man, what could I say?" He looked at me for an answer, but I didn't have one. In a bit his head sagged forward again. I wriggled around until I could get comfortable with his head resting on my arm, and then I just sat like that until long into morning, while the old man slept and slept and slept, and I just sat.

And the next day, and the days after that, you'd think none of it had ever happened. We walked the roads as usual, talking a bit more, as I've said, but we never once talked about our night in the byre, and there was never another bloody word about his Jailly Doura. Oh, I might have asked, and he might have answered, but I didn't think I wanted to know a thing more about her and him and their child than I already knew, thank you very much.

No, I wasn't *jealous*—please, do me a favor—but I was
fourteen and he was mine, that's all, whatever that means
when you're fourteen. He wasn't my father or lover, he
was just mine. And if I *was* jealous, I had a bloody right
to be, only I wasn't. Just big and ugly, the same as
always.

One thing different, though. At night, usually when he
thought I was asleep, he practiced a new song over and
over. Or maybe it was an old one, for all I could tell—he
kept his voice so low and his south-coast accent would get
so thick that I couldn't make out one word in ten. Even
when I really was asleep, the slidy, whispery music
always filled my dreams full of faces I'd never seen, animals I didn't recognize. It sounded like a lullaby people
might sing in some other country; like my lucky coin
that's worth something somewhere, I've no doubt. Never
had dreams like that again.

We did get to Davlo that spring—Sirit Byar went out of
his usual way to make sure of it. There was nothing for
him there—he didn't bother with even a single night at
the Miller's Joy, but stayed with a farmer while I went on
alone. I found Desh Jakani at his smithy, and he told me
that my father hadn't been into the Miller's Joy for more
than a month now, and that he'd been thinking seriously
of going by our farm any day to look in on him. "Never
the same man after you ran away," he told me. "The spirit
just went out of him, everybody says so." My father
hadn't had much spirit in him to begin with, and Desh
Jakani was a liar born, but all the same I scrambled up
that mountain track as though a rock-*targ* were after me,
really thankful that I'd come home when I had, and
wishing with all my heart that I were anywhere, anywhere
else in the world.

The way had disappeared, completely. I'd always kept
things cut back at least a little, but everything—the path,
the pasture, our few poor fields—everything was smothered in foxweed, ice-berry brambles, and *drumak*. I
looked for our *rishu* and the two Karakosk horses, but
they were gone. The door of the house hung on one hinge.
My father squatted naked in the doorway.

He wasn't mad, like Sirit Byar's Jailly Doura, or even very drunk. He knew me right away, but he didn't care. I picked him up—all cold bones, he was—and carried him into the house. No point in going into what it looked like; it was just the house of a man who'd given up long ago. When I left? Like enough. Likely Desh Jakani was right about that, after all.

My father never spoke a single word during the two days I stayed with him. I put him to bed, and I made soup for him—I'm no cook, and proud of it, but I can make decent soup—and managed to get some of it down his throat, while I told him all about my travels with Sirit Byar, the things I'd seen with him, the people I'd met, the songs I'd learned. I think I sang him every song I knew of Sirit Byar's during those two days, including "The Good Folk," the one that started the brawl in the Miller's Joy so long ago. He listened. I don't know what he heard, because his eyes never changed, but he was listening, I know that much. I swear he was listening.

I even told him about the salt-meat boy. That was on the morning of the third day, when I was holding him steady on the chamber pot. That's when he died, trust my father. Not a sound, not a whimper, not the tiniest fart, he was just dead in my arms, just like that. I buried him at the doorstep, because that's the way we do in Davlo, and left the door open for the animals and the creeping vines, and walked down into town one last time to join Sirit Byar.

What? What? You should see the look on your little face—you can't wait to know if we ever went to Credevek together, ever tried a second time to sing Jailly Doura back from wherever her poor ragged mind had been roaming all this long time. Well, let me tell you, for the next two years, Sirit Byar saw to it that we didn't go anywhere near Suk'hai, let alone Credevek. He'd have us veering back south as early as Chun, never mind who expected him where, or what bounty he might be passing up. When I asked, he only grunted that he was getting too old to trudge that far uphill, and anyway those folk were all too tightfisted to make the extra miles worthwhile.

Wasn't my place to argue with him, even if I'd been of a mind to. I wasn't.

Those were good years, those last two we had together. My strength had caught up with my size, and I could have carried the *kiit* all day by a couple of fingers. We tramped every road between Cape Dylee and Karakosk, between Grannach Harbor and Derridow, him writing his new songs in the air as we went, and me eyeing every pretty boy in every town square as boldly as though I were some great wild beauty who'd been the one to do the choosing all her life. There wasn't one of them as lovely as my salt-meat boy, and they didn't all come bleating after me by night—no fear about that—but I'll tell you one thing, Sirit Byar never had to sing anybody to my bed again, no bloody fear about *that* either. You're almost sweet when you blush, chicken-wrist, do you know that? Almost.

Yes. Yes, yes, we did go to Credevek together.

It was my doing, if you want to know. I won't say he'd never have gone without me; all I *will* say is that he hadn't been back there for—what's that make it?—seventeen years, so you figure it out. What put it into my head, that's another story. I wanted to see her, I know that. It started as a notion, just a casual wondering what she looked like, but then I couldn't get it out of my head, it kept growing stronger and stronger. And maybe I wanted to see him, too, see him with her, just to know. Just to find out what it was I wanted to know, maybe that was it, who remembers?

So that last morning, after we'd been to Chun—I remember it was Chun, because that was one place where Sirit Byar did sing "The Juggler" in public—and came once more to the Fors na'Shachim crossroads, I said to him, as casually as I could, "That peddler yesterday, the man we traded with for the new kettle? He spoke of trouble on the Fors road. I meant to tell you."

Sirit Byar shrugged. "Bandits." One fairy tale's true, anyway—there wasn't a high-toby in the country would have laid a hand on Sirit Byar or lifted a single copper from him. They used to come out of the woods some-times, bashful as marsh-goats, and travel along with us a little way, hanging back to encourage him to try over a new song as though they weren't there. They couldn't make him out, you see. I think they felt he was somehow one of them, but they couldn't have said why. That's what I think.

"Plague," I told him. "Fire-plague, broken out all down the Fors road between here and Dushant. He said the only safe route south was the Snowhawk's Highway. It's a good road—we can follow it as far as Cheth na'Vaudry and then cut west to Fors. We could do that."

Sirit Byar looked at me for a long time. Did he know I was lying? I've no more idea than you have. What *I* knew was that fire-plague hits the south coast, his country, at least once every ten years, people die in hundreds, thousands sometimes. He said at last, "We would have to pass through Credevek."

I didn't answer him. We stood silent at the crossroads, listening to insects, birds, the wind in the dry leaves. Then Sirit Byar said, "Azdak." Not another word. He took the *kiit* from my hand and set off toward Credevek without looking back. Limp or no limp, I had to trot to catch up with him.

So there's how we came to Credevek, which is a strange place, all grand lawns, high stone houses, cobblestone streets, servants coming and going on their masters' errands. No beggars. No tinkers, no peddlers. A few farm carts, a few children. *Quiet.* The quiet sticks to your skin in that town.

Sirit Byar marched straight down the main street of Credevek, with me trailing after him, not knowing what to do or even how to walk if I wasn't carrying the *kiit*. People came to their windows to stare at us, but no one recognized Sirit Byar, and he never looked this way or that. Straight through the town until the paved streets and the stone houses fell away, nothing much after but meadowland gone to seed, a few pastures, and the brown Durli Hills in the distance. And one big wooden house snugged down into the shadows between two foothills— you could miss it if you didn't look sharp. Sirit Byar said,

"If we travel by night, we will reach the Snowhawk's Highway before noon tomorrow."

I said, "That's where they live, isn't it? That's where Jailly Doura lives."

Sirit Byar nodded. "If she lives still." He turned to look at me, and suddenly he reached out to put his hand on the side of my neck, right here. My hair, the roots of my hair, just went cold with it. He said, "Between that house and where we stand, there's our journey. That's what the god of wanderers was saying to me. Whatever happens in that house, this is why we met, you and I. I would never be here, but for you. Thank you, Mircha."

I didn't know what to say. I just said, "Well, I wanted to get out of Davlo, that's all." I tried to take the *kiit* back—I mean, it was my *job,* carrying it, from the first day—but he wouldn't let me. He swung it to his shoulder and we started on our journey.

And it was a longer journey than it looked, I can tell you. By noon, which is when we should have reached the house in the foothills, it hardly seemed any closer than when we'd first seen it. Barely this side of the sunset, it was, before we'd done with trudging through empty, stony defiles and turned up a last steep road that ran between two huge boulders. There was a man waiting there. He was short and old, and the little that was left of his hair was as white as Sirit Byar's, and if he wasn't exactly fat, he looked soft as porridge, and about that color. But he faced us proudly, blocking our way like one of those boulders himself. He said, "Sirit Byar. I knew if I waited long enough."

Now. I have to tell the rest slowly. I have to be careful, remember it right, so you can set it down exactly the way it was. Sirit Byar said, "Aung Jatt," and nothing more. He just stood looking down at the other man, the way the high, shadowed house looked down on us three. Aung Jatt didn't take any notice of me, which is difficult. He said to Sirit Byar, "You cannot see her. I will not allow it."

"It has been fifteen years," Sirit Byar began, but Aung Jatt interrupted him. "And if it had been fifty, she'd still not be healed of you, healed of your music. I told you

never to return here, Sirit Byar." You know how, when
you grip something too tightly, it starts shivering and slipping in your hand? Aung Jatt's voice was like that.

Sirit Byar said only, "I must sing for her once more."

"Oh, aye, once more," the old man answered him. "And
when you have sung your songs of love and ghosts,
dragons and sailors, and gone your way again, who will
stay behind to piece what's left of her into some kind of
human shape *once more?*" He mimicked Sirit Byar's
deep, hoarse voice so bitterly that I giggled, I couldn't
help it. Aung Jatt never took his eyes off Sirit Byar.

"She did not know me for three years after you were
here," he whispered. "Three years. What possessed me to
let her listen to you? What made me imagine that the
music of the father might keep her from trying to follow
the child? For three years she wept in the dark and ate
what I pushed under her door—for two years more she
said no word but the child's name, over and over and
over. For five years after that—" He made himself stop;
you could hear his throat clicking and grinding. Sirit Byar
waited, blinking in the setting sun.

"Fifteen years," Aung Jatt said presently. "There are
times even now when she takes me for you, do you know
that?" He grinned like a dead man. "You might think that
would hurt me, and in a way it does, because then she
sometimes tries to kill me. I must always be watchful."

Sirit Byar closed his eyes, shook his head, and started
to move around Aung Jatt, up the road toward the house
beyond. Aung Jatt stopped him with a palm gently against
his chest. He said, "But she has stopped calling for the
child. She usually sleeps through the night, and it has
been some while since I had to feed her. And she hates
you far more than I do, Sirit Byar."

You couldn't be sure, because the sunlight was slanting
off the windows, but I thought I saw someone moving in
the house, just for a moment, the way you can see a
feeling flicker across someone's eyes and be gone again.
Aung Jatt went on, "She hates you because she knows—
she *knows*—that the child would still be alive if you had
defied her parents and stayed with her. I know better, but

there." He chuckled and patted Sirit Byar's chest with his fingertips. He said, "Did I tell you when you were here before that it was a boy? I'm growing old, I forget things."

Sirit Byar said, without looking at me, "Come on, big girl," and put Aung Jatt out of his way with one arm. Aung Jatt made no protest this time. He was still smiling a little as he watched us step past him—I say *us*, but he never saw me, not for minute. He didn't follow, and he didn't speak again until we were on the stone steps that led to the front door. Then he called after us, "Beware, Sirit Byar! The second floor is her domain—when you are there with her, you are in the moon. The servants will not ever climb the stair, and should she come down, they scuttle away into corners like beetles until she passes. Beware of her, Sirit Byar!"

I heard Sirit Byar's scornful grunt next to me—after six years, there wasn't a grunt or a snort of his I couldn't translate. But I wasn't scornful, I'll tell you that much. I said I'd never been frightened, and it's true, but madmen—madwomen—make me uneasy, if you like. Madwomen in the dark make me very uneasy. Sirit Byar pushed the door open. Just before we went inside, I looked back at Aung Jatt. He was standing exactly where we had left him, and he was laughing without making a sound.

It was a fine, proud house, certainly—and remember, I've slept in a palace. Felt bigger inside than outside somehow, and it felt *soft*, too—lots of thick Tahi'rak rugs and drapes and those buttery cushions they sew in Fors out of traders' old saddle blankets. Hardly an inch of floor or wall showing: the whole place was made like a cradle, like a special box you keep something special and breakable in. Servants slipped past us without a word, or anyway their shadows did, for I couldn't hear their footsteps, nor our own, come to that. I couldn't hear the front door swing shut, or any sound from the outside once it had. What I did hear was someone breathing. It wasn't Sirit Byar, and it wasn't me—I don't think either of us had breathed since we came through that door. Sirit Byar touched my shoulder and nodded me left, toward the stair. You'd expect a house like this to have a grand spiral stairway, but this was just a narrow little one, not room enough for the two of us to go abreast. Sirit Byar had to hold the *kiit* tight against his side to keep it from hitting the railing. I followed him, not thinking too much, not feeling anything, because why not? Where else was I to go right then?

It was different on the second floor. Deep-sea cold, it was, and thick with twilight, old stale, mushy twilight filling our eyes and ears and nostrils, like when you get smothered in the bedding when you're asleep, and then that's all you can dream. The breathing was all around us now, no louder, but quickening, eager. There wasn't another sound anywhere in the world. Sirit Byar stopped on the landing. Clearly, loudly even, he said, "Jailly Doura."

The breathing never faltered. Sirit Byar said again, "Jailly Doura. I am here."

No answer. Where we stood, I could make out a chair, a wall, another chair, a gray face floating in the air, the gray mouth of a corridor. Sirit Byar looked left and right, trying to guess where the breathing might be coming from. My eyes were growing used to the dimness now—I saw that the floating face was a portrait hanging on the wall, and I saw other paintings, and lamps and braziers as tall as me, taller, all unlit, and a great dark chandelier swinging overhead. The corridor lay straight ahead of us, with high double doors on either hand. Sirit Byar said, "This way," and went forward like a man moving in his own house in full day. I hurried after him. I didn't want to be left behind, left alone in the moon.

He never looked at any of the doors, only strode along until the corridor bent right and opened out into a kind of—what?—well, like an indoor courtyard, I suppose. There must have been an opening to the sky somewhere, because the twilight was thinner here, but I still couldn't see as far as the walls of the place, and the little warm night wind I felt on my face now and then made me wonder if it *had* any walls. There were a couple of benches, and there were pale statues in alcoves—and, of all the bloody things, a tree, set right into the floor, right in the middle of the room. A *sesao*, I think, or it might have been a red *mouri*, what do I know about trees? I certainly don't know how Aung Jatt ever watered and nourished the thing, but its trunk disappeared in darkness, and its branches reached out almost as far as the bench where Sirit Byar had calmly sat down and begun turning the *kiit*. I stood. I wanted my feet under me in that house, I knew that much.

The breathing still sounded so close I thought I could feel it sometimes, and yet I couldn't even be sure where it was coming from. Sirit Byar looked up into the tree branches and said, "Do you remember this song, Jailly Doura?" He touched the *kiit* with the heel of his hand, to get a sort of deep sigh out of all the strings, and began to sing.

I knew the song. So do you—if there's one song of Sirit Byar's that the wind carried everywhere, and that clung where it landed like a cocklebur, it was "Where's My Sandal?" Right, that funny, ridiculous song about a man who keeps losing things—his shoes, his wig, his spectacles, his false teeth, his balls—and that's the way people sing it in the taverns. But the melody's a sad one, if you whistle it over slowly, and people don't always sing the very last verses, because those are about misplacing your faith, your heart. Nobody ever sang it the way Sirit Byar sang it that night, quiet and gentle, with the *kiit* bouncing happily along, running circles all around the words. I can't listen to it now, never, not since that time.

He spoke to the tree again, saying, "Do you remember? You always liked that song—listen to this now." And his voice, that damn fisherman's growl of his, sounded like a boy's voice, and you'd have thought he'd never trusted anyone with his songs before.

He sang "The Woodcutter's Wife" next, that odd thing about an old woman who doesn't want to die without hearing someone, anyone, say "You're my dear friend, and I love you." She goes from her husband to her

children, then to her brothers and sisters, and finally she
hears the words from a tired village whore who'll say
anything for money. And yet, when she does say it for
money, somehow it comes out true, and the old woman
dies happy. Not a song I'd choose, was it me trying to
woo a madwoman out of her tree, but he knew what he
was doing. About songs, he always knew what he was
doing.

I think it was "The Good Folk" next, and then "The Old
Priest and the Old God." By then it had gotten so dark in
that strange courtyard that I couldn't see the tree, let alone
Sirit Byar. He took flint and steel out of one pocket, a
candle-end from the other, and made a little sputtering
light that he stood up on the bench beside him. He sang
the song about the lady made out of flowers, and he
sang "Thou," the one he wrote for his sister, and even my
favorite, the one about the Fox in the Moon. Never moved
from where he sat in his tatter of candlelight, no more
than I did. I just stood very still and listened to him
singing, old song on new, one after another. I could hear
Jailly Doura's heart beating somewhere near, as well as
her breathing, both quick as a bird's—or a *shukri*'s—and
one time I was sure I could smell her, like faraway water.
Twice Sirit Byar asked, "Will you show yourself, Jailly
Doura?" but no chance of that. So he just sang on to
someone he couldn't see, making his magic, drawing her
in through the dark, so slowly, the way you can sometimes charm a dream into letting you remember it. That's
magic too.

Then he sang the lullaby. The one he'd been practicing
every night for two years. I remember a bit of it, just a
little.

*"Don't fall asleep,*
*don't close your eyes—*
*everything happens at night.*
*Don't you sleep—*
*as soon as you slumber,*
*the sun starts to ripen,*
*the flowers tell stories . . ."*

She made a sound. Not a moan, not a cry, not anything with a name or a shape. Just put down that she tried very hard not to make it. It came out of her anyway.

When she hit him, she knocked the *kiit* out of his hands. That time he couldn't save it—rugs or no rugs, I heard it crack and split, heard eighteen double courses yowl against stone. I just caught a lightning flash of her in the candlelight: matted gray hair flying, eyes like gashes in dead flesh, gaunt arms flailing out of control, beating her own head as much as Sirit Byar's. Something bright flickered in her hands against his throat. The candle fell over and went out.

The darkness was so heavy, I felt myself bending under it. I said, "Jailly Doura, don't hurt him. Please, don't hurt him." I could hear the *kiit* strings still thrashing and jangling faintly, but nothing more, not even the dreadful *breathing*. Nothing more until Sirit Byar began to sing again.

*"Don't you sleep—*
*the marsh-goats are singing,*
*the fish are all dancing,*
*the river asks riddles . . ."*

You couldn't have told that he was singing past a dagger, or a broken piece of glass, or whatever she had been saving for him all this long while. He sounded the way he always did—gruff and south-coast, and a little slower than the beat, and not caring about anything in the world but the song. He might have been back in the Miller's Joy, sitting on a table, singing it to fighting, bawling sots; he might have been trying it over to himself as we trudged down some evening road looking for a place to sleep. He sounded like Sirit Byar.

He sang it through to the end, the lullaby, so I knew she hadn't killed him yet, but that was all I did know. I couldn't see anything, I couldn't hear anything, except the footsteps beginning to shuffle slowly toward me. They dragged a little, as though she'd somehow taken on Sirit Byar's limp. I'd have run—all bloody *right*, of course I'd

have run, that's just good sense, that's different from
fear—but in that crushing dark the steps were coming
from everywhere, the way the breathing had been at first.
My knees wouldn't hold me up. I sat down and waited.

Close to, she didn't smell like a distant river at all, but
like any old hill woman, like my father. She smelled lifelong tired, lifelong dirty, she smelled of clothes sweated
in and slept in until they've just *died,* you understand me?
I know that smell, I was born and raised to it, and I'd
smell just like that now if I hadn't run off with Sirit Byar.
What chilled my bowels was the notion that a wealthy
madwoman, prowling a grand house among terrified servants, should smell like home.

When I felt her standing over me, with the stiff, cold
ends of that hair trailing across the back of my neck, I
said loudly, "I am Mircha Del, of Davlo. You should
know that if you're going to kill me." Then I just sat
there, feeling out with my skin for whatever she had in
her hand.

Her breath on my cheek was raw and old and stagnant,
a sick animal's breath. I closed my eyes, even in the darkness, the way you do when you're hoping the *sheknath* or
the rock-*targ* will think you're dead. I was ready for her
teeth, for her long, jagged nails, but the next thing I felt
was her arms around me.

She rocked me, chicken-wrist. Jailly Doura held me in
her sad, skinny arms and bumped me back and forth
against her breast, pushing and tugging on me as though
she were trying to loosen a tree stump in the ground.
Likely she didn't remember at all how you rock somebody, but then I don't remember anybody ever rocking
me in my life, except her, so I wouldn't ever have known
the right way. I did have an idea that it was supposed to be
more comfortable, but it wasn't bad. And the breath
wasn't so awful, either, when you got used to it, nor that
hair all down my face. What was bad was the little whimpering sound, so soft that I didn't truly hear it but felt it in
my body, the broken crooning that never quite became
tears but just shivered and shivered on the edge. That was

bad, but I kept my eyes closed tight and helped her rock me, and Sirit Byar began to sing again.

It doesn't matter what he sang. I know some of the songs in my bones to this day—bloody well *should,* after all—and there were others I'd never heard before and never will again, no matter. What matters is that he sang all night long, sitting by his shattered *kiit,* with a mad-woman's grieving for his only applause. Jailly Doura went on rocking me in her arms, and Sirit Byar sang about merrows and farmwives and wandering Narsai tinkers, and I'll be damned if I didn't fall off to sleep—only a little, only for a moment now and then—as though they were really my parents putting me to bed, just the way they did every night. And stone Azdak only knows what Aung Jatt thought was going on upstairs.

Dawn came suddenly, or maybe I'd been dozing again. It was like staring through rain, but I could see the court-yard around us—there were walls, of course, and a few narrow windows, and the tree wasn't *that* big—and I could see Sirit Byar, looking a bit smaller than usual him-self, and white as his own hair in that rainy light. Jailly Doura was still holding me, but not rocking anymore, and sometime in the night she'd stopped making that terrible silent sound. If I turned my head very slowly and care-fully I could see most of one side of her face—a thin, lined, worn face it was, but the nose was strong and the mouth wasn't a dead slash at all, but full and tender. Her hair was a forsaken birds' nest, thick with mess—well, about like mine, as you can see. Her eyes were closed.

Sirit Byar stood up. His voice was a rag of itself, but he spoke out loudly, not to Jailly Doura this time, nor to me, but to *someone.* I couldn't tell where he was looking, what he was seeing. He said, "This is my last song. Take it. I make this bargain of my own will. I, Sirit Byar." He stood silent for a moment, and then he nodded once, slowly, as though he'd had his reply. Oh, chicken-wrist, I can still see him.

I'm not going to sing you the whole song, that last one. I could, but I'm not going to. This one dies with me, it's supposed to. But this is the ending:

*"Merchant, street-girl, beggar, yeoman,*
*king or common, man or woman,*
*only two things make us human—*
*sorrow and love, sorrow and love . . .*

*Songs and fame are vain endeavor—*
*only two things fail us never.*
*Only two things last forever—*
*sorrow and love, sorrow and love . . ."*

By the time he finished, it was light enough that I could
see Aung Jatt standing in the courtyard entrance. Behind
me Jailly Doura stirred and sighed, and as I turned my
head she opened her eyes again. But they weren't the
same eyes. They were gray and wide and full of surprise,
curiosity, whatever you want—they were a young
woman's eyes in a tired grown face. Maybe I had eyes
like that when I was first traveling with Sirit Byar, but I
doubt it. She said softly, just the way he'd said it to
me, "There you are." And Sirit Byar answered her, "Here
I am."

Careful now, both of us, chicken-wrist, you and me.
Jailly Doura looked down at me in her arms and said—
said *what?* She said, "Are you my daughter, little one?"

"No," I said, "No, no, I'm not. I wish I were." Then I
was horribly afraid that I might have lost her again,
saying that, driven her right back to where she'd been, but
she only smiled and touched my lips and whispered, "Ah,
I know. I was just hoping for a moment, one last, last
time. Never mind. You have a sweet face."

I do not have a sweet face. There are ugly people who
have sweet faces, much good may it do them in this
world. I have the face I want—a dirty, mean wild
animal's face that makes people leave me alone. Fine.
Fine, I wouldn't have it different. But if ever I wanted in
my life to have sweetness that somebody could see, it
would have been then. I stood up, cramped and cranky,
and helped Jailly Doura to rise.

She was small, really, a tiny gray barefoot person in a
mucky ruin of a gown that must have cost someone a few

gold *lotis* a long time ago, and that a beggar wouldn't have wiped his nose on now. She was as shaky on her feet as a newborn *nilvi* colt, but she wasn't mad. I looked over toward Aung Jatt, trying to beckon him over to her, but he was staring at Sirit Byar, who had stumbled down to one knee. Jailly Doura was by him before I was. She knelt before him and took his face between her hands. "Not so soon," she said. I remember that. She said, "Not so soon, I'll not have it. I will not, my dear, no. Do you hear me, Sirit Byar?"

You see, she knew better than I what he'd done. He had given up his last song to the gods, the Other Folk, whatever your people call them. And a bard's last song has power, a last song is always answered, as this one was—but what becomes of the bard when the song is over? Sirit Byar's face was a shrunken white mask, but his eyes were open and steady. He said, "Forgive me, Jailly Doura."

"Not if you leave us." she answered him. "Not if you dare leave now." But there was no anger in her voice, and no hope either. Sirit Byar made that half-grunt, half-snort sound that he always made when people were being a little too much for him. He said, "Well, forgive me or no, you are well, and I've done what was for me to do. Now I'm weary."

I wanted to touch him. I wanted to hold him the way Jailly Doura had held me all night, but I just stood with my fingers in my mouth, like a scared baby. Sirit Byar smiled his almost-smile at me and whispered, "I'm sorry the *kiit* broke, big girl. I wanted you to have it. Goodbye." And he was gone, so. Aung Jatt closed his eyes himself, and began to weep. I remember. Jailly Doura didn't, and I didn't, but old Aung Jatt cried and cried.

I buried him, and the shards of the *kiit* with him, under the threshold of the house, as I'd done with my father. The others wanted to help me, but I wouldn't let them. When I was finished, I scratched a picture of Azdak, god of wanderers, on the stone stair, and I walked away. So now you know where Sirit Byar lies.

There's no more worth the telling. Aung Jatt and Jailly Doura, wanted me to stay with them as long as I liked, forever, but I only passed a few days at the house with them. What I mostly remember is washing and washing Jailly Doura's long gray-black hair in her bath, as the Queen's ladies used to do with me, four of them at a time to hold me in the tub. I always hated it, and I've not put up with it since, but it's different when you're doing it for someone else. You don't wash fifteen, sixteen years of lunatic despair away in three days, but by the time I left Jailly Doura could anyway peep in a mirror and start to recognize the handsome, dignified mistress of a great house, with servants underfoot like *dai*-beetles and a husband who looked at her like sunrise. I don't begrudge it—whatever was hers, she'd paid double-dear price for it, and double again. But I'd have liked Sirit Byar to see her this way, even once.

When I left, she walked with me down to the two great stones where we'd first met Aung Jatt, a hundred years ago. She didn't bother with saying, "Come back and visit us," and I didn't bother promising. Instead she took both my hands and swung them, the way children do, and she just said, "I would have been proud if you had been my daughter."

I didn't know how to answer. I kissed her hands, which I've never done with anybody except the Queen, and you have to do that. Then I swung Sirit Byar's old sea-bag to my shoulder, and I started off alone. I didn't look back, but Jailly Doura called after me, "So would *he* have been proud. Remember, Mircha Del!"

And I have remembered, and that's why the fit took me to have someone set it all down, the only true tale of Sirit Byar you're ever likely to hear. No, I told you I don't want it, what good's your scribble to me? I can't read it— and besides, I was there. Keep it for yourself, keep it for anyone who wants to know a little of what he was. Bad enough they mess up his songs, let them get *something* the right way 'round, anyway. Farewell, my chicken-wrist—here's your twelve coppers, and another for the sweet way you blush. There's an ore barge tied up at Grebak, waiting for a good woman to handle the sweep, if I'm there by tomorrow's eve.

\* \* \*

*"The Last Song of Sirit Byar" was written as an excuse to return to the world of my 1993 novel,* The Innkeeper's Song. *I don't write sequels—or epic trilogies, for that matter—and once a story's told I've always moved on to something as different as I could make it. But in this case I found that I actually missed this world I'd made up in a backward sort of way (no maps, no charts, no genealogies), as much as I missed the people I'd lived with for a couple of years before I sent them on their way. So, as an experiment, I imagined a character based pretty much on my old hero, the great French* chansonnier *Georges Brassens, and imagined him into that world. Mircha Del, the narrator, on the other hand, exploded into my head with her first raucous, outraged words. That happens once in awhile, if you're very lucky.*

# ROUNDELAY
## *Mary C. Pangborn*

Mary C. Pangborn was born August 12, 1907 in
New York City. She studied biochemistry at
Yale University Graduate School, and worked
as a research biochemist with the New York
State Health Department of Albany from 1934
to 1970, when she retired. She has always, on
the side, been a wannabe writer, but no pub-
lisher was ever interested. Period.

Somebody's father had generously donated a huge roll of
gilt paper for the Christmas decorations of the third-grade
room. That was the beginning of it.

Miss Jacobs was watching of course. You didn't worry
about blunt-pointed scissors, but you had to be sure
nobody piled up wobbly chairs to stand on, and you never
knew what else they might think up. She was having fun,
too; no lessons this afternoon—they were free to do anything they liked to pretty up the room for the party, and if
some characters on the school board had to label it "Creative Activity," why, nuts to them. The kids wouldn't be
stopped by a spot of name-calling.

It was Ellie Bingham who started it, as usual. She said,
"Let's make a paper chain! A *big* one, all around the
room!"

It happened every time. Start with a new bunch of kids
in September, and by the third day, the boiling pot would
have thrown up a leader (sometimes two or three, and
then you got politics, as it has been since the days of the
caveman). Oddly enough, the others usually didn't resent
Ellie's bossiness. She seemed to know when to stop short,

stop pushing just before they got mad enough to push back. Something like an athlete's sense of balance? She might be a pretty girl someday, you couldn't tell; now, she had a goblin look—sharply pointed face, black eyes snapping, untamable curls cut in a short mop. She was holding up a strip of paper for approval. "Think that 'll be big enough?"

She got several shouted *yes* votes, and then Davy Harris challenged her: "It's *too* big." Katy Jones, the peace-maker, offered: "Bend it into a circle and *then* let's see."

Ellie put the ends together between two fingers and held it up. There was a short concentrated silence, then several cries of—"Okay, okay, let's get started!" But Ellie wasn't satisfied. She let the strip fall open, took one end and twisted it once, then reached quickly for the paste and fastened it so. "Look, look now! Miss Jacobs, look! Isn't that prettier?"

Ruth stared, trying to remember—where had she seen—? Oh. "Yes, it's lovely, Ellie. Do you know what that is?"

"What? It's just a paper ring."

"It's a special kind of ring. It's not a circle any more, is it? It's called a Moebius strip."

"A *what* kind?" Davy Harris sniffed. "Funny silly name!"

"It's a man's name," Ruth explained. "A German name. The man who invented it."

*"Invented?"* Ellie gave her that blank stare; grown-ups are silly! "What's to invent? Anybody could do it, I just *did.*"

"Yes, dear, but I suppose it took a genius to study the—the math part of it. Look, it doesn't have any inside or outside, it's all the same. Isn't that interesting?"

"It's *what?* Lemme see." Davy grabbed. Ellie shriek-ing, "Don't tear it!" He didn't. He ran his finger gently around, around—"Hey, wow, that's right! The whole thing is an outside!"

"Is *not,* it's all an *inside,* stupid."

Katy said, "It's not either out or in, it's just *there.* Isn't it, Miss Jacobs?"

"Why—why, yes, that's very good, Katy."

Ellie reclaimed the ring, with authority. "We must make *all* of them like this," she announced. "Then it will be *all* special. Come on, everybody make one, take turns, get in line."

But Davy had to make laws, too. "We don't have to call it that ugly name, though." Ellie ignored him.

Somebody yelled, "You made that up, didn't you, Miss Jacobs? Nobody could be named Mubbius!"

And the inevitable chant started, a brief spasm of bedlam;

*"Mubbius Pubbius—"*

*"diddley-gubbius—"*

*"skee-legged, sky-legged, bow-legged MUBBIUS!"*

(Oh, yes, the perfect round: serpent with tail in mouth. Hey, Ruthie, watch your spelling, girl, let's not mix up math and myth.)

She stood back calmly, waiting, and sure enough Ellie brought them to order: "Shut up, dopes, come on, get with it! We've got to make this whole chain today!"

Ellie's father taught English over at the College. She never said "We gotta"—probably she couldn't. Professor Bingham was a pleasant, mild-mannered man—mild, that is, except when his ear caught someone misusing "hopefully" or "fortuitous" or some other victim of current fashion. Then his wrath could become Homeric. Mrs. Bingham was a power on committees. Ellie was an only child; she caught the full force of whatever it was, heredity or environment, never mind trying to sort that one out. She would probably become a senator, or a college president, or—

"Miss Jacobs, could we please have another pot of paste? We need to work from both ends so it goes faster."

"Certainly, Ellie. That's a very good idea."

The chain grew and grew. . . .

Grew into loops over all the windows and halfway around the blackboard. Ruth said brightly, "Now, isn't that lovely! All ready for the party. Come, children, it's almost time for your bus. Hats and coats."

Ellie flung out both arms in a gesture embracing the

universe. "But it's *not* ready!" she wailed. "It must go all around the room and meet! One bi-i-ig chain!"

"Well, we'll see, dear. You'll have time to do some more in the morning."

There was a big roll of paper left. Ellie grabbed the scissors. "Look, everybody, we'll each take some home and make more pieces, then we can put them together tomorrow. Here—"

Authority is sometimes required, even with modern methods. Ruth took the scissors firmly. "Now, Ellie, that's enough. Let's say anyone who wants to take a piece home may have it. I'll cut some for each of you. Now, who would like one?"

"God rest you merry, gentle—folk."

Ruth tried to check the crazy lurch of her pulse at the sound of the deep, warm-laughing voice from the doorway. The room filled with happy shouts of welcome. "Hey, Mr. Morris! Come, come see what we've done!"

Ruth gave him the official smile between teachers. "Hi, Bernie. They've been getting the room ready for the dance. Come, children, mustn't miss the bus."

"Our dance, yes." He leaned beside the door while the shrill crowd boiled past him. Square, dark, chunky, not exactly handsome, beginning to get bald at the front (but who cares about *that?*) He had led the kids into a love of music—even those who seemed to be nearly tone deaf. Ellie was the last out, clutching a roll of gold paper. "We'll have the song just perfect, Mr. Morris," she told him kindly, "You'll see."

"I know you will." Quiet fell with shattering impact as the last of the children vanished down the hallway.

"Peace, it's wonderful." Bernie grinned that sudden flash of comradeship, making your heart turn over, and wandered to the nearest window, where the free end of the chain dangled. He lifted one loop and turned, raising startled eyebrows. "What the hell! How did they hit on *this?*"

"It was Ellie, it always is. She just happened to do one like that, and they were off to the races."

"You know what it is?"

"Of course, I told them. They were fascinated. Ellie wants it to go all around the room and meet."

"Oh, she does? You think that's wise?"

"*Bernie!* Whatever do you mean? A paper chain—little kids—"

"Right, that's all it is. Do they plan to take it past the door?"

"Oh, that's easy. I'll have Nick bring the stepladder. Scotch tape on the top of the casing, nothing to it."

"Mm. Somebody will have to climb. Maybe I'd better come and help. I've got a free period in the middle of the morning."

"Oh, Bernie, would you?" (Lovely! As if a girl couldn't climb a stepladder! He's only a couple of inches taller than I am. Well, three, maybe.) "If they really do make it that long. I suppose they'll get tired of it before they finish."

"Not with Ellie driving them, they won't. That song and dance they've been practicing for their party, that round, 'Three Blind Mice.' You'll be surprised how well they manage it; they don't get the separate voices tangled up at all. One or two of the little demons can actually sing. But this, now." He moved his finger slowly around the paper loop. "I almost wish they were doing some other song."

"But why? They love it, and you know it's too late to change. The mice even have costumes, just caps with ears, but—"

"That settles it, of course. Did you ever notice that a round is a sort of musical Moebius strip?" Over his shoulder, still fingering the paper loop, "Have dinner with me, Ruthie?"

Lovely, so lovely, to sit at dinner together in this quiet booth, the chattering world screened off; sharing, finding things to talk about, so easily (but I could cook him an even better dinner than this!) She felt nearer twenty than twenty-seven, and, well, not exactly beautiful, but something better: knowing she didn't have to be. (It does happen. Sometimes. To some people. They say. If only.

You couldn't help thinking. But. Don't be silly, Ruthie, you know perfectly well this is nothing but.)

Morning of the day, and Bernie did come as he'd promised. To the business of fastening loops of paper chain over the door he brought a portentous solemnity of dedication. It was astonishing how many children did bring homemade loops of paper chain, carefully piled into brown paper supermarket bags so they wouldn't crumple—all the mothers had evidently thought of the same system. Ellie insisted that all the chains must be inspected, loop by loop. "*You* must look at them, Miss Jacobs," and she did, conscientiously, dreading to find an imperfection that would require criticism (please, Lord, no storms and tantrums today!) but all was well. Apparently you could easily get into the rhythm of creating Moebius strips and go on and on. . . .

"Now *you* could make the last ones," Ellie offered generously. "Look, it needs about three more." Startled and pleased (yet why should it also be frightening?) Ruth responded warmly, "Thank you, Ellie, I'd love to. You all watch and make sure I do it right."

And the chain was long enough. Over the back of the piano, across the brightly tinseled Christmas tree in the corner, looped along the top of the shelves on the inner wall, and here, beside the door, the two ends hung limp, waiting. Ellie cut the paper for the final ring. No one challenged her right to be the one who joined the ends. Ruth watched her holding the two pieces, one in each hand, studying them with a concentrated frown, a dedicated artist who must get this brush stroke, this word, this note, exactly right. She gave one of the ends of the chain a twist before she slipped the joining loop in and reached for the paste. "There!" She looked up in triumph. "Now the whole *thing* is special! See?"

Ruth did see, and felt a thoroughly ridiculous tingle at the back of her neck. What happens if you make a Moebius strip out of a whole chain of Moebius strips? How silly, it's nothing but gilt paper! still, she was glad Bernie hadn't seen it.

She forgot about it in the hustle and burly of the day, until it was time for the dance.

The whole day had gone well—no fights, no tears, not even any spilled lemonade, and only the normal amount of mess from the ritual of little presents around the tree. (It's possible, I suppose, that on one day of the year they all turn into little angels.) And now the dutiful audience of parents had been successfully herded into the huddle of seats squeezed into a corner for them. How room had been found for them was a genuine fourth-dimensional puzzle. But there they were, and there was Bernie taking his place at the piano.

*. . . three blind mice . . .*

All in line at first, and then, as they started to sing, joining hands and moving into a circle. At least, you expected it to be a circle, but it was cleverer than that. Miss Beeman had worked over it as though preparing a professional ballet company for a Broadway first. They wound slowly into a tightening spiral, singing, the frantically jumping mice penned into the middle. The mice had supposedly been selected by lot; only Bernie knew how they just happened to be the three who couldn't sing. Triumphantly, the separate pieces of the round came together at the right moment as the spiral closed:

*ev-er see-such-a sight-in-your life*
*as three blind mice!*

Some ill-informed parents began to clap, and were firmly rebuked by the piano as the round picked up again without a hitch; now the dancers were unwinding, leaving the mice clutching each other dramatically in the center. Bernie's left hand was having a lot of fun with those chords; did he think he was giving a Bach recital? Unwound, a circle now, not yet joined.

The room was beginning to swim and blur a little. Ruth leaned against the wall, dismayed. (I ought not to have skipped lunch—not a headache now, no, please! And what's happening to the music? Someone playing a recorder? Something wrong with my ears—)

They were supposed to join hands, completing the circle, at the final shout of "Mice!" Now Ellie should reach to Davy at the other end and—

She twirled on a single beat of the music, changing hands, so that as they completed the round she was the only one facing outward, while all the others looked to the center of the ring. She had given the whole circle a Moebius twist.

And this was supposed to finish the dance. The piano stopped, but that other voice—some kind of woodwind, certainly—went on and on, growing louder, as though closing in from a distance, and Ellie's shrill insistent voice rose to meet it, pulling the children into the song again:

*"Three Blind Mice!"*

Round and round they pranced, frantically singing, possessed; and Ruth felt the room spinning with them. Bernie had risen, leaning on the keyboard, annoyed and alarmed. There was some kind of mist over by the window, not a grayness, more like a dazzle of light; a shape in it— someone outside trying to look in?—and out of nowhere the impossible music grew and grew, many-voiced now, picking up the melody and playing with it as though all the ancient gods were leaning out of their separate heavens and laughing together.

And there he was, the Piper, taking shape out of the sun-dazzle: straight out of a fifteenth-century picture, pied double red and purple, feathered hat cocked sideways; his face was hidden behind the hands that held the pipe. The reedy tune came clear, strong; behind him a swirl of stained-glass colors, an unfamiliar landscape of hill and forest beyond the open window—(*What?* You don't have open windows in December, it's not—)

Ellie was straining toward him, dragging all the children after her, singing, singing—they had all risen at least three inches off the floor, floating toward the Piper, into the window, into legend.

Through the fog Ruth saw Bernie's frightened face—she wasn't mad, then, he was seeing it too. She saw him fumbling and tearing at the paper chain over the piano. She reached for the nearest bit of chain behind her and tore it apart. The tiny sound of tearing paper was magnified into a howl and crackle of static as the music stopped.

Stopped; but not before Ruth had caught a glimpse of a further twist of the loop, above and beyond the pied piper— the vast shape of that other Piper, the ancient one, the goat-foot, the horned god, making ready to set *his* pipe to his mocking lips.

. . . nothing, then. Children standing about, grinning happily, accepting their parents' lighthearted applause. Had none of *them* seen or heard—anything?

Professor Bingham had taken off his glasses and was polishing them, slowly, with a faintly puzzled frown.

And Ellie? She stood lost, solitary, empty-handed, staring out the window. "Oh!" she wailed, "oh, look, look!" And then, happily, "Hey, look everybody, it's snowing!"

And it was all over. The people were going, and nothing had happened except another Christmas party. Ruth found herself compulsively counting the children as they went out, and was absurdly relieved to discover they were all there.

Bernie was examining the hanging paper chain, carefully tearing more holes in it. Ruth protested weakly: "It's—it's nothing but trash for the janitor to clear up."

"I know. Just to be on the safe side."

(Safe? Oh yes, the children. But. Who wants to be *safe?*)

She said, "It didn't happen, you know."

Now he would give her a quizzical look and say, "What didn't happen?" Or something equally sensible.

He turned away from the limp harmless fragments of gilt paper and came to her; carefully, gently, he untwisted her tight-clenched fingers. "No; no, I suppose it wasn't a happening, exactly . . ."

Grave, thoughtful brown eyes studying her, wondering (oh, was it possible?) what it means when two people can see together into the same fourth dimension. "Let's go, honey. What we both need right now—first—is a drink."

*I don't know how it can be possible to describe how one decides to write a particular story. Those constantly flickering mind-sparks that we call "ideas" sometimes condense into crystals, and the crystals may collect into a larger shape, a structure; then you say, yes, try that for a story. There might sometimes be an external happening to start the crystallization process, but if there was any such in this case, I don't remember it. I haven't anything to say about the story except: here it is.*

# SPACE STATION ANNIE
## by Cynthia McQuillin

Cynthia McQuillin has sold thirteen stories to date and has just completed her first novel, a fantasy about a singer with a gift for psychic healing. Her most recently published works include "Humphrey's Dilemma" (*MZB's Fantasy Magazine*); "Cat's World" (*Catfantastic III*); "The Virgin Spring" (*Sword and Sorceress XI*) and "Shadow Harper" (*Sword and Sorceress XII*).
Due out in 1996 and 1997 are: "Daelith's Bargain" (*Sword and Sorceress XIII*) and "The Stone-Weaver's Tale" (*Sword and Sorceress XIV*).

"Damn rich-kid, transient brats!" Annie Keeley swore, remembering how their voices had taunted her as she ducked into the dimness of Trace's Three Satellites Lounge. "Space Station Annie! Space Station Annie!" God, how she hated that epithet! She would never forgive Bram Tyler for writing that damn song. Annie was certain he'd done it out of spite, to punish her for the breakup of their spectacularly unsuccessful affair the previous year.

She'd been on her way out even then, and he was an eager, young up-and-comer. At first he'd been wonderful—seeming sympathetic and supportive. They'd shared some fabulous duets back then, on and off stage. But as her popularity waned and his began to grow, he became short-tempered and distant, criticizing everything she did or said. When Annie finally figured out that Bram's career was what their relationship was really about, she dumped him.

God, he'd been furious when she told him to get out! She almost smiled at the memory of his perfect, always-so-in-control expression contorted in childish rage. But he'd gotten even, and in spades. Without meaning to, Annie found herself humming the first verse of his bitter prophetic ballad:

> *"Annie sits by herself in a bar, with no friends.*
> *She thinks of her past and dreams, now and then.*
> *Once she had beauty, but you can see in her eyes*
> *That life has grown bitter, love holds no surprise."*

The performer in her had to appreciate the song's sweet, poignant melody, even though she resented the accuracy of the caricature he'd drawn. But she hadn't been like that till *after* he'd written *Space Station Annie*.

*I don't have time for this!* Annie told herself sternly as she slipped onto a stool at the bar and signaled Mike, the bartender, to bring her a flask of syntha-scotch. She usually didn't drink before a performance, but she really couldn't afford to be all wound up tonight, not with a major talent scout coming in from Titan Station. It had taken her three months to convince Jodan McKaye to come out and take a look at her; she certainly didn't want to blow it now.

Setting the half-emptied flask down on the bar, Annie leaned back to gaze out of the viewport, waiting for the alcohol to take the edge off her anger. Trace had named the lounge for the orbital transmitters which hung like huge Christmas tree ornaments in graceful formation just beyond the big polyglass window. The view was spectacular, though its impact had long ago ceased to affect her. Contemplating their ethereal symmetry as she took another hit, Annie sighed, then motioned to Mike to bring her a vid-link.

"Only one drink, Annie. Trace's orders," he said when she asked for a second flask.

"Thank you, Nana Mikey," she muttered as she jacked the link in for a private hookup. It wasn't like she was a lush or anything.

Deftly fingering the keyboard, Annie signed on-line to
scan the current gig-list. There was nothing she could use,
mostly private parties or thinly disguised ads for live sex
performances. If only she could get a spot in one of the
class lounges. Switching to com mode, she put through a
personal query to her agent.

"Annie, how nice to hear from you," Mark Chang said,
when she finally got his secretary to put her through. But
he looked far from pleased.

"I want to know why Martin Trudeau over at Club Paris
was so surprised to see me, when I dropped by to follow
up on that audition you were supposed to be lining up."

"You know how it is, Annie. Things slip through the
cracks sometimes." He spread his hands in a helpless
gesture.

"Yeah, but they're always *my* things, Mark, and I'm
damned sick and tired of it!" He flinched visibly as she
glowered.

"Look, Annie, you've had a long run, longer than most,
in fact. You should be happy with that. Hey, I'll be the
first to admit that you've made a lot of money for the
agency over the years, and that's why I've kept you on,
but. . . ."

"Get to the point, Mark!"

"I was trying to let you down easy, but you force me to
be blunt. I'm running a business, Annie, not a charity.
That means I've got to go with the clients that pull in the
big credit."

"Fine, then you can do without my ten percent! From
now on I'll handle my own bookings." Her eyes flashed
sparks as she hit the document-copy/file key on her terminal. "Computer, ret-scan and voice ID Annie Janice
Keeley ident 3745p."

"ID verified . . . waiting."

"Log cancellation of contract 2904478-4 Keeley,
Annie J. as of this date on verbal acceptance, ret-scan and
voice ID Mark T. Chang." Annie's voice was calm,
almost cold. "Do you agree, Mark?"

"Okay, Annie, if that's the way you want it!" He leaned
forward in the view screen to key his own terminal.

"Computer, retinal scan and voice ID Mark Thomas Chang ident 7998m."

"ID verified . . . waiting."

"Log cancellation of contract 2904478-4 Keeley, Annie J. as of this date. I hope you're happy, Annie!" He signed off without waiting for her reply.

*Good riddance!* she thought acidly. He'd come crawling back when she reestablished herself, and then he could just go hang with everyone else who'd deserted her.

"On my tab," she called to Mike as she headed backstage to change for the show. How dare Mark treat her like some broken-down failure! She'd fought her way to the top once before; she was still good enough, and young enough to do it again. Mark, Trace, those damn kids, she'd show them all.

Sometimes she really hated this business. But it hadn't all been heartaches and jerks. She'd met some really wonderful people along the way, too. Annie smiled, as she always did when she remembered Mikhail Sevranski. The ambitious young engineer had been the first real love of her life. But it was no use daydreaming about might-have-beens. Mikhail had drifted out of her life a long time ago, just like so many other good things had.

As she sat down at the makeup table to study the slightly magnified image the light-mirror threw back, Annie couldn't help thinking about him, though. She'd done that a lot since her breakup with Bram. Mikhail had been everything the vain young singer wasn't—sensitive, gentle, and earnest. They had met at the dive where she was working on Luna Station when she first started out. He applauded much too enthusiastically at the end of every set and bought her a drink after the last one. The rest was magic. They had six months together, then Mikhail was assigned out to one of the mining stations, and Annie had become famous.

"Show time!" she said to her reflection, clearing away the romantic cobwebs. "Can't blow it tonight, Annie girl. This could be your big break."

Wriggling into the auraglow skin-tights she performed in, Annie shoved her station togs into the locker she shared with Casey Polaski, accidentally knocking a holo-poster off one of the shelves. It unrolled to display a beautifully detailed picture of Bram Tyler performing at the Metro. The egotistical little twit was everywhere! She couldn't get away from him, anymore than she could get his Goddamned song out of her head. *Why did he have to make the melody so haunting?* Annie thought, stuffing the poster back into the locker. She wished she'd written it herself! Actually, she wished she'd written anything in the last year.

Once, the songs had flowed through her like water from a mountain spring. But the more disillusioned she'd grown, the harder it was to feel the music inside of her. Now her inner voice had been stilled completely. She wanted to blame Bram for that, too; but the truth was, she'd been losing it all along. That was why the fans had deserted her, and that was why she'd lost her contract with Global Arts. In her more rational moments Annie recognized that fact, but this wasn't one of those moments.

Returning to the light-mirror, Annie squeezed off a shot of syntha-scotch from the pint flask she kept tucked away in the back part of the top drawer. Just a hit to quiet her nerves. But the pump was clogged so she only got a mouthful of alcohol-laden mist. *Just as well,* she supposed, tucking it away as she wondered where Casey was. It was almost time for the first set.

*Christ! Don't let Trace make me go on early tonight. That's all I need!* Annie thought angrily as she began dabbing on her foundation. She had spent the rest of this month's wages on a quickie juve job just two days earlier, so she'd look her best for McKaye; but it was already breaking down. *Damn!* Her face was beginning to take on that look of character that marked her as well over thirty, and that was death for a performer these days. Anyone who was even moderately successful could afford to look twenty-five forever.

"You're going to have to start putting that stuff on with a trowel if you don't get up to the clinic for a real treatment soon," Casey said as she shimmied through the tight space of the dressing area, already in her costume.

"It's about time you showed up," Annie snapped, stressed to the point of irritability. Intent on her reflection, she hadn't even heard the door click open.

Casey was a bar-companion by profession, shilling drinks and listening while the customers spilled their troubles. It was cheap therapy, but it helped keep the station workers sane. The big redhead had a special understanding with the boss, so he let her sing a few numbers in the show to keep her happy. She was a little on the mouthy side, but the patrons liked her. *Probably because she bounces,* Annie thought uncharitably. But then, the woman could hardly help that she was so lavishly endowed.

"You need grav units for those things," Annie said, as Casey elbowed her way up to the table.

"Don't I wish," she laughed good-naturedly, pushing up the amplification on the mirror field so she could put the finishing touches on her makeup. It was far more elaborate than Annie's, almost garish. Without asking, she snatched Annie's glitter hypo from the table, twisting on the spray setting to highlight her eyes. Then she turned it down to a narrow field, to give herself a beauty mark on the right breast.

"Whoops, that's my intro music!" Casey squealed, dropping the hypo. Then she paused suddenly in midflight, fixing Annie with a look of desperate appeal. "Is it all right if I do *Luck is a Jade* tonight?"

"You can't be serious, Casey! You know I always open with *Luck,*" Annie groaned. That last thing she wanted with Jodan McKaye coming was to change her set.

"Oh, please, please, Annie. It's such a great number for me. I've already had Zale program the music in my key, and it's too late to change it now." She was fairly dancing with anxiety.

"Okay, okay," Annie sighed. "Go on. Tell Zale I'll open with *I Only Dream of Going Home.*"

Annie could hear Casey rolling into a really torchy version of *Luck is a Jade* as she put the finishing touches on

her own makeup. It was the last song she'd written after
Bram—the last song she'd ever write if she didn't pull
herself out of this slump. The cynical tone of the lyrics
had mirrored her own growing cynicism and despair as
*Space Station Annie* began hitting the space ways. As
much as Annie hated to admit it, Casey did more for the
sultry blues ballad than she ever had.

Taking a moment to compose her thoughts and prepare
for her performance, Annie stared into the mirror and
calmly examined her reflection. It was the same face
she'd seen there for over forty-five years: frizzy blonde
hair, hard green eyes—like jade and onyx pebbles; high
aristocratic brows and a wide sensuous mouth. She was
tall for a woman, and her body was fit and lean from
working out daily on the grav-track. Yes, she was ready
for her comeback. *Come on, Mr. McKaye, just give me a
chance!*

Casey still had two more songs to go, but Annie was
too nervous to wait backstage, so she slipped out front to
see what the house looked like. She expected a good
crowd since it was Friday and Trace's was the only bar
open. There wasn't enough trade for the big places to
bother with till Saturday, after everyone had rested from
their double shift weeks.

At first glance it looked like the usual batch of young
rowdies. There was no sign of McKaye yet, but she
noticed a group of older men sitting at a table near the
bar. They must be pretty high rollers, judging by their
choice of beverage. Bottles of real Scotch went for big
credit out here. Their clothing, which was about ten years
out of date, marked them as out-system returnees. Very
successful returnees, exactly the sort of customers Trace
liked his employees to cultivate.

Casey bounced offstage to a brief but affectionate
flurry of applause as the light curtain rippled down to
cover her exit. When the holo-image cleared the field
again, Annie was onstage, leaning seductively against the
synth unit whose housing was detailed to look like a real
old-time grand piano. The operator ran his fingers lightly
over the keyboard, bringing up a rainbow light display

along with the delicate chime of a wire-strung harp and the haunting, distant lilt of a bagpipe. The sound of the pipes died as she began to sing, leaving only the harp for accompaniment.

*"Well it's great to be a spacer,*
*When you roam from star to star.*
*Takin' any ship that gets you there,*
*Till you don't know where you are.*
*And all the girls are beautiful,*
*But you don't care anyway,*
*'Cause none of them are human,*
*And you never really stay."*

The music spoke of the roving souls of Ireland who carried their homeland in their heart; but the words told the rollicking tale of a young man off to seek his fortune in the space ways and his reversals of fortune—first as a cargo hauler, then a smuggler, and finally as a barkeep.

*"I sell smuggled booze to spacers now,*
*Who don't know where they're bound,*
*And they always talk of goin' home*
*When they buy another round.*
*But it was me who chose to take the road*
*And sing my own damn song.*
*Now, I only dream of goin' home*
*When there's somethin' goin' wrong."*

Jodan McKaye came in about halfway through the number. Annie flashed him her best smile when she finished, then went right into her fast-paced, hard-edged patter. By the time she started the next number, she'd warmed to her performance considerably. *I'm really on tonight!* she told herself as she moved seamlessly from song, to patter, to song. Her voice was pure and lilting, reflecting the character and mood of each piece she sang. But then, it was never her voice that betrayed her.

Near the end of the set, Annie's confidence began to fade as she sensed she was losing the audience. She signaled Zale to substitute one of her surefire hits, for the heartwarming ballad she usually used to close.

"Come on, Annie," one of the techs in the front row called, "Do something we haven't heard."

"Yeah," his companion laughed. "We're getting tired of the same old hard-luck songs."

One of the men from the table in the back stood up, and moving with catlike quickness, took the instigator by the shoulder. Annie couldn't hear what he said, but both hecklers were suddenly silent. But it was no use. She looked back to McKaye just in time to see him shake his head, and rise to leave. The last two lines of "Space Station Annie" leaped unbidden into her mind as the music died away.

> *"When she takes a bow, though you never pause,*
> *In the back of her mind she still hears the applause.* ²

But she did hear applause, she realized, almost laughing at the absurdity of it. Looking toward the bar, Annie saw that the five men at the back table had actually gotten to their feet and were putting their hands together with remarkable fervor. As she slipped from the stage, Trace caught her eye and gestured for her to join them. Her heart wasn't in it, but she nodded anyway.

The returnees sat talking and laughing among themselves as Annie approached the table. She noticed that the one who'd quieted the two techs, a short wiry man with the most amazing shock of radiation-whitened hair, was looking at her with confident expectation. *Great, I could use a little ego massage,* she thought to herself, mustering a smile as she approached. Unlike the spacers and station workers, he wore a neatly clipped beard.

"Thank you for your assistance, Mr. . . . ?" she said holding out her hand.

"Sevan," he said as he rose to take her hand. "Mack Sevan. I'm the Commerce Liaison for the delegation from Cade's World. We're on our way to the Colonial Policies Conference at Earth Prime." Rather than merely gesturing for her to sit, he pulled out a chair for her, an old-fashioned courtesy she'd always liked. "And these are some of my colleagues."

Annie smiled at each man as he was introduced, but

never took her eyes from Sevan. He had a handsome, rugged face and a boyish sort of charm that she liked right off. His eyes flashed blue-green, like a high mountain lake in the dark setting of his face, and his teeth gleamed like ivory in a warm, open smile. Sensing something more than mere fannish enthusiasm in the way he looked at her, Annie made the usual pleased-to-meet-you noises with a ring of sincerity she hadn't bothered with in a long time.

"Annie Keeley," he said at last, grinning like a kid. "I can't believe it's really you."

His manner seemed more like that of an old friend than a fan, and there *was* something familiar about him.

"Have we met before, Mr. Sevan?" Annie gave him a searching look.

"It was a long time ago, before I shipped out for Kelly's Edge." He named a section of the frontier she'd heard mentioned quite a lot in the news recently—something to do with a new medicinal herb or an agri-product. It didn't matter; what was important right now was the way he looked at her when he said, "But I'm still your biggest fan."

"He's not kidding, Annie," the man he'd introduced as Tad Mangan said.

"Well, that's very flattering, Mr. Sevan." A genuine smile trembled tentatively on her lips, then settled in to stay.

"It's Mack to my friends, who were just leaving. Weren't you?" He looked pointedly around the table.

"Well, I guess we could go over that presentation again," Tad said, when one of the others began to protest. "It was really a pleasure to meet you, Annie. You have no idea how much your songs have meant to us over the years." The sentiment was echoed all 'round as they made their departure.

"As I was saying," Mack continued, once they'd gone. "Please call me Mack. I do hope we can be friends."

"I'd like that, Mack," she returned his smile.

When he raised his hand for service, she was amazed at how quickly a waiter appeared. "Champagne," Mack ordered. "None of that squirt-gun stuff, either. I want a bottle of Brut, if you have one. If not, your best bottle of wine."

Annie could hardly believe her eyes when Mike produced a bottle of Cordon Negro Brut from behind the bar, and served it himself. She dearly loved champagne and hadn't seen a bottle in so long she couldn't even remember the last time. Mack grinned even wider when he saw how her eyes lit up.

"That's pretty expensive stuff," she said.

"This is a special occasion."

"It must be pretty special coming home after all this time."

"No, Annie. *You* are the special occasion. Coming back to Earth is no big deal for me; I like it just fine out on the Edge." Then his tone softened and he grew suddenly serious, *"I only dream of going home when there's something going wrong."*

"Just like the song, Mack?" Annie teased, catching herself just in time. She had almost called him Mikhail. But the flash of recognition faded as she studied his face more closely. This self-assured stranger bore only the most superficial resemblance to her first love. Mikhail had been a pale, soft-featured boy with a cherubic body and thick, curly black hair. His voice had been very different, too—soft, almost melodic. Mack's was deep and gravelly. Only their eyes were the same, blue-green.

"Yup, just like the song," he agreed, seemingly oblivious to her confusion as he poured the champagne.

Annie sipped at the sparkling liquid to cover her consternation. The bubbles tickled her nose as they burst, breaking the spell that held her. Suddenly she laughed, sounding almost like Casey.

"That's better," Mack said. "You look like a kid when you laugh. It makes your eyes sparkle."

"I feel like a kid when I drink champagne," she replied, smothering a giggle.

"Let's make a toast," he said with a mischievous twinkle in his eye. "To new beginnings."

"To new beginnings!" She touched the rim of her glass to his, then drained its contents. But Annie found herself once again studying his face as he carefully refilled their glasses.

"It's getting rather crowded in here," Mack said in annoyance, drawing her attention to the scruffy lot of mech-workers that had just come off shift. Five of them had plunked themselves down at the next table and were staring at Mack with open curiosity. It wasn't every day someone walked into the Three Satellites Lounge and ordered champagne.

"I have a compartment over at Central Hostelry," he said.

"Actually, I have another set to do," she replied, frowning slightly at his offer. By station rules, the only "partners-for-hire" were the androids in the company bordellos, but some of the bar-companions and entertainers were known to pick up extra money in their sleep compartments. She hadn't sunk that low, not yet.

When she started to rise, he put his hand on her arm. His fingers were hard and strong; he could easily have crushed her slender bones, but his grasp was gentle, barely enough to detain her. Annie found the sensation of such controlled strength mildly exhilarating.

"You don't *have* to do anything." His gaze was intense. "Spend one hour with me, Annie, anywhere you want. You won't regret it."

Annie would have sworn that her experience with Bram had destroyed her capacity for trust. But there was something about Sevan which drew her to him, the promise of something she couldn't quite fathom. She needed to get out of this limbo Bram's song had put her in, and get back into the real world. *McKaye is probably my last chance,* she thought bitterly as she stared into this stranger's weathered face. What did she have to lose?

"I'm taking the rest of the night off, boss," she called to Trace as she saw him coming out of the stockroom. He started to protest; then, seeing who her companion was, he changed his mind.

"Okay, but don't make a habit of it. I'll let Casey go on again. She's been after me to let her do more stuff anyway."

*Of course,* Annie almost laughed out loud, wondering how soon Trace was planning to ease Casey into her spot. But somehow it didn't matter. Nothing mattered anymore, except what Mack had to say to her.

They agreed to meet in the Hydroponics Section after Mack dropped by his hotel to pick up his duffel bag and some food while Annie changed into her station togs.

"Here you go," he said, offering her a burger and a plasti-pack of limp, greasy fries.

"Thanks," she smiled at him, setting the food down between them on the metal bench.

"God, it's great to have real food again," he laughed around a mouthful of burger. "Even tank-grown drek like this. You get pretty tired of ship rations when you're used to the fresh stuff."

"I'm afraid I wouldn't know," she said, nibbling on a fry. "It's been quite a while since I've had money for luxuries like fresh food." Annie sighed, breathing in the fresh air from the garden tanks. "I should come here more often, it's very peaceful."

"It is," he agreed looking at the tidy rows of greenery, "but it's nothing compared to being out in the open, with a mossgrass plain rolling out from your front porch like a Pastaan carpet, and the spring·sky so blue you think it'll burn out your eyes. Now that's something worth getting up for in the morning."

"Your home?" Annie asked, setting down her empty soda flask. The burger, as much of a treat as it was, was too well done and she wasn't really hungry. She rolled the remains in the plasti-wrap and deposited it back in the bag with the empty fry pack.

"It's more of a vacation place than a home now, a cabin I have out near Presquill. That's a trading center at the foot of the Kilgarrie Range. We've struck up quite a lucrative trade with some of the locals there. The *sedai,* which is what they call themselves, aren't real bright, but they're incredibly clever with their hands, and very friendly. One of the things we're here to do is make sure they get registered as protected sentients with the Planetary Council.

"I started out with a little bar up there when I first came to Cade's, but I don't get back there nearly as often as I'd like."

"Sounds like a nice place," Annie said, glancing down at the duffel he'd set carefully on the floor beneath the bench. She could have sworn it just tapped her foot. "Have you got something alive in that thing?"

"Oh, that," Mack replied with a chuckle, opening the shapeless sack to reach inside and pull out something that looked like a cross between a cat and a ferret. "It's only Mrs. Henderson," he said, smoothing the plush, honey-colored fur. "She's a Cadine Burrow Cat. They form a pretty strong bond with you if you raise 'em from kits, and I don't like to leave her alone for too long. That's why I wanted to pick up the bag.

"She's completely tame." He offered her to Annie, who gingerly accepted the strange creature. Settling Mrs. Henderson into her lap, she stroked the triangular head. The Burrow Cat snuffled briefly at her fingers and began to purr. The species was either nocturnal or subterranean she guessed, watching how Mrs. Henderson squinted at the grow-lights overhead.

"I think it's too bright for her," she said, as the creature tried to burrow under her arm.

"How thoughtless of me!" Mack said, returning Mrs. Henderson to the duffel bag, which he left partway open so she'd have some fresh air.

"Burrow Cats are night predators. In the wilds they dig tunnels. But they're just as happy in a pile of blankets or a bag."

"She's adorable, Mack, but you didn't bring me out here to sell me a Burrow Cat."

"No, I didn't. Sorry, I've been enjoying myself so much I didn't think that I might be wasting your time." He took a breath, then started into his pitch.

"I own a chain of entertainment centers at Vedor's Port on Cade's. But I'm also in the public relations business—that's why I'm with the delegation, and I worked Phobos

Station for five years to make my stake before I shipped out. I'm telling you this so you'll see that I pretty much know what's what both in-system and out. And I'm here to tell you that there are some incredible opportunities on Cade's World for people looking to make a fresh start."

"I've thought about shipping out," Annie admitted. "But that takes a lot of money, which I don't have. But even if I did, why should I risk my neck out in the middle of nowhere? I need to make a comeback *now,* I don't have time to work my way back in from the high frontier. This is where the industry is and it's going to stay that way, at least in my lifetime."

"You might be surprised," he said, arching his brow. "The colonies have grown considerably in the last twenty years. Cade's World isn't all that primitive, and Kelly's Edge is expanding like you wouldn't believe."

"What's your point, Mack?" Her tone was more impatient than she had meant it to be, but her patience was wearing thin.

"Things are changing, Annie, and faster than you think. As humanity moves out to the stars, we're taking culture and the arts with us. The exodus has already begun. Believe me, it's my business to know. The sharp ones and the hungry ones are already out there pushing, and they're the ones who'll shape the future of the entertainment field, you can bet on it!"

Annie sat up straighter. "What kind of market are you talking about, Mack?"

"Several million now, in ten years—billions. It's not common knowledge, Annie, and I probably shouldn't be telling you this, but Cade's World is on the verge of an expansion breakthrough. Our agri-coms have produced four new varieties of high-yield grain hybrids and dozens of new pharmaceuticals that are going to be hitting the market as soon as they come out of test-quarantine in about two years. When that happens, Cade's—which is already a self-supporting colony and a major transport hub—is going to become a boom world. People will be rushing to settle there from all over the Edge, as well as from Earth itself—"

"And they'll want booze and entertainment," she finished. "But what does that mean to me? Once the market's grown enough to attract the big time pop-heroes I'll be just another has-been, forced to move farther and farther out onto the frontier to stay ahead of total failure."

"You used to have more faith in yourself, Annie." He shook his head. "Besides, things aren't like that on the Edge. People aren't interchangeable, disposable units like they are here. You just don't know! He paused for a moment, trying to find the right words.

"Look, I know it all sounds like 'blue sky and roses' to you now. God knows, when I first signed up to work stations, I was all full of hopes and dreams that died before I ever made it out. But I found a new life on Cade's World, and I learned how to dream all over again. And, Annie, you can, too!"

"I appreciate that you're trying to help, Mack," she said, rising to pace with an exasperated sigh. For some reason, his assurances only made her feel more trapped and hopeless than ever.

"Look, Annie, I know what it's like."

"No, you don't!" she rounded on him. "You can't possibly know what it's like for me. To you I'm just some image on a holo-recording, or voice on an audio. You listen to my songs and then you think you know me, but you don't."

"You're wrong, Annie. Dead wrong." Standing, he took her by the shoulders and turned her so that her eyes met his. "I *do* know you. I know the Annie Keeley who's not afraid to live life the way she finds it. The woman who keeps on fighting for what she wants no matter what anyone says or does to stand in her way.

"I know you think you've lost that spark of creativity that kept your dreams alive, but you haven't! You still have the same clarity of vision and sensitivity that allowed you to sing people's dreams into reality for all those years. I know you do! That's your special gift, Annie, and no one can take it away from you."

"But they have!" she blurted, pulling away from him. "Don't you see? I've lost it. I haven't written a song in

over a year." He started to speak, but she cut him off.
"The Annie Keeley you're talking about doesn't exist
anymore, Mack. She's dead." Annie turned away, shoulders slumped in defeat.

"She could live again, if only you believed in her,
Annie." He reached out to turn her back to face him.

"It's easy for *you* to say that," she said pushing him
away again, harder this time. "But I'm the one who has to
live with the wreckage when all your pretty promises
shatter into reality!"

"Damn it, Annie! Sit down and listen to me." He
pushed her down onto the bench more forcefully than
he'd meant to, and for a moment they sat glaring at each
other. Before either of them could speak, Mrs. Henderson
erupted from the duffel bag and into Annie's lap. Chur-
ring with concern, the Burrow Cat stood up as tall as she
could and patted Annie's cheek with one leathery little
paw, startling her out of her angry reply.

"Oh, dear," Annie laughed despite herself. "She's so
upset." The Burrow Cat nuzzled up unto her shoulder and
burrowed under Annie's hair, wrapping her in a small
furry hug. Then she began making a rhythmic humming
sound. "Does she do this a lot?"

"I've never seen her do anything like it before." Mack
seemed truly perplexed by Mrs. Henderson's behavior.
"But they are low grade empaths—that's why they bond
so closely with humans, and they're very protective. She
knows I care about you, so I suppose she's trying to make
you feel better."

"If only I had this kind of effect on agents, producers,
and audiences." The Burrow Cat began to purr, and Annie
sighed, feeling inexplicably better as wave after wave of
comfort seemed to envelop her.

"You could," he smiled a little sheepishly at her, regret-
ting his outburst the moment before. "I know you don't
believe it yet, but on Cade's World you're practically a
legend, or you *could* be with a little judicious management." He raised both eyebrows and made a kind of
hopeful funny face.

"Seriously, Annie, every émigré who passed through a

station on their way to the new frontier remembers the
gutsy blonde with the haunting voice, who seemed to be
singing only to them. Your visions gave us something to
cling to when things got too hard, or too lonely. But more
importantly, Annie, you gave us a sense of our own history, and that's something we still need, now more than
ever."

"Oh, Mack," she started to say when a curious kind of
double vision overcame her. Her face grew pale as she
looked into his steady gaze, and saw another, younger
face form around those oh-so-familiar blue-green eyes. It
was like looking at a negative image she realized, but this
time she was sure. His pale skin was weathered to a tan so
dark that it made him look almost Indian, and his curly
black hair had been bleached and straightened, but his
eyes were still the same and so was his belief in her.

"Mikhail!" Her voice was almost a whisper. "I just
couldn't believe it before. My God, it's been so long!"
She had imagined this reunion so many times recently
that it seemed unreal.

"Annie," he murmured, voice choked with emotion as
he reached to embrace her.

"Why didn't you tell me it was you, damn it?" she
scolded, only half as cross as she sounded. "And for
God's sake, why did you change your name? Are you in
some kind of trouble?" Her voice softened suddenly with
concern.

"Nothing like that," he smiled, stroking her cheek.
"Remember I told you that when I first started out on
Cade's World I had a bar out in Presquill. Well, the *sedai*
couldn't pronounce Mikhail Sevranski. Mack Sevan was
the closest they could get. After a while, it kind of stuck."

"That doesn't explain why you didn't tell me."

"Pride maybe, I don't know!" He waved his hands in a
helpless gesture. "Besides, I wasn't sure you'd want to
see me after I just disappeared like that."

"Men!" she said, raising her eyes to the ceiling. But the
exasperation drained from her when he made the same
funny *harumph* face he always had, whenever she caught
him dissembling. "So, you finally came back."

"I said I would."

"I remember. You were going to work the station for three years, then send for me as soon as you got a steady post." Her expression softened. "What happened to us, Mikhail?"

"You suddenly got very famous, love," he said, sitting back with a weary sigh. "I couldn't bear the thought of watching you slip away an inch at a time, so I decided to just let you go."

"Without even asking what I wanted?" Undaunted by the reproach in her tone, he looked into her jade-cool eyes and laid his hand over hers.

"I couldn't have lived in your world, Annie, and I didn't have the courage to ask you to give up your career. How could I, after you'd worked so hard? Honestly, would you have followed me to Cade's World if I *had* asked you?"

"No, I would have tried to keep you here," she said at last. "How did you get to be so smart, Mikhail?"

"Living on the Edge teaches you to value the real things in life. Honesty is one of them, like the honesty in what you wrote. Your songs are real, Annie! They're alive and well out there on the Edge, waiting for you to come find them, if you're only willing to take a chance."

She wanted to say yes, but she couldn't seem to speak the word.

"What's wrong, Annie?" His voice was gentle. "What's holding you back?"

"I'm afraid, Mack." She was back in the present again. This man was no more Mikhail Sevranski than she was the Annie Keeley he'd met in that second-class lounge on Luna Station so very many years ago.

"You were afraid when we first met," he said softly, as though reading her mind. "But you thought I didn't know. It was failure you were afraid of then. What is it now, Annie?"

"Hope," she smiled crookedly, one little tear slipping down her cheek. "That's funny, isn't it? All these years hopes and dreams have kept me going, kept me alive. As long as you have a dream, you can always find some way to hang on. But when you can't even dream anymore. . . . Enough of this!" she said gruffly, trying to cover the intensity of her feelings. "Take your beast back. I can't think while she's trying to run emotional interference." But Annie's hands were gentle as she took Mrs. Henderson down from her shoulder and passed her back to Mack, who stowed her back in the duffel.

"How did you know, Mack?" Annie asked, when he sat back up.

" 'Space Station Annie' made it out to Cade's World about five months ago. I could have killed that bastard Tyler when I heard it, but I knew that wouldn't do any good. When I found out that you weren't recording anymore, and that you'd stopped writing. . . . Well, I had to come."

For a moment he looked almost apologetic, then an ingenuous smile spread across his face, and he said, "You know, I went to a lot of trouble, Annie. You have no idea the strings I pulled to get into that delegation. I think you owe me at least a shot at promoting you." His smile had blossomed into the most infectious grin.

Annie was smiling despite herself when she finally said, "All right, Mack. Go ahead and make me an offer."

*I wrote the song "Space Station Annie" about ten years ago at the request of some people who were developing a theme park based on a space station holiday. The funding fell through, but the song was recorded on various collections, the last of which was a tape entitled "Uncharted Stars" which also features the other songs from the story. Annie's plight, a manifestation of one of my own deepest fears, haunted me for years as health problems gradually made professional appearances impossible for me. Writing this story was the perfect opportunity to resolve some of my feelings about songwriting and performing, and to get to know a little more about Annie, who isn't me, but who might have been.*

# SWAN SONG
## by Lyn McConchie

Lyn McConchie runs a small farm in New Zealand. She became a professional writer in 1990 and, since then, has sold over 70 stories in five countries. This includes work in *MZB's Fantasy Magazine* and *Catfantastic III* and *IV* anthologies, as well as stories in four of the five crime anthologies appearing from Australia's Artemis Press to date. She has had two historical novels published, a nonfiction book about the amusing incidents that take place on her farm, and most recently her *WitchWorld* collaboration with Andre Norton, *The Key of the Keplian,* which was recently listed by the New York Public Library as one of the Best Books for Teenagers for 1995.

On a World where everyone sang, T'Chree was an anomaly. Had she lived elsewhere she would have been counted as beautiful. Her thick plush fur shone with youth and health. Her claws curved perfectly over dainty fingertips, and her lithe, slim shape was grace itself. In the eyes of her human friend, she was indeed beauty, but to T'Chree herself she was ugly. On a World where a beautiful voice outweighed any looks, nothing could make her lovely. As a small cub, she had once announced,

"One day you'll all come to listen to me. I'll be the most wonderful singer you ever heard."

Her parents had hushed her swiftly. Already it was likely that her voice would shame the family. All those bloodlines, all the great divas. Why, some had traveled to other worlds, sung before great Rulers, honored and respected. Their glorious voices had been immortalized in the alien recordings. T'Chree's uplifted voice had been known to scare Aras under their hides. It hurt the ears, making her parents wince and wonder if she was a changeling.

But one person was always a consolation to T'Chree at these times. Her human friend, Ruth. The humans had purchased a house next door to T'Chree's family estate when Ruth was still a baby. Side by side the two had grown up, each supporting the other in sister-friendship. They had been nine Hajacycles when they vowed blood sisterhood, small hands cutting slender wrists and young voices uttering the solemn oath. Through childhood the child and cub were inseparable, although now that they were grown, work to some extent divided them.

T'Chree's voice had not improved as she grew older. She had begun to understand her failure as quite a small cub. She heard it in the muttering behind her back. In the quiet laughter that began to be heard whenever she tried to sing. Apart from her sister she withdrew. At least to Ruth she was not a jest, something to giggle about and whisper over. Now they were adult, Ruth worked for her father in his trade office and T'Chree had obtained a job as Collator in the Capital's Folklore Museum. It kept them apart much of the time. The Museum was well outside the trade suburbs, a dusty lonely job, where T'Chree sorted out moldering manuscripts and transferred the writing to computer storage. Many of the ancient writings she treated dated to times when her people had just begun to explore neighboring worlds. Some were even earlier.

Ruth worried about her; her friend was becoming more and more of a hermit. Leaving to go to work before others rose, returning after they had eaten their evening meal.

"It isn't good for you. Come out and eat with me. We could see one of the new holodramas?"

"And have all point me out as that daughter of the Sheeecar line who cannot sing?" T'Chree said bitterly.

"More likely they wouldn't even recognize you. You've lost weight, your fur is harsh, and your claws look ragged. I daresay the museum loves the hours you work, you must be running the place single-handed. But it still isn't good to spend all your time underground. You need to get into the light now and then."

"All right, I'll come. Just expect me to say I told you so if I'm right."

She was. But she had underestimated the depths of Ruth's fury when a casual comment caught her ears. She hauled her friend away, a small purring giggle breaking from her as she did so.

"Ruth, Ruth, you can't start a fight here. The peace-keepers will have your claws for it."

"Didn't you hear what he said?"

Whiskers drooped as her friend slumped slightly. "I heard. Why do you think I didn't wish to come."

"You—you mean it's ALWAYS like that?"

"Yes."

"But, WHY? On our home World—"

"I know. On your home World it doesn't matter if you can't sing. You can do a thousand other things. But what if, on your home World, a female is so ugly every passerby stares. What if one look at her makes any male feel sick. To you, singing is just something else some can do well and others can't. On our World it is what draws a mate. To any male the moment I open my mouth I proclaim myself the most ugly of all females. No male would accept a mate who cannot sing. What sort of lineage is that to give his cubs? We were together so often, just the two of us. You never before saw how it is."

"I suppose not. They all thought your voice might change with puberty, didn't they? Then, just before that, I was sent off to Earth for schooling. I've been back three years, but we only seem to see each other at our homes?" Her voice went up in a question at the last.

"Now you know why," T'Chree informed her wryly. "Don't worry about it. Let's go and eat at your place. We can watch the viewer." They did so with T'Chree musing all evening how good it was to have one friend to whom she was acceptable. Yet, despite the knowledge of her voice, she continued to hold to her dream of the great

Auditorium one day. When she began the job, it had been only the means to an end. Out there the alien races were bewildering in their diversity—and their abilities. She would train her voice, learn all she could, then seek out someone from them who could give her back the dream. To live, one requires hope. That hope was all that kept her alive through the laughter, the ostracism, and slow bitter fading of her youth. Her money went to teachers. She learned the scales and the projection of her voice. The words and music to the greatest songs of her world.

She watched as one by one her childhood contemporaries were claimed. Some to marriage with males who cherished the voices that united them. A couple of the most fortunate to careers in song. A tragedy for another whose throat was injured in an accident. He killed himself as soon as the healers said he had lost the fine voice he had possessed. T'Chree had heard that news with a savage amusement. Was it better to have had and lost or to be like her?

She continued to train. Youth drained out of her as the years revolved past. She had the finest theoretical knowledge of any singer on her world. Driven by her demons of hope she learned it all. The careful breathing, the pacing of a song in tempo, the words and harmonies of the most difficult music. She did the exercises alone, deep in the caverns where the ancient materials of her work were stored. She had long since won a grudging respect from her teachers. They shuddered at her voice, but applauded her stubborn desire to learn. They could give her no hope, but generously, they no longer mentioned the waste of her money they considered the training to be.

They, too, had come to see the value of the hope which kept her alive. Sometimes they used her refusal to give up as a goad to their other students. They spoke no name, but everyone guessed of whom they told the story. It made T'Chree more outcast without her knowing it. To refuse to accept that she was crippled made those who knew her nervous. Others so cursed had run mad through the streets. Killed those whose voices they knew to be superior. Long-repressed pain and resentment curdled into a fury of pain and rage.

As people withdrew from her, T'Chree only worked the harder. Without friends, she had time for her work and her obsession. She would wander out to the edge of the great desert to look up at the stars. She would force her voice to sing the songs she had learned so painstakingly. To her own ear her voice was not unpleasant. She could tell that it was not first rank. But the nuances that made her family shudder slipped past her. There were times when she wandered and sang the night away.

It was on a night like that as she sang that hope first started to fade. All the years, all the money poured out on her teachers. Yet she was still no closer to finding the aliens who could give her the dream. Her singing had not been the only thing she worked hard at. Often she had remained long hours at her console, calling up records of other worlds. These had been studied, all the subsections relating to medical skills and voice gifts. Nowhere had she found a race who could bring the dream. She bowed her head as she walked, no longer forcing her voice into song. Should she surrender? Give up the fight she had waged against herself for so long? It would be easy to die and her family would be grateful to be rid of her.

But some stubborn core refused the question. To die now would be to negate all the bitter years. To waste that strength she had displayed. By now she knew of her teachers' use of her as an example. She understood how it had driven her people farther from her. Yet the bitterness that engendered made her strong. If her whole life was delusion and failure, yet she could show them how she died. She would not give in, would not allow those who whispered and laughed to triumph. If she must live a hundred years unable to sing, she would do so. She would neither suicide nor run mad so they could shrug and say they'd always known it would happen one day.

She began to spend more time at her manuscripts. Her voice training had gone as far as possible. Now she had only to keep up the exercises. Yet she knew with sorrow that time was trickling past her. If she found nothing in the histories of other worlds, it would soon be too late. Voices; even the most carefully hoarded of them, decay with time. Hers would be no exception. In a few more years, the flexibility would start to vanish, the highest part of her range to drop. She had perhaps another five years, before the tool she had crafted turned a blunter edge in her hands.

Then events worsened. Ruth had stood by her down the dusty unhappy years. But now she must leave for Earth. Like T'Chree, Ruth had never mated. She ruled her family's trading house now, but the signing of a new agreement called her home for a time.

"I'll be gone almost two years. I'm going to miss you."

T'Chree could only nod. She would miss her friend far more. Ruth was the only friend she had.

It would never have occurred to T'Chree to beg Ruth to stay. To head a trading house was to have great responsibilities. But oh, Goddess, she would miss the strength of her only sister-friend. The knowledge that to Ruth the lack of voice did not matter. It was T'Chree who was loved. It had been her presence that had kept the daughter of Clan Sheeecar strong.

Ruth clasped hands. "You'll write and so will I. Time will pass and I'll be back." Her fingers tightened. "Promise you'll be here when I return." Neither spoke of why the promise was asked, nor of why T'Chree hesitated before swearing.

Then the human was gone and T'Chree was alone, with only family about her, but few of them caring. Her mother loved her still; with Ruth gone, her dam was the only one T'Chree could turn to. But as the year crawled past, the older female sickened. Soon she was gone, leaving her daughter completely alone. That was bad enough, but when evil comes, it never comes alone. Word ran through the clan that one was to return to it. A cousin would come home. I'Chria. I'Chria with her voice that transcended the angels. They had always hated each other. Once the younger female had realized the power of her voice, she had used it to bait and torment her cousin.

If only Ruth had been here. She smiled at the memory.

Of a human girl hurling herself at the fastidious I'Chria, rolling her over and over in mud. Ruth had sat up triumphantly.

"There. Now you look the way you are inside. If you ever speak about my sister like that again, I'll do the same."

There had been something of a row about that. I'Chria's sire and dam had not appreciated their daughter returning in such a state. But Ruth had spoken out. Repeated the words I'Chria had said and shown again her anger and outrage on a friend's behalf. After that T'Chree's cousin was silent when the human was about, not so silent when she was not. The older woman remembered the sneers. The effortless way that her cousin had sung, daring her to follow. She recalled failure, bitter as ashtan root in her mouth. She stood in her cavern amidst her manuscripts and wept.

In her heart she heard the great songs; she strained in her mind. Yearning to hear her own sounds twining about the lift and run of the music. Her throat ached. She wanted to sing as the great Divas, those whose recordings were the treasure of a planet. To give to her people and hear their applause come crashing back. To feel her voice raise them from ordinary things into a world where all was beauty. To drown them in a song so sublime they would never ever forget that moment. To give, to pour out everything she had ever learned or dreamed. To do that even once, she would trade all the years of her life remaining.

She wiped her eyes and returned to her work. There was room here to sleep. Better a hard bed here than return to a home where her cousin would be holding court. She immersed herself in the piles of moldering parchment. Hummm! An interesting reference. Where had she seen something like that before? Idly she dug into her memory and blinked. Surely she'd run into that legend at some time. Deft fingers flickered in quick command. The computer unrolled its treasures of reference obediently, as she leaned forward to study them.

T'Chree smiled to herself. A legend, a child's tale for

children. But what if it was true? Madness overwhelmed her as she flung back her head, howling with wild laughter. By all the Gods at once, had she been hunting in other worlds all these years for something which had been under her nose the whole time? She buckled down to work. Flicking through the heaps of ancient writing in search of one specific reference. Bit by bit she pieced together the stories. Once there had been another race to share this world with them. A race who could grant her people's dearest wish. Yet the payment asked was so terrible that in the end the Elders had risen to drive them out. The other race had gone, seeking a planet where their offer might be accepted in peace.

T'Chree fell back in her chair. If they had gone—there was no record of where, not even a direction. But then her mind was whispering.

"When they built the dam at Shanya, there were those who would not leave their valley. They chose to remain and become one with their land. What if—what if there were those amongst this race who felt the same? Perhaps deep in the mountains and deserts, a pocket of the others still lingered. Able to grant wishes, to give the dream to those who sought them out to clasp hands in the bargain."

Her throat ached to sing, her desire to hear her voice flow in utter beauty tore at her. It had to be or all her life had been nothing. If she must die striving, then that was only right. For a tenday she ripped knowledge from the manuscripts. Garnering every hint, every tale, every reference in her quest to find a direction. Finally, gaunt-faced with hope, she leaned back. The Yerlan Mountains, it had to be. And it was all so terribly logical. The region was believed to be waterless although some rain did fall there. The mountains themselves held a valueless mineral that distorted powercasts. They could only be reached on foot past the Agrave Desert, and who would bother?

But she must prepare. To do this she had to be in excellent physical condition as well as having sufficient gear to travel. She went home to where her cousin held court. A cousin left baffled by T'Chree's indifference to all the gibes cast her way. Methodically, the female ate and slept

while gathering the things she would need betweentimes.
Then, in the depths of a moonlit night, she departed.
Behind her, she left a sealed letter. The seal would not
release until she was dead. By then, she would not care,
but all should be in order. It was her last gift to an
uncaring people. Even her office had been left neat.

Desert travel left her exhausted, but she forced herself
on. For the dream she would do anything necessary. Her
beast died at the foot of the mountains and she slashed its
throat to drink the blood. She must have all the moisture
possible. Then she climbed deep into the savage peaks,
chose a place, and stood. Carefully she warmed her voice
with scales, then short runs. Finally she began to sing and
into the song she flung everything she had. All the years
of training, all the bitterness, the pain of memory and iso-
lation, the terrible driving need to sing or die. Her voice
faded into silence and she waited.

From behind her a soft voice spoke. "Do you come to
make a bargain? Do you know the bargain we offer?"

She spun and went to her knees in shock. Gods! How
could such an alien thing stand before her, live on her
own world. Then the words penetrated and she took up
her fear to thrust it from her. This was the giver of the
dream. How could it be anything but beautiful to her?

"I come to make a bargain. As for the bargain you
offer—" She began to recite the belief she had put
together from the ancient tales and the being nodded.

"That is true. It is four generations of your kind since
one dared to clasp hands with us on that."

She was curious. "Is it permitted to tell me who it
was?"

A head inclined graciously. "It was S'Tachen of Mirrormene. He came to us saying that he was the last of his
line. That none would mate with him for the ugliness of
his voice. That he would have killed himself, but that with
him died all hope for continuation of his family, his
blood. We made the bargain."

"Yes." Her voice was low as she recalled the story.
S'Tachen had wed and his wife had produced a son and
then a daughter. Then the man had vanished, but his

family had grown and flourished. The stories said that his voice had been sold on record to other worlds for sums that had enriched his family beyond measure. She had heard the recordings herself. It was true that his voice had been among the greatest her world had ever bred.

She smiled wryly. Her world had indeed bred that voice, but not quite as she had always believed. She nodded to the being.

"I know of the one you name. But how do I explain the change in myself?"

"How did that one explain it?"

T'Chree remembered. "He claimed to have been off-world. To have been foolish enough to eat a strange plant that scoured his throat. For days he could not talk, when at last he could, his voice was as it was on his return."

"This was never questioned?"

The woman shook her head. "It would not be. He also said that it might be a gift from the Gods to prevent the death of his line. The pious would not question the will of the Gods. The practical would not question the results which brought great wealth to our people. Any others would be hushed by the pious and the practical."

"Then let you think up a story to match his, and follow. We will care for you while preparations are made." His orbs were kind, "You may change your mind at any point."

"Have any done so?"

A faint sound that might have been alien laughter. "No, those who have come so far will never change their minds. Yet, if you do—you may go free."

T'Chree followed him in silence. She doubted the truth of that but was wise enough to say nothing. She was conducted to a small chamber hollowed into rock. There, after she had been given food and water, came those who would question further.

"Tell us of your life?" She told. "Yet you have trained for a voice you do not have?" She had. "That was wise. what we can give is the raw material, and already you have refined it."

Her voice shook. "Then you will make the bargain?"

"You know your life will be short once it is done, perhaps two or three years, no more?"

"I know." She stretched out her hands to them. "What does it matter if I can sing. I will have those years, stand on a platform, and know it is my voice that moves those before me to tears. I will have the finest voice of any on my world. My family will revere my memory. And—" Her voice broke harshly. "I will no longer be outcast, isolated, and feared. For those years I will live a lifetime in glory." The veiled heads before her bowed. "I swear none shall know how this happened. At the last I will come back to the desert and you may have what is left."

"Then the bargain is made." Strange five-fingered hands slid out to clasp her own. "Eat and sleep again. In the morning we will come to make final our agreement."

They came and what was to be done was accomplished. She was provided with food, water, and another beast. One of the beings handed her a crystal.

"This, too, is a record. Wear it whenever you sing. Our children will remember your name, hear your voice when you yourself are silent at last. Know that we honor you far more than ever your people did."

She bowed in answer, goading the beast into a walk. She did not look back as she descended the mountain trails. The desert was almost crossed before she decided which lie to tell. Then she halted. With a heavy branch from a shriveled tree she struck herself across the throat. And again until all the skin was blackened with bruising. She camped three days, then went on. Against the swelling and soreness the crystal was cool. She lengthened the chain on which it hung. It appeared to be no more than a pretty crystal, worthless like the desert and mountains.

She smiled at the thought. The land had its own secrets, so did the crystal, and now, so did she. She returned to her work and her family. With a scriber she explained her bruising and silence as a fall across rock. Her throat had felt strange ever since, but she was sure there was no damage. Her family was incurious. Only I'Chria taunted her that she was becoming clumsy as well as ugly and voiceless. T'Chree ignored her, revenge was about to be so very sweet. Two weeks later she decided to begin. In private she had tested her voice already. The bargain had been kept.

Now she wandered about the garden, weeding and clipping the dead heads from the Rosen. She allowed herself to hum. From the corner of her eye she saw her father stop and listen. She allowed her sounds to broaden into soft words. A song from Mirrormene, into the words she allowed her voice to flow, each word distinct but so soft one might strain to hear. Her father strained, face intent. She permitted him a little louder voice to hear. She hid a bitter smile as he vanished abruptly. He returned with others.

She let them listen also for a little, raising her song so they might begin to know what she was. It was interrupted as he strode across the grass: his hands seized her shoulders.

"Come with me."

She freed herself firmly. She had been independent for more than half her life now. She would take orders from him no more. He'd made it plain she was worthless to him long ago. An ugly daughter with an uglier voice. Let him beg. She strolled away, leaving him to stand baffled. After that, he haunted her as did others who had heard her song. She allowed them to hear more, as the days passed. Finally he came to her as a supplicant. The family needed her gift.

I'Charia's voice was failing in its promise. No one else of the blood had sufficient voice to bring in the wealth the family needed. Her cousin's voice was excellent, but it was weak. The woman could sing only a few times each year in concert. Now, although she was young for it to happen, the upper registers were beginning to fade. T'Chree was conducted to the family song room. There, for the first time, she permitted them to hear the voice she had bargained for. It was glory, wonder, all the things she had dreamed of as she watched them submerge themselves in the sound.

Her father made the arrangements. Collected the

money, and engaged the other musicians necessary. She sang. Great soaring wild flights of sound that tore at the listeners until they wept. The applause thundered on until it seemed forever. Another concert; the acclaim mounted as she was compared to the great Divas of old. Songmakers wrote songs for her, musicians composed music, and the people of her world came to listen and venerate. It was all she had ever wanted. Each concert seemed to lift her higher, with each time her voice was finer. But only she knew the reason and that she kept to herself.

She had long since made her plans. She would know when the time came. But, before that she had a task, she would live long enough to accomplish that. To dedicate it to the child, girl, woman she had been. She hunted, listening to songs and music until she found him. A musician whose songs could tear the heart from a listener. Then she summoned him.

"Write me a song."

"The honor of your asking is mine. What shall I write?"

"Write me a song cycle. The tale is of one who was voiceless. Make the pain burn in your words. Let the music tell of her grief; the words, of how she was outcast in a world that values none who cannot sing. Let it be a song to bring weeping in all who hear. Show them the mirror of their own cruelty."

"It will take time. Such a song must be perfect."

"You have three moon cycles. Go! Return when it is done and tell no one of this. It shall be my final song." His head came up sharply. "Yes, my voice will fade again soon. I am too old to sing as I have been. But, before that, I will have a song to make them know what the years have been."

She stared after him as he left. Her voice was unfading, but he would believe the lie. He did, laboring over the cycle of song until he ached with weariness. But, for that glorious voice, he would work the nights down into day. Three months later he came to her. He thrust the work into her hands and stood by as she read.

She turned to her father. "Give him all I made last night."

"Are you mad?"

"No, he has written a work which will make our name live forever. Wealth will pour from other worlds into ours. I am the voice; he is the music. Together we shall be more than a singer has ever been. Give him all I made. It is no more than his due."

"When will you sing my work, Diva?"

"When I have studied it. But I shall sing it alone."

"Ah." He understood. She would follow custom. Many of the greatest had done this, one last song, sung alone, then death so their voice should never fade.

Throughout the months as she sang, she had written to Ruth. Letters had flown the stars to keep them together, but of the bargain she had said nothing. The last letter had given a date. A time when her friend would return, but it would be too late. T'Chree wept for that. She would have wished to see the human who was sister-friend to her one final time. Only Ruth, of all, had ever loved her for herself alone. Only Ruth, and she could not—dared not—tell her of the bargain.

She sang several times in the weeks that followed. But never the song he had written. Each time her joy at her voice grew stronger. She bathed herself in the swell of sound, surfed the notes that flowed from her mouth. Her eyes were avid on the faces of her audience. She lived her music as they did, feeling the memory of her voicelessness die. She would not be recalled as she had once feared: as an outcast and a nothing. They would remember her forever and she would leave them one last song.

The time was upon her and she knew it. Preparations were made and she took up the machine that would be impressed with that final song. The beast was packed; without farewell she slipped into the night. One day into the desert she set a timer, laid out the machine she needed. Then she sat to wait. A night, and another, and the figures came out of the dark.

"It is time. Are you content with your bargain?"

She remembered the glory of her song. The fulfillment after the barren years. "I am content."

One reached out to touch her throat. She broke the chain, handed the crystal to it. Within her something stirred. She stood, moved to turn on her machine, then she flung back her head and sang. The song yearned, it wept and burned, and spoke to any who heard. It was pain and sorrow in crystal sound. It tore at the heart and mind with words so grieving, music so poignant, that even those with her wept, alien but understanding the passion she shared. The pain was becoming worse as she sang, but she took it to use. Sharpened it to edge her voice, to color the power with which she sang.

Pain became a thing apart, fuel for the fire that consumed her. The song crested, then slid down to a softer note. For those who hoped there was always a chance. Live on and dream, work for the dream. Music swelled again as she spun into the final portion of the cycle. Triumphant, her voice lifted. She had prevailed, the dream had come to her, and even death itself could not silence her now. Dimly she was aware of her flesh parting, blood spilled, draining all of her, but she sang on.

The song ended on a wild note that seemed to hang shimmering in the air. Alien fingers flicked off the machine. Then, from around her, began another song. A repetition of the last portion. She sang with it once more, but this time smaller voices blended with hers. She lifted on the sound; she was weakening, but still she sang. Hands took hers, holding her upright, love flowed from them into her. Her body should lie in the desert but the crystal would keep her song alive. Let her own people find the machine and have that much of her. She crumpled as the last note came from her mouth.

Dimly she heard the makers of her bargain leaving. Soft small voices still sang the last part of her song again and again. She smiled weakly. She had not mated, born no cubs, but those who sang were her children. Still blood drained from her and she lay back, cradled on soft warm sand. Her clan would not search for ten days. It was the custom. She mourned only one person she must leave behind now. Ruth, sister-friend and companion through so many of the dusty years. The years when there was only hope and that fading. She wished she could have sung for Ruth. Seen her sister's face light up in delight at the sound of song.

She gazed up at the stars, moonlight spilling over her fur. Then she shivered. A sound. Goddess, let me die swiftly. I do not wish to be eaten by things of the desert while I still live. A face hovered over her. T'Chree smiled up. So—the Great One was merciful. At the last she had sent a vision to comfort her daughter. A hand clasped hers.

"Keep still."

"I cannot move, mhaa, it does not matter. I am glad that you will be with me at the end." She allowed herself to slip away into the bright darkness that reached out. Her ears did not hear the exasperated sound above her limp body. Did not feel the swift fingers that worked or the touch of the cunning robot pincers that flicked over her torn flesh. At length Ruth sat back on her heels. That should keep her foolish sister from leaking all her blood onto the sand. She spread blankets and rolled T'Chree over, tucking them in about her. Then she lay back on her own.

She'd guessed more than T'Chree had known. Letters between friends always told more than one realized. And while her friend was clever with a computer, Ruth was better. With a faint memory to guide her, she, too, had followed the path and understood the possibilities. She had arrived weeks earlier, but her friend had been singing about the World and not known of her coming. She had followed T'Chree into the desert, guessing at something of her intent. She had watched in horror. Afraid to interfere. Those things might kill them both, but if she waited—she had. She was in time, but from the song she had heard that glorious voice was strained. Never again would it sound as more than passable. She had given T'Chree life, but would her sister be able to live it with much of her voice gone once more?

Beside her the limp figure stirred. "Ruth, mhaa, sister, it was you in truth. What have you done?"

"Saved a sister too silly to save herself."

A weak laugh. "Ruth! None but you would say that." The laughter faded. "You saw, you heard?"

"Yes. Lie back and drink this."

T'Chree gulped obediently. "Ruth, are you back for good?"

"If I wish."

"And if you don't?"

"I have other places, other Worlds where we trade." Her hand tightened over furred fingers. "Why not come with me. There are a thousand Worlds out there who will not care if you sing like an angel or do not. Come with me, the skies are wide, and—" She paused. "And I have been lonely without you this past time. Come with me and leave sorrow behind."

She found her clasp returned. "I have given all I can to my clan," T'Chree said softly. "Now it is time I gave to myself and to the mhaa I owe my remaining time. I will come. Let all believe I died here."

"In the morning we'll head for the Port. I can get you a passport and clearance at once and in my surname."

"Ruth? You mustn't ever speak of 'them.' It's important."

"I know. I'll say nothing." Nor would she, the woman thought. Somewhere, some other time to come there might be another like her mhaa. She would not take all hope from them. She reached over to tuck in the blankets more securely. They would have so much fun together. She and her sister-friend. The stars were theirs now, the stars and all the years remaining. In the morning she would get T'Chree to the mount she had brought. The crystal could stay where it was. Together with the bloody sand it would convince the clan not to look for her.

She grinned. If she knew that lot, they wouldn't look too hard anyway. They'd never valued their clanchild. Their family would live well on the recordings of T'Chree's songs, particularly that last. Let them have that. It was all they had ever wanted of someone who had had so much more to give. She stroked the fur of her mhaa's arm. All the stars and all the years. She had the best of it. Her last thought was of the bargain-makers. Where were they now?

Under the wide starlit sky a line of veiled figures skimmed the sand. Across a patient beast a roll of soft fiber was bound. Tiny figures clung to it, crooning the song over and over again. Gratitude washed the hearts of their elders who listened. Once again new life was brought to their kin in the high mountains. Born of a terrible bargain for those who made it. But there would always be those to make it willingly. Behind them the machine stood that bore the final songs. Those it held might change a World's thinking, but not yet. The line wound up into the foothills, lost to view. The song faded.

*I wrote this story following the collision of two trains of thought. One—the vague memory of a survey in which Olympic athletes were asked: if they could take a drug which would guarantee a gold medal but which would kill them ten years after, would they take it? A very high percentage said they would. They were then asked the same question but with only one year to live after the medal. An astonishing number would still have taken the drug. The other thought was my lifelong desire to be a singer when I can't carry a tune in a bucket. From these two things "Swan Song" was born.*

# HEAVENSIDE SONG
## by Warren C. Norwood

Warren C. Norwood started writing when he was nine, published his first poem when he was fifteen, and his first novel, *The Windhover Tapes: An Image of Voices,* when he was thirty-six. That novel garnered him two John W. Campbell nominations. So far in his career he has published many poems, short stories, and a dozen more novels, as well as a lot of nonfiction including books on how to play the mountain dulcimer. He teaches writing and has seen thirty-six of his students professionally published. He and his writer-wife Gigi live near Dennis, Texas with two dogs, two cats, deer, wild turkeys, armadillo, raccoons, bobcats, and as many hundreds of birds as Gigi can lure to the feeder.

Shelley whistled her way through her days because, "You may not sing," Father had said. "You're just a girl, and girls are never allowed to sing."

He almost smiled—at least Shelley had looked for a smile, but his mouth only made words, not smiles. Father held his arms wide and his bushy eyebrows arched over deep-brown eyes. His eyes didn't smile either.

"Great-grandfather Ponder did not travel his whole life with Fallwell in that leaky old can of a gen ship to build a new home where girls would be allowed to sing." Like sailfeathers his arms sank to his sides. "When you're old enough, or when you are a bride-pledge, you may dance the dance of nine veils. When you're ready, you may play the dulcimer or flute."

Father leaned forward, his voice quiet and steady, his eyes piercing hers. She dared not move. She knew that if she moved, his big puffy hands would grab her in an instant and lift her off the stool.

"You may even attempt the temple blocks, although I never heard a girl yet with any rhythm. But you *may not* sing. Not even your bedtime prayers. Do you understand me?"

Shelley nodded but kept eye contact. She was five ages old, but she knew everything she needed to know about paying attention to Father.

That had been fourteen ages before. Now, Shelley was nineteen ages old, old enough to dance the dance of nine veils. "Not for the men, not for bride-pledge," Annabell, her sister, had whispered deep in darkness on the night Shelley asked for instruction. "Dance only for our Mothers and Grandmothers."

No matter how well Shelley ever understood her sisters, she wished she could talk to them about her songs, too, but she dared say nothing. Instead she went to temple, and as she knelt at the end of the line outside the sacred alcove waiting for her turn in the booth, she remembered the first time she had shared her secret of song. On her twelfth ageday, her day of womanhood, she had come to this very temple and this very compassion booth and prayed aloud, "Dear Kuan-shi-Yin, I need your help."

"Speak, child," the familiar ageless voice had said.

Shelley knew Kuan-shi-Yin wasn't real, that she was just the bodhisattva-computer of compassion for all women, the one whose name meant She-Who-Hears-All-Cries-Of-The-World, but Shelley didn't care. "When I play my dulcimer in my room or even when I play my flute behind the screen to entertain while the Fathers eat, I . . . I hear words in my head."

"You have always heard words, child, since you were a little girl—and usually words you should not have heard." the voice said. Kuan-shi-Yin sounded amused.

"I know, but these words are lyrics to the songs that have no lyrics, lyrics to the songs—"

"Lyrics to the songs that are forbidden to have lyrics?"

"Yes," Shelley said, startled by the interruption. Kuan-shi-Yin had never interrupted her before.

"Sing one of these lyrics for me," Kuan-shi-Yin commanded.

After a long moment of hesitation, Shelley forced the words out of her mouth, barely conveying the melody.

> *"Late in the evening*
> *In moonfall and rise,*
> *All the girls sing*
> *Sweet truth and lies."*

*Sweet truth and lies?* Shelley heard words like that almost every time she played, words that echoed in every dulcimer tune, words of paradox and question that she had never, could never—"What do they mean, Kuan-shi-Yin?"

"I cannot say. But they are good words. Keep them."

*Good words? Keep them?* Again Shelley was startled. She never knew where the words—"Do my sisters or Mother or my grandmothers . . . Do other women ever . . . I mean, have they heard words like that in their heads?"

"Sometimes," Kuan-shi-Yin answered.

"Then why don't they talk about them?"

Shelley waited for an answer, but instead received only Kuan-shi-Yin's usual words of parting. "Try to understand things, and be kind to all you meet."

That memory left Shelley feeling unusually relaxed and she was glad, because there were still several women between her and the compassion booth. She recalled how at age nine she had tried to confront the problem head on. She had been playing her dulcimer for two years and was ready to expand her repertoire.

"Why won't they let me play all the songs?" Shelley had asked her grandmothers.

"Women only play women's songs," Grandmother Also had said. Her blue eyes with their bushy silver lashes always looked sad when she talked. "If you sometimes hear your brothers and the men singing in their courtyard, or after evendrink, you must close your ears. You must never listen to their songs."

"Why, Grandmother?"

"It is forbidden, as all men's things are."

"But why?"

"Because it is the Fallwell way," said Grandmother Ponder, her eyes and eyebrows and hair all the same intense black despite her age. "Because little girls are taken away if they sing."

"Dear," Grandmother Also said, taking her hand, "the men's songs are too powerful for girls." Suddenly her face relaxed and her deep wrinkles softened. "If girls started singing, the world would turn upside down. Don't even think about it."

Of course Shelley memorized every piece of song she heard her three brothers sing. She memorized every fragment of harmony that drifted through the house in the mornings. She memorized every wisp of melody that floated up from the courtyard. She memorized every bit of lyric she managed to hear after evendrink when the men gathered in their courtyard around the old Teller to watch yet another version of *The Sage of Earth*. Every song she heard, she memorized . . . words and all.

The words were a problem, though, a problem Shelley didn't understand. Many of the men's songs were made up of nonsense words, like *hey, ho and nonny no, yokata-yakata-pocketa-rocketa, ring-a-ding-doo, boola-boola,* and *Cum-by-yah millyord.* The words she did understand were mostly about fighting and drinking, or kissing and sex and other things she thought were silly until her fifteenth age. Then she fell in love with Roland DeVries and realized she had no songs to express her love to him . . . and wasn't meant to have any.

So, soon after she fell in love, on the eve of her sixteenth ageday, Shelley went to see Kuan-shi-Yin.

"I'm in love," she announced as soon as she finished her ritual chants.

"You are of the right age."

"I'm making up new songs. I change the men's melodies, and put my own lyrics to their songs, lyrics that suit me." She waited a long moment before Kuan-shi-Yin responded.

"You must be careful never to sing them aloud."

"They're love songs."

"Of course they are, dear. You must be especially careful not to sing those aloud. Love songs are very powerful." Kuan-shi-Yin's voice sounded old that day for the first time in Shelley's memory.

Four periods later she sat crying in the compassion booth. "He's gone. He moved half way around the world because his father found him a job." She blew her nose. "And his mother found him a *bride-pledge*." Shelley sobbed louder and snorted into her bandanna, wondering how her life could have gotten so miserable.

"What about your songs?" Kuan-shi-Yin asked when Shelley finally calmed down.

"I sing them to myself . . . over and over." Tears rolled down her cheeks.

"Then life goes well with you."

"These are new songs. They're songs about my sisters and Mother and grandmothers—even our foremothers."

"Sing for me."

Shelley blew her nose one more time, cleared her throat, sat up straight, then sang,

*"Daughters of Fallwell, born to the mission,*
*Traveled to Heavenside far long ago.*
*Some came of guilt and some of contrition,*
*And some out of love only women can know."*

"Very interesting. What made you write that?"

"I don't know. You know how . . . songs come into my head. Lyrics tag along with every melody I hear. Sometimes I hear music and sing prayers to the melody."

"I've heard you sing the chants to me."

Shelley leaned forward on the kneeling bench and laid her forehead against the cool grille. "I know you've heard. You're the only one I *can* sing to. It's almost like there's some well inside me full of music—full of songs—and the well is overflowing. They're part of who I am."

Now three ages later, on the brink of performing the dance of nine veils, Shelley came to Kuan-shi-Yin one more time looking for guidance and relief.

"My songs," she said, skipping the usual prayer of salutation as she knelt in the familiar booth, "they come all too quickly and all too often. I never know when they're going to spring from my tongue."

"I have told you before, these are dangerous things. You must never, never let the men hear you sing your songs. Never. Never, child. Do you understand?"

"Yes. I mean, no. I mean I don't understand. Why are they dangerous? Why are these songs I want to sing so dangerous?"

"Just trust that they are."

"I can't." Tears filled Shelley's eyes. "I came here as always, willing to trust you, but I can't. Not any more, Kuan-shi-Yin. The only things in this world I *can* trust are the words. You're a computer. The men are bureaucratic idiots. My sisters and mother—"

"Be careful, child. You will go too far."

"—and grandmothers are bound by traditions that make no sense . . . that I don't understand."

"You must trust me."

"But Kuan-shi-Yin, you're just a computer. Probably built by men and—Oh! Great Mother help me. They know, don't they? The men . . . they know. Oh . . . please, no. They have access to all your memory. You tell them—"

"*Hush.*" The word rushed from the speaker grille.

Shelley fell back against the padded wall. Energy coursed through her as though she had touched an electrical wire.

"I promise you, child, no man touches my memory or even knows of my true existence. They think I am a computer, also."

"But . . . but you are, aren't you?"

Kuan-shi-Yin sighed.

"Aren't you?"

"You dance in five days, correct?"

"Of course. You know that."

"Practice well, Daughter. You are greatly blessed. May you bless the world."

*Daughter, not, child? Bless the world?* What did that mean? And why didn't she answer my question? Shelley wondered as she mumbled her final prayers before leaving the booth. If Kuan-shi-Yin wasn't a computer, what was she?

That night as she lay abed, Shelley dreamed that she met herself coming through a mirror wearing a white robe trimmed in red and black.

"You are a singer," her other self said with a smile.

Shelley could only nod.

"So sing." The other self dissolved and an old crone stood before her wearing a black robe trimmed in white and red.

"Who are you?" the old crone asked.

I am a singer, Shelley thought.

"Then accept your miracle. You must sing when it is time. For now you can whistle."

Shelley awoke with a great sense of calm. She whistled as she prepared for the dance of the nine veils, the dance she would dance for her sisters, her mother, her grandmothers, and a hundred relatives and very special female friends. She whistled as she practiced. She whistled as she rested. Shelley whistled until the day before her performance when, in the middle of a twirl she started singing.

> *"On a night as deep as it was long*
> *My daring love broke out in song."*

"What are you doing?" Annabell cried as she jumped up from her chair.

Words poured straight from Shelley's subconscious to her tongue.

*"And some said right and some said wrong,*
*On Heavenside the next morning."*

"Stop it!" Panic filled Annabell's voice. Fear filled her eyes like a bonfire in the night as she reached to cover Shelley's mouth.

Shelley grabbed her arms. "No, sister, I won't stop it. I can't stop it." Anger flowed through her in wonderful waves of energy. "I'm a singer. I've been singing all my life . . . but only to myself and Kuan-shi-Yin. Tomorrow night I will sing for you and our Mother and Grandmothers." Even as the words escaped her mouth, Shelley was amazed by what she said.

"But you can't, you must not." Annabell trembled. Tears spilled from her eyes. "You're the late child, Mother's Blessing. You must not sing. They'll take you away!"

"I know," Shelley whispered, wondering what darkness they would take her to, "but I must sing. And besides, we'll be in Mothers' Hall and the men won't know." Just saying that seemed to give her strength. "Listen to me, Annabell. I don't understand this any more than you do, but I know that I have to sing, and I know that you must not warn them. You must not tell. You must promise me."

Annabell's black eyes looked away. "I cannot."

"You must. Please. Promise me."

"All right," Annabell said softly.

"Say, I promise."

"I promise." Her voice was barely audible. "Granmamma help us. Granmamma help you."

"Yes," Shelley said, hugging her sister to her. "Granmamma help us." She had always disliked the diminutive names for the Great Mother, but suddenly Granmamma sounded comforting.

That night, Shelley fell asleep almost immediately. She dreamed of deserted hallways that echoed with voices. She awoke to visions of women standing row upon row in their dark gowns, their open mouths producing a sound like a howling wind. She fell back asleep and dreamed voices. The voices chased her, again, and again, and again, until she pushed herself out of bed well before her usual time and headed for the kitchen to break fast. Deep inside she knew she would only shame herself and her family by singing. But deep in her soul—

"Good morning, Daughter," her mother said as Shelley entered the kitchen.

"Good morning, Mother," Shelley said, giving her mother a kiss on the cheek. The cheek was wet. Fear pulled Shelley's stomach into a knot. Had Annabell told? "Mother, you've been crying. What's wrong?"

"Nothing that won't fall away like your veils when you dance tonight, precious." Mother stood. "I will be busy most of the day, but I will be in the front row this evening."

"I hope you'll be proud of me," Shelley said, surprised by the tremor she heard in her voice.

"Of course I will. You are my bravest daughter." She caressed Shelley's face with a deeply wrinkled hand, then left the kitchen.

What did she mean by that? Shelley wondered as she prepared her food. Does she know? Does she think I should do it? Does she think I should sing?

All day long as Shelley sat in the open room and received guests, she wondered how much her mother knew. Friends and relatives, almost one hundred women, stopped by to kiss her cheeks and bless her for dancing. Shelley smiled and thanked them with the Buddhist invitation, "Come with open hearts to the sutra of dance." But she doubted they would bless her when the day was over.

Four of her five sisters blessed Shelley twice each, but each seemed to have an odd look in her eye, and Annabell never came at all. Shelley was twelve ages younger than her closest sister, twenty ages younger than Annabell, yet it was with Annabell whom Shelley had formed the strongest bond. Her absence only added to Shelley's tension.

After one final rehearsal, a bath, and a light meal in the early evening, Shelley changed into her red dance dress and the white, red, and black veils with her sister

Leeann's help. Shelley always felt like an alien compared to Leeann and her normal life. She couldn't imagine Leeann ever wanting to sing, yet at the same instant Shelley sensed that Leeann could make beautiful music. "Where was Annabell today?" Shelley asked as calmly as she could.

"Ill, at least that's what she told Mother."

"And what do you think it was, my oldest sister?"

"I think her marriage is bad for her health."

Shelley sighed, and in her own sigh, she heard Kuan-shi-Yin's sigh. "I fear for her. Rashan beats her, you know."

"Everybody knows," Leeann said, stepping back to look at Shelley, "but there's nothing we can do about it. It is Husband's Right."

"In all my nineteen ages I don't understand that."

"Perhaps after tonight you will." Leeann's face masked any reading. "Come, it is time."

All too soon Shelley stood trembling behind the curtain on the stage of Ponder Mothers' Hall. Fear and pride and anger and dignity coursed through her veins. All too soon the curtain opened and the lights played on her poised body. Her trembling shrank to the pit of her stomach. All too soon the music called for her to rise, and Shelley danced.

She danced the introduction to *The Goddess*, the first movement of the nine veils. She danced without thinking and without effort, the steps and figures having been taught her since she could walk. But this dance was more than an accumulation of play-party steps learned as a child. This evening she danced as though her body flowed on currents of harmony she could feel, currents that lifted her, turned her, and set her gently back down.

Through the joy of it all she felt old familiar words bubbling up inside her, and Shelley knew she could not escape them and did not want to. She knew that if she was fated to sing, these were the words that had to be sung.

As she sank in a controlled spiral and threw off the first

white veil, lyric poured from her soul and she sang "The Mothers' Prayer" from the chanted litany she had learned as a child:

*"My sisters and Mother and grandmothers, too,"*

A gasp rose from the audience.

*"The call is for now, and the call is for you,"*

"Yes," someone shouted.

*"To rise up and join me and sing your heart's song,*
*To live as right women or die by the wrong."*

"Blasphemy," a male voice screamed, breaking the sanctity of Ponder Mothers' Hall.

Someone raised the house lights. The audience was on its feet, one hundred women in dark gowns, mostly the crimson and purple of the Ponder Family. Annabell with a gold patch over her right eye stood in the front row between Mother and Grandmother Ponder. The whole audience swayed and sang, *sang with Shelley* as she, too, rose gracefully to her feet and repeated the verse.

*"My sisters and Mother and grandmothers, too,*
*The call is for now, and the call is for you,*
*To rise up and join me and sing your heart's song,*
*To live as right women or die by the wrong."*

More male voices shouted from the side of the hall, but just as quickly they were stilled in a flurry of dark robes.

*"The Great Mother watches our Heavenside life.*
*She blesses our children and eases our strife,*
*And as She-Who-Hears-All shows us the chance,*
*The sutra of movement, the worship of dance."*

One hundred voices sought and found their natural harmony, and Ponder Mothers' Hall swelled with joy as the women sang the familiar words together, words that before they had only chanted in the monotones of worship. For the first time since she learned the prayer at age two, "Mothers' Prayer" made sense to Shelley.

She spun off a red veil as the rear doors flew open.

Father strode into Ponder Mothers' Hall leading a party of ten or twelve men including her brothers and brothers-in-law. Behind them came a flood of women in dark robes—red, blue, brown, green, black, solids and stripes and checks, robes of other houses and other halls.

"Cease this blasphemy!" her father shouted. In a moment he and his party disappeared under a swarm of crimson and purple, and the music soared.

Shelley spun into a brief pirouette and kept dancing and singing, unable to stop, carried on the flow of energy, woven into a trance of power so strong she could not have broken free if she had wanted to.

Because it wasn't just her. It was the voices of hundreds of women, singing in liberation, praising the Great Mother through prayer and song and Shelley's dance, until the fall of her ninth veil and the final sweet echo of Amens.

Shelley stood in a daze as relatives and friends swarmed up to hug her. More women poured into the back of the hall. Some carried weapons. Some pushed bound men in front of them. Some escorted men who were greeted with smiles and hugs.

Shelley didn't understand any of it. But she knew that whatever happened on this evening, thousands of women would one day sing songs about it.

*When my two favorite Annies invited me to write a story for* Space Opera, *I quickly accepted, then sat down and wrote "Heavenside Song." I think this story reinforces the messages I try to give repeatedly to all the girls and women in my life: Trust your heart and your gut feelings. Be willing to go against the flow if that's where your heart leads you. Don't wait or watch for outside approval—especially from men who aren't very good at giving it anyway. Trust yourself. Trust your skills and talents. You can accomplish great things following these guidelines. My wife says I'm always empowering women, and I think that's as accurate a summary of my intentions as you can get.*

# DRIFT
## by Steven Brust

Steven Brust was born in November, 1955, and
currently lives in Minneapolis, Minnesota. His
latest novel is *Freedom and Necessity,* a collaboration with Emma Bull.

It was just after 1:00 in the afternoon when I walked into
the ProSound Studios, research facility of Myron Clay,
Chief Development Engineer for Lodestone Industries
and designer of the Groovemeister 1.

The reception area looked like a Victorian drawing
room, with cherrywood paneling and a neat little secretary at which sat a secretary. I gave him my name, and he
pointed the way to Studio 4, which looked like a living
room done in Swedish Modern—a long, white couch, a
glass table, a 13-inch TV set embedded in a dark wood
cabinet, a few chairs that matched the couch, and, where
you might expect a mirror or a painting, a long window
that looked into the booth. The speakers (eight of them)
were concealed in the wall, and a few microphones hung
from the ceiling like light fixtures.

The Groovemeister—light blue fake ceramic shell,
about three feet long, a foot deep, and eight inches high—
sat on the coffee table. Jacky Hanks, looking just like his
picture on the cover of the August '15 issue of *Today's
Percussion* only older, sat on the couch next to Myron,
who seemed smaller than he used to be, a little more bald,
and with a bit more of a squint. A metal drum sat on the
couch between them. Jacky and Myron stood up as I came
in. Myron introduced us. Jacky's hand was limp and his
smile was shy.

"I love the way you play," I told him.

Jacky looked flustered and sat down in a simple, straight-backed chair to the right of the Groovemeister, facing the sound booth.

Myron told Jacky, "I invited her in case she wanted to write a story about, you know, the bet."

Jacky shrugged.

"You want to tell me about it?" I asked.

"Sure. Come with me." I followed Myron back into the booth while he gave me a short version. I got the full story over the next three days. It went like this:

When Myron heard who had arrived at his studio, he immediately had Jacky shown in—Myron had spent hours listening to "Sensing the Soul" and programming the aesthetic into his creation. He was proud of his work, and wanted to show it off. "Come to see the beast?" asked Myron.

Jacky grunted—he was never at his best with words.

"It's been doing great stuff for us," he added.

Jacky grunted again.

"You wanna see it?"

"Yeah," said Jacky.

Myron led the way into Studio 4, where he'd been doing his testing, and pointed out the Groovemeister. It was, in fact, one of the first production models, not a prototype. Myron began explaining it. "We made it this size mostly so it would be easy to swap boards in and out—the next version will be about the size of a cigar box. These are the lines in—they receive the signal and make all the adjustments as well. There's no separate programming like in the old machines. I can control the whole thing from the board, or just fire it up and let it go. The musicians play, and it figures out what the right drum part is. You can have it play along if you want, or just insert the data into the mix. It understands dynamics, both leading and following, and when to play ahead of the beat, when to play behind it, and when to play on top of it."

Jacky grunted and stood over the Groovemeister, staring.

"Of course, you can program it just like the old machines, or leave it anywhere in between. It can—*what the fuck are you doing?*"

What Jacky was doing was playing the Groove-meister—his way. He was tapping it with his hands, his fingers, his fingernails, and his elbows, laying out an East African seven against nine. Myron screamed, "Get your goddamn hands off it!"

Jacky stopped, looked at Myron, and grunted, "Lousy resonance."

"Get the hell out of here before I break your fuckin' neck," suggested Myron.

"Bet it couldn't keep time in a wheelbarrow," said Jacky, turning to go.

"You bet," said Myron. "Heh."

"That's right," said Jacky over his shoulder. "I bet."

"Okay," called Myron, getting more and more irritated. "What do you bet?"

Jacky stopped and turned back. "Twenty bucks," he said naming all the cash he had on him. This was after the reevaluation of '28, but before the one in '33, so twenty dollars was enough to buy about two weeks' worth of groceries for one person, or a meal in an okay restaurant. In other words, not much.

"Shit." Myron paused for a moment, then said, "What are we talking about betting on?"

Jacky thought for a while, then said, "Twenty bucks that I can keep a steadier beat than that thing."

"You're just being stupid. A metronome can keep steadier than meat."

"Nope. They drift."

"Everything drifts—but doesn't drift enough for the human ear to detect."

"Enough for *my* human ear to detect."

"Bullshit. The Groovemeister is more accurate than a Synchograph, and they're guaranteed to within five hundred ticks."

Jacky looked blank.

"One tick," said Myron deliberately, "is the transition between energy states of the cesium 133 atom."

Jacky still looked blank.

"Nine billion, one hundred and ninety-two million, six hundred and thirty-one thousand, seven hundred and seventy ticks make up a second. The Synchograph is accurate to within five hundred of them. The Groovemeister is better. Much better."

"So?"

"The brain can't detect variations in tempo of a ten thousandth of a second."

"Mine can," said Jacky Hanks.

Myron stared at him for many, many ten-thousandths of a second before saying, "Horsepucky. How would we check it, anyway? If you lose, you'll just say . . . no, wait. I still have the cesium clock working. I could run a line to the analyzer in the booth, and we could it measure it down to . . . I'll have to adjust for the length of the line. Call it twenty-three feet. Uh . . ." Myron smiled suddenly. "I could do it."

"Good," said Jacky.

"You serious?"

"Yeah."

"Well, hell, let's set it up, then."

Jacky grunted and put his twenty out on top of the Groovemeister. Myron elaborately put two tens on top of Jacky's bill, and went back to the booth to hook up the cesium atom beam clock to his computer, called up the analyzer, and introduced them. Then he picked up his phone and called me.

I came out of a deep, hangover-induced sleep, and didn't wake up until he said the words, "Jacky Hanks;" the next thing I knew I was dressed and in a cab heading for the studio.

While they were waiting for me to get there, they set up the microphone for Jacky's drum, adjusting the range and the spread, and testing the response, and setting the speakers in the room to follow Jacky's movements and keep pointing at his ears. They also set the Groovemeister and the computer in the booth to pick everything up, testing the laser signal from the mike to the booth three times because Jacky didn't trust it.

Then they sat there waiting for me, and not saying anything until I arrived. Myron, as I said, gave me the short version of all of this.

"Thanks for inviting me," I said when he'd finished. I started getting excited, both at the idea of a great story, and at the prospect of watching what was about to happen.

"My pleasure," said Myron. "A story about it would be good for us."

"However it turned out?"

Myron snorted.

"Are you recording?" I asked him.

"Do I look stupid enough not to be?"

"Sorry."

For you techies, Myron had pointed an EV 2416-I at Jacky's drum, a Syrian metal dourbakee made in Pakistan with a 10-inch antique Remo fiberskin head. He made sure the mike was set for the circumference of the drum, set up the receiving software, and verified the signal from the computer to the Groovemeister. "Its ears are working," he remarked.

"I think this is going to be very interesting," I said.

"I hope so," said Myron.

Myron powered up the Groovemeister and ran it through its diagnostics. He hit some keys and tapped the screen of his computer, setting the Groovemeister to "respond, synch, live, hard-tempo." At 1:58 he started the recording program and announced, "Rolling. Whenever you're ready, Jacky."

I've listened to the recording of that session more times than I can count, and I can now identify the rhythms, the instruments the Groovemeister was simulating, and recall my own reactions at the time.

The first sound is Jacky's grunt to acknowledge Myron, and then, drum between his knees, Jacky laid down a simple 6/8 at 120 beats/minute, playing lightly on the edge. The Groovemeister came in and matched it, producing a sound like a ceramic version of Jacky's own drum.

Jacky, who was staring at a spot just above the window into the sound booth, smiled.

He began popping some of the off-beats, and throwing in the bass sound from the middle of the drum until the 6/8 became a slinky Arabian 4/4; when the Groovemeister picked that up, with a sound like very light drumsticks on a closed high-hat with good Zildjian cymbals, Jacky laid a solid three against it.

I inhaled sharply.

"What is it?" said Myron.

"I'm impressed," I said. "Your machine—it's figured out the polyrhythm and how to embellish on it."

"That's right," said Myron, sounding smug. I didn't look at him—Jacky was too fascinating when he drummed. Not his hands, though they moved with a fluid beauty, but the joyous intensity of his expression. He was not what you'd normally call good looking—tall, gangly, with a misshapen nose, wearing a light-colored, long-sleeved shirt with a drum key visible in outline in his breast pocket. But the rapture on his face was irresistible. I wished I'd taken the time to put on something more interesting than a flannel shirt and a pair of jeans.

They played with the three against four for nearly two minutes, before the Groovemeister, taking the lead for the first time, changed its tone to deep but tightly tuned tom-toms and began subdividing. Jacky laughed softly and cut the time in half, then in half again, then, putting the drum under his left arm without dropping a note, began pounding out a straight, demanding four with hard slaps in the middle of the drum, while the fingers of his left hand closed the rhythm with whispers against the edge.

The Groovemeister acknowledged it, then went into a calypso five using a simulated 1940s Rogers snare drum sound—it made me think of rum and dancing until daylight and Harry Belafonte. Jacky shrugged and continued playing the straight four—just letting the polyrhythm come around to the big *one* every twenty measures. Jacky softened the inflection, but kept the rhythm constant.

After seven minutes of this, they both shifted, as if on cue, to a very fast Turkish nine. The Groovemeister generated the bass sound of a Tupan with tight calfskin heads tuned a fifth apart.

"Jesus Christ," I said.

"Shut up," said Myron, and a few minutes later the nine resolved itself (of its own will, it seemed to me) back into the closed 6/8 with which they'd begun.

"They slowed down," I said a little later.

"No," said Myron. "They're playing half-time—the tempo is the same."

"If you say so."

He was right, too, although I didn't find that out until much later when I listened to the recordings. Myron checked the levels again, then lit a cigarette. The screen of his computer held only a single window, which logged the strength of the signal.

"How long have they been playing?" I said.

"Most of an hour."

"Mmmmm. Doesn't seem that long."

I almost asked Myron to put his cigarette out, but instead I gave up and asked him for one. He lit it and handed it to me.

In the studio, Jacky smiled again. He was holding down an Iraqi 10/8 with his right hand, his thumb doing the bass while his fingers slapped the off-beats; it was an odd rhythm, almost like a 6/8 but containing a surprise 16th note at the end, so it sounded like a three-legged drunk walking down an icy hill. With his left hand, he sometimes pressed the head to change the pitch; at other times he struck at his own rhythm with patterns of five, six, or seven. The Groovemeister used a conga sound to close the 10/8 in a constant roll, with a woodblock sound to answer the fills.

I couldn't get enough of watching Jacky. He wasn't a superstar by the usual definition of the word, but players knew who he was, and so did critics. There were even preposterous stories circulating about him. For example, there was the story that when he was three days old, just back from the hospital, he began slapping out a 7/8 (*One*-two-*one*-two-*one*-two-three) at 80 beats per minute on his crib and held it for over an hour. Or that when he was two weeks old he set up a salsa beat by shaking a rattle and striking it on his crib on the accented beats. No, I don't believe those, but, watching him play, I wondered.

Jacky switched the drum so it was between his knees again and started doing finger rolls into the *one* and out of the *ten* each measure. The Groovemeister led the way gradually back to the 6/8 at 120 beats per minute; it matched the sound of Jacky's dourbakee. Jacky thought that was funny and gave a laugh that we could hear in the booth.

"I'm hungry," said Myron.

"Me, too."

"Pepperoni, onion, and olive?"

"How 'bout green pepper instead of the olive?"

"Okay. I'll order it."

"You have beer?"

"I have beer."

"Good."

"You want one now?"

"No, let's wait for the pizza."

This whole time I'd been staring fixedly at Jacky, who seemed to be living in some other world. My eyes were getting tired. I stopped watching long enough to use some eye-drops.

Both drummers, responding to some signal only they understood, went into a continuous roll that sounded like waves breaking; no discernible rhythm was apparent at first, but gradually they came out of it into a very gentle, pulsing 8/4, queerly broken up into twos and threes, with an odd emphasis on the offbeat after the seven. The Groovemeister played the timbale, which earned it a slightly scornful look from Jacky. They both played with this for a while; then they broke it up differently and began switching parts. The Groovemeister generated the sound of an East African slit drum. Jacky laughed again. I decided I liked his laugh.

He had a timeless and placeless look—like he could have been any age and of any background. In fact, he was born in 1971, which would make him just about sixty years old, and born in Lakota, Ohio, to Lillian Hanks, who conducted the Lakota Symphony Orchestra, and

Julio LaPrince, a jazz pianist and studio musician. If rhythmical skill is hereditary, I guess he had every reason to be good; if it is environmental, the same applies.

The pizza arrived. I neither looked at nor tasted the two or three pieces I ate, though I remember how good the beer felt on my throat. Jacky was playing the side of his drum, implying a swing 5/4; the Groovemeister was playing low-pitched tom-toms, very sparely.

The story of Jacky's first encounter with a drum machine, in which, at age six, he attempted to destroy it with a hammer, has a certain poignancy, although, like the other stories, there's no evidence that it actually happened. Certainly, it is possible; in 1977, when Jacky was six, drum machines were becoming common enough that one of his parents could easily have brought one home, probably a Simmons STS 1000 or something like it. Such machines were little more than programmable metronomes with a limited synthesizer; it wasn't until the 1980s that machines were developed with the capacity to respond to tempo changes, much less play behind or ahead of the beat.

I wondered if that story were true. I'd played around a bit with doing a story on Jacky before. I'd never written it, but I'd done some research, and I knew enough about Jacky's history to make the story plausible, if doubtful.

Jacky got his first gig at the age of nine, when he played with the Lakota All-Stars, a band thrown together to back up singer Shirley Demero, who was in town for a local jazz festival. Mr. LaPrince had been asked to play keys, and he agreed if they would audition Jacky. "The Kid" passed handily, and the All-Stars stayed together for eight years, with Jacky on drums for the first six. He left in the summer of '86, when bandleader Lippy Sullivan suggested picking up a Roland 505 and, "freeing Jacky up to work around it." Jacky packed up his kit (a set of Tamas with one rack tom, a thirteen-inch crash ride and a fifteen-inch sizzle) and walked without saying a word.

I said, "What time is it?"

Myron looked around for a clock, before remembering the one on the computer. "About 7:45," he said.

"You should check the analyzer; there's no way he didn't slip by now."

Myron laughed. "Christ. You're right. I completely forgot the bet. I'm minded to let him keep the money—bet or no, that's one hell of a show."

"Check it," I said.

I heard the click of the keys as Myron called up the analyzer. A moment later, against a background of 9/8 against 10/16, at 240 beats per minute, with accented 32nd notes, I turned to look at him. His face was white.

"He hasn't slipped," said Myron.

I stared at him. "Don't be ridiculous. How far did you go down?"

"To the limit of the machine."

"What's the limit of the machine?"

"The machine, Clara my dove, is sensitive to ticks. Roughly one ten billionth of a second. I couldn't go quite that far, because you lose something in the time it takes the signal to get from the cesium clock to the analyzer. The analyzer has to account for that. So we're accurate to within twenty ticks, which is roughly two times ten to the minus eight, or two nanoseconds, or, uh, a five hundred millionth of a second."

"Huh? That's just silly. The sound of the beat lasts at least—"

"The analyzer ignores the leading and trailing edge of the beat and marks the center. We don't lose much accuracy in marking the center—I built the analyzer myself for testing the Groovemeister."

I licked my lips. "And he—?"

"Yeah."

"My God!"

"Yeah."

"He isn't human!"

"He's human," said Myron.

I stared at Jacky through the window. After a while I said, "His right leg."

"Huh?"

"No matter how fast or slow he goes, his right leg just keeps going at the same tempo. That's how he does it."

"Yeah," said Myron. "That explains the whole thing."

"Don't be sarcastic. Should I bring him some food? Or at least some water?"

"Sure."

I brought out some pizza and a glass of water. He wasn't interested in the food, but he took the glass with his left hand, maintained the beat with his right, drank half of the water, and handed me the glass with a smile.

When I got back to the booth, I said, "Did he slip while he was drinking? I'd feel awful if I distracted him."

Myron checked. "No."

I watched him drum.

Two years after leaving the Lakota All Stars, Jacky quit school, left home, and began traveling. He made his way to Brazil, where he worked as a percussionist at carnivals and studied with South American drummers. He then managed to get hired onto a cruise ship, the *Sally S.*, by which means he eventually arrived in Morocco. He spent four years avoiding war and traveling throughout the Mideast, working as a poorly paid studio musician and absorbing North African rhythms. He next spent three years in India studying the North Indian tabla, after which he took what, in one of his infrequent letters home, he called, "a long, slow summer vacation in Jamaica" that took two years.

For the record, I was born a few days before Jacky's ship landed in Morocco.

By the millennium, when Jacky was almost thirty years old (and I wasn't quite eight) he had also visited Japan, China, and the Balkan Republic; and he had cut two discs. The first, "Easing Down the Shady Side," was recorded with some of the greatest jazz players of the era; the second, "Inside Down," was his famous first solo percussion work. In his travels, he mostly supported himself by performing on the streets with whatever hand-drum (or random piece of material) he could find; he was almost unique among drummers of the day in having no interest in collecting instruments. To Jacky Hanks, anything was a drum if it sounded good and wouldn't hit back.

This was around the time that the term "meat drummer"

came into vogue, and the phenomenon was leaving as the term was entering. Even bands that had built their reputation on live performances were phasing the "meat" out of their percussion sections.

Jacky returned to North Africa, where he spent six years with an Iraqi Sufi master (whom he never named, at the master's request). By the time he reemerged in the West, the Synchograph (or "Sink-or-Swim," as studio musicians called it ) was an industry standard, and the age of the meat drummer was all but over. This was when he cut his disc, "Sensing the Soul," which, in the words of jazz and *Worldbeat* critic Marta Durring, "made every percussionist in the world throw out his old programs and start over." Although "Sensing" was never anything like a chartbuster, it was an instant sensation among percussion programmers; Marta's words were scarcely an exaggeration.

I came back to the present, and realized that it was two in the morning—we'd been there for twelve hours. I suggested calling the whole thing off, just for the sake of Jacky's health and so everyone could get some sleep. But Myron just shook his head, at which I felt relief—I hadn't really wanted it to stop.

I sighed. "Want some weed?"

"Need you ask?" said Myron.

The drummers (I discovered I was now thinking of the Groovemeister as a drummer, not a machine) were playing very softly—Jacky's drum was under his arm again, and he was using feather touches on the head in a kind of a jazz feel, changing time signatures every couple of measures. The Groovemeister was playing a small kick drum, a hi-hat doing quarter notes, hitting the bell of a cymbal and throwing in an occasional snare hit on an offbeat. I found that my head was rocking forward, and my imagination was supplying saxophone, piano, and stand-up bass.

After "Sensing" was released, Jacky spent several years on a continuous, worldwide quest for bands who both played the sort of music he was interested in, and still wanted a live drummer. The quest was painful and almost fruitless, except for a few brief stints in Eastern Europe in which he, in his own words, "Did some good gigs and damn near starved to death."

For my part, I had given up on writing poetry by this time, had found and lost Jesus at Antioch College, had spent my summer in the Southwest sweating my way through a neo-pagan revival group, joined Earth Spirit, wrote and edited their journal, switched my major to journalism and ecology, transferred to the University of Minnesota, tried hallucinogens, recovered, and was desperately trying to get a degree so my mother would get off my back. I had resolved that if I ever got another letter starting, "Clara, dearest, I'm worried—" I'd probably commit some horrid antisocial act.

Jacky starting playing ahead of the beat, going to a more '80s and '90s rock feel. The Groovemeister hung back, creating a tension that seemed to stretch and stretch, until it gave a flourish of tom-toms and landed, still with the same sounds, right on top of Jacky's rhythm. I heard myself giggling, and noticed that Jacky was grinning widely. I felt very pleased that I had gotten the joke—it was as if I were in the know or something; Myron was still staring at his screen.

They quieted down after that, and the Groovemeister slowly worked back to a tom-tom sound, and deepened it. Jacky nodded and matched it, waiting.

By the time Jacky returned to North America he was fifty-five years old, with a weather-beaten face, and the reputation of being the top human percussionist in the world. It was around this time that our paths first crossed, when I, ironically enough, wrote a review trashing his performance, although that wasn't the point of the column. I was then living in New York, writing for the *New Voice* and, having recently abandoned Buddhism, was considering becoming a Jew in order to better follow up my fascination with the Cabala. The *New Voice* sent me up to the opening of L5 to cover the concert by the Grateful Dead, which I quite correctly panned. I said then, and still believe, that when every member of a band has retired and been replaced, it is past time to pack it in, and

my column wondered if those who booked the concert
were aware of what sort of message they were transmitting along with the signal of the concert itself. It was only
years later, when I began studying Jacky's history, that I
discovered that he, along with Taro Hart, had drummed at
that show. I'm sorry to admit that I didn't notice the percussion at all.

The column was well received in music circles, and
was one of the reasons I was able to make the syndication
deal, which, in turn, gave me the leisure to begin my first
book, *Music Without the Muse: Jazz in the Late '90s,*
which was published in 2024.

I looked over at Myron, who was frowning and staring
at the screen. He reached out as if to adjust something,
and then changed his mind. He caught me looking at him
and said, "What?"

"Nothing," I said.

The Groovemeister had thinned out its sound even
more—now there was only the ting of the bell of a
cymbal, and Jacky was playing with a ragtime feel,
hinting at almost familiar melodies. The Groovemeister
picked up and the sound again, coming in with a straight,
square, thick, full sound like the rhythm section of a New
Orleans brass band when traps were brand new. Jacky
wore a lopsided grin.

It was around the time my book came out that I met
Myron Clay, who had just finished the prototype of what
would become the Groovemeister 1, and we lived
together during most of '24, and parted amicably enough
early in '25. I'd studied music all through school because
I loved it; he had begun studying music only when he
became fascinated by the hardware, and I think it was
always the mathematics of music theory he enjoyed most.
He was a pure techie, I guess. He went from cars to
bridges to computers to drums machines over the course
of thirty years, but I didn't think he ever really understood
the joy of coherent sound, any more than he ever needed
affection from people. I still thought of him as a sweet
man, though, and I was pleased to notice that I'd broken
him of the habit of combing his hair over his bald spot.

At just about the time Myron and I were breaking up, Jacky returned to Lakota and spent some time with his parents. Then he headed for New York, hoping to lead a revival of live drummers—an effort that earned him many friends, a few enemies, and no success whatsoever.

After several years, frustrated by his experiences in New York, Jacky walked into the ProSound Studio in Manhattan—home of Lodestone Industries and the Groovemeister 1, which had been released earlier in the year as the most complete and modern drummer yet created. He introduced himself and asked to speak to the lead development engineer: Myron Clay.

Dear Myron.

"Thanks," I said suddenly.

"For what?"

"Calling me."

"You're welcome."

We listened to more drums. They had long ago left New Orleans, and the Groovemeister, which was still sounding like a full trap set, had set up a rhythm and blues feel, with a quarter-note ride on a cymbal; Jacky was doing finger rolls against it, creating a dreamy feel like a blues club at four in the morning.

The next thing I knew, Myron was waking me up and it was 4:00 in the afternoon. "We've been sleeping," he said.

"I guess so."

I tasted my mouth, pulled out my mirror and smeared on some under-eye cover goop. I listened to the drums. After a while I said, "What are they doing? They're just flailing away."

"Listen a little longer," he said.

"There's no beat."

"Sure there is. They just aren't playing it. It's—" he gestured in the air, pointing out the missing beats that they were playing off of.

"You're right," I said eventually. Then I said, "Proud of yourself, aren't you?"

He smiled. "Shouldn't I be?"

As we listened, over the next few minutes, the room

was gradually filled with the pounding of Japanese Koto rhythms. The Groovemeister had the sound right. Jacky's face was expressionless, his eyes just barely open. Myron brought up the analyzer again, then made it vanish. I looked at him, and didn't need to ask.

I said, "This is like being there when history is happening."

"Yes," he said. "It's just like that."

I brought Jacky more water, and stood below Mount Fuji, watching the clouds part around it.

When I met Myron, he was a short, dark-haired, slightly paunchy man of about fifty, with permanently red eyes from staring at computer terminals and circuit boards. He told me that he was fixing cars before he could walk, which is probably not much of an exaggeration, considering what his father was like the one time I met him. It's a long road from fixing cars to designing the state-of-the-art drum machine. Or maybe it isn't. As I listened, it really hit for the first time just how much Myron must have learned about rhythm.

I watched him watching the contest, and I couldn't tell what he was thinking. The Groovemeister was now playing bells—striking, clear, and spare—while Jacky worked against them with finger rolls in a sort of 6 into 4.

"You have one tasty machine there," I said.

Myron shook his head and didn't answer. I've never been able to tell what Myron is thinking—this is one reason we didn't last more than a few months.

By 2023, when we met, he had gone from computer engineering to theoretical electronics to electronic design, and had already pretty much designed the Groovemeister. His first name for it had been "The Dynagroove," and advanced publicity had gone out under that name, until someone pointed out that this was the name of an RCA recording label from three-quarters of a century earlier, and RCA would probably not be amused. The techs had been calling the prototype, "Antonio the Groovemeister," or even, "Tony" for over a year by this time, so, when Myron was called at 11:30 at night by a desperate marketing agent who needed the new name *right now,* "The

Groovemeister" was all Myron could come up with. Myron was never at his best at night; this is another reason Myron and I didn't last. He never, ever, referred to his machine as "Tony."

After another few hours, I asked, "What are they saying?"

"Tabla language. They're both talking the beats. Or, rather, playing one, and talking another."

"I've read about that, but never run into it."

"I programmed the Groovemeister for it."

"It seems to fit."

"Yeah."

For a while, then, I was caught between watching Jacky and watching Myron. Jacky was a joy; Myron was a puzzle. His eyes seemed bright and alive like I'd never seen them, then he would shake his head and look almost gloomy. At first, I thought he was hearing mistakes by his machine, and I tried to listen for them and match them to Myron's mood changes. Abruptly, between one beat and the next, I remembered that Myron had taken what he could from "Sensing the Soul" and built it into his machine. While I was listening to a pair of brilliant drummers exploring the world of rhythm, Myron was listening to the difference between his interpretation of an aesthetic and the original—to the difference between his brain and Jacky's hands.

When I realized that, I felt an odd sort of disgust mixed with pity; but as the drummers gradually dropped out of the tabla talk and returned once more to the gentle 6/8, to which they waved as to an old friend before passing by, I decided that Myron could no more help who he is than Jacky or I could help who we were. And if there were one right way of listening to drums, why did my mind wander in time to the music?

We ordered more pizza for breakfast, and listened.

Over the next twenty-four hours, we journeyed to East Africa, to Polynesia, to China, to West Africa, to Croatia, to South America, across the breadth of Europe, to North America, and to North Africa. Some of these places I recognized at the time, many I filled in later, listening to the recording. I had long ago lost any sense of connection to reality; I was just a pair of ears. Sometimes I'd be aware that I was grinning broadly, other times I'd find that I was just staring without focusing. Jacky would smile and introduce melodies by muffling different parts of his drum, the Groovemeister would harmonize while subdividing the notes even finer. Jacky would frown and, by bouncing his right hand very lightly off the surface while striking sharply with his left, make his drum phase; the Groovemeister would slide under the phasing. Jacky would laugh as if the machine had made a clever joke and replay the melody in 13/4.

I brought him more water; he refused more food.

It was at 11:31 on the morning of the third day that I stood up amid the beer cans, cigarette butts, and pizza boxes, and said, "You've got to stop this. He's killing himself."

Myron looked up at me blankly and wide-eyed. "I—"

"You what?"

"He can stop when he wants to. Look at him. He's smiling again."

"He'll smile himself right into the grave."

"Let them go."

"No," I said, and reached over to the keyboard. "How do you shut this down?"

"Don't."

"If you don't tell me, I'll just start punching buttons."

He grabbed my wrist and held it tightly. This was the first time he had ever touched me other than affectionately, and it hit me like a bounced check notice. I stared at him, then burst out with, "What the hell's your problem? If he hasn't slipped now, he isn't going to. Call it a draw."

Myron let go of my wrist and looked at the computer. He muttered something under his breath, then brought up the analyzer again. He stared at it for a long, long time.

"What is it?" I said.

"It isn't a draw," said Myron.

I waited for him to continue.

"The Groovemeister," said Myron slowly, "is supposed to be accurate to within two hundred ticks, okay? That's good. I mean, that is really, really, fucking good. No one, no machine, has—"

"Myron."

He stopped and swallowed. "Yeah. Well, it drifted, you know. I mean, just a bit. About forty ticks, and that's over seventy hours. That's better than the specs call for. That's—"

"Drifted?"

"All machines drift. So do people, you know. I mean, give anything enough time, and measure it finely enough, and there's going to be some drift from the starting tempo. You can't have a machine—"

"What drifted?"

"The 120 beats per minute. The Groovemeister has speeded up, like about forty ticks, that's some impossibly tiny fraction of a second, okay? That's one second in about two million years. That's *nothing*—"

"The time between beats is shorter?"

"Just theoretically. You could never hear it. It—"

"And Jacky?"

"He's drifted, too. I can't tell how much because the analyzer has a margin of error—"

"Less than forty ticks?"

Myron licked his lips. "Yeah."

"Then Jacky won."

Myron straightened his back and nodded. "Yeah. He won."

I stared at him for about fifty billion ticks, then said, "Jesus Christ!" I reached over, realized I still didn't know what to do, and said, "How do you cut the thing off?"

Myron hit a button, and PFL appeared on top of the screen, with "GM" and "JACKY" below it. I touched Jacky's name, abruptly silencing the Groovemeister. Jacky matched the shut-off, making it a dead stop more powerful than rhythm, then resumed, by himself, wrapping himself in a smile and a West African polyrhythm that I couldn't begin to understand. I opened the door into the studio as he dropped the volume and worked his way back into the 6/8 at 120 beats per minute.

"Jacky," I said. "Jacky, you can stop. You've won. You held steadier than the Groovemeister."

"Hell," said Jacky in a whisper that I could barely hear above his soft drumming. "I know that."

He played softer and softer. "The thing ain't bad, really," he said, still whispering. "But it's got no soul."

His hands came gradually to rest and the room to awful silence; then the drum fell from his hands, making a muted thud when it hit the carpet, and Jacky pitched forward onto his face, slapping the carpet himself and producing an ascending run of three eighth notes as he landed with knees, shoulders, and face. The mike managed to pick it up and we were still recording; I've listened to those three eighth notes about a thousand times.

Myron came up next to me and stared down at Jacky. "Call an ambulance," I said. Jacky lay perfectly still, on top of his drum, breathing easily and still smiling a bit. I looked at Myron, then stared at Jacky's hands and wondered why I wasn't crying and why Myron was.

While Myron called the ambulance, I transmitted the tracks of the session to my computer at home. I thought about erasing it from Myron's, but he wouldn't know what to do with it anyway.

Jacky didn't die, but he didn't quite recover either. He did a few jazz gigs after that, but never recorded again.

Myron resigned from Lodestone Industries in '32 and joined the Winterland Laboratories, where they were working on a project to cut time even finer than the cesium atom beam clock. As far as I know, he's still there; we haven't run into each other since the studio.

In '35 I published *Sound of the Beast,* which stayed on *The New York Times* Bestseller list for eight weeks. I've been working on a biography of Jacky Hanks that something tells me I'll never finish; I'm too close to the subject, I guess. I've been writing my column, and I've spent a great deal of time listening to drums. I keep thinking about releasing the recording of Jacky's last session, but I haven't done so. I've given copies to friends, and I hear that the bootlegs have been spreading.

Jackie died in the winter of '36. I attended his funeral,

though not many did: I heard that he wanted it that way. I met his old Sufi master, who showed up and drummed for the funeral, but I won't release his name either. I presented myself to the family as an old friend, which wasn't really true, but I saw to it that Jacky's dourbakee was interred with him in the family plot, and that he was buried with a drum key and forty dollars in the breast pocket of his light colored, long-sleeved shirt.

*I wrote this story recursively . . . I was wandering around my kitchen and said if I'd written it, I would want to write it this way, and just kept going until it was done. It brings together my passion for drums and my long-standing tolerance for folk music.*

# A HOLE IN THE SKY
## by Margaret Ball

Margaret Ball lives in Austin, Texas, with her husband and two children. She has a B.A. in mathematics and a Ph.D. in linguistics from the University of Texas. Recent publications include *Changeweaver, No Earthly Sunne,* and *Lost in Translation.* When not writing she makes quilts, plays the flute, and feeds the pets.

Melissa didn't really worry when she started wearing the bui-bui, the black head-to-foot veil that all decent women on Linganya Island wore. Sure, it was hot, but even if she'd gone around in shorts and a halter top she'd have been hot. She was awkward in it, too; the chin-strings kept slipping off, and she never quite mastered the quick one-handed flip with which you were supposed to get a fold of cloth over your face whenever a man approached. But nobody laughed at her for being as clumsy as a little girl in her first bui-bui. And there were certain advantages. She *could* wear ragged shorts and a halter top underneath, for instance, since nobody was going to see anyway. And she worked out a way of carrying her tape recorder on a strap over one shoulder, under a concealing fold of black cloth. Everybody in Linganya knew she was taping them anyway, so it wasn't really an unethical field method, but when they *saw* the tape recorder it distracted them. They would talk about their cousin in Nairobi who had a television, not that you could pick up anything on the TV since EAPTV went off the air, or about some other one of the marvelous machines that had been breaking down and disappearing ever since Achana.

Achana meant divorce, or separation, or simply going different ways, or something like that. Mama Aisha, who fussed over Melissa and tried to make her eat more good coconut curry, said it meant the end of everything. Sheikh Hamed said Mama Aisha didn't know everything, and one good thing about Achana was that they didn't have any more to do with the mainland and all those crazy upcountry Kikuyu and Luo and Meru and other tribes and their wars. So perhaps it meant Independence. And apparently the tribal wars upcountry had kept Nairobi from noticing Achana, or anyway from doing anything about it. Yet.

Melissa wasn't sure where that left her, politically speaking. The research permit that allowed her to stay in the country had come from the East African Union, which had broken up before she even got here—too many of the organizers died, first of AIDS and now, lately, of the new blackspit, the mutated version that was even worse than its three predecessors. Her temporary papers were stamped in Nairobi, and she was supposed to report there every three months for a renewal, but as far as she knew you couldn't even *get* to Nairobi these days.

Not that it mattered—for the time being. She'd fought and argued and begged for three years to get this chance to do her field work on Linganya, the one island where nobody had ever been, the one that was special in some way that nobody could explain, the one that kept itself to itself so thoroughly that they said even the language was different. "Those people, they're crazy," the man in Nairobi had told Melissa. "They talk the old pure Swahili of three hundred years ago. You can't even understand them."

Melissa nodded and didn't argue. She'd grown up in a holler of the Blue Ridge so far back people told the same kind of stories about it. When she got to the University of Virginia she'd been told that her kinfolks had to be tied down to get shoes on them, that their chief amusements were bootlegging and feuds, and that they spoke pure

Elizabethan English. She knew all that was lies, and she figured the truth about Linganya would be just like the truth about Possum Creek—not nearly so romantic and a lot more interesting. Linguistically speaking.

So far, she'd been half right and half wrong. They didn't speak seventeenth-century Swahili, but the dialect had diverged enough from the mainstream to give her plenty of material for a dissertation. That, she'd been counting on. What she hadn't been counting on was that it was so complex, preserved so many forms that had never made it into the grammar books, that it took her two months to figure out the inflections. And even then she didn't *understand* anybody. The man in Nairobi was right about that.

All the people in Linganya seemed to care about was singing. They did a little fishing, had a few fields of yams, but these were like hobbies. Their *job,* everybody's job, was to squat in a circle and sing monotonous quatrains to a set of four different and simultaneous drum rhythms.

That is, it was the men's job. The women cooked the fish and yams and braided each other's hair in interesting patterns and grated coconuts into a sweetish white paste and preserved chopped-up mangoes in salt and talked. Melissa hung around with her tape recorder and captured as much of their conversation as she could, and whenever anybody noticed her standing with empty hands they gave her a coconut to grate or some dried fish to pound or some other job. All the households were like one big extended family—again, just like Possum Creek—and Melissa figured that her role in the family was that of the slightly retarded second cousin once removed that everybody made allowances for.

Only three things really worried her. One was that she was running out of cassette tapes and batteries, which meant she was going to have to make the bus trip to Mombasa sometime soon. Another was that she couldn't transcribe the dialect on the tapes, because somehow the incessant drumming and singing of the men got mixed in with the women's talk and made a confused noise that kept her from picking out individual words. She hoped that when she got home, somebody in the computer lab would be able to do a signal enhancement on the tapes and get the words clear for her and get rid of the drumming, which now went on all the time, even in her sleep.

And that was the third thing. When she was awake, she knew perfectly well who she was. Melissa McCoy of Possum Creek, no, of the University of Virginia, linguistics graduate student, collecting examples of the Linganya dialect for her dissertation. And if the best way to collect examples was to wear a black bui-bui and let the old women of the village treat her like a retarded relative and give her cooking tasks to do, fine. She could return at night to her solitary hut and light the kerosene lamp and write up her observations and know who she was. Melissa. Not a Linganyan. A foreigner, *mzungu*, somebody who would go back home some day when all the fuss about Achana and the upcountry tribal wars calmed down, when she had enough material to write her dissertation.

Sometimes, after she finished writing her notes, she turned down the lamp and sang to herself, quietly, and pretended she was a little girl in the mountains again. When she sang the old songs, "Do Lord Remember Me" and "Will the Circle Be Unbroken" and all the rest, she could imagine the cool clean air of the Blue Ridge Mountains and she knew exactly where she had come from and who she was.

But when she slept, the drum rhythms got into her sleep, and so did the songs.

*Risala siwe ajizi*     *enenda kwa wenye chewo*
*Ukenda siwa mkazi*     *mtafute mwendaniwo*
*Mwambie eshe simanzi*     *dira ashike ziliwo*
*Kuno kuzima kwelewo*     *haiwi kwisha uhunzi.*

*Runner, don't linger*     *go to those above*
*do not delay*     *go to your friend*
*tell him not to fear*     *hold fast to the compass*
*the cooling of the tongs*     *doesn't end the forging.*

In her dreams it made perfect sense. She dreamed in KiLinganya and she understood everything and she knew why the songs and the drumming had to go on, why that was more important than anything else in the world. She was Mlisa Mlinganya and the drums beat with the rhythm of her own heart.

And then she would wake up and say to herself in English, "I've got to go away for a while." In Mombasa there would be other *wazungu,* foreigners from Europe and America. She would talk to them and read the six-week-old issues of *Time* and *Newsweek* with all the pages about African affairs cut out by the censor and she would remember who she was.

Then Sharif Ahmed Musali, who sometimes came to Linganya with a dhow full of rice and cloves and other things that didn't grow on the island, brought the man from upcountry, and suddenly Melissa didn't have a choice any more.

The stranger wore city clothes, pants with an iron-hard crease down the legs and black pointy-toed Italian shoes and one of those big multicolored tunics with embroidery 'round the neck that everybody back home thought were authentic African dashikis. And he talked city talk, too, the cut-down, no-inflections trade Swahili that Melissa had studied back in Virginia, before she found out it didn't have much in common with the elaborately inflected and subtle language of Linganya. So they brought her in as a translator. Melissa was proud and pleased about that, at first. She figured being a translator ought to upgrade her village standing, say from Retarded Cousin to Crazy Aunt.

"Big bad news upcountry," the stranger said. "No planes. No more way to get away, nowhere to go anyway. Land falling apart everywhere. *Achana.* All the *wazungu* gone. Everybody dying of the blackspit."

It took Melissa five minutes to rephrase that with all the inflections of KiLinganya, and then Sheikh Hamed waved one old, knobbly hand and said tiredly that they already knew all that, and if there wasn't anything else, would the gentleman mind if he got back to work?

The other men of Linganya were still sitting in their circle, drumming and singing their endless songs about keeping the forge hot and watching the compass and holding the sky and—

Holding the sky? Melissa hadn't heard that one before. Not that it mattered. None of the songs made any *sense* anyway. But there was a hole in the interlocking drum-patterns. They did need Sheikh Hamed there, adding his seven-thirteen beat and his cracked old voice. It sounded *different* without him. Melissa felt vaguely uncomfortable.

Then the stranger vomited black bloody spit all over Sheikh Hamed's bare feet and two fan-bearers and a couple of children who'd been squatting at the sheikh's feet, and Melissa found out that taking care of the sick and dying was, as might have been expected, women's work.

Melissa McCoy didn't want to do it, didn't want to take off the stranger's clothes and discover that his pants were soaked with another black and bloody discharge, didn't want to carry sea water so Mama Aisha could wash his body decently before they buried him. But carrying the buckets slopping over with salt water was better than actually *washing* the flesh that decayed even while Mama Aisha cleansed the stranger for burial. And however much Melissa McCoy screamed and gibbered inside her head, Mlisa Mlinganya was firmly in charge of her body.

Mlisa Mlinganya carried the salt water for the stranger, and then for the two children he'd vomited on, who died within hours. And then there were more bodies. The multiple overlapping drumbeats got thinner. Day and night blended together. Occasionally Melissa McCoy said in her head, in English, "Wash yourself every time you go for water. Salt water's a disinfectant. Don't touch the bodies. Don't let them vomit on you." Then the silly *mzungu* woman went back to wailing inside her head that they had to get out, *now,* and Mlisa Mlinganya hitched up her black bui-bui and got on with carrying the water.

At the end of one trip Mama Aisha wasn't there to tell her to go back and hurry about it. She was lying on the

straw mat where she used to sit and read the Koran, and
there were pools of black blood and black runny feces all
over the straw, and her face was falling in like a col-
lapsing balloon.

Melissa McCoy set her bucket down and started crying.
Mlisa Mlinganya started back for more water, to wash
Mama Aisha and to wash the blackspit away, but some-
body called to her.

It was Shiekh Hamed. He had collapsed over his drum.
Nobody else was in the circle; nobody alive, anyway.
Mlisa Mlinganya noticed a couple of bodies that ought to
be moved, but she couldn't think where they would go.
All the yam fields had been used already, and the rest of
the island was solid coral rock.

"You must leave here, my daughter," Sheikh Hamed
whispered. Melissa McCoy, inside Mlisa's head, noted
that she'd been promoted to a fairly high place in the
family. "It is necessary that I should be staying with my
family and that I should cause those falling ill to be cared
for in decency," said Mlisa Mlinganya. In KiLinganya it
was just a matter of three verbs and a few dozen ending
forms tacked on to them, but you had to get all the suf-
fixes in the right order. She had to concentrate to make
sure it came out right.

"Don't act like a stupid *mzungu*," said the sheikh. "You
*wazungu* don't die of the blackspit, I don't know why, but
you can be some use now. It's a man's job, but you're the
best I've got. Anyway a *mzungu* woman is practically the
same as a man."

Melissa decided not to explain about the milder form of
blackspit that had swept the United States after the army
liberated Somalia for the fourth time, and her theory that
the three weeks she'd spent throwing up tarry black stuff
had immunized her against this version of the blackspit.
She also decided it would not be a good time to talk to
Sheikh Hamed about Women's Liberation. Mlisa Mlinganya silently applauded both decisions, folded her
hands, and waited for the sheikh to explain just what it
was he wanted her to do.

"You have to get my son." The sheikh turned his head

aside and spit out a pool of black gunk. "Baraka. He went to the city. He knows the chants. Somebody has to keep the chants going."

Melissa had to admit that after weeks and months of being driven crazy by the incessant drumming, she almost missed it now. Still, she couldn't quite see that singing and drumming were the most important things in the world. Getting out was the most important thing.

"I don't know if I can get to Nairobi," she said. "But I'll try."

"Not Nairobi, stupid woman," Sheikh Hamed said. This time he forgot to turn his head. The blackspit dribbled out of his mouth and down his front. Melissa's stomach heaved at the smell. Funny, you'd think she'd be used to it. "Mombasa. You take the bus. Even a stupid *mzungu* should be able to ride a bus to the city. Baraka. Mwembe Tayari. *Mombasa.*"

Then his head fell forward and a flood of blackspit covered the drum. Melissa stood for a moment, listening to the flies buzzing around the other bodies, and then she put on her going-to-the-city cotton skirt and blouse and went down to the spit of coral rock that stuck out and made a little harbor for the island.

Sharif Ahmed Musali was there with his dhow. That made as much sense as anything else. He made some noises about the bad luck of having a woman on his boat.

"You brought me here on the dhow," Melissa pointed out.

"Yes, and look what happened. Besides, that idiot who made me bring him here last month brought the blackspit. I don't want to get it."

"*Wazungu* don't get the blackspit," Melissa said. "If we did, I would be dead by now, wouldn't I?"

The water slopped rhythmically against the sides of the dhow. Behind them Linganya was silent for the first time in Melissa's memory.

There was still a bus. It was half blue and half rusty naked metal, and the blue half said "APTIST MISSION BU" in white letters, and the axles were bent so that it jiggled in a seven-thirteen rhythm like Sheikh Hamed's drumming, but it was running. Sort of. It jounced over the coral rock that passed for a road while the driver kept up a running commentary on *wazungu* who came to Africa and made roads and airports and electric power plants and then went away and left everything to fall to pieces.

"You put something in place, you got to keep it going," he said over and over.

At Malindi he ran out of gas—petrol, they called it here—and stopped. "This is as far as this bus go," he announced. "They all crazy in Mombasa. You crazy, too, *mzungu* girl, you want to go there. Anyway, I got no more passengers. I think I retire from driving bus, lie on the sand and watch the water until the blackspit kill me."

Melissa offered to pay him more to take her all the way to the city, but he just got out of the bus and walked away, toward the sound of the sea, leaving the APTIST MISSION BU in the middle of the road.

Melissa started walking south. She couldn't think of anything else to do. After a while a jeep full of men in blotchy black and green uniforms pulled up and the men made gestures for her to get in. She sat on the edge of the front seat, clutching the dashboard to keep from falling out when they hit ruts, and the men laughed and chatted. At first, when they were talking about the panga gang they'd met up the coast and how they killed the gang members by spitting them on their own machetes over a fire, she thought they must not realize she could understand them. Then they started talking about what they could do with a crazy *mzungu* woman, and looking sidewise at her, and she realized they didn't care if she did understand them.

While she was waiting for a chance to jump out of the jeep they kept talking, crazy talk, impossible talk: everything was breaking down, they said. The *land* was breaking apart. *Achana,* they kept saying, *Achana,* as if that were some kind of explanation. It was happening to the *mzungu* countries first, the land breaking apart and drifting away like clumps of kelp in the ocean.

"It'll happen here, too," one of them said. "But later."

"It won't happen," another spoke up. "Not as long as they keep singing on Linganya."

"Everybody is dead on the island of Linganya," Melissa said, using the KiLinganya verb form that meant caused-to-be-dead-by-something-not-human, and the driver of the jeep swerved and hit several ruts at once and she fell out without even planning to. He stopped and stared down at her.

"You Mlinganya?" he demanded.

Melissa nodded while trying to get her feet under her. One hip hurt like hell, but she didn't think anything was broken. She didn't think she could run fast enough to escape, though.

"Should have said so. You look like a *mzungu*. What's the matter, you got a skin disease or something? Come on up. Nobody hurt you. Not Mlinganya."

Melissa figured if she ran, they would decide she really was the *mzungu* woman she looked like. Anyway she was tired and hot and where would she run to? She climbed back in the jeep, somewhat stiffly because of the ache where she'd landed on her hip, and the soldiers drove her the rest of the way to Mombasa without talking or joking or even looking straight at her. Once the driver asked if it was true that everybody was dead.

"They died of the blackspit," Melissa repeated. "Sheikh Hamed sent me to find his son Baraka."

Mombasa looked like a burned-out, bombed-out war zone. They drove through empty streets with shattered windows where the stores of the Indian traders had been, past scarecrow figures poking among the trash on the streets and dead bodies lying in pools of black vomit. But Mwembe Tayari, the old-clothes market under the mango tree, was still busy and lively.

"You better stay with us, Bibi Mlinganya," the driver said. "Everybody dying here. We die, too. First go to good place, have drinks, find prostitute. Die happy. We take care of you."

Everybody in Mwembe Tayari was silent while the jeep was there, but as soon as the soldiers reluctantly drove off, leaving Melissa there, the traders started shouting and pulling on her sleeves and offering to sell her "authentic Africa carvings."

Melissa pulled her bui-bui out of her shoulder bag, unrolled it with a flick of her wrist, draped the black cloth over her head and raised the chin flap to cover the lower part of her face. "Did you think I was an *mzungu* tourist?" she demanded in KiLinganya, the language that was like Swahili but that allowed the question to carry additional inflections of scorn, boredom, weariness, and impatience-with-lowly-slaves. "Take me to Baraka bin Hamed, who sells the *khanga* cloths."

Baraka was a thin black man wearing European clothes and gold-rimmed glasses with one cracked lens. He looked as though he should have been teaching school-children to chant Koran, not selling brightly patterned cloths with flowers and proverbs printed on them.

"This is not a good place for you," he said when Melissa found him.

"I know," Melissa said wearily. "I'm going home. I just had to find you first." Her shoulder bag was heavy with all the tapes she'd made on Linganya. Everything else she'd left behind on the island of the dead.

Baraka shook his head gently. "Home? You have no more home, Bibi Mlisa."

"I'll just take a cab to the airport. . . ." Melissa's voice trailed off and she realized that she was very tired and dizzy. Maybe she was catching the blackspit after all. Eventually the virus had to mutate into a form she wouldn't be immune to.

"Eat," Baraka said. "Rest. Then you will tell me, and I will tell you." *Everything we both need to know,* it was that form of "tell."

Melissa nodded wearily. They squatted in the back of the stall, in the multicolored shade of pink and purple and orange khanga cloths draped overhead, and ate curried something from tin bowls that had to be sent back to the cooked-food stall when they were finished. She told Baraka what had happened and what Sheikh Hamed had asked her to do, and she used his exact words because in KiLinganya you don't shorten or rephrase anything unless you can be absolutely certain you aren't changing a shade of meaning, and Melissa didn't kid herself she was that good yet.

When she was through, Baraka looked up at the sun shining through the colored cloths for a moment. Then he explained, gently but very clearly, that there were no planes at the airport, and nobody to fly them if there had been.

"There has to be *some* way to get home!"

"I really do not advise it," Baraka said. "We saw, before EAPTV stopped transmitting."

He told the same kind of story the soldiers had been telling, and Melissa didn't believe it for a minute. Countries, whole *continents*, didn't just break up and disappear.

"You put something in place, you got to keep it going," Baraka said, just like the bus driver. "You *wazungu* are good at starting complicated things, but you lose interest. You forget. You don't train anybody else. We don't have any electricity in Mombasa since the last engineer caught the blackspit."

"I don't see what that has to do with—" Melissa began, but Baraka was already on his feet. "I don't have time to explain it. We can talk on the way north."

"I'm not going back to Linganya!'

The colored lights shone out of Baraka's cracked glasses, splintering apart into bits of pink and purple and orange without connection. Drifting apart, falling apart, and a hole in the center.

"Seem to me," he said gently, "you have no other place to go."

Or, since he was speaking KiLinganya, he might have said, "This place is the only one for you." Because the same verb form worked both ways.

After that things started going blank, with clear bits now and then, like a dream. In one part of the dream they were driving north in a very old VW bug with holes and sticky stains in the seat cushions, and Baraka was singing in a monotonous way that made Melissa think, drifting the way she was beginning to do, that she was back on

Linganya and the circle of elders was singing and drumming. She had to learn a whole new set of verb forms when she asked about the singing; not present, not past, not future. A tense-no-tense that meant whatever it was had always been happening and always would.

"But they were wrong about that," she said into the heavy night air that enfolded them, "or else I didn't understand the verb system. There was a lot I didn't understand."

The car jounced over sun-baked ruts, and she saw the abandoned half-blue bus in front of them. "He ran out of gas," she said. "Petrol. Whatever. Do we have enough gas?" She leaned over and tried to inspect the gas gauge, but it wasn't working; the red needle lay on Empty.

"We don't need petrol," Baraka said, and when he stopped singing to speak the car engine stuttered and almost died.

Melissa drifted off into sleep. When she woke, Baraka's voice sounded hoarse, and so did the car. "I have tapes," she said. "If that would help."

Baraka shook his head. *"Wazungu,"* he said pityingly. *"Machines."*

"We're riding in one," Melissa pointed out, but just then someone rushed out of the darkness, black skin gleaming in the headlights, yelling and waving. *Panga gang,* she thought, but she couldn't see any machete; and when Baraka stopped, the man kept waving and pointing off into the blackness beyond where the car headlights could reach.

They got out of the car and walked forward carefully, one step at a time, until their feet teetered on the edge of black nothingness.

"It has begun," Baraka said.

"Road work," Melissa said. "Earthquake. Subsidence."

There were dhows on the beach, the man who had stopped them said. There would always be a boat for WaLinganya returning home. Was it true, he asked? Had the blackspit killed everyone on the island? Had the song stopped?

"The song sings itself," Baraka said, using the tense-no-tense that meant always and forever, and the man seemed happier.

Perhaps the dhow sailed itself; Melissa couldn't tell. There was a sail that the man helped Baraka raise, and a hint of movement in the heavy air, and it was totally crazy to be going off like this into the darkness, but she was beyond reasoning. She fell asleep again, and when she woke, the boat was in Linganya's little curved coral harbor and Baraka was handing her to shore.

He seemed to know exactly where to go through the darkness. She followed the sound of his steps, and memory filled in where they were: now passing Mama Aisha's courtyard, now the mosque, now they were in the village square.

Baraka knelt and gently moved an old man's head from a drum covered with black vomit. Melissa's last bucket of sea water still stood beside the mosque, the one she had been carrying when Sheikh Hamed died. She sluiced off the drum and Baraka picked up the seven-thirteen rhythm, at first raggedly, then gaining power and assurance.

Melissa thought it was a little lighter around them. But Baraka was tired. He kept pausing and coughing, and every time he coughed, the growing light died down.

"I have tapes," she said again.

Baraka shook his head.

"I know the songs," she said. "I wasn't trying to learn them, I was trying to write a grammar of KiLinganya, but the songs got into everything. Can a woman sing? A *mzungu* woman?"

Baraka shrugged. Melissa started singing the first thing she thought of, the only song that was right for Linganya Island on this morning that was no morning—the forge song that sounded lonely and hopeless without the other drums backing up their two voices.

*Listen to the names        of all the islands*
*Pate, Siu, Faza            Linganya of the songs*
*Listen to the names        of the sea and the sky*
*the cooling of the tongs   doesn't end the forging.*

The sky was definitely lighter now; light enough for her to see the big cracks and gaps in it. Not clouds. Just places where there was nothing, like where the road had ended last night. The sharp edges of jagged black places that you could fall into forever cracked open the smooth dim blueness of almost-dawn. Things falling apart.

> *We are singing the fire        we are singing the iron*
> *We are holding the earth    we are holding the sky*
> *Linganya is singing            we are still singing*
> *the cooling of the tongs    doesn't end the forging.*

She thought the cracks in the sky were closing as they sang, just a little.

*This story has been quietly growing in the back of my head since the years I spent studying Swahili dialects on the coast of East Africa. Clumsy attempts to dance in time to complex rhythms of wedding dances, the diatribe of an African civil servant who thought us* wazungu *criminally irresponsible for having burdened his country with a technical infrastructure they could not maintain, and the night when some villagers warned me that the road I was traveling on ended in a thirty-foot-deep pit . . . all these ingredients came together while I was considering how much time we* wazungu *spend discussing God as the Creator of the universe, and how little we think about the effort it takes to maintain a system once it's put in place.*

*Considering how much time and effort and attention is required to maintain a houseplant or a dog, never mind a child or a career, isn't it reasonable to wonder if somebody somewhere is working quietly at the upkeep of the universe?*

# THE IMPOSSIBLE PLACE
## by Alan Dean Foster

Alan Dean Foster was born in New York City and raised in Los Angeles. He has a bachelor's degree in Political Science and a Master of Fine Arts in Cinema from UCLA. He has traveled extensively around the world, from Australia to Papua New Guinea. He has also written fiction in just about every genre, and is known for his excellent movie novelizations. Currently, he lives in Prescott, Arizona, with his wife, assorted dogs, cats, fish, javelina and other animals, where he is working on several new novels and media projects.

"But I could swear I heard singing last night."

Matthew Ovatango scratched the place on his forehead where his short, tightly curled hair began as he gazed out across the night-swept vastness of Kaokoland. They had camped in the shadow of a smooth hillock of gray granite that very much resembled a gigantic ball of elephant dung. Beyond the battered but indestructible Landrover lay the immense reaches of the Hartmann Valley. Sere yellow grass carpeted the endless plain. Not far to the west, the southern Atlantic Ocean gnawed remorselessly at the lonely sands of the Skeleton Coast.

The nearest town, if such it could be called, was Opuwo, a two-hundred kilometer roadless drive to the east. In these barren reaches lived few trees, and fewer people. Howard had come, deliberately and with photography aforethought, to one of the most godforsaken corners of the Earth in search of solitude and marketable photos. Thus far they consisted entirely of landscapes. No one lived in this lonely corner of Namibia except a few wandering Himba and their cattle.

So how could he have heard singing in the chill and perfect night?

"Perhaps it was a pied crow." His guide stirred the fading fire with a stick. The bark of Bushman's Candle collected earlier in the day flared briefly at the fringes, the waxy exoskelton of that remarkable plant perfuming the night air as it burned.

Rising, Howard turned to gaze into the darkness. Half a moon transformed the nearby inselberg, a mountain of sculpted granite boulders like the one beneath which they were camped, into a fantastic imaginary fortress. It reminded him of the massive walls of Sacsayhuaman, the plundered Inca fortress outside Cuzco, in Peru.

But it was only a pile of rocks. The people who had first inhabited this land had raised up nothing more elaborate than crude, temporary huts of shattered rock and reed.

He was turning back to the fire when he heart it again.

This time he whirled sharply and took a couple of quick steps away from the crackling blaze. "Don't tell me you didn't hear that! Your ears are sharper than mine, Matthew."

The guide eyed him appraisingly. "A pied crow, Mister Howard, sir. If you trust my ears, then trust my words."

The photographer strained to hear more. "That cry wasn't like any crow call I've ever heard."

"And the pied crow isn't like any crow you've ever seen either, sir." Patiently the guide stirred the pulsing embers, cajoling them to renewed life. "You sit yourself down and get warm, sir. Tomorrow we will drive down toward the Hoarusib and look for the desert elephants."

Howard let his glance linger a moment longer on a landscape that seemed to rise up into the stars. Then he disappeared into the tent. Moments later he reemerged with electric torch, canteen, and camera.

Ovatango's lips tightened in the soft glow from the fire. "You shouldn't leave camp, sir. Especially at night. Easy to get lost here."

"I know what I'm doing, Matthew." Howard slung the camera strap over his neck, hooked the canteen to his belt. "I've done plenty of night photography in strange places, just last month in Etosha. I can always follow the fire back to camp. Get some rest yourself. You're going to be doing a lot of driving tomorrow."

"This isn't Etosha, sir. This is the Skeleton Coast. Etosha is civilized country compared to here. There is a reason for its name, you know. Just last year two men illegally prospecting for diamonds on the Coast got lost. They had been here before, they 'knew' the country, and they were well-equipped. A private plane spotted their Landrover and a government patrol came out to look for them. They had become lost in the fog and driven around in circles. When their radio didn't work, they tried to walk out. It took two weeks to find the bodies. The jackals and hyenas had been at them."

"Don't worry about me." Howard started off in the direction of the looming inselberg. "I'm not afraid of hyenas." He grinned. "Maybe I'll catch the sunrise from the top of the rocks. I like being on my own, Matthew."

The guide didn't smile back. "No one comes to this place who doesn't, sir. Please be careful. You are my responsibility. I am not worried about you meeting a hyena. But what if you step on a horned adder or a dancing white lady?"

Howard kept his eyes on the circle of ground illuminated by the flashlight. "I won't be climbing any dunes, Matthew. This is all rock and gravel here. And a dancing white lady," he added, speaking of the ghostly white tarantula of the Namib sands, "would be more frightened of me than I of it."

The fire didn't shrink behind him so much as it was swallowed up. The immense dark stones that he soon found himself striding among all looked exactly alike—sleek and curved as if polished by some titanic gem tumbler. There were no trees, of course, not even a salt bush. Only in the sand rivers could trees find enough subterranean water with which to sustain themselves.

The shifty weight of his canteen was a reassuring

presence on his hip. The damp chill of night would give way to the rising heat of early morning. He found himself slowing, the guide's words shadowing his thoughts. What if the fog did advance this far inland tonight? The famous mists of the Namib could instantly reduce visibility to zero. No fire could light a way back to camp through it. Furthermore, there was no water to be found in this country for a hundred kilometers in any direction, from the Kunene River up on the Angolan border to Cape Frio camp . . . and maybe not water there either.

But the night was crystal clear, the stars devoid of flicker, and though his athletic years were behind him, he felt confident he could outjog an advancing fog, even on unfamiliar terrain.

It was the lack of landmarks that gave him pause. Even in broad daylight it was easy to get disoriented out here. Many did, and many died. He dug in his pocket and relaxed a little. It was unfair of him not to have shown Ovatango the luminous compass, but it would be amusing to see the guide's face when he strode confidently back into camp.

He was ascending now, using the pale light to find his way. Here he had to be extra careful. A deceptively gentle, smoothly weathered ascent could terminate abruptly in a sheer drop of a hundred meters or more. Sand whispered under his hiking shoes, each step a small voice telling him to *shush, shush,* as *if* the land itself was admonishing him to respect the unparalleled silence and solitude.

He thought he must be nearing the summit when moonlight suddenly broke through the rocks off to his left. There was an opening there and he turned toward it. Over a black granitic curve that bowed up into the sky like a black clavicle he trod, then down into a frozen stream of sand, and up once again.

Then he stopped, his lips parting in wonder. It was not a gap, a break in the rocks he'd come upon, but an arch. An absolutely lunatic geological phenomenon.

He'd seen arches before, and photographed them. In the American southwest, in Australia, in Morocco. Always they were fashioned of sandstone, easily weathered through by the wind. But he was not looking at sandstone now. He stood within a garden of solid, impermeable granite.

The Namib was the oldest desert in the world, and the wind here had aeons in which to work. No more than seven or eight feet high at its maximum, the opening in the rock was longer than a football field, tapering in height to mere inches at either end. The bridge of rock itself was fifty or sixty feet thick and at least as broad—a sleek-flanked rope of black stone flung by the hand of a perverse geology across the crest of a low hill. The result was a long window in which a man could stand with his head scraping the rock ceiling while gazing out across an endless flat valley. Moonlight bathed the horizonless reaches in pale silver.

His fingers throbbed from gripping the camera too tightly. He let it rest against his chest. There was no way he could capture the phenomenon at night. That would have to wait for daylight, and a wide-angle lens. Very wide.

Then he heard the singing again, and knew despite Ovatango's disclaimers that it was no crow that had ever lived.

Crouching without knowing why, he advanced toward the upper end of the fantastic arch. As he ascended the slope, a figure came unexpectedly into view. He froze, watching and listening. So mesmerizing was the unexpected sight that not once did he think of his camera. For Howard this was unprecedented.

The woman was short, no more than five feet tall, and naked save for a modest loincloth. She was not black, but a very beige or dried apricot-color. Her black hair was sliced flat in a neat crewcut and her eyes were almond-shaped. Though she looked almost Mongolian, he knew she was not. He had seen her people before, though more often in the southern part of the country.

She had a beautiful voice, though he recognized neither her words nor the language from which they sprang.

Arms outstretched, she was half singing, half chanting.

At first he thought she was singing to the moon, but she was too far beneath the arch for that indolent disk to be visible from where she stood. She had to be singing to the rock itself. Or to something on the rock.

The song stopped, the delicate hands lowered, and she was looking straight at him. She made no move to cover her nudity, nor did she seem in the least afraid of him. This, too, was typical of her people, who from his brief acquaintance he knew to be bold and confident.

"Hello, big darling. You have found me out, so you might as well come up here." Her English was rich and flowing, as if she were pronouncing every vowel with her whole throat.

He hesitated, wondered why he was hesitating, and then resolutely climbed up to stand beside her. She had taken a seat on the curved floor of the arch. Feeling it was the polite thing to do, he crossed his legs and sat down nearby. Despite her semi-nudity, she gazed back at him openly, frankly. The smooth skin of her breasts hovered beneath the slim arms she rested on her knees, their sleek curves mimicking that of the rock itself.

"I heard you singing. My guide didn't want me to come."

"But you are a man who does not like to be told what he can and cannot do. I like that."

He coughed gently, the cold invading his throat. "You're very direct."

"A property of my people."

"You're San?"

"No. Khoikhoi, or as most people say today, Nama. The Bushmen-San are very close to us." For the first time since he'd sat down her eyes left him, to question the darkness from which he'd emerged. "Your guide is not Nama."

"No. Herero."

"Ah. That explains it. A Nama guide would not have brought you anywhere near here. This place is sacred to the Khoikhoi. Only a very few know of it. My grandfather was one who did. Also," she added with a startlingly white smile, "the Herero and the Nama do not get along. It goes back a long ways, and has a lot to do with cattle."

He smiled back. "Trouble in Africa often does."

"You are an unusual man, Mister . . . ?"

"Howard. Howard Cooperman. My friends call me Howie."

"Howie is too weak a name for this place. I will call you Howard."

"Your English is very good. Surely you don't live around here?"

"No one does. Only memories live in this place. I am an accountant for the First National Bank of Windhoek." She waved a hand toward the southeast. "That way."

"I know. Hundreds of miles of nothingness. That's why I'm here. There aren't many places left in the world where you can find nothing."

They were both quiet for a while then, sharing the kind of total silence Howard had only experienced before inside a cave. Not a bird called, not an insect chirped, not the muted roar of a distant aircraft disturbed the upper atmosphere. Civilization of any sort was very far away.

"You want to know what I'm doing here, dressed like this, or rather, undressed like this, singing in the middle of the night. But you're too polite to ask." She traced an outline on the bare rock. "I am singing praise songs. The old songs, which my grandfather taught me."

"It was very beautiful," he told her. "You sing to the rock?"

"No." She giggled softly, and her laughter was like water in the desert. "Why sing to a rock? Look above you."

Tilting back his head, he brought the beam of the electric torch up . . . and lost his breath.

The underside of the arch was completely covered in the most exquisite primitive paintings he'd ever seen. Both the ancient bushmen and their cousins the Khoikhoi had left such paintings all over Namibia and Botswana, planting pigment throughout the Khalahari and Namib Deserts. Only weeks ago he'd spent several days photographing the most famous of them at Twyfelfontein.

But this was grander, much grander. Everything had been executed on an overpowering scale. Their outlines incised into the rock and then filled with color, hundreds of animals paraded across a canvas of a million tons of flying granite. Pacing the great herds on either side were the famously fluid stick figures of the ancient hunter-gathers who had lived side-by-side among them.

The animals and people and paintings dated from a time long ago when this part of southwest Africa was much wetter and lusher, when the people called the Strand-lopers hunted oryx and springbok and impala on the beach and rivers like the Secomib and Nadas still reached the sea. Ten thousand and more years ago, when the game and the grass covered the land as far as the eye could see. Before the Namib took over this part of the continent and the South African army slaughtered what animals remained.

"No one's ever photographed this before." He stood awestruck by the skill and accomplishments of the ancient painters. "I know: I would have seen pictures." Despite the chill his fingers were moist against the hard body of the camera.

"No. You can be the first. Or you can help me."

He blinked and turned back to her, the light flashing in her onyx eyes and making her turn away sharply.

"Sorry." He lowered the beam and then, on impulse, clicked it off.

"Thank you." In the shade of the arch she was a shadow herself now. "I need a man."

"You *are* direct."

The bubbling laughter echoed again. "Not like that, though I wouldn't refuse you. I need a man to dance for me. It has to be a man. The women sing the praises. The men dance."

"I don't understand, but if you need a man to dance for you, why not one of your own people?"

She leaned toward him. "Because they are all afraid."

The cold of the Namib night jumped suddenly closer, like a dancing white lady spider on the hunt.

"What are they afraid of?"

"They have been told that the old ways are wrong and that they must all become modern. I am modern, I have a good education and a modern job, but I also had a grandfather. He brought me to this place when I was a little girl, and showed me the dances, and because of him I was never afraid. My grandmother taught me the songs.

"When I was old enough, I started coming here as soon as I could get away. First from Gibeon, where I was born, then from Keetmanshoop, where I went to school, and now from Windhoek, where I work. Sometimes a boy or a man would come with me, but they wanted to dance a different dance. Sometimes I danced with them, sometimes not." Eagerness infused her voice.

"You come from a far-off land. You have no fears of the old ways, no prejudices. You heard the singing and came of your own free will. I think you are special, Howard. Special to this place and special to me. If I sing, will you dance?"

He shook his head. This was too bizarre. But if he could get her to pose for him in the morning, she would make a magnificent image, framed in the impossible arch with the great valley stretching out before her.

"I'm not much of a dancer, Miss . . . ?"

She didn't stand so much as flow to her feet. "I am Anna Witbooi. My grandfather was the greatest of the Khoikhoi elders, a direct descendant of Heitsi Eibib, who was the first of our people. I will sing the true praise songs and you will dance. I can show you the steps, but I cannot dance them myself. The women sing, the men dance.

"First you must take off your clothes."

It seemed crass to be self-conscious in so pure a setting. He folded his clothes and laid them in a neat pile, all but his briefs which she told him he could retain. It was cold and he hoped he wouldn't start shivering. The damp chill didn't seem to bother her at all.

"Like this." Standing so close he could feel the warmth of her, she started to dance.

The movements were simple and not impossibly precise. More of a rhythmic stamping and turning than anything else. All he had to do was keep time to the chanting.

"All right," he finally told her. "I'll give it a try. Just don't expect too much. But I want something in return. Tomorrow, when there's light, I want to take some pictures of you."

"Yes." She was teasing him. "Tomorrow you can take pictures of me."

"Just one question. Why do you do this, come out here year after year, to sing to a bunch of old paintings?"

"Because the praise songs need to be sung. Because of tales my grandfather told to me. Because I know in my heart that there can be nothing to fear from a place as breathtaking as this."

Having said that, she began to sing.

At first he felt silly, prancing about in the altogether, but the feeling passed quickly. There was no one here to laugh at him or point accusingly. The steps felt natural and he entered into the unbounded spirit of the moment with increasing enthusiasm. Dancing pushed back the damp night and warmed his body. He began throwing his arms up and out, careful not to scrape his fingertips against the unforgiving ceiling.

He hoped he was doing well, but he couldn't tell. Anna had her eyes half closed and her own arms outstretched as he'd first seen her. Her voice echoed and quivered with words so ancient they had never been written down. They bounced off the smooth rock as he twisted and twirled, his feet rising and falling, the bare soles only occasionally smarting from the isolated pebble that marred the otherwise perfectly smooth floor of the majestic gash in the mountain.

A gleam caught his eye that did not come from his torch. Just a little to the left of his head a family of giraffe etched in eternal stone and tinted white and red was glowing with a ghostly light all its own.

"Don't stop," she whispered urgently, somehow working the admonition into the sing-song of the chant.

He missed a step but managed to recover. The glow within the rock was the palest of efflorescences. Head tilted back, he strained on tiptoes until his face was only inches from the ancient painting. He couldn't tell if the light was emanating from the primordial pigment or the granite beneath.

"Faster!" she hissed at him, snapping him out of his awed stupor.

His knees lifted with her voice. Muscles long disused strained to comply. He found himself whirling with an abandon that verged on madness, the self-control of a lifetime fled, as if he no longer cared for anything save keeping step and time to her singing. The light in his eyes was internal, but that which had begun to illuminate the entire underside of the arch pulsed within the living rock itself as each painting, each patiently rendered etching began to throb with the light of a dozen candles.

Bushmen's Candles.

It was a tossup as to whether his legs or his balance would give out first. It turned out to be his legs. Calves aching, thighs trembling, he settled slowly to the smooth rock like a tin top winding down. The pure air refreshed his lungs as he drew in long, deep breaths. He was utterly, completely exhausted.

"Sorry . . ." he managed to wheeze, "I'm . . . sorry, Anna. I can't go anymore."

"But you did fine, Howard. You did very fine." As she knelt beside him, her warmth spread over his ribs like a blanket, burning where she placed her hand on his shoulder and squeezed with the strength of old iron. "Look."

He raised his eyes. As far as he could see the Namib night was alive with massed game. Like runaway construction cranes giraffe clans loped along above great herds of gemsbok and blue wildebeest. Rare, black-faced impala mixed freely with zebra, while families of warthogs scurried along underfoot. Four-legged phantasms, a clutch of albino springbok cropped contentedly at the thick grass. Somewhere a lion coughed into the night, and a leopard cried, lonely.

Thousands of them there were, surging and bawing and mewling and eating, the endless veld on which they trod a carpet of muted green in the moonlight. Close by but hidden, a river flowed, its own special music sweet behind the stark curtain of night. Eden it was not, but it was close.

"What . . . ?" he started to say, but she put a firm finger to his lips, hushing him as she tucked her body against his.

"The men dance, the women sing," she whispered. "This is the picture my grandparents wanted me to paint. Look at it, drink it, keep it always with you. Me too, if you want. You're a distinct man, Howard Cooperman, and I'm tired of being an accountant."

"What's that?" He pointed excitedly. Graceful as ballerinas, the small herd paraded into view from amongst the wildebeest, elegant heads bobbing in time to their rumps. The front half of each body was striped, the back portion an unbroken shade of roan.

"Quagga," she told him. "They say that the last ones became extinct in the nineteenth century, but my great-grandparents saw them in this country as late as the 1920s. Another secret of the Nama."

Howard gaped. A quagga stallion turned to consider him and snort challengingly before moving on. It showed no anxiety at their presence. No fear of ever having been hunted. The stallion was a sublime and noble memory of recent Earth, of not-so-very-long-ago Africa. Howard forgot about his camera, useless in this light anyway, and used his eyes.

Eventually he returned his attention to his companion. It was the dancing, he knew. The dancing and the music. They had placed him in some sort of trance; a trance he wished would never end but which he knew soon must.

"Will they still be here when the sun comes up? Will you?"

Her face, speaking to both Asia and Africa, turned up to him, and she offered him that utterly natural, thoroughly guileless smile. "If you want me to, big darling."

Somewhere far away, in a place of mystery and wonder, he heard a voice saying, "Of course I do," and realized it was his own. He commended that voice for its honesty, just as he commended his lips to hers.

Matthew Ovatango looked all the next day and well on into the evening before getting on the radio and calling for help. Planes flew out from Sesfontein and scanned from the air, but it was a couple of days before two Land-rovers full of rangers could arrive from Otjiwarongo and begin to search on foot.

They found a well-equipped Landcruiser registered to an Anna Witbooi of Windhoek. Its tank was a quarter full and there were three jerry cans of petrol in the back end. Protected from the omnipresent dust by a plastic laundry bag, a severe black business suit with fluted white blouse hung from a hook above the passenger seat. From the empty vehicle they tracked petite footprints to the base of the inselberg, and from there climbed up and discovered the great arch. But there was nothing to indicate that Anna Witbooi or Howard Cooperman had ever climbed that far.

Eventually the search was called off, as were many in that part of Kaokoland and the Skeleton Coast, and the respective parties were officially notified. But the place was not forgotten, for awed anthropologists came to study the magnificent etchings which decorated the underside of the impossible granite bridge. They took measurements and made drawings and carefully photographed the deft incisions which extended from one end of the arch to the other, wishing only that more than a few lingering flecks of paint had adhered to the stone.

Sprinkled among the hundreds of animal etchings were the slight, easily recognizable silhouettes of people, the ancient hunter-gatherers who had always followed the now vanished herds and whose most accomplished artists had decorated a thousand similar localities throughout southern Africa, though perhaps none so expertly as this. The images carried baskets and babies, spears and throwing sticks.

The youngest member of the largest party of visiting specialists pointed out that the berry-gathering basket being held by one male figure looked suspiciously like a Nikon. She and her colleagues had a good chuckle over that around the campfire that night, and their laughter lingered in the pure and empty air like a fragment of song.

*The Impossible Place isn't impossible. I've been there. Certain specific parts of the planet are so extraordinary, so astonishing, that the problem isn't how to write about them, but how not to write about them. I'd been waiting for an opportunity to utilize this particular spot in a story, and this thoughtful volume provides it.*

*Should you wish to visit it yourself, the directions are simple. Fly to the Kunene River, on the border of Namibia and Angola, head downstream until you reach the dry Otjinjange stream, get in your Land Rover and head west toward the Skeleton Coast. You'll find The Impossible Place in the Hartmann Valley, between the mountains and the sea. Good luck, and good dreaming. . . .*

# EVER AFTER
## by Paula Lalish

Paula Lalish lives happily ever after on a small island in Puget Sound, Washington. Two-thirds of her children are grown. Her husband and one son remain with her on five acres of nettle and hemlock, orchard and garden, where most of the noise they hear is noise they make themselves.

Here comes the bride, a white schooner sailing down the aisle, her nylon net spinnakers spread to catch the breeze. The twin daughters from her second marriage stalk ahead, looking sullen, strewing flower petals like gardeners salting for slugs.

Cindy surreptitiously wipes her sweaty palms on her skirt. The organist delivers the final crashing chords of "Lohengrin" and signals her with a wink. She opens her mouth, and the butterflies that have been trapped inside her stomach float up and out, transforming themselves into the opening strains of "Ave Maria."

She casts her voice over the audience like a net, gently ensnaring them. Leaping up the first tricky arpeggio, she is amazed as always at how the clammy panic of stage fright disappears once she's actually singing. Closing her eyes, she rides the crest of the melody and begins the gentle slide down the farther slope.

BANG! The church doors burst open. A distorted voice burbles through a loudspeaker, "Music Police! Everybody freeze!"

Cindy's butterflies turn to stones. Her eyes snap open. The organist dives for the vestry door, the maroon spikes of his hairdo sticking out in a perfect cartoon caricature of alarm. A dozen policemen storm the aisle, riot guns drawn. Two burly officers clamp their gloved hands under Cindy's armpits and haul her outside. To her chagrin the media are there: a many-tentacled monster snapping her picture and shoving microphones in her face.

"Cindy! As the first person arrested under the new Artistic License Law, how do you feel? Your thoughts!"

"Did you intend to make a test case of yourself?"

"Cindy! Reliable sources report that you ate porridge for breakfast this morning. Did your diet in any way influence your criminal activity?"

The policemen shove her into the back of a waiting paddy wagon. The organist is already there, in handcuffs. His nose is bleeding and his nose ring dangles askew and he has a bruise on one cheek. "The exits were sealed," he tells Cindy. "We never stood a chance."

The bride and groom are hustled in after Cindy, followed by the twins. "Does this mean you're not getting married after all?" one of them asks hopefully.

Cindy begins to cry. The organist lends her a bandanna. "There's been a mistake," she whispers tearfully. "This wasn't supposed to happen."

"That's what they all say," the arresting officer replies, slamming the door.

Down at the station, they are booked and finger-printed—the bride and groom for soliciting; Cindy for performing without an artistic license; the organist for the same, plus resisting arrest. The twins aren't charged with anything, but since they are just in town for the wedding and don't know anyone, they are allowed to stay. The desk sergeant herds everyone into a cell.

"Hey, wait a minute," the organist pipes up, "Don't we get to make phone calls?"

"Keep your hair on," the sergeant snaps, then bursts out laughing. "If you call that purple cactus on your head, hair!"

Cindy, who has begun to think the organist is sorta cute, in a weird way, is offended. She flashes him a sympathetic look; he winks back. *"Illegitimati non carborundum,"* he says philosophically. She blushes, wishing she had paid more attention in French class.

One by one, the sergeant escorts them to the phone booth. After Cindy's turn, she begins pacing back and forth.

"Did you call your mother, dear?" the bride asks. "No, my fairy godmother," Cindy whispers.

"Couldn't hear you, dear," the bride says. "Have you got a touch of laryngitis?"

The door bursts open. Cindy jumps up expectantly. A gorilla comes in carrying a large flat box. "Somebody order pizza?" he asks.

"Over here," the organist waves, checking his watch. "Damn, twenty-eight minutes. Two more and it would've been free."

"Do I smell anchovies?" The sergeant bustles over. "Ooh, and pepperoni! Hey, I'm starving—can I go halvesies with you?"

The organist nods agreeably. The sergeant thrusts some money at the gorilla, who says mechanically. "Thank-you-for-choosing-Go-Go-Gorilla-pizza, the-pizza-you'll-go-ape-for," and departs.

"Anyone else?" the organist asks. But Cindy is too upset to eat, the bride warns the groom about his cholesterol count, and the twins turn up their noses at the anchovies.

The sergeant pulls up a chair and reaches between the bars for a large drippy slice. With the first bite, his eyes roll up in ecstasy. "I gotta hand it to ya," he says happily. "You may be a freak and a scofflaw, but you sure know your pizza."

"My band invented it," the organist says. "We call it 'Downwind is Deadly.' It's the extra garlic and jalapeños that deliver the *sine qua non*."

"Band?" the sergeant asks suspiciously. "You aren't one of them folksingers, are you?"

"Heck, no! None of us can carry a tune. Why, we hardly even play music. We just turn our amps all the way up, brown out the neighbors' TV reception, and make the dogs howl," he explains.

Mollified, the sergeant says, "Oh. I guess that's okay. By the way, I'm Sergeant Latschki. But my friends call me Sarge."

"Ugh," says the organist, shaking hands through the bars.

"What?" Sarge pulls his hand back.

"My name's Ugh. Well, it used to be Hugh, but I dropped the extra 'H' when I joined a nihilistic post-grunge band."

Sarge thinks this over. "Tell me, why'd you do it?"

"What, change my name?"

"No. Break the law. Why'd you go hire yourself out as a musician? You musta known you'd get caught."

"Oh, mine is the all-too-common tale of today's at-risk youth," Ugh says cheerfully. "High school dropout, forced into dead-end minimum-wage employment at McRoadkill, bought a black-market keyboard and taught myself to play, saw my chance to make a little easy money and I took it. Didn't think I'd get busted my first time out. Too bad I didn't get the money up front," he adds wistfully, "I was gonna get my belly button pierced." He shrugs at the whims of fate, and winks at Cindy.

"Jeez, that's rough." Sarge helps himself to another triangle of pizza. "There oughta be a law against—well—I dunno. But it seems to me there oughta be a law against *something*."

"There already is," Ugh points out. "There's a law against practically everything. That's why I'm here. I thought the new Artistic License Law didn't go into effect until next Saturday."

"It's a good law," Sarge bristles. "It ain't right, untalented people committing public atrocities and getting away with it! You wouldn't go to an unlicensed doctor, would you? Then—"

"Calm down, Sarge. I agree. People like me shouldn't be allowed to take music into our own hands, or set our own standards for what is art. We need to be stopped. Don't you agree, Cindy?" He gives her another sly little wink.

"I—" Cindy sings. POOF! There is a blinding flash. Everyone gapes at the apparition hovering in midair: a dumpy, rosy-faced old woman with untidy hair and a magic wand, wearing a pink poly-blend jogging suit and Doc Martens. Folding her wings, she settles next to the empty pizza box.

"What took so long? Get me out of here!" The words burst from Cindy's mouth at full volume, to the tune of *Greensleeves*.

> *"It feels like it's been at least a year*
> *Since I faxed you to come rescue me*
> *'Cause in jail's not where I want to be."*

Heads swivel from the old lady to Cindy and back again.

"What happened to her laryngitis?" asks the bride.

"Hey! You her lawyer?" Sarge demands.

"Certainly not!" the old lady replies with dignity. "I'm her Fairy Godmother."

Sarge scowls. "How come she rates a Fairy God-mother?"

"Well, it's a long story—mind the sleeve, dearie, that's brand new. Got it from the Sears Wishing Book, do you like it?"

Cindy sings a C-major scale, "I-I want to go-o *no-ow*."

"How come she's singing instead of talking?" Ugh asks.

"Well, I see I'm going to have to begin at the beginning," Fairy Godmother says, looking pleased at the prospect. Cindy groans, a musical slide down to low G, but takes a seat and resigns herself to waiting.

"Once upon a time," Fairy Godmother begins, "poor Cindy's mother died and her father remarried. Cindy's stepmother had two daughters of her own, and oh, my! Didn't she play favorites! The stepsisters got new gowns and tickets to all the balls, while Cindy got the chores and hand-me-downs and a bed of ashes.

"Then one day Cindy's teacher, suspicious because the dear lamb was always falling asleep in class, called Child Protective Services. They hired her a sharp attorney. Well, he saw that Cindy would never find justice in the mortal court system, where it would be her word against the stepmother's, so he brought her suit to Faerie Court.

"The Queen found in Cindy's favor, and granted her three wishes. The stepmother and stepsisters were condemned to dance all night every night for a year in glass shoes three sizes too small.

"Because Cindy's under age, the Court appointed me as Godmother ad litem. She has to use up her wishes by her eighteenth birthday, which is midnight tonight."

"And you bungled the first," Cindy blurts, to "The Star-Spangled Banner" this time,

*"you incompetent lout!*
*So I'm wasting my sec-*
*Ond wish getting bailed out!"*

"What was your first wish?" asks Ugh.

Frustrated, Cindy resorts to whispering. "To be a famous singer. But I didn't wish to sing *everything*. And I certainly didn't wish to be arrested." She throws Fairy Godmother a murderous look.

Fairy Godmother shrugs.

"What I want to know," Sarge says to Cindy, "is how come a singer? Why not something practical, like a big sailboat or a million dollars or extra wishes?"

"Nix on the extra wishes," Fairy Godmother informs him. "That's always the first thing you mortals try. The Blessed Realm'd be bankrupt in a week if we hadn't invoked a 'no wishing for wishes' clause."

Cindy ignores her. She takes a deep breath and searches for an explanation to Sarge's question. It comes out on a haunting melody reminiscent of Mimi's aria in the third act of *La Boheme*. "You know how you feel when you go to the dentist and he can't find a single cavity?" she sings plaintively. Sarge nods. "Or you stay up all night studying the wrong chapter for a test, and just when you realize your grade's going right down the toilet, you find out the test has been postponed? Singing's like that, only more so. It's like—it's like—well, you take this big gulp of air and then music pours out of you like ginger ale from a tap. It's just the best feeling in the world. Better than when your stepsister comes home from a date with spinach stuck between her teeth. Better than shopping." She lingers over the last note lovingly. Everybody sighs.

Ugh winks at her. Sarge looks thoughtful. Fairy Godmother flexes her wand and says, "Now for your second wish—"

"Hold everything!" Sarge interrupts, "Just wait a dog-gone minute. If a rotten childhood is grounds for free wishes, *I'm* entitled to some! I wanna make an appearance in this Faerie Court of yours."

"Done," says Fairy Godmother, flicking her wand. Instantly they all find themselves standing—or hovering—in the opalescent brilliance of Faerie. Achingly beautiful creatures sweep by on gossamer wings, scarcely sparing the bewildered mortals a glance.

"Look at those *dresses*," whispers one of the twins. "Where's their mall?"

Cindy stamps her foot, a wasted gesture, since there is no ground. She shrieks operatically, "I wanted to go *home!*"

"Oh, but you didn't *wish* to go home," Fairy Godmother replies sweetly. "You only wished to be out of jail."

"Oh, fine!" Cindy sings hotly,

*"Be that way! Weasel out if you must*
*On a slim technicality—*
*I might as well've stayed in the ashes and dust*
*Till my Prince came to rescue me."*

"Excuse us a moment," Fairy Godmother says to the others, drawing Cindy aside.

"Listen, young lady," she hisses. "Don't pull that spoiled-brat act on *me*. So you had a rotten childhood; *get over it*, okay? And don't blame me, or your stepmother either, if you don't know how to make a wish. You should have paid more attention when your poor teacher was trying to teach you how to say what you mean. You wanted out of jail, I got you out. Right?"

"Yeah, I guess," Cindy pouts, in a minor key. "But now I've only got one wish left."

"Then for heaven's sake make it a good one! And quit embarrassing me. Now, there's our summons," she adds, harking to the distant peal of a carillon, "Come on."

"To Faerie Court? Again? I don't want to."

"Well, you have to. All mortals entering the Blessed Realm must appear before the Queen, and that's flat." Fairy Godmother waves her wand and Cindy finds herself flying with the others toward the Royal Palace. As they float along, Ugh says, "What's the Faerie Queen like? Is she as fabulously beautiful as they say?"

"Well, um," Cindy dithers melodically, "It's a matter of opin—"

"Here we are!" Fairy Godmother trills happily, halting them before the gates of the Palace. Turreted and buttressed, it rises dark and mysterious into the eerie perpetual twilight of Faerie.

"Doesn't look like this thing'd pass a building inspection," says the groom. "What's it made of, anyway?"

"Oh, all sorts of wonderful things," Fairy Godmother replies. "Alabaster, adamant, amber, ambition, gold, pearl, spiderwebs, moonbeams, daydreams, gingerbread, chocolate, and those little colored sprinkle-things that come on cupcakes. Windows of watermelon sugar. See? Better than rose-colored glass, because if they break you can eat them."

"Can I have a bite?" asks one of the twins, reaching for a curlicue of gingerbread.

"Don't touch that!" cries her mother, slapping her hand away. "Remember Hansel and Gretel!"

"But I didn't get any lunch," the girl sniffles. "I was saving room for wedding cake."

"Never you mind, dearie," Fairy Godmother soothes her. "You can ask the Queen for a lifetime supply of cake, when your turn comes."

"You mean we all get a wish?" asks the other twin.

"Of course. It's a time-hallowed tradition, going back to the first mortal ever to stumble into Faerie by mistake. He took one look around, recovered from his fright, and immediately begged a boon. Refused to leave without one, in fact. We've since learned that all you humans are like that, bless you! Can't go anywhere without wanting to take a little something back home to show the folks. A hotel towel or seven years' good luck, it doesn't really matter. Just so long as you can prove you've *been* somewhere."

They jostle inside and begin the long march toward the Queen's throne, on a plush carpet which seems to grow plusher as they advance, until they are struggling like jungle explorers through a dense growth of red carpet fibers higher than their heads. "Wear-dated," Fairy Godmother points out. "The Queen believes in quality."

Ugh, leading the party, suddenly pitches forward. The others tumble after him, landing unhurt on a floor of polished marble at the very feet of the Faerie Queen, sprawled on a carved onyx divan, painting his fingernails a divine shade of lavender.

"Oh, goody, *mortals,*" he says in a bored voice. "Couldn't somebody just send out for sushi?"

The humans pick themselves up and glance uncertainly at Fairy Godmother. "Don't mind him," she says. "He's just feeling a teensy bit cross since his lover left him for a pro football career. He won't eat you."

"Goodness, I should think not," says Faerie Queen, arching his exquisite eyebrows. "Not without some salsa and a whole lot of beer.

"Why are they here?" he asks Fairy Godmother. "Can't they see I don't feel well? Make them go away."

"Shame on You," she chides him. "The Queen of Faerie can't afford to waste time sniveling."

"I could if these pesky mortals would ever leave me alone," he replies petulantly. Fairy Godmother folds her arms and looks at him. "Oh, all right, let's get on with it, then. Who's first? Not the little warbler! She was just here! Back for more wishes already? Greedy, greedy, greedy!"

"I—" sings Cindy.

"Ooh, look, a wedding party! Well, that's more like it; I adore weddings. I always cry. Was it lovely?"

"Actually," says Fairy Godmother, "it hasn't happened yet."

"We'll save them for last, then. You, the fellow with the anchovy breath and the tacky uniform. What do *you* want?"

Sarge gapes at the Faerie Queen, momentarily speechless. Fairy Godmother says, "Just the usual: compensatory damages for a deprived childhood." Faerie Queen points the tiny paintbrush at him.

"What makes you think We care about your childhood? Why don't you go to your parents for compensation? Hmm?"

"It wouldn't do any good," Sarge mutters, "They don't have anything I want. They deprive themselves worse than they did me."

"Oh, dear," sighs the Queen. "I was afraid of this. You're going to have to explain. And that means we're all going to have to listen." He waves the brush, and suddenly everyone is seated in comfy chairs.

"Real leather upholstery," Fairy Godmother whispers to Cindy, "From the Spiegel catalog!"

Sarge takes a deep breath. "Your Honor—Your Greatness—Your Grace—"

"Just get on with it," Faerie Queen advises, applying the polish to his toenails. "And *try* to make it interesting."

"Yessir. I mean Ma'am. I mean—well. See, my story of hardship begins at an early age. I was born at the Woodstock Festival, in a converted school bus. My parents named me Peacelove Freedom Mellowblossom Hendrix Latschki.

"They were itinerant sandalmakers, until one day during one of their frequent 'religious experiences,' they had a revelation that it was cruel and speciesist to exploit animals for their hides.

"So they became organic farmers. We moved to this

hick town in northern California where all the other boys had normal names like Tommy and Jesse and Billy. Their moms made them school lunches of bologna sandwiches and Ding Dongs. I got tofu enchiladas.

"I was sixteen years old before I got my first pair of store-bought blue jeans. My parents didn't believe in them, because they were a byproduct of the Industrial Revolution that separated humankind from the soil and killed off our right relationship with Mother Earth."

"True," says Faerie Queen.

"I don't care! I wanted things other boys had. I wanted a G.I. Joe and an air rifle and *television!* Do you know what my parents did for entertainment?" He struggles with his emotions. "They had *hootenannies!*"

"No!" the bride and groom exclaim together. The twins listen up, thinking it must be something really perverted.

"Yes! They'd invite their tie-dyed friends over to the bus with their crummy twenty-dollar guitars, and sing folk songs!" He is shaking. "God, I bet if I heard 'Kumbaya' once, I heard it a zillion times."

"Oh, I feel your pain," says the groom.

"You do?" Sarge asks, surprised.

"Well, no, not really. But by saying I do, I'm setting up a mode of receptivity between us, where your inner child becomes free to trust my outer grownup."

"Say what?" asks Ugh, scratching his head, with another wink at Cindy. Shyly, she winks back.

"Solly is into Reactional Analysis," the bride explains. "We both are. We met at a seminar. It's this terrific new therapy that shows how everything that goes wrong in your life is somebody else's fault."

"Hey, I'm talking about myself here, if you don't mind," Sarge reminds her.

"Well, of course you are. That's the first thing we learn in the seminar. All anybody ever talks about, no matter what they're saying, is themselves. We also learn that today is the first day of the rest of your life; that people are basically good at heart, but don't loan out your credit cards; and a group hug helps everyone have a nice day!" She stops, mulling over what she has just said. "Golly, it doesn't sound like four hundred and fifty dollars' worth, when you put it like that," she adds doubtfully.

Sarge turns back to the Queen. "Your Honor, I've never known a normal childhood. While other boys my age were dropping cherry bombs down public toilets, I was learning to meditate. While they were smoking stolen cigars and puking their guts out, my parents took me to peace marches. I was denied the ordinary formative experiences of youth.

"And girls! Forget it. I never stood a chance. Would you have gone out with a guy like me?" he asks Cindy. She looks him over critically: bad haircut, Clark Kent glasses mended with tape, and that please-don't-kick-me puppydog look that guys always get when they know a girl is going to turn them down.

"Gee, it's so nice of you to ask," she croons a lullaby, "But I'm waiting for my Prince—"

"You see? This is what comes of being raised in a non-sexist environment. It may work fine for running a food co-op, but it sure doesn't work on the babes. They want some curly-haired smooth talker who knows how to open car doors and help them with their coats, all that stuff my mom taught me was degrading to women."

His story earns him a round of sympathetic looks from everyone but the Queen, who looks up from his pedicure disdainfully. "You think *you've* got romance troubles? Try being Queen for a day! Oh sure, everyone loves you, till you've fulfilled all their wishes, and then it's 'See you later, alligator'! Why, if I had—"

"Your Faerness," Fairy Godmother says, with a forced smile, "Are you forgetting Who You are?"

Faerie Queen jams the brush back in the bottle and tosses it away. It becomes a long black slug, which crawls slowly off, leaving a glimmering trail of slime. The Queen sulkily rearranges his gorgeous legs on the divan and stares at Sarge.

"Oh, all right," he says at length. "We find in your favor. You may have three wishes."

"Only three?" Sarge wheedles. "It's gonna be awful hard to rebuild my life with only three wishes."

Faerie Queen raises one imperious hand. "Nevertheless, if We were you, We would take them and go. That is, if We didn't wish to spend eternity as an out-of-tune guitar at a be-in." Sarge blanches, takes the three wishes, and disappears.

Faerie Queen casts a jaundiced eye on Ugh. "What about you? Want to sue your parents for a rotten childhood? Everyone else is doing it."

"Not really. I just came along for the ride. Fact is, my parents were pretty decent to me. I managed to mess up my life without any help from them."

"Oh, I feel your pain," says the groom.

"You do?" Ugh and Faerie Queen ask together.

"You bet. I also suffered at the hands of too-kind parents. They never spoke a cross word to me, or each other. They gave me anything I asked for: a pony, a drum, summer camp. They let me stay up late on school nights and bounce on my bed and spoil my appetite before dinner. Mine was a golden childhood. It ruined me!" He bursts into angry sobs.

"But what went wrong?" Ugh asks.

"Wrong? They set me up! I thought life was going to be a never-ending trip to Disneyland. Then I grew up and got out in the world and discovered cutthroat competition and professional jealousy and people who just don't care about my happiness! My parents filled me with false expectations. If anyone deserves compensatory damages, I do. I wish I'd been born to a regular, contentious, dysfunctional family so I would've known what to expect!"

"Forget it," Faerie Queen says, "No wishing on the past."

"Yeah, I might've guessed," the groom mutters. "Not even magic works out for me."

"Oh, cheer up, Solly," says his bride. "Things aren't so bad. After all, we've got each other, don't we? And don't forget the girls—it's not too late to give them the kind of childhood you missed."

"Sure, Sol," one of the twins says. "Just in the brief time we've known you, we've already saved up tons of great stuff for when we're old enough to have our own analysts."

"Really?" He sniffs and wipes his eyes. "You mean I'm not a total failure?"

"Not yet," says Faerie Queen dryly, "But there's still time. And now," rising grandly to his feet and spreading his glorious wings, "I'll show you some magic!" he points at the groom.

Solly cries out, clutching his pot belly as it melts away. He grabs his scalp—lush wavy hair is crawling across his bald spot. The shiny places disappear from his rented tuxedo, which tailors itself to his newly impeccable physique.

The bride hardly has time to be amazed before Faerie Queen points at her. She screams. She shifts and shimmies inside her gown like a python in a pillowcase. At last she and the gown come to a standstill; the gown is two sizes smaller, the bride three. It fits her, no longer like a tourniquet, but like a glove. The groom's eyes bulge appreciatively. The twins whistle; they have been magically cured of their overbites.

The Queen flings out an arm. Ugh finds himself seated at the bench of an organ whose pipes stretch up to the pale dome of Faerie. He pulls out all the stops and leans into *Jesu, Joy of Man's Desiring*.

Cindy picks up the melody. For all the bellowing grandeur of the organ, she finds her voice easily equal to it. From somewhere a chorus of fairy voices fills in the harmony and she sings, sings, and it is everything she has ever wanted, except for fame and money and a cute boyfriend.

The music ends. Everyone is a little out of breath, even Faerie Queen. He pronounces the happy couple husband and wife. He snaps his fingers. Pink doves appear from nowhere and flutter around the newlyweds, and then—a blackout.

When the lights come back on, the wedding party has vanished. "Off to the Club Med honeymoon of their dreams," Faerie Queen says. "And the brats are at an upscale coed summer camp. They'll spend the next six weeks learning to ride horses and hold their liquor and French-kiss."

Fairy Godmother says, "All very nicely done, as always, Your Faerness. But it's nearly midnight and Cindy's got one last wish."

Ugh smiles encouragingly and winks. Suddenly Cindy knows exactly what she wants.

"If you please, Mister Queen," she says demurely, "I wish you would turn Ugh here into a handsome Prince."

"Okey-doke," says Faerie Queen, with a mystical swishing of hands. There stands Ugh, scarcely recognizable, in a to-die-for plum-colored velvet suit with gobs of lace at the wrists, thigh-high purple leather boots, and his hair in cascading ringlets. He winks at the Queen.

"Hubba-hubba," gasps Faerie Queen. "This time I think I've outdone myself." He scatters fairy dust all over himself and Ugh; they fall in love on the spot.

"Darling," says Ugh, "There is one teeny little wish I'd like to make."

"For you, sweetcakes, anything," Faerie Queen vows.

"This tic in my eye," Ugh says, winking again, "It's been driving me nuts all day. Could you please get rid of it?"

"Your wish is my command." Faerie Queen takes his true love by the hand and flits away.

"Come on, Cin," Says Fairy Godmother, "I'll give you a lift home." But Cindy sinks down onto the Royal Divan and sings plaintively,

*"Once I had three wishes but now I have none;*
*Oh waly, oh waly, this isn't much fun.*
*I wanted some fortune and fame and romance,*
*But each wish was bungled; I stood not a chance.*

*I wish I could unwish each wish that I blew*
*And start fresh tomorrow with wishes anew.*
*But I know it won't happen, of that I am sure,*
*And I think all you fairies are full of manure."*

"Nonsense, dearie. All your wishes came true, you know, in their fashion."

Cindy throws her a baleful look.

"Really. Ugh *did* turn into a handsome Prince, and you *did* get out of jail—"

"Big DEAL," sings Cindy.

"And you've been famous for—" she checks her watch, "—five hours. That's a lot more than the fifteen minutes most people get."

"What do you mean?" Cindy sings ominously, to the opening notes of Beethoven's Fifth.

"Well, surely you remember the news reporters? As the first person arrested under the new Artistic License Law, you made the six o'clock news. And the eleven o'clock as well, in some viewing areas."

Cindy's mouth drops open. As long as it's open anyway, and "On Top of Old Smokey" has just popped into her head, she sings:

*"You mean I've been wasting*
*My time in this place*
*While back home on TV*
*They were showing my face?*

*Why didn't you tell me?*
*My stepsisters would've*
*Dropped down dead from envy,*
*And I think that they should've.*

*Oh, fame it is fleeting,*
*And mine it is fled.*
*I've an urge to take aspirin*
*And crawl back in bed."*

"Now, now, don't be angry. I'm not a Fairy Godmother for nothing, dear; I programmed your VCR for you. You'll be able to enjoy the experience for years to come."

Cindy makes a face.

"And," the old lady continues, "When you get home I daresay you shall find your answering machine swamped with calls from Oprah, Geraldo, Donahue—everyone will want you on their show."

Cindy sits up.

"Not to mention the supermarket tabloids. Your name will soon be a household word. If you play your hand right, you can have fame for the rest of your life without singing another note. Unless, of course, you'd rather."

Cindy's face is shining. "Oh, I thank you! Oh, I thank you! I tha-a-ank you!" she warbles to "The Hallelujah Chorus."

Fairy Godmother says modestly, "Don't mention it, dearie, it's all in a day's work." She waves her wand, and Cindy is standing on the sidewalk in front of the police station. Hordes of fans wearing pink "FREE CINDY" T-shirts are chanting her name. She turns to flash Fairy Godmother the victory sign, but the old lady has vanished.

Reporters thrust their microphones in her face, begging for a quote. But the voice she hears, strangely familiar, reaches her from the edge of the crowd. She turns, and there stands Sarge. It takes a moment to recognize him; he seems . . . different. Why, he's *handsome!* How come she never noticed before? And there's something about his sloppy haircut and his tape-mended glasses that's incredibly dear. She finds herself running toward his out-flung arms.

"Darling!" she cries, "I love you!"

"I know it," he replies gladly, "It was my first wish."

She raises a hand to her throat. "What's happening to me? I'm not singing any more!"

"Isn't it great?" Sarge beams adoringly at her. "That was my second wish. I knew how upset you were not to be able to talk normally. So I wished that you could!"

Cindy turns around. The legion of admiring fans, the reporters, the news vans are breaking up and drifting away like summer fog. No one, except the besotted Sarge, is paying her the least attention.

"You undid the whole wish!" she rages at him. "My fame, it's gone, just like that!" She stares at his beautiful face, torn between the anger that makes her want to hit him and the lust that makes her want to undress him.

Sarge is giving her the please-don't-kick-me puppydog look which, for the rest of their long days together, will evoke powerful mixed feelings in her. "I was only trying to help," he mumbles.

Cindy sinks down on a bus-stop bench. Resting her chin in her hand, she thinks things over. Anxiously, Sarge takes a seat beside her.

At long last she sort of smiles. "Maybe things aren't so bad," she muses. "At least we've got true love. And my stepsisters still have to dance every night in those tight little shoes."

"And we've still got one wish," Sarge adds.

Cindy grabs his arm. "We do? We do! That's right! Oh, this time we'll be very careful what we ask for! Let's see, I'll wish to get my fame back, only I'll make sure to stipulate that I only have to sing when I *want* to, and—what's wrong?" for Sarge is looking mournful again.

"I was gonna wish for a sailboat," he says longingly. "I thought it'd be the most romantic thing, just the two of us, sailing off into the sunset together."

They look at one another, overcome with love and conflicting ambitions. They just sit there for a long time, holding hands, slowly coming to realize that this is what it's like to live happily ever after.

*Why do all the old fairy stories end in the same place? What does it mean to live "happily ever after?" I wrote this story out of my own muddled understanding of what happiness is. I used to think that it was the big exclamation point at the end of a sentence, the culmination, the big payoff. But more recently, I believe that happiness doesn't really kick in until after the pronouncement of those famous last words, "THE END"; that the best sort of happiness lies in simply realizing that you get a second chance.*

# SOULFEDGE ROCK
## by Suzette Haden Elgin

> Suzette Haden Elgin is the mother of five and grandmother of nine children. She lives in an underground home in the Ozarks, built by her husband, where she returned after retiring from the Department of Linguistics in the University of California. She works in various media forms, including science fiction-music and art, as well as fiction and nonfiction. She also consults for medical professionals. She is the founder of the Science Fiction Poetry Association and the Linguistics & Science Fiction Network, which she currently heads.

Her name was Lark, but Woodpecker would have been more appropriate; *pecking,* not the announcement of joy-in-the-morning, was her style. The present target of her determined beak was her own mother, and she'd been at it now a while.

"The only accurate word for it, Mother," Lark said, peck ... peck ... pecking, "is 'scandalous.' It's *scan*dalous!"

Caroline took another bite of her salad, keeping her eyes on the lettuce, which was especially nice this year, and answered patiently; patience happened to be *her* style. "It's only been a couple of minutes, dear," she said, "since you told me the only accurate word was 'obscene.' I remember distinctly."

"TSK!" Lark clucked, sharp and quick. "Mother, this is *not* funny!"

"I hear you," said Caroline. "Please go on, Lark."

"Please go on?"

"You will, you know. You will go on. And on."

The scowl on Lark's face would have made some people laugh, the way it screwed her features into a tight and ugly knot. But Caroline Emberhall, thirty years of experience with her daughter under her belt, maintained the same courteous and neutral expression she'd assumed when the tirade began. There was always the hope, she reminded herself year after year, that Lark would outgrow this unpleasant habit and take up a more rational sort of communication. Her optimism was based on the fact that Caroline herself had only begun to be a civilized person after she turned forty; there was still time. She had unfortunately been unable to convince Lark's former husband to wait for the transformation. Much as he respected Caroline, much as he assured her he valued her opinions, much as he would miss her, he had gone right on with the divorce. In spite of all Caroline had told him about her own wild and worthless younger self.

"Mother," Lark said fiercely, stabbing a baked potato with her fork, "do you know what it reminded me of?"

"It?"

"Your shameful television caper, Mother! Do you know what it reminded me of?"

"No, dear," said Caroline.

"It reminded me, more than anything else, of a *zoo!* There you are, the keeper, in your long white coat. And there *they* are, all the poor patients, on display for every yahoo with a television set to gawk at, while you put them through their tricks! I do *not* understand, Mother, how you can bring yourself to do something so cruel, so shameful, so outrageous, to people who, God knows, already have suffered more than enough! You're supposed to be a professional, Mother, a woman of education and skill and sophisticated knowledge—how can you treat them like *cir*cus animals, the way you do? How can you *do* that?"

Caroline's first inclination was to make some sort of mild remark directing Lark to make up her mind between the circus and the zoo. It was her usual habit to let Lark

rave on until she wore herself out and to say nothing at all
that might energize her further, because when she had
exhausted herself it was sometimes possible to get
through to her with a sensible sentence or two. And
because it was quicker, of course; arguing with Lark only
inspired her and rewarded her, and prolonged the misery.
But the sudden glimpse she got of the expressions on her
granddaughters' faces as she looked up from her plate
changed her mind. Letting Lark turn the air blue till she
tired of it was the quickest and most efficient way to
move on to some other subject, but letting her frighten her
children that way was something else entirely. *Bestir
yourself, Caroline!* she told herself sternly. *Less laziness!
More gumption!*

"That will be quite enough, Lark," she announced, in
the same voice she used to quiet rowdy wards. And then
she turned and spoke to Andrea and Charlotte, in the
voice she used to reassure *frightened* wards. "Littles," she
told them gently, soothingly, "it's all right. Really! You
must not worry about this."

"But, Grandmother, we *saw* you with all those sick
people! Mama let us watch with her!" Andrea was eleven,
and took everything very seriously; her hands were tightly
clenched on the edge of the table as if to keep her from
sliding out of her chair. "And she explained it to us,
Grandmother, as it went along . . . how it was like putting
all the sick people in cages and selling *tickets!*"

*Ah, yes,* Caroline thought. Lark would have provided a
running commentary. *"See what she's doing? Isn't that
awful? Did you see that, girls? Look at what she's doing
now! Did you hear that? Do you see what I mean? Do you
understand? You must tell me if you don't understand!
Are you paying attention? Do you see what she's doing
now?"*

Sometimes Caroline was tempted to ask her daughter
smartass useless questions, like *"Why do you hate me so
much, child?"* and *"What did I ever do to you to make you
treat me this way?"* Maybe something that opened with
*"After all I've done for you, Lark Ellen . . ."* This was one
of the times. It was truly rotten of Lark to have done that,

with Caroline not even there to offer the two little girls an explanation or a less lurid version of what was happening.

But of course Lark perceived her behavior as keeping Andrea and Charlotte safe, protecting them against their dangerous tendency to assume that people might have good reasons for what they did; she had done it not to betray her mother but to shield her young. And so Caroline fought off the temptation, indulging herself with only the one thought: *"You, Lark, are a narrow-minded and intolerant vicious little bitch; I love you, but I sure don't like you."*

Aloud, she said, "Andrea, and Charlotte, too, I'm sure that your mother intended to first tell you that some people might see things the way she was describing them to you, and then she meant to go on and tell you that those people were wrong, and explain to you what I myself would have said if I'd been there. I expect that something distracted your mother, so that she forgot to do the second part. That happens, you know. People get distracted and forget things."

She glanced at Lark briefly, saw the younger woman draw a breath in preparation for the next pecking-to-death, and went right on talking so that she would not have that opportunity.

"It's true, kids," Caroline said, "I do go into the wards of the hospitals and take TV crews with me, so that people can see how I use Soulfedge to communicate with patients who aren't able to talk. That's true. I do that. It takes away some of their privacy; that's also true. I don't like that part of it, and I wish it could be avoided. But there's a good reason why I have to keep on doing it, any time I get a chance." *Any time I can wheedle and plead and convince a producer, whose only real desire is for a show about serial murderers born of cannibal parents and afflicted with leprosy, to follow me into a medical facility.*

"What good reason?" Charlotte demanded, scrunching her face up just like Lark. *"What* good reason, Grandmother?"

Both girls were, naturally, modeling their communication on what they saw and heard their mother do; Caroline was home too rarely to counteract that very much. And nine-year-old Charlotte was learning the model more successfully than her sister was, poor child. She would expect everybody she encountered to dislike her immediately. And they would all respond to that by obliging her, which would reinforce the expectation. *See? Mama was right!* Poor child.

"All over the world," Caroline answered her, "in hospitals and schools and clinics, in every kind of place where sick people go, there are people who can't talk any longer."

"Because something awful has happened to their *brains*," Andrea put in.

"Yes. They got sick, or they got hurt, and something in their brain, something that has to do with talking, got damaged. And that's a terrible thing to have happen to you, because it shuts you away from other human beings. It makes you qualify for the label—it makes you an *aphasic*. You can't tell anybody what you need, then, or how you feel, or what you're thinking about."

"Poor things!"

"Yes. Poor things. It's a very sad thing, aphasia. Pray that you will never be an aphasic, because it's *hard* to bear and to cope with."

"Yes, Grandmother. But—"

"I am sorry to interrupt you, Charlotte," Caroline said, "and you may interrupt me sometime, if you like, in return. I want to tell you *why* I do what I do—and then I'll listen to what you and Andrea have to say. The problem is, most people don't know that when something goes wrong with the part of the brain that lets you talk, the part that lets you *sing* is often still okay. They don't know that many many aphasics *could* communicate if the words were sung instead of spoken. I have to spread that information so that people who right now are in a sort of communication prison can be set free from it. I have to make it possible for people out in the world to see and hear, with their own eyes and ears, how patients who can scarcely say even a word can carry on a conversation if the words are sung."

"*Very* dramatic, Mother!" Lark snapped. "Such clever images! But let me tell *you*—"

"And now," Caroline said, sailing on, "I have interrupted your mother as well as you, and she is also entitled to interrupt me back sometime. I'm almost through, dears. I just want you to understand that getting the information out is too important to set aside because of the problem of privacy. If I didn't believe that with all my heart, I would never . . . never . . . put the patients on television."

"Oh, so the end justifies the *means,* does it, Mother?"

"In this case, Lark, yes, it does. Just for a while. Just until I can be reasonably sure that the information is out."

"Mother, you are just making excuses . . . rationalizing. You *know* you are!"

"Lark, you've never seen a person who's spent ten years unable to say a single word, or only a handful of words, suddenly realizing that though talking is impossible, what needs to be said can be *sung!* I have seen that. I have seen that joy. That recognition of freedom. If you had ever seen that, Lark, you'd agree with me—we have to make sure everybody knows."

"They should all know about the music language, you mean!" Charlotte piped. "Every single one of them should!"

Caroline sighed. It happened every single time. No matter how many times she explained, no matter how carefully, the media always called it a music language. It was sexier that way, they told her.

"It's not a music language, Charlotte," she said.

"But they *said!*"

"I know. But they said wrong, darlin'. Soulfedge isn't a language, only a very useful code."

"Mother," Lark objected, "the girls really do *not* want to hear about your sacred distinction between a language and a code!"

"Yes, we do!" Together, like a duet. "Yes, we *do!*"

"Well, I don't," said Lark emphatically. "Finish your dinners, both of you, and no more nonsense!"

Both girls stared at her, weighing the odds; Caroline could hear the wheels turning in their heads. Suppose they defied their mother had insisted on hearing about it, how heavy would the penalty be? How long and how fierce the pecking?

"Tell you what," she said swiftly. "After dinner I've got to go do an hour's worth of stuff in the garden . . . I've got perennials to deal with, and weeds. If you two kids will come out with me while I do that, I'll explain the whole thing—while your mother does the dishes, so she won't have to be bothered with it. Fair enough?"

"And while we're there," Andrea demanded, still clutching the table, "will you teach *us* how to do it?"

"Will I what?"

"Will you teach us to talk the music language? Will you? Please, Grandmother?"

"*Really,* Andrea!" Up till then Lark had only been agitated; now she was genuinely annoyed. "Do not *bother* your grandmother with one ridiculous idea after another! She is a very busy woman; she does *not* have time to teach you ridiculous little girls Soulfedge!" She turned, fuming, to Caroline. "*Really,* Mother! *Now* look what you've done!!"

Caroline stared sadly at this child of her body. *I do not blame Jack for divorcing you, Lark Ellen,* she thought. *I might very well divorce you, too, if I had that option.*

"Of course I will," she said aloud. "I should have thought of that long ago. We'll start tonight." And she added, "It will take more than just one lesson, mind you, even though it's only a code. Think about Morse Code . . . it takes a long time to learn. Soulfedge has more than four hundred words and phrases. But we'll start, and see if you like it, and then we can go on with it another time if you want to."

She smiled at Lark, and put her full energy into projecting the message: *Do not start carping about my putting crazy ideas into your children's heads. Please, Lark.* But she did not turn out, suddenly, to have telepathic powers.

"Mother, will you please do me a favor? Will you

please not start filling my children's heads with your crazy ideas? Would you promise me that, please? They have to grow up in this world and get along with other people and find a way to earn a *living,* they can't be off chasing windmills like *you!*"

Caroline did not point out to her daughter that it was Lark who had trouble getting along with people, or that it was Caroline, with her crazy ideas, who earned a living for Lark and for her children.

*Give her ten more years,* she told herself. *And then, if she does not show signs of changing for the better, you will be fully justified in throwing her out on her useless little rear.*

"I'll remember that, Lark," was all she said.

The garden was cool and shaded in the autumn light, with the sun low in the sky; it smelled of sage and rue and garlic chives and basil and dill. The trees were ablaze with scarlet and gold and the glorious red-orange that she loved beyond all other colors. Caroline went down on her knees in the grass, thankful for it all, willing to risk any tick tenacious enough to still be lurking there this late in the year and this far from the woods.

"Come ahead, ticks," she said briskly. "I'm ready for you!"

"Are there ticks?" Andrea bit her lip and stepped back from the edge of the perennial bed. "Mama says look out, we'll get Lyme disease and be crippled for life. . . ."

"If there are," Caroline told her, "they'll go for me, down here in the grass with my bare skin. You and Charlotte are quite safe."

"Grandmother," warned the child, "Mama will be mad if *you* get Lyme disease, too!"

"She'll say you should have had better sense," Charlotte summed up. "She'll say it's your yard and you should know how to look after yourself. That's what she'll *say,* Grandmother!"

"Charlotte? Andrea?"

"Yes, Grandmother?"

"Do you want a Soulfedge lesson or not?" *Never mind*

*the distinction between a human language—which is infi-
nite, and can never be listed, no matter how much time
you have to do that in—and a code. Let that pass.*

"Yes, ma'am! But—"

"I'll be careful," Caroline assured them. "I'll watch out
for the ticks. You have my word on it. Now shall we
begin?"

"Hush up, Charlotte," said Andrea anxiously, "or you'll
make Grandmother cross and she won't *teach* us!"

"Good point, Andrea! Excellent! Ready?"

They both nodded, and Caroline bent to her work, both
the weeding and the teaching.

"Soulfedge," she said first. "There was a way of
learning singing once, called *solfeggio;* The woman who
constructed Soulfedge called it Solfeggio, but some re-
porter got it wrong and it's been Soulfedge ever since.
Her name was Norinda Blannes, and she was one of my
professors when I was in graduate school. If you want to
know more about that part of it, ask me sometime and I'll
tell you. Right now, though, let's just learn . . . oh, let's
learn half a dozen bits of it, for starters. Some useful
expressions. Ready?"

"Ready!"

She sang the first one at them, slowly, so they could
remember what they heard. *Solmido* for the notes; plain
old "la, la, la," for the words. That was hello and good
morning and good evening and greetings in general. *Sol*
. . . and then down a major third to *mi* and down another
major third to *do*. First three notes of the good old
unsingable "Star-Spangled Banner."

"Can you sing that back to me?" she asked them. "It
means hello." And she sang it for them again, and waited,
and was greatly pleased when they both gave it right
straight back to her. They sang with their mouths almost
closed, staring down their noses at the ground, the way
children who are always told "For heavens *sakes! No*body
wants to hear you do that *cat*erwauling!" are inclined to
do. But they could both carry a tune, and their pitches
were good. It shamed her to think that she'd spent so little
time with them since Lark came grumpily home that she

hadn't really known what to expect. *I must do better than that*, she thought.

"Hello," they sang at her. "Solmido! Hello!"

"Hello!" she sang happily back.

"Why don't you sing 'hello' instead of just going 'lalala'?" Andrea asked her, and Charlotte put in her two cents worth, observing that that would be a lot more sensible.

"Because Soulfedge isn't English," Caroline said, giving a yank to the middle of a whopping mat of carpet weed. "People who speak French would have to sing 'Bonjour' and people who speak Spanish would have to sing 'Buenos dias' and so on. And all the melodies would have to be the same size as the words in the languages . . . lots of problems, you see. This way, what matters is the tune. If the only sound you can make is 'ah,' even if all you can do is hum, as long as it fits the tune it means the same thing."

*Even*, she thought, remembering Mr. Willis Fortune from Little Rock, *if the only sound you can make is the word 'shit.'* 'Shitshitshit,' Willis Fortune would sing when he saw you, all three notes right where they were supposed to be. And 'shitshitshit' on the three notes that meant farewell and good-bye, when you left. It would be far better, she knew, if she just didn't mention Mr. Fortune; Lark would have a conniption fit. It had not been Mr. Fortune's fault that damaged brains are so often left with only a few bits and pieces, and those so rarely the *appropriate* bits and pieces. He had been a lovely man; she had no intention of letting Lark peck at him.

"Now here's how you do 'good-bye'," she said instead. It was *sol*, then *do* twice. "Sing it with 'la,' or hum it, or . . . whatever you like. As long as the notes are right."

It was almost two weeks before Caroline got out to her garden again, and she'd spent no more time at home in those two weeks than was her usual practice, in spite of her resolve. There was always a new place to go, a new group of stubborn and disapproving medical professionals to convince or get past somehow, a new paper to write—

for people who, hyperliterate and multidegreed though they were, could not read a single note of music and had never been taught solfeggio.

The girls had seen her off in the mornings with soldodo and welcomed her back in the evenings . . . so late it was their bedtime, usually . . . with solmido. Lark had assured her, in among the imprecations, that they sang the other things they'd learned back and forth at each other all day long, driving her out of her mind, and she *hoped* Mother was *sat*isfied. But there'd been no time for another lesson. *Soon,* she promised herself. *Soon.*

Fortunately there'd been a hard frost that had discouraged the weeds, but the garden was a mess all the same. She stared at it, shaking her head, wondering why it wasn't possible to get Lark to do a little something out here once in a while, remembering at once that that was more trouble than doing it yourself, trying to decide what to tackle first. Because she loved gardening, she decided to just begin and go on till she got as close to the end as she could get, and she settled to it, humming happily to herself. Considering what she'd been doing last time she was here, it wasn't surprising that she was humming the first three notes of the "Star-Spangled Banner," over and over.

And that was when she heard it.

It knocked her back on her heels, stunned into silence, the clump of dead brown leaves and stems she'd been pulling together dropping from her hands. *I have been working much too hard,* Caroline thought.

In the wild years she so deeply regretted now—except that remembering them kept her from being the sort of constipated shrew Lark was, and perhaps that was some good come out of them after all—high and flying on a blessedly pure brand of LSD she'd had access to, she had seen and heard and smelled and tasted and felt things wonderful beyond any power of words to describe. That was long ago, but it was a strong indication that she had more imagination than was strictly necessary for human survival; she was just one very lucky woman that she had never been given the dirty drugs that were the luck of the draw and that she'd had no real interest in drugs, even then. *You did not hear what you thought you heard, Dr. Emberhall dear,* she admonished herself. *Snap out of it!*

But she was a scientist. You have to make the test, if you're a scientist, however impossible the hypothesis may seem, and so she looked off into the distance and sang it. *Solmido!* "Hello!"

Caroline kept a basically tidy garden, despite the weeds. The only rocks to be found there were rocks she had set down in their places with her own two hands, for their beauty. And all three of those rocks gave it right back to her, clear and true, higher pitched than her notes, but absolutely clear and true. *Solmido,* they sang, just the notes, reminding her of flute notes.

"Hello!" sang the rocks.

Caroline walked carefully over to a huge sycamore tree that she dearly loved for its peeling bark and the way it glowed like finest marble when its leaves had all fallen. She sat down on the ground, braced herself against its trunk, said a prayer—*Please, Holy One, may I wake up now*—and sang the greeting just one more time. *Remember, you coward,* she told herself, *people reacted this same way to the idea that* germs *exist, once upon a time!*

The three rocks knew the other items she'd taught Andrea and Charlotte, too. Perfectly.

"Mother," said Lark, "this is the *craziest* thing I have ever *heard!* It's *November,* for heaven's sakes! You will get snowed in and not be able to get back here until *spring!* Are you out of your *mind?*"

Caroline smiled at her. "I hear you, Lark Ellen," she said politely, as she dialed the number.

"Yes, that's correct," she told the travel agent, who appeared to feel the same way about this that Lark did. "Yes, I do indeed want to book a flight to the Grand Canyon. Yes. Even if it is mid-November. Just get me the tickets, please, and I'll stop by and pick them up tomorrow afternoon."

She paused and listened.

"Yes," she said. "My daughter mentioned that I might get snowed in. That's all right."

"Mother!" Lark fussed as Caroline hung up the phone. "Will you please stop and think this over? You can't *possibly* mean to go trekking off to the Grand Canyon *now!* You'll miss your *con*ference! Mother, there's nothing at the Grand Canyon but a lot of big old *rocks!*"

Caroline went over to her child; she took Lark's face firmly between the palms of her two hands, one to each cheek. It was something that almost always got the person's attention, if it was safe to get that close.

"I hear you, dear," she said, inclining her head toward her daughter. Holding her with her eyes as well as with her hands. "I hear you."

*I was pleased beyond measure to be asked to write this story. Most people are unaware that those whose language abilities have been damaged by illness or trauma can often sing far better than they can speak, and I think that's a serious information gap—it's something that should be widely known, so that those who need to communicate with language-impaired persons can give music a try. It may not help, but often it does, and it requires no machines or drugs or medical instruments; singing is free, and it works when the power is off. This story gave me a chance to try to get the word out about this, and I'm grateful for it. (As for the rocks, I have a rock myself that spoke to me, just once; I keep it close by just in case it happens again.)*

# SCARBOROUGH FAIR
## by Elizabeth Ann Scarborough

Elizabeth Ann Scarborough won a Nebula award in 1989 for her novel *The Healer's War,* which was based on her experiences as an Army nurse in Vietnam. She has collaborated on three books with Anne McCaffrey, with the most recent being *Space Opera.* She lives in Washington with three cats, Kitty-bits, Mustard and Peaches, and a kitten named Popsicle.

"Yes, madam, I know very well where you are. I *asked* for your name," the taxi dispatcher said, patiently but firmly, as to a child or an intellectually challenged entity. Like an American tourist dumb enough to visit an English seaside resort at the end of October.

"My name is Scarborough and I'm also in the town of Scarborough. There's a connection there, see?" I was patient, too, even jovial. I understood attitudes about tourists. I live in a small, charming Victorian seaport town on the Washington coast. Several times a year and particularly in the summer and at Christmas, it becomes impossible to find a parking place or a seat in a restaurant in my own town. That's how overrun it becomes with people from other places in search of atmosphere, scenery, and gifts (or so the Chamber of Commerce hopes). "Part of my family used to be English, see," I explained further, getting into the role so that her preconceptions about how shallow and trite I was would all be validated and we could get on with finding me a cab.

"The Prince of Wales Hotel, was it, then, Miss Scarborough?" she asked quickly, afraid I'd tell her my life history and expect her to invite me for tea, no doubt.

"You got it."

"Heading where?"

"The beach I guess."

"The strand, then," the woman corrected me haughtily.

"Look, lady," I said, tired of the game. "I'm not stupid. I speak English. I watch PBS. I know for an absolute fact that beach is a perfectly legitimate word, in England as well as American, for a beach. What are you, a taxi dispatcher or a—a—" I couldn't think what profession would possibly employ someone to be deliberately rude over two equally correct word choices.

"Ahem. The walk is actually quite pleasant, if you don't mind a bit of wind," a voice at my elbow said.

"Great. I like wind. I'll walk," I told the telephone, and hung it up. Then I turned to see who had spoken. A white-haired lady looked up at me with bright Delft-blue eyes. She wore a navy coat with a paisley silk scarf draped over the shoulders, and a powder blue-and-white afghan in a lacy pattern tucked over her knees between the wheels of her wheelchair. It was one of the old-fashioned wooden kind you used to find in VA hospitals. She was still very pretty, her bones fine as a bird's, the lines in her face delicately etched.

"Thanks," I said.

"Think nothing of it. I couldn't hear the other end of the conversation of course, but from your response it seemed like quite unprovoked rudeness. As is eavesdropping, I suppose."

"My voice carries well," I said to cover her apology. "How far is it? To the beach I mean."

"Not far at all if you go down the road and across the bridge. It's quite scenic, even now. There's rather a steep hill but there are steps in several places and there's also the funnicular."

"The what?"

"The little tram that goes up and down the hillside. It's called a funnicular."

"Are you a local?"

"No, but I used to spend every summer here when I was a girl."

"I'll bet it was really beautiful then. I only saw a little coming to the hotel from the train, but it looks like it's been a gorgeous place."

"Ah, yes, it was before the war. When the baths were in operation, the gardens were in bloom year round, the promenade was always filled with strollers and evenings in the hotel dining rooms were like fashion parades."

"Just like Agatha Christie," I said.

"You're a mystery fan, then?"

"Oh, yes. And I wanted to come here only partly because my family has the same name. The other part was all those Christie mysteries where the whole family was returning from or going off on their hols at Scarborough."

"Just as we did," the lady said, then twisted slightly in her chair to greet another lady, somewhat younger, who was just getting off the elevator. Lift. "Oh, here's Daisy now. My sister, Daisy Jacobs, Miss Scarborough."

"Ann," I said. "Nice to meet you, Miss . . ."

"It's Mrs. Jacobs actually, but do call me Daisy," she said with a little sniff, after which she mopped her nose with a crumpled tissue. Like her sister, she was dressed for the outdoors, but she wore gray wool trousers and a beige coat with a little beige felt hat over her lightly tinted strawberry blond hair. She was obviously younger than her sister, her face rounder and her build sturdier. Her eyes were puffy and red-rimmed behind big, stylish tortoise-shell glasses.

"Nice to meet you, Daisy," I said.

"And I'm Eleanor Porter," my new friend said. "Daisy, Ann is here for the first time, finding out about where her family comes from. Isn't that nice?"

"Pretty typically American, I guess," I said. "But you can't get much more direct. I mean, it's not like my name's Smith or something."

"No, Scarborough isn't awfully common," Daisy agreed. "There's an exhibition down on the strand, but I don't know if it's open or not this time of year. We've never been at this time before. Only during the summer, for the fair."

"There really is a Scarborough Fair in *this* Scarborough then?" I asked.

"Naturally," they both said, a little puzzled.

"Well, I mean, I thought it was just a song. Then there's a Ren Faire in Texas by that name but . . ."

"A what fair?" Daisy asked.

"A renaissance faire, where they reenact medieval times, only they skip the unhygienic bits," her sister informed her. "There was an article about it in the Sunday supplement. Do you know, Daisy, before we tend to business, I think it would be nice if we showed Ann something of the town. Do you think we might?"

Before I noticed that Daisy was looking doubtful I blurted out enthusiastically, "Oh, would you please? If you spent your childhood here, you'd know all about it. It would be so much more fun . . . that is, if you don't mind."

"I should love to," Eleanor said. "But I can't get about much these days without assistance."

"Well, I don't see why we shouldn't, if you're sure we wouldn't be imposing on your holiday, Ann," Daisy said. She sounded as if courtesy really were her only concern.

"Oh, no. I'd love it."

That settled, Daisy and I maneuvered Eleanor's wheelchair down the handicapped-inaccessible entrance of the motel. A forty-year-old bellboy belatedly bestirred himself to help us, and then we set out down the grand promenade, as Eleanor called the thoroughfare which swept past dozens of once-stately Georgian edifices similar to our own hotel.

Our hotel and all of the others faced the sea and the cliffs leading down to it. The promenade followed the shoulder of the cliff, which was beautifully landscaped in deciduous trees now wearing their fall wardrobes and busily showering their gold and auburn leaves on the ivied terrace. A little path zigzagged down the hill to the Spa and we stopped to look.

The Spa was an imposing building, even seen from

above. It resembled a Victorian conservatory—lots of glass in the walls, a la Prince Albert's Crystal Palace, little domed towers at the corners and a large central tower in the middle. A red-brick courtyard joined the building with a semicircular-shaped cloister and an oval domed enclosure surrounded by fancy tiles. At the far end of the brick courtyard lay an empty pool, large and round, with a tiled bottom. "Did they bathe there?" I asked.

"Oh, no, that's only a fountain," Daisy said with a little cough. "The baths were in the central area. Of course, they were used most often by adults who felt in need of taking the waters for health reasons. The sea was much more exciting for us as children, though the water was very cold indeed."

"When you're young, you don't seem to mind as much, though," Eleanor said wistfully.

"I know," I said. "The water in the Sound, where I come from, is so cold it makes my bones ache and I can only stay in a second or two, but the kids will run in and out of it all day long."

"It wasn't so much the swimming, really," Eleanor said. "It was that one met all of one's special summer friends year after year—the same families came to the same hotels and the same spots on the beach and did the same things. It was very—comforting. As if we had one life most of the year and an entirely different identity for summer. So many memories." She twisted in the chair to look up at Daisy. "Yes, dear, you do see why I don't mind staying, don't you?"

"I suppose, but I still don't see why you can't come to stay with us."

"You've no room, darling, and you know it. It will be just like the old days to be here again, only I'll not have to leave this time."

"I wish you'd reconsider. The hotels aren't what they used to be, especially the ones that have been converted for nursing homes. Some of them are desperately delapidated."

"That's why you'll help me look until we find one that

isn't, dearest. But I do insist it have a decent view of the sea and the promenade."

I hated to think of our hotel, with its one miserable lift, its seven stories of steps, and its one-bathroom-to-a-floor toilet facilities being turned into a nursing home. I was a nurse before I started my present profession and the thought of trying to tend to bedridden and incontinent patients under such conditions did not appeal to me. The places looked like fire traps, and even our hotel, a three-star one, was crumbling around the edges and in need of paint. "Are you unable to live by yourself now?" I asked. Maybe it wasn't polite to ask so soon after I'd met these ladies, but when you've spent several years of your life asking total strangers when they had their last bowel movement, questions about health no longer seem particularly private or personal.

The wind tried to snatch the scarf from Eleanor's coat but she caught the silken square and proceeded to tie it around her head. "I don't see why not, actually. I've been coping with life in this chair since the war."

"It's your blood, dear," her sister said, as if reminding her of something about which she surely needed no reminding. "The doctor said the clotting was very dangerous, with your heart condition, and that someone really must be around to watch you at all times."

"I can't feel my legs, you see," Eleanor said to me. "If I injure them by playing polo in my chair or something ridiculous like that, the medication I'm taking for my disorder could cause me great damage before some responsible adult took me in hand."

I nodded. "I've been a nurse. It does sound like a good idea for you to be with someone in case you need help." I still hated to think of her in those moldy old hotels, though.

"So I thought, what better place for my personal elephant's burial ground than Scarborough, where we were so happy?"

"You said you'd been a nurse, Ann. Did you quit when you married?" Daisy asked her own untactful question, changing the subject.

"Oh, no. I kept working after I got married," I said, not dropping a stitch and ignoring the implied question about my marital status. "My husband and I were building a cabin in the woods in Alaska. But about the time I got divorced, I decided to start writing."

"Do you really?" Eleanor asked. "What do you write?"

"Fantasy novels."

"For children, then?" Daisy asked.

"No, for adults—or children in some cases. They're stories based a lot on folklore and fantasy and in my case, on folk songs. That's one reason I'm here. It's always tickled me that my name had a folk song about it, so I wanted to see the place."

"Fascinating," Eleanor said. "I once had a friend who loved folk songs and told wonderful stories. Mostly about Ireland."

We strolled across the causeway, as the ladies called the bridge that topped the high stone wall separating beach from cliffside town. There were no swimmers out today, of course. A surfer or two with wet suit and board, a lone sea kayak, and the bright sails of two wind surfers showed against the white-plumed silvery water.

The waterfront was a disappointment. Daisy and I eased Eleanor's chair aboard one of the funniculars and paid our 99 pence. The little tram car then descended a track down the steep cliffside to beachfront level. Other than the seascape, only the architecture was wonderful—wrought-iron-edged awnings over a long boardwalk. The multi-domed, many-sided, red brick colossus that was the old Grand Hotel towered from beachfront to high above the tallest buildings in the clifftop town, dominating the skyline.

"Of course, it's been so long since we've been here that I didn't have occasion to notice then," Eleanor said, "but the nice thing about being at a health spa is that so many things are accessible to wheelchairs."

"Except the hotels," Daisy said stiffly. "I didn't find them to be at all convenient."

"One can't have everything. I'm sure the ones that have been turned into nursing homes have been adapted accordingly. Daisy dear, I do intend to spend my last days here."

"Very well."

"There are a lot of video arcades here, aren't there?" I asked. They were, I suppose, beachside fun for the kiddies, along with the shops selling cold drinks and ice cream and tacky souvenirs. It was no worse than places in the States, but I've never spent much time in those places. It seemed a shame to me to lure kids to the beach so they could turn their backs on the sea and sand for virtual battles with coin-generated foes. Oh well, it was supposed to be good for eye-hand coordination.

"There do seem to be, don't there?" Daisy said. Eleanor was lost, looking out to sea again. "There didn't used to be, but there was always something of the sort, though not so loud and with so many flashing lights." Clanging and flashing still issued from a couple of the places, though many of them sported "Closed" signs.

"No, it wasn't like this. It was lovely then, meeting our friends year after year. At night there were fairy lights all along the strand. Remember, when we were small, how Eamon claimed the lights really were the lanterns of fairies?"

Daisy didn't smile.

"And later, when we were older, for those moonlit strolls. . . ."

"You were older," Daisy said, with a sniff that wasn't entirely her cold this time. "I was still a child."

"It was so romantic, Ann, you can't imagine," Eleanor said. "Just the fairylights and the stars and moon shining on the ocean, the warm sand, and a friend you'd known since childhood suddenly so very intensely interesting. Of course, when the war broke out, we couldn't have our fairylights anymore. In fact, we . . ."

"We stopped coming altogether then. I remember you cried for weeks when Father said it was too dangerous," Daisy said, and began coughing hard. "Oh, dear. This wind is aggravating my cold, I'm afraid."

"I'm becoming rather tired myself. You must excuse two old ladies, Ann. I understand there's some sort of historical exhibition here now—there—that Millennium thing. You'll probably enjoy that. And do try to see the main part of the town. It's a bit of an arts colony these days, I understand. But now I think we must go back and rest."

A taxi was passing then, and I insisted on putting them in it and paying the fare in advance, thanking them for their company.

"Perhaps we'll see you at dinner," Eleanor said.

"I'll try to see the exhibition before closing time, that is, if it's still open," I told her. "I'll probably be going down for dinner about six."

"Lovely," she said, and their taxi drove away at a neck-breaking speed, as if the driver was so glad not to have to maneuver his way through crowds that he celebrated by pushing the edge of the envelope.

The exhibition was far down the beach, away from the rest of the attractions. Halfway there I was picked up by a shuttle bus with bright slogans and no passengers at all. The driver, a middle-aged man, looked profoundly bored, but in answer to my question said in a thick Yorkshire accent that aye, the exhibition had not closed and I might find someone there if they hadn't gone to tea already. We sped far down the beach, past all the businesses and the cliff containing the skeletal remains of the castle, to a fake Tudor cottage with its atmosphere destroyed by a large sign saying Millenium.

The door was open and I poked my head in. I didn't see anyone to sell me a ticket, and called out. Someone called back from the bowels of the building, "Go on 'round, then, and I'll catch you on the way out."

It wasn't exactly Disney World or even Madame Toussaud's, but it was more interesting than I would have expected from what I'd seen of the town so far. Apparently we Scarboroughs had a Viking in the woodpile—one Skardi, as he was nicknamed for his harelip. I was glad they hadn't translated his affliction when they named the town. He founded the village, which became a center for pottery, a medieval seaport and a meeting place for tradesmen—the origins of the fair. There was more about the castle, though they didn't mention the murder of King Edward's gay lover there, an interesting tidbit I'd picked up in an English history class. A particularly vivid diorama featured the slighting of the castle by the Roundheads during the Civil War (I kept seeing boys in blue and gray even though I knew it was a different Civil War).

There wasn't too much about the fair after that, except that they said it continued. The most recent history all concerned the healing waters of the spa and the bombardment of the town by the Germans in 1914. It was rebuilt then and the posh clientele of the spa were joined by middle- and working-class people on holidays. The ladies were probably from a fairly well off middle-class family, I thought. I paid on my way out and bought a few souvenirs, and could not stop humming the Simon and Garfunkle tune all the way home. I wondered if they had researched the original ballad, as I had, to know how appropriate the very old song was for an ancient Viking settlement.

It was dark out by the time I emerged from the exhibit and the wind was wilder and colder, so I popped back in long enough to phone a cab—I got a better dispatcher this time. I arrived just in time to go to my room, deposit my souvenirs, and rest my feet a moment before dinner.

Eleanor was engaged in a heated discussion with a waitress when I arrived. "That's ridiculous," she was telling the woman. "No one was seated at this table when I arrived, there was no reserved sign, and I wish to look out at the sea."

"You were assigned a seat by the wall over there, madam," the woman said.

I clucked my tongue as I arrived and pulled out a pad and pen, "Oh, dear, my editor failed to mention this," I said, ostentatiously flipping over a page as if I couldn't believe what I'd read before. "A three star hotel that assigns seats to its guests as if they were schoolchildren. I don't think so! That's probably worth the loss of two stars at least."

The waitress turned and glared at me, and I gave her my biggest, most American smile. "Hello, I'm Elizabeth Ann

Scarborough. I've been traveling around England for the *New Yorker* Fine Dining supplement, but there seems to be some mistake. I certainly don't think the *New Yorker* would give a high rating to a restaurant that denies the best seats to its diners when the dining room is entirely empty. And it might also appear to some critics that your wish to make this lady take a less desirable and visible table might smack of discrimination against her as a person of disability. The *New Yorker* would frown on that. A lot."

I said this in my loudest, ugliest American tones, throwing my not insubstantial weight around, and as I suspected, another woman, older than the one I faced and not wearing a uniform, hurried forward to say, "Is everything to your satisfaction, Miss Scarborough?"

"If I'm not to be arbitrarily assigned a table not of my choosing in this empty dining room."

"You may, of course, sit anywhere you like."

"Then I believe I'll sit here, and enjoy the lovely view at the table my companion has already selected. May we have our menus please? And some bottled water?"

They left and the older woman returned with both the menu and the water. When she'd gone again, Eleanor and I both allowed the giggles we'd been suppressing to sputter forth.

"Jolly well done," she said, patting my hand approvingly.

"Will Daisy be down soon?"

"No, poor dear. She came here to help put me in care and she could do with some herself. She feels much worse than I do." She picked up the menu and browsed. "I'm ravenous. Let's see, the lamb or the veal?"

"I'm sort of in the mood for anything with parsley, sage, rosemary, and thyme," I said, half singing the last as in the chorus of the Simon and Garfunkle tune. She didn't react for a moment.

"What dish would that be, then?" she asked when she had finished scanning the menu. "Sounds appallingly overseasoned. Rather like tossing in the whole herb garden."

"It was a joke," I said. "You know, like the line in the song."

"I'm afraid I don't know," she said. "What song would that be?"

"Scarborough Fair," I said.

"There's a song about it? How lovely. You must sing it for me sometime."

That was perhaps the wrong thing to say, since I'm a shameless extemporaneous a cappella singer. However, I have always maintained that singing in conversational tones should be every bit as acceptable as conversation in conversational tones and no more intrusive to adjoining tables. Since there were no other diners at adjoining tables anyway, I sang her the song.

She brooded all through the soup course without saying anything, leaving us to sip and slurp in silence. Finally she patted her lips with a napkin and said, "I've been trying to place that song. It sounds so very familiar. Wherever did you learn it?"

"It's vintage Simon and Garfunkle! A monster hit in the sixties. I loved it because after it came out, everybody could pronounce my name. I'm surprised you haven't heard it before."

"We never listen to popular music, only classical. Perhaps it's only the tune I know and it was taken from something in a larger work?"

"Could be. Although actually, a lot of classical pieces have bits that were adapted from popular folk songs of the day."

"Is that so? How very interesting," but she sounded vague and she was staring into the distance again, as if ours was a three-way conversation. Then suddenly her eyes were back on me, and she was smiling, though her tone was surprisingly cautious, as if testing its weight on a shaky-looking ladder rung, when she said, "A pity, really, that they put such modern words to it. They make no sense at all, do they?"

"Actually, they do," I said, warming to one of my favorite topics and pleasantly surprised to find such a sympathetic listener. "It's not really a modern song at all, just a modern version of a much older ballad that's collected in the Child Ballads as one of the Riddles Wisely Expounded. The original version was called The Elfin Knight—and various other things. And Scarborough isn't always the town, or even usually. But the theme is the same. The man asks a woman to do an impossible thing if she wants to be his true love and she thereupon asks him to do an even MORE impossible thing if he wants to be hers. Which didn't make much sense until I read about it in Wimberly's folklore book. Am I boring you?"

She had been looking out to sea again and could have been halfway to New York from the far-off expression on her face. But at my questions, she returned her attention to me with a troubled-seeming smile. "Not at all, dear. I'm simply reflecting on how people are always putting riddles between themselves and their true loves. Not just in ballads either. People do that in real life all the time, don't they? 'If you *truly* care for me you'll do or won't do thus and so.' Tests, I suppose. Is that what your song is about? Because it's all rather sad. You can lose someone very precious by expecting them to jump hurdles that are too impossibly high."

I nodded. "The song about the Lady of Carlisle always struck me that way. She wanted her boyfriends to fight a lion to get back her fan. I'd have told her to take a flying leap if I'd been them."

"Yes, I can see the temptation. You've made quite a study of these songs, then, have you, Ann?"

"It's a lifelong interest. I've written three books about the story songs, actually. And I promise not to go on and on about it until I make your eyes glaze over. But, since you really love this place and may end up spending the rest of your time here, I thought you might like to know the rest of what Wimberly had to say about the Elfin Knight."

"I would indeed. It had never occurred to me that the words might be riddles for that purpose, but it makes sense. When times are uncertain, as they so often are, bloody-minded young people feel they have some sort of right to ensure their mates are suitable. Possessed of the proper survival characteristics. Rather cold, that. But romantic love wasn't quite the consideration it is now I suppose, and it's quite practical to know if someone is loyal enough to play one's game, intelligent enough to understand the puzzle, and ingenious enough to solve it."

"That's true of some of the riddle songs—early versions of the False Knight of the Road have answering verses that are actual solutions to the problems so that the person answering wins the prize—either a lover or staying out of hell, depending on the version. And the Riddle Song I know from when I was a little girl has solutions in the song. But the riddles in the Elfin Knight are so hard they would have been impossible back then. And they're answered not with solutions, but with other riddles."

She laughed. "A bit like life, then. Always answering a question with a question. And so typical of people unsure of their ground. Throw up impossible obstacles, and if your love can somehow magically overcome them, then you can be sure. But one never can be sure really, can one? Not until it's much too late. Why—oh, why—are we so afraid of each other?"

Die-hard enthusiast that I was, I wasn't listening to the nuances in her voice, the longing, the regret, the sadness. Insensitive as any fan telling me what was wrong with one of my books, I took the opening she gave me and plunged ahead. "In the original of the Elfin Knight, fear definitely entered into it. The Knight in the song is a supernatural figure who wants to carry a girl to the underworld. Wimberly says that according to another expert named Baring-Gould, this dates back to an old Norse or Teutonic tradition during a time when plighting a troth was such serious business that a girl owed her loyalty to her lover even after he was dead—so much that he could drag her back to the grave with him if she couldn't answer his riddle with a harder one. So she wasn't *trying* to be his true love, she was trying to escape being dragged back to the grave with him. Kind of a "Fatal Attraction" sort of thing."

"Ah," she said and seemed to be giving it so much

thought that I was wondering if I had a real folk music convert on my hands.

"It's really those impossible riddles that stay pretty constant in all the versions of the song," I told her. "And that's the difference between the Elven Knight riddles and those in other riddle songs."

She sighed, deep and shuddering and looked very tired. I wondered if she was beginning to feel unwell again. "Pity," she said. "That the riddles are so impossible."

"Well, they were when they were dreamed up. These days I don't suppose they would be. What with new technology and so forth. If you just fudged on the interpretation a little. The shirt for instance."

"I beg your pardon?"

"You could make a shirt pretty much like it says in the song. Mind you, not an Armani or anything, but a rough upper garment could be made by getting a length of cloth—I suppose that's what cambric would be and tearing it or cutting it with a laser tool instead of a knife or scissors. . . ."

"And what would you hold it together with? Staples, perhaps?"

I shrugged. "Hot glue. Then you could have it dry cleaned and it wouldn't have been watered or had wind blow on it—suppose you'd have to provide the cleaners with the thorn yourself."

"And how about the acre of land the woman asks for?"

"Well, they reclaim land from the seas in a lot of places—it's expensive but it's done. As for the planting and harvesting, nanotechnology. . . ."

"My word! You Americans!" she said.

"That's just my science fiction side coming out," I said.

That brought us up to dessert, or "pudding" as Eleanor called it.

Eleanor had changed the subject entirely, asking about my life in Alaska and my marriage. "Are you married?" I asked, when I'd given her the *Cliff Notes* version of that portion of my life.

"No, I never did," she said sadly. "I retired ten years

ago from the civil service. I was very lucky to find a position with my disability."

"So you've basically been a career woman, then?"

"I was engaged once, before the war. But we parted over politics and—and then he was killed, you see. So many were."

"Yeah, Vietnam was kind of the same for women my age in the States," I told her.

She was quiet all through dessert, and then said, "I met him here, you know. We were children together, Eamon and I. You'd have liked Eamon, Ann. He was musical, like you. A lovely singer, one of those soaring Irish tenors. Sometimes I hear him still, in my dreams. We were going to be married. We meant to announce our engagement during the Fair here, when we were all together for the summer again. But then the War broke out and the Irish Republic declared itself neutral. Eamon's father had been conducting his business in London for some time, but chose to return with the family to Ireland at the start of the War. Father was furious. Although he had always said that Daisy and I might marry as we liked, he had never really approved of Eamon's family and called the Houlihans traitors. Eamon and I met on the beach, as our families were angrily packing to leave. He asked me to elope and return to Ireland with him. I demanded to know why he was running away to Ireland, why he couldn't join up and protect us from the Nazis like every other real man. He said he would defend me with his life, but for reasons that should be obvious to me, he didn't care to extend his protection to my country. We had a horrible row and—that was the last time I saw him."

"What happened?" I asked.

She nodded. "Without telling me what he was going to do, he went right off and enlisted and was promptly killed en route to the front. I only learned of it months later. I was in uniform myself by then, driving ambulances and so forth. Until my jeep got hit. That was when I lost the use of my legs. Our parents were killed in the bombings in London. So you see, there was no use in falling out, no use in spoiling our last good time together here, and no use my giving up Eamon, for I never was fit to marry anyone else after, even had I wished ... no, no, don't protest. You don't know, You've no idea what it was like."

I did, a little, having been a nurse in Vietnam—but I hadn't been injured as she had, hadn't lost someone I loved as much. I always thought of the English as being just an earlier, maybe a bit stuffier, version of Americans. I kept forgetting how devastating it had been for them to have both World Wars on their doorstep, killing not only soldiers, but civilians. I reached out and laid my hand over hers and hoped she wouldn't think it terribly, gauchely American.

She didn't cry openly, though there were a few tears. She must have shed so many.

"So that's why you wanted to come back here when you couldn't live alone anymore?"

She nodded. "Daisy hates the idea, but I keep thinking, perhaps if I become senile, I'll remain in the dream I have of seeing him again, of being here and young and in love ... though I'd settle for old and forgiven. Ann, dear?"

"What?"

Her face was brightening. "You're so very clever, knowing about that song and figuring out how to solve the riddle of the shirt. Do you think we might, between us, do what you suggested and perhaps ... I don't know. I just feel that I should like to do something of the sort."

"I was going to leave tomorrow to visit a friend in Romsey for Halloween."

"Of course, you must do as you think best, but it would mean so much to me."

The lady had had a very hard life and was getting ready to spend the rest of it in a mangy old hotel to be near the memory she wished to honor. What I had told her about the song had apparently given her an idea for a little ritual gesture that would give her a sense of closure on something that had caused her pain throughout her life. My friends at home in Port Chetzemoka are always doing that kind of thing, but usually for a lot less important reason. I didn't figure it would hurt me, and my friend Marjorie in Romsey really wouldn't care one way or the other. "Okay, sure."

She sighed as if terribly relieved at my agreement and said, "One other little thing. I'd rather Daisy didn't know. She'd think I'm getting feebleminded as well as just feeble. I shall tell her to rest an extra day tomorrow and that you have agreed to let me show you the town properly."

The fabric store had a bolt of white linen that cost the earth, but was the closest thing we could find to cambric, a kind of French linen, or the other fabric mentioned, Holland, which was linen from the Netherlands. This linen was made in Sussex, but it would have to do. When the woman began to cut off a piece, Eleanor bought the entire remnant, so that it wouldn't have been cut.

"Now where would we find a laser knife in a Yorkshire seaside town, I wonder?" I said aloud.

"I've another idea. Could we not wrap a sort of shirt perhaps, since we've so much fabric? Rather like the Indian saris?"

And as soon as we got our hot glue gun at the local artist's supply store, that's exactly what we did, with Eleanor serving as model and me as draper-gluer, right there in the mostly deserted store. We were both laughing and swearing, me roundly and Eleanor with a surprisingly unladylike "bloody hell" once or twice. The sales clerk, a boy of about twenty who had previously looked extremely bored, said, "I say, that's going to be a smashing mummy costume. You'll be the hit of the masquerade."

The draping and gluing accomplished, we had a shirt of sorts, and all we had then to do was persuade the local dry cleaners to ignore the unorthodox nature of our garment and to give us their extra fast service—a goal accomplished by an under-the-table ten pounds in addition to that they normally charged.

Before the woman hauled the "sark" across the counter, Eleanor said, "Wait," and stuck a thorn into one of the folds. "That's not to come out, now," she told the woman, who looked as if she'd like to put as much distance between herself and us as possible.

After that, we had a very nice stroll along the beach. The day was one where the sky changed every two minutes, the brisk wind whisking mountain ranges full of clouds across the horizon, then sweeping it clear until the next buildup. The air was full of moisture and ozone and the salty, fishy smell of the beach. Eleanor had a friendly conversation with the tinker man who offered the pony rides—his grandfather had been the one to offer pony rides when Eleanor was a child, she learned.

We enjoyed a late lunch of hot dogs, soft drinks, and ice cream in one of the tacky little waterfront places instead of at our hotel. The plan would be to then go back and pick up our "sark" before the dry cleaning establishment closed.

But Eleanor started to fade then. "I'd best return and check on Daisy," she said. "Do you mind picking up the sark yourself?"

I assured her I didn't and suggested she get some rest. We were going to sneak away from the hotel at about eleven thirty, after Daisy was asleep, and I would wheel Eleanor to the beach where she would present her offering. We were hoping for high tide to take it out right away. I felt slightly silly, but it was fun and I knew it would be a great anecdote to share when I wrote home.

Eleanor returned to the hotel in a cab, but I took the funnicular back up to the town and hired a cab out to the castle hill. Very little remained of the castle and the walk was too far and too steep. But the side trip occupied me until time to pick up the sark.

The thorn was still in it, and it was clean. The clerk shook her head as I held up the unlikely garment for inspection. "Halloween costume," I said. "Our mummy's very particular about her shroud."

I stepped back out of the dry cleaners into a sudden, driving wind, flinging sheets of rain over everything. Fortunately, the sark was in a protective plastic bag. I ducked back inside, pulled my rain poncho out of my shoulder bag and slipped it over my head, then tucked the bag with the sark underneath it as well. Instead of battling my way back to the hotel, I headed for a restaurant I had seen around the corner. Hot dogs and ice cream left an empty place and I didn't want to battle the snooty dining room staff again.

Somewhere in the distance a siren announced a. that a speeder had been apprehended, b. that a fire was being fought, or c. that someone was on their way to the hospital. I voted for c. in a town so full of nursing homes. I wondered which one Daisy and Eleanor would select. The rain hadn't lightened at all even though I took plenty of time finishing my meal and had dawdled a while longer reading my tour book over tea. I called a cab, and fifty minutes later, it still hadn't arrived. So I fought my way against the wind back to the hotel, sloshed my way to the lift, and on to my room where I hung up the sark, divested myself of my wet pants, shoes, and socks, which I arranged over the heated towel rack, and let the poncho drip into the tub. Then I fell exhausted onto the bed and let a pit of sleep close over me while the wind whistled around the building and rain assaulted the pane of my window.

I awoke, confused, in the darkness, to the sound of a knock at my door. "Ann, dear?" came a whisper. "It's Eleanor. It's eleven fifteen. Are you awake?"

I jumped up, pulled on my extra pair of trousers, and went to the door. My hair was still damp. Eleanor sat in her chair, dressed much as I'd seen her to begin with in her coat and scarf with her little lap robe.

"Maybe this isn't such a good idea tonight," I told her. "It's pouring out there."

"Nonsense, it's just a bit of rain."

I pulled the sark out of the closet. "Here it is. Now that you have it, can't you do what you want any time?"

"Spoken," she said. "Like someone young and healthy. Please, Ann. I've no idea how long I'll be able to do this. Come on now. There's a good girl. Stop whining and let's get on with it."

I knew it all along. I knew that I was nuts taking an elderly British lady, wheelchair-bound and with a heart condition, to the beach in the middle of a storm at midnight on Halloween. It simply didn't seem like very good judgment, even at the time. But she wouldn't take no for an answer, and if I hadn't gone, I felt sure she'd try to go alone. As it was, she couldn't have done any worse if she had.

"At least let's call a cab," I said.

But she shook her head stubbornly and I pushed her out into the rain, then dragged the wheelchair backward down the steps, a technique we'd used earlier in the day. I could hardly see and I really wished I'd brought mittens. My hands were already cold and numb on the handles of the wheelchair.

It was all downhill to the beach, however, and we had an excellent tail wind, my poncho making a kind of sail. The sark was tucked beneath Eleanor's lap robe. Except for the white mares' tales of the waves, the water was utterly black. The sky boiled with black on steel-gray clouds. When the wind pushed an opening for the clouds or the high, full moon. Dead leaves whipped wildly around us until we got to the beach, and then it was wet sand that sprang up to sting us.

Eleanor said nothing. The tide was high, as we wished, yard-high waves crashing onto the beach.

"You want me to put the sark in the sea for you?" I asked Eleanor.

"No, dear. Not yet. I want you to sing the first part of the song, about the sark. Would you do that please?"

No one ever has to ask me twice to sing so, though the wind tore every note from me before I quite had it out, I did as she asked.

I'd got to the bit about the "wash it in yonder dry well" part when I noticed someone walking out of the water, an aura of shining water still clinging to his outline. One of the surfers in his wet suit, out for a highly stupid midnight surf, I thought at first.

I took a breath, meaning to wait until he'd gone.

"*Ann,*" Eleanor said urgently, shoving the wheels of her chair to propel herself toward the man. Her scarf tore loose from her head and went flying, as did the lap robe, leaving the sark twisting in a ghostly fashion on her lap. *"Keep singing."*

"Guy's going to think we're nuts, Eleanor, singing in this kind of rain."

"Nonsense. Eamon's Irish. And he's been singing the same song to me in my dreams for years. That's where I knew it from, you see. Trust me, Ann. He will understand about the sark. . . ."

But I couldn't remember any more. It didn't matter. The man was closer now, and I saw that instead of a wet suit, he wore a vintage military uniform. Just one stripe. As he drew nearer, the wind rose even higher and tore the sark from Eleanor's hand. She let it go, opening her fingers deliberately to let it fly at him. He caught it and let it fly out to sea like an oversized gull. He was almost close enough I would be able to make him out clearly, though his face was still in shadow.

Then, suddenly, a blast of wind roared between us, knocking me to my knees in the sand, and when I could look up, it was to see a huge wave come slamming down on us all.

I screamed and dived for the wheelchair, hanging onto it with all my might as I snorted seawater.

As the water drained backward again I scuttled toward the sidewalk, pulling the chair, but even before I could see clearly again I knew it was empty.

The waterfront, the road, the shops, all were totally empty of people and cars. I ran along the beach, trying to see, calling for her, but I never saw a sign, not so much as a hand or foot of her or the man she claimed was Eamon. Nor did I see the sark, except perhaps, unknowingly, amid the tossing whitecaps.

Finally, when I'd called all I could and looked until I was certain she was beyond my help, I returned to where I had left the chair, to find that it, too, had washed away.

I half thought I'd wake in my bed at home, as if I'd lived through a particularly weird and exceptionally wet nightmare, but I was awake and shaking with all-too-real cold by the time I forced my way back through the gale, up the hill to the hotel, which was as close to other people and help as any place. I rang the bell for the concierge, rang it and rang it but without response.

Daisy, I'd rouse Daisy, I thought. How would I tell her what I had allowed to happen to her sister? I didn't know, and I certainly couldn't explain about sarks and songs and strange military men. But I did have to get help, someone to search for poor Eleanor. Eleanor had told me their room number, and I found it and pounded my frozen hands against the wood. The door opened immediately and the night clerk stood there. Beyond her I could see Daisy, sitting forlornly on the bed. "Daisy, I'm sorry, but we have to get the police. Something's happened to Eleanor."

The concierge just stared at me and I pushed past her to kneel beside Daisy, who seemed not to hear me. "You have to listen to me. Something terrible has happened to Eleanor."

Daisy shook her head and when she lifted it, I saw that she wore a sad little smile. "Not so terrible, really. It's spared her the indignity of the nursing home. I had no idea you'd be so upset, Ann, or I'd have made sure someone told you. Did you only just hear?"

"Hear nothing, I saw!" I said.

"You've been at the funeral home? Oh, I knew I should have kept vigil, but I've been feeling so ill and Eleanor really had no belief in all that superstitious nonsense."

The concierge was glaring at me. "Miss Scarborough, I think you should return to your own room. I've just given Mrs. Jacobs the sleeping draught the doctor left for her this afternoon when he came to officially declare Miss Porter's death."

"Death? This afternoon?"

Daisy reached up and touched my sleeve. "Oh, you poor dear, did you think it had only just happened?"

"I did hear sirens," I admitted.

Daisy nodded and patted my hand. "It must be a great shock to you. Eleanor was enjoying your company so much. You couldn't have known how close she really was to death. Neither of us knew for sure, of course, but I felt, when she asked to come back here, that it was almost time. Thank you for keeping her such good company on her last day."

How could I tell them that I'd been with her not an hour ago? That I'd seen—thought I'd seen—her carried away by a wave, and a man. I stumbled for the door like a zombie, but Daisy said, "Wait," and turned to the other bed, where she fumbled in an open suitcase.

She held out a worn black-and-white folder to me. "Scarborough Faire" the heading said. It seemed to be a little pamphlet advertising the event. "This was one of Eleanor's mementos. Since you were both so intrigued with the fair here, I think she'd like you to have it." She closed my hand around the brochure and I returned to my room.

I just lay there in my wet clothes upon the bed for hours, listening to the hammering wind and rain. At last, the pane of glass began to lighten just a bit, and the wind to subside, enough for me to hear what I thought were voices on it, a tenor and an uncertain alto, singing, "Then you'll be a true love of mine. . . ."

*While I dislike the song "Kansas City" and many other songs with the name "Annie" in them, I've had a fondness for "Scarborough Faire" ever since Simon and Garfunkle released it in the early '60s and suddenly people knew how to pronounce my cumbersome last name, previously a subject of punful speculation. Later, I learned this song was not only a legitimate Child-balladizing, authentic folksong but related to one of the oldest riddle ballads ever collected, "The Elven Knight." Riddle ballads came to my attention when I was intrigued by Jean Ritchie's recording of "Fair Nottamun Town" with all of its contradictory lines, though earlier I had heard Burl Ives sing the Cherry Without a Stone song, one of the more popular and simpler riddle songs. According to Wimberly's book on folklore in the Child Ballads, riddles in these old songs came from a Norse tradition whereby a woman who was engaged was pledged to her betrothed even beyond the grave, and if the ghost wanted to come and drag her down with him, she had to outriddle him to defend herself.*

What all this has to do with Scarborough I don't know, but I visited the town in England in 1994 and learned that it was once a Viking (aha! Norse!) settlement named for a Viking who was named Skardi because of a scar from a harelip—thus the town was called Skardi-borg, or Scarborough. There was a Faire—a hiring fair where people often found apprentices, goods, and true loves. The town on the whole, however, was much more Agatha Christie-esque than medieval in appearance, hence the tone of this story.

# THUNDERBIRD ROAD
## by Leslie Fish

Leslie Fish was born and raised in an excruciatingly dull, boring suburb of northern New Jersey, and escaped into reading science fiction at an early age. She escaped next to the University of Michigan, where she majored in writing, art and grass-roots political activism. After that, she held a dozen bizarre jobs before becoming a full-time science fiction folkmusic performer and writer. She's published half a dozen albums of her music, about a dozen short stories, and coauthored *A Dirge for Sabis* in collaboration with C.J. Cherryh. She now lives in Phoenix, Arizona, along with a typewriter, a computer, three guitars and six cats.

Mazatzal Peak lies some fifty miles northeast of Phoenix, Arizona; you can see it from Route 87. The turnoff is hard to spot—just an unmarked dirt trail leading out into the desert—and it takes me a couple of tries to find it. My battered old Jeep can handle the road, but it's a rough ride: five miles of uphills and downhills, in the hammering heat, through the blinding yellow dust. From what little I can see of the passing landscape, even the cactus looks withered and shriveled.

The road ends against the slope of the long mountain. I pull up at the first serious rocks, kill the engine, wet down my bandanna and tie it bandit-style around my face while I wait for the dust of my arrival to settle.

Not that the dust really settles, these days. Here it is

Spring Equinox, and the dust hangs in a constant dry mist over the southern half of Arizona. It coats everything, choking all creatures that breathe, blotting out the stars and even the moon by night, smearing and darkening the sun by day. Dust, the enemy: drought, the cause. It's been two years since the last rain.

I'm here to change that, if I can.

Seeing that the air's as clear as it's going to get, I slide out of the Jeep, take the keys, and set the bar-lock on the steering wheel. Gods know, there could be car thieves even this far out of town. There are people desperate enough to steal any working vehicle with sufficient gas to get them out of the desert, hopefully out of the state, to any place where there's water. I've seen respectable real estate dealers lose everything and go over the edge, steal cars and run to Los Angeles, become beggars there rather than hang on here in the deep desert, in this drought.

Half the state is dying of thirst, and something has to be done—something, anything, no matter how crazy.

What I'm planning is crazy, according to half my ancestors: the mechanistic, rational Palefaces. My other half says that this is desperately needed, and what do I have to lose by trying?

My life, maybe. One bad fall up in those rocks is all it would take. Or one misstep in the ceremony . . .

Never mind. Move. Pull the paper-wrapped package out of the cooler chest. It's still frozen. Good. It'll thaw out during the climb, be just about right when I reach the peak. Stuff it in the backpack along with the bowl and magical gear. Now go.

I walk toward the steepening slope and begin the climb. It's easy enough as mountains go—all age-shattered rock and talus, no special equipment needed—but it's a long haul, especially in this burning, dust-choked weather.

Too much time, while I climb, for thinking: worrying, doubting like a proper Paleface.

How much am I deluding myself? How much of psychic work is ever real, solid, provable? What really happens when I go into trance-state, sing, and . . . reach?

I see visions, and they're usually true; but how much of

that is good guessing, based on forgotten clues dredged up from my subconscious? I can pick up or send thoughts and feelings: but again, how much of that is just good guessing, mine or the other guy's? Move small objects with thought: could I be tipping the table, or breathing hard on the object, or some other unconscious trick? Images seen in trance: how many are real, how many only psychologically symbolic?

This is the curse of the rational scholar. No matter how massive the evidence grows, I can't see the mechanism—so I can never be truly sure afterward.

Of course, I can make myself sure while I'm doing the work; years of practice have accomplished that much. Leap of Faith, Suspension of Disbelief, kidding myself—I can do it. Only before, and after, do the doubts come.

Be reasonable, they say. Look at this objectively.

Go meditate and sing on top of a mountain, out in the deep desert, in killing 110-degree heat, in the middle of a monstrous drought. Sure. Sunstroke, thirst, a bad fall—I could die out here, and my bones wouldn't be found for a century. Write my epitath in advance: here lies a superstitious idiot who died of carelessness while trying to magick up some rain.

But if I don't even try, and the drought goes on, everything else will surely die.

Plenty of people have died for less justified faith, trying to accomplish far worse things.

I love my land, and I'll risk my neck to save it. It's as simple as that. Walk on.

The slope grows steeper, and now I have to climb. Both hands, both feet: the pattern falls into a jagged rhythm. The rhythm picks up a tune. Soon enough the words will come, and this, too, is part of my magical system. Let it happen.

*The rain won't come, and the land bakes dry.*
*The sun burns red in the dust-thick sky.*
*Before the life of the Earth can die,*
*Go walking on Thunderbird Road.*

The dust thins, the air cools a trifle with advancing height, and I finally reach the peak. I drop and sprawl for long moments on the narrow pier of stone, catching my breath. The tune wanders steadily through the back of my mind, and I keep it rolling there. Meanwhile, I can afford to take a drink. Careful—don't drain the canteen. Some water will be needed for the ceremony, and some for getting back down again. The wind blows lightly, thin and hot.

The heat and thin air make recovery slow. I use the time to pull out the telescope and take a good look at the land below me.

It's all yellow dust, empty and still. At this season it should be green, hopping with jackrabbits and prairie dogs and the occasional deer and antelope. Now . . . even the scrub pines are dead, even the cactus dying, and nothing moves.

The far-off highway lies empty, dust-drifted. Everyone who hasn't left the state stays indoors whenever possible during the day. The few surviving ranchers have given up on water-guzzling Whiteface cattle and gone to Longhorns, buffalo, Saharan goats, or desert mustangs. The remaining farmers have switched to drip-irrigation, greenhouse planting, water-hoarding crops. The hanging-on city folk have covered over their swimming pools for water storage. All who stay, for love of the land or personal orneriness, have accepted the drought's terms. There's no more war between man and nature: we live with the land or we don't live at all.

*The weak ones run, and the smart ones hide,*
*Hoard their water and stay inside,*
*Battened down for the long, hard ride—*
*Waiting on Thunderbird Road.*

And here I sit on Mazatzal Peak, at the headwaters of the dried-up Salt and Verde Rivers, source of the waters for half the state. If the drought breaks anywhere, it must break here.

So get up and to work. I have only a few hours until sunset, and eagles don't fly at night.

I find the effective center of the rock platform, mark it with my pack, then collect enough stones to outline my circle. Open the pack, take out the essentials and stack them close at hand. The big, lidded, metal bowl is difficult to set level. I open the waxed paper package, empty its sloppy contents into the bowl, and put the lid on. The weight holds the bowl steady. Now I take up my string-and-peg compass and start building my circle, my psychic castle.

From now to the finish, I must believe everything. Afterward I'll believe nothing, analyze everything. That's the only way to walk the line between the two worlds: rational and mystic, Newcomer and Old People, White and Red, outer world and inner. I survive by balancing as the seasons balance.

Mark the circle with stones (for Earth, matter), then with sprinkled pollen (life, air, space—gathered from every plant I could find in the Phoenix Valley), then water (time, emotions, life of the desert) dropped sparingly from my canteen. Now, fire (passion, energy)—a poured circle of mixed vegetable oil and grain alcohol. Finally, the cornmeal (food, life, fertility), and draw the five-pointed star (unity of man, mind and nature) of my Paleface ancestors. Pieces of different traditions, yes, but they blend well. Like me, I hope.

And through the slow circle-building, the song replays, grows, adds words in my mind.

*Paths of the sky,*
*Roads of the mind,*

Now the fire-cup in the center of the pentagram: fill it with prepared charcoal, light it, sprinkle on the incense (spirit, mind, psychic power), then light the fire-trail of the circle. Yes, it catches readily (good sign) and flares, surrounding me with a ring of low blue flames. Circle complete.

Now inhale the fumes, breathe in the long-conditioned rhythm, drop deep into trance. Let the song wander on.

*Ways of the spirit
The wise can find*

. . . Yes, it's working. Awareness of body drops away, and I am all Mind. I feel the walls of my circle like an open-topped castle of iron, my awareness spreading like smoke, ranging above the peak and across the sky. See the parched land and its struggling life. See the dust, the heat, the glowering sun.

And see the hot, hard, vast pyramid of high-pressure air, crouching above the land like a cougar over its kill, holding off the wet winds from the Pacific and the Gulf of Mexico. See it: a monstrous configuration of pressure and heat. Recognize the unnatural energy that holds the invisible giant cone in place.

This is no natural drought.

Some intelligent mind made this. Some mind—and it has a human feel—deliberately broke the cycles of snow and rain, built this huge cone of high-pressure air that deflects the water-bearing winds, and maintains it even now. Someone made this happen, keeps it happening, wants the cities and farms and ranches and all the life of the land to die.

Who has that much psychic ability—and that much hate?

No matter. What one mind made, another can unmake. I can see the pattern, its strength and its weak point. It can, in fact, be broken easier than a natural high-pressure zone. My strategy will work. I can end the drought.

. . . But only if I can reach the Mind whose power I need.

*Through that land
Where the tracks are blind,
Hunting on Thunderbird Road.*

I know he exists. I've hunted through the scattered accounts in odd corners of various libraries, and drawn my own conclusions. All myths, all enduring legends, are grounded in fact. He can help me, if I can persuade him. He's out there somewhere, pursuing his eagle-patterned life over a hunting-range as wide as the whole state and more. There may be only one of him per generation, but there's always at least one. Find him, call him, persuade him . . .

*Walk this Way,*
*And find that One . . .*

Damn. Something impinges on my spread consciousness, something close and intelligent, but not what I'm trying to call. A man, coming nearer, climbing the mountain right now.

Oh, hell, I'll have to deal with him.

I set the pattern of my Call along the psychic paths, keeping the tune and rhythm of the song running through the back of my mind. Set it to work automatically, maintained by no more than my presence, life-energy, mindset, though most of my conscious attention may be elsewhere. I withdraw enough of my awareness from deep trance to deal with the intruder.

Soft ringing of bells, pebbles slipping from under softshod feet: he's here. It'll take a few seconds yet before I can energize my body, turn my head, open my eyes to look—but I can see him plainly enough as he stops, stares, comes padding cautiously toward me.

He's medium-short, has long black hair like mine, angry dark-brown eyes. He's dressed in the old style, like me: headband and loose cotton blouse, close trousers and knee-high desert boots, waterbag and medicine-bundle, ritual knife of obsidian and a practical handgun in a belt-hung holster.

There the similarity ends. His headband isn't a simple bandanna like mine, but woven of thongs of dyed leather, ornamented with carved bones and multicolored feathers. His medicine/magic pack is of hand-sewn deer-skin. Around his neck hangs a Navajo-patterned necklace of silver squash-blossom forms and massive turquoise nuggets. The belt that clasps his waist is Hopi-style silver conchos with inset black symbols, mostly stylized serpents and suns. The silver rings on his fingers are of Zuni work, more sun-patterns but realistic and elaborate. From the fringes of his boots hang spherical copper bells and feathers beaded with coral, fossil shell, and Apache Tears. His skin is the deep copper-red of the Old People, mouth set in a grim and concentrated line.

He's a shaman, a trained medicine-man, and I can feel the wave-front of his determination, his power, his surprise and annoyance at finding me here ahead of him.

Patience: he can clearly see what I'm doing. He'll understand, and give me the professional courtesy of waiting until I'm finished. . . .

But he doesn't. He stalks slowly counterclockwise around my circle, sniffing like a coyote. I feel his questions probe, rude and impatient, at the barriers of my psychic castle. He wants to know what I'm doing here. He has considerable power, and no restraints on using it. He's felt his way far enough through my shielding to guess that I'm busy with a Summoning. But there his attention slides away, impatient. He doesn't know or care *what* I'm Summoning. Anger, arrogance, impatience: a bad combination for a medicine-man.

My neck joints crackle as I turn my head, raise a finger to my lips, politely signal for silence.

Defying custom, common sense, and magical protocol, he asks aloud, "Who are you? And what are you doing here?"

The air reeks of his hostility, and I've done nothing to provoke it. He can't even drag out that old excuse of "Whites trespassing on sacred ground," thank you. For one thing, to be blunt, one can't tell that I'm not entirely of the Old People until I open my giveaway-blue eyes. So what's his complaint, except that I was here first?

"Shh," I say aloud. "My name is Jan Teiner, and I'm praying for rain."

Instead of cooling, his anger flares. "Teiner! I've heard of you; they call you Chantayna the Spellsinger, down in the city. You got a big reputation among the White-eyes, but that doesn't cut any ice out here."

Gods, it's worse than I thought: professional jealousy, with more than a touch of racism. I'll have to disengage enough awareness to deal with him on an intellectual level. Reinforce the pattern once more, let the song flow.

> . . . *Who knows the Ways of*
> *The rain and sun . . .*

I open my undeniably blue eyes and look straight at the intruder. "Some people call me that. I make no claims for myself, except that I came here to pray for rain."

He looks just as I envisioned him, with the addition of homemade bracelets of fossil-coral beads. Passing tourists might call him "ethnic" and "quaint." I call him a dangerous magician, loaded for bear.

"So you think you're a rainmaker, huh?" He laughs, not pleasantly, and stalks slowly around the borders of my circle. He doesn't quite dare to break the ring, but I can feel the desire, the constant anger, the scorn.

Why? And why now? He knows, from testing my barriers, that I have some ability. In a drought like this a shaman should be grateful for any help, however weak or alien. Could he be so jealous as to want all the credit of rainmaking for himself, even to the point of refusing help?

"Call this a rain-charm?" he sneers, inspecting my circle. "It's garbage! Bits and pieces of the real thing, glued together with a little New Age wafty mysticism. Look: you've got a circle of stones, not colored sand. And burning booze? Firewater was a Whitey invention! The five-pointed star—a purely European symbol. This is a cheap rip-off of the real native magic. Go play your games on gullible Whitey fools in the city, if you want, but keep them the hell off our sacred ground."

He pokes at my circle with his toe, but doesn't quite touch it.

My internal alarms are going off. It takes effort to keep partly detached, even in light trance, maintaining my circle, not letting anger rise and distract me—

—As he clearly wants it to do. Direct assault—using classic scorn, doubt-induction, irritation, distraction—trying to weaken my intent and break my circle.

Again, why? And why with such easy lies? Does he think I'm that ignorant, that the old "sacred ground" trick will work on me? Or that I haven't done my homework about this site? I know very well that the whole Earth was sacred to the Old People—but some places more than others, and Mazatzal Peak wasn't one of them. The Red Men didn't separate the sacred and worldly as Whites do, but this place is no more "sacred ground" than my backyard in Phoenix.

Is he afraid of what I'm doing? Does he think I'll work it wrong, turn a rain-spell into something harmful? Or is this just a smoke screen for the same personal power-jealousy?

Or is it blind race-hate? The gods know, the Old People have reason to resent the Newcomers for taking most of their land, much of their livelihood, now maybe even bits of their magic. But would that outweigh the need for rain, for survival, for the life of the land itself? Unbelievable!

Better reinforce my Call again.

> *. . . Who brings the wind*
> *Where his long wings run,*
> *Flying on Thunderbird Road.*

I answer, keeping calm and rational—a technique handed down from the ancient Greeks, yes, we White-eyes have some useful ancient traditions, too. " 'Purity' of tradition isn't the point. Anyone who understands the Art can use tools from any time and place, so long as they fit together and serve the purpose. My purpose here is to bring rain. What's yours?"

That last is a shot in the dark, but it strikes home.

"My purpose here is to preserve my people!" he shouts, face darkening, fists clenched. His sincerity rings like a bell—but with a muffled undertone. He has another cause that he's not telling.

"Then our tasks are the same," I reply fast. "Help me bring rain, and save everybody."

A reply leaps—I can feel it—to the front of his mind, but he muzzles it fast. His mouth shuts like a trap. His eyes narrow, shields rising behind them. "*I* don't mix traditions," he snaps. "It doesn't work. You're just in the way. Get out of here."

Silent alarms ring again. This time I've caught him in a flat-out lie.

"If you practice only pure, traditional magic," I answer, "why are you wearing amulets from at least three different tribes?" I point to his visible gear. "There's Zuni work, Hopi, Navajo—and what else?"

That catches him. He takes a step back, scrambling furiously for a counterblow. I feel his pressure on my circle loosen for a second, and take the opportunity to strengthen my Call. Against the hypnotically repeating tune and rhythm I chant silently: *Come, oh, come. . . .*

"They're all Pueblo tribes," he recovers. "Their medicine traditions are the same. Who do you think you are, to pick and choose?"

"I've already told you who I am. Who are you to judge magic?"

"I'm Carl Natonhey," he grins, as if I should know the name. "Also called Bloodhawk."

Whoa, there's another inconsistency! No magician of any system gives away his True Name to an opponent. "Bloodhawk" surely knows that. It's a trick; he's tossed me a harmless nickname, seeing if I'll be naive enough to pounce on it, be distracted. But I won't.

"Did you think I was asking for your True Name?" I laugh back at him, "or giving you mine?"

For an instant, a blank look slips across his face.

Aha! Caught him! It wasn't really a trick; he just didn't remember the concept of True Names. He knows, as I do, that overmuch attention to labels can distract a magician from the real power: the psychic meaning behind the words.

Yet the traditions of the Old People put great emphasis on True Names; it's one of the traps in their system.

And he didn't think of it!

All the details fall into place: the mixed-tribe jewelry, the political buzzwords, the cultural arrogance as fierce as the virtue of a reformed whore. Now I see him clearly.

"You're no tribal man," I strike back. "You weren't raised on the rez, and you don't live there now. You weren't any tribal medicine-man's proper apprentice; you learned from several teachers, from books, from experimentation—just as I did. This is no sacred ground, and you've got no religious argument; it's all pure politics. You're just playing Red-man Activist for the ego-boosting—and in the middle of a killing drought!"

He turns pale under his copper tan—and reaches for his gun.

I whip mine out first.

He has the sense to freeze right there, with his revolver barely clearing the leather.

"Put it away, and I'll do the same," I say. "This is neither the time nor the place for gun-dueling, not when we both have work to do."

He slides his gun slowly back into the holster, not taking his eyes off me. I do likewise. We're back where we started. Mexican standoff. Physically, anyway.

His fury beats on my shields, shockingly heavy. He's not in trance-state, not properly grounded, can't breach my circle—but the amount of power, even like this, is astonishing. I've never met anyone with so much raw psychic talent.

"No, I don't live on the rez," he growls, regaining control. "Why should I, when the fight's out here? No, I didn't learn from any one medicine-chief; I learned from as many as I could find. And damn right I'll fight in the middle of a drought! Do you think hard times make Whiteys steal any less? Now get the hell off this mountain, and let me tend to business!"

There's something wrong here, something too urgent about his "business," something he doesn't want seen or known. And why doesn't he want me to finish my ceremony?

"A true medicine-chief would have more patience, could wait until I'm finished." I can't resist adding: "This time, Bloodhawk, somebody else was here first."

"We were always here first!" Oh, that pushed his buttons; here comes the classic sermon. "The Whites came as invaders, destroyers, land-thieves, plague-spreaders—"

I let him rave on, taking the opportunity to check my circle and Call again. Yes, the barriers are still holding and the Call pulses out steadily, rolling with the rhythm of the music in my mind. If the Mind I want is anywhere within reach . . .

"—a history of slaughters, lies, land-thefts, broken treaties—" Bloodhawk's still preaching, as if everyone didn't know the story, as if it never happened to anybody else.

"Yes," I cut in. "And the Old People had better than three hundred years' warning. They knew that the White Man was coming, and that the White Man was dangerous, ruthless, numerous, bigoted, lying and land-greedy: the single biggest threat that the Red Man ever met."

Bloodhawk stops to listen, pleased to hear me agree about the sins of the invaders, as if my own Chippewa/Dutch/whatever ancestors couldn't have said the same.

"And still," I throw in the kicker, "All the tribes and nations just couldn't give up their old rivalries, couldn't forget their treasured old feuds and internal wars, not even to unite against the White Menace. That weakness defeated them, kept them separated and squabbling, let the White Man pick them off one by one. They squabbled in the face of a greater menace—just as you're doing right now: fighting me, instead of joining forces to fight the drought."

Something behind the eyes, something hidden, almost surfaces—then darts away.

"The Whites played on that," he snaps back. "They played divide-and-conquer, just like everywhere else they went. Just ask the Irish, or the Israelis, or the Moslems of

India. It's an old trick, and the Red Man was innocent enough to fall for it."

*Innocent?* I wonder. The Apaches, the Iroquois, the Sioux—and, yes, the Chippewa—I could call them many things, but "innocent" isn't one of them.

"But not anymore!" Bloodhawk proudly hammers a fist on his chest. The Navajo necklace bounces and jingles. "Today, we've learned better."

Again, that undercurrent of something concealed, something at cross-purposes.

"Here in Arizona, Red Man didn't do too badly," I point out. "The 1680 revolt kicked the Conquistadores out of everything but Tucson. The Apache were so mean that White Man had to buy them off, clean deal. The Navajo were tough enough to keep White Man off their lands entirely. This is where the Old People held on best, out of the whole country. So why are you, here and now, so furious about White Man's sins that you can't call a truce even with a half-breed—not even long enough to join forces against the drought?"

That darting, secret purpose flashes close to the surface.

"Because the Whites stole the Phoenix Valley!" he shouts, throwing a piece of the truth at me like a stone. "The confluence of the rivers, some of the best farming land in the state—hell, that city's water system is based on the old Hohokam irrigation ditches. The Whites stole it, and we want it back!"

". . . You want Phoenix. The whole Valley of the Sun."

Right there, I see it; the passion in his tirade let it slip. That cone of power, holding back the wet winds: the psychic signature on it is Bloodhawk's. He's the one with that much power—and that much hate.

"You did this," I whisper, stunned. "You set the . . . the curse that caused the drought. All this dying . . . *you* did it."

He clenches his fists and grins like a coyote about to pounce. The gloves are off. He won't let me walk off this mountain alive, not with that secret.

I wonder if I can draw and shoot fast enough to kill

him. No; his hand is too close to his holster in expectation. He'd beat me to the draw.

"Yes," he admits. "I did it. I have the power. Just try making your little junkyard spells against that."

He kicks a scuff of dust across the boundary of my circle, dimming an inch of the fire.

I've got to stop that before he muffles part of the circle, or nerves himself up to step across it.

"Instead of dead dust," I drawl, trying to sound amused, "why don't you toss some living creature through that barrier and see what happens?"

He stops, hesitates, thinks for a moment. I see his eyes drop, flick over the ground. Then his hand darts down. He comes up with a tiny lizard, a little gray sand-skink, held by the tail. The tiny creature wriggles frantically, certain that it's been caught by the world's biggest cactus-owl. Bloodhawk grins, and tosses the little lizard into the circle.

As it flies above the fire, even before it lands, the skink goes into convulsions. It hits the ground on its back, still writhing, as if shocked by an electric stunner—or a heavy static charge, which is closer to the truth.

Yes, my circle still holds.

Bloodhawk takes a respectful step back.

The skink jerks a few more times, then lies still. I pick it up, reassured to feel that it's only unconsciouses—but I won't let Bloodhawk see that. I tuck the tiny creature into the shadow under my knee, set it on its stomach, and surreptitiously stroke its back, hoping the little lizard will recover soon.

"Why did you do it?" I ask Bloodhawk, while he's still off balance. "You have to know what your drought's doing to the land."

"Can't you guess?" he recovers. "To drive the Whites away, of course! Greedy fools, wasting water: can't live without their precious lawns and golf-greens. That city uses more water in a day than the whole rez does in a month."

*It has a lot more people, too,* I think, but don't say.

"—Wallowing pigs, can't live without wasting water.

When there's no more to waste, they'll go. They're going already, back to Los Angeles, or New York, or the Midwest, or whatever water-rich place they came from. When the last of them are gone, then I'll break the sky-wall and let the rains come. Then, and not before. Try telling that to the Chamber of Commerce!" He laughs, long and ugly.

"Try telling it to the Inter-Tribal Council," I stab in the dark again. "They just might believe you."

He cuts off the laughter as if he'd thrown a switch, frowning. "They didn't believe me when I offered them the tactic, two years ago. That bunch of old women. They made it clear that even if they did believe, they wouldn't go along with it. Too tied up in Whitey economics, didn't want to lose the trade, the tourist market, crap like that."

"So you did it on your own?"

"Damned right." That ugly smile is back. "If they've figured it out yet, they haven't so much as sent word to me—let alone sent another medicine-man to try undoing my work. Think you can do what they can't, or won't dare?"

I ignore the challenge for the moment. We both know this will come to a wizards' duel soon enough, and I'd rather avoid that as long as I can. "I see the end of that road," I say instead. "When you pull this off, when you come back with the biggest scalp ever, you'll be Medicine-Chief of the whole Southwest."

A slow, powerful smile is his only answer.

I have to keep calm, can't afford to be afraid now, but it's sobering to realize just what I'm dealing with. His talent is massive, his training obviously thorough, and his ambition utterly ruthless.

In a straightforward contest of power with him I'd lose, no question. My only chance is to make this a duel of wits. Right now, all I can do is stall for time. And Call. . . .

*Come, oh come. . . .*

"Aren't you forgetting a few things?" I try, briefly feeling out my Call again. It's still working, and he still hasn't noticed. "Not all the Palefaces have left, or intend to leave. Some of those Newcomers have fitted themselves to the land, adjusted to it, learned to live with it, just as the Old People did. Those of us who learned from the land, let it shape us, we're not exactly what you'd call White anymore. We're sure as hell not just invaders anymore. We're part of the land, too. You'll never drive all of us out."

"Bull," he snaps. "Another six months, maybe another year with no rain, no snow, no water—believe me, they'll go."

He means it. I realize now, that's the reason he came up here: the thing he didn't want any witnesses to see. He plans to renew the cone of standing air, his curse, for another season at least. The implications are horrifying.

"Bloodhawk, do you have any idea what another year without rain will do to this country? When there's no water left for the Whites, there'll be none left for the Old People, either. The animals will die. The plants will die. Even the topsoil will turn to dust and blow away. What about them, Bloodhawk? They weren't consulted, and they're not part of your war. Do you intend to kill them, too?"

"The Whites will go first," he insists, refusing to believe. "As soon as they're gone, I'll let the rains come."

"And when the land thrives again, the Newcomers will start to trickle back. Then what? Will you make a drought again? How many times will you play this game?"

"As often as necessary." He pulls the medicine-bundle off his shoulder, and starts reaching into it.

I can't keep him distracted much longer. "And meanwhile, how many of the plants, the animals, the other Old People, will die for your war?"

"Enough will survive." He dismisses the whole problem, pulling the bundle open. "They always do."

"How many is 'enough'? How many of your brothers will you kill?"

"I have no brothers," he says, pulling out a feathered hoop.

"You don't care about any of them, do you?" I can see

his whole pattern now, and it's appalling. "You don't care about the life or spirits of the land, or even about your own people. You just want to take the Phoenix Valley! You'll have your victory, even if you celebrate it from an altar of bones in a land of ashes."

He only shrugs, and opens the bundle the rest of the way. I see enough to warn me what to expect: the painted bones, the patterns cut into the gourd rattles, the dried snakeskins, the pouches of colored sand. . . .

"Get off the mountain," he says in passing, as if it no longer matters. "Run while you can. I'll draw my circle around the whole peak. Your circle will be crushed inside it—and you, too, if you're still here."

He means it, and he can do it.

Would he really let me run away, not drop rocks out from under my feet, not hit me with a small landslide, let me survive to get home and warn someone who might listen? I don't think so.

I wonder what it's like to die of magic, of psychic force, of Bloodhawk's' drought-curse. Like strangling, maybe—or thirst, or burning. He won't make it easy, or fast; whatever his original tribe, there's more than a little of the Apache in his nature.

I can't run, can't let him win, can't let the land die.

"I'll stay," I answer. And I promptly dive back into full trance, tighten my shields one last time and put all my strength into the Call. It's my one hope now.

*Sky-spirit, storm-spirit,*
*Chief of the high winds.*

How long before my Call is heard and answered? How long will my shields hold against Bloodhawk's power? How long will I last after that?

Behind me I hear the jingle of copper bells, the dry clatter of snake rattles shaken in a gourd, the clicking of pendant bones, a whisper of barely-voiced chanting, carefully-placed shuffling steps—all moving away. I needn't look to tell what he's doing; he's dancing his circle around the peak, enclosing my circle within it.

Dancing: using kinesthetics to draw on the power of his whole nervous system, as I use my music. No doubt he's also scattering colored sand, or pollen, or possibly powdered bone behind him. I can feel the unphysical pressure rise.

When he closes that circle, I'll be in serious trouble. I don't have the sheer power that he does. I don't dare leave off my Summoning to reinforce my circle's walls; that would only prolong the inevitable collapse anyway. All I can do is send for help and hope it arrives in time. Sing silently, reach, reach. . . .

*Sky-lord, shadow-maker,*
*Come, oh come.*

I hear the jingle and rattle as Bloodhawk's dance comes circling back. He'll close the first circuit in another moment. Will he cut off my Call, attack, or gather more power first?

Ignore him and concentrate. Reach through the music. . . .

And far off, at the thinnest edge of my Call, I feel the touch of another mind.

It's psychic. It notices me. It answers.

It's not human.

It's bright, wordless, massive, alien—like no mind I've ever met. It would be terrifying, if I could afford to let myself feel fear. I have to keep Calling to it, sweetly as a lover. I might as well be fishing for dynamite.

*Come, wind-rider. Come, cloud-striker.*

The touch strengthens. That impossible mind approaches, inrigued. He comes, but from how far? How long will he take? Can I last?

The heat/pressure around me thickens abruptly. I'm suddenly thirsty, dust-choked, burning, throat too dry to whisper a word if my form of magic needed it.

Bloodhawk has closed the first circle.

But I can still feel that oncoming mind. Bloodhawk

hasn't closed me off, not yet. He's more concerned with raising his power, casually crushing me under it, than shutting off my Summoning.

Gods, he still thinks I'm just trying to Summon rain! He doesn't know what I've really Called, just knows that he's stronger than I am and hasn't bothered to look further. I still have a chance.

> *Spirit of the winds of the burning lands,*
> *Come, oh, come. . . . And hurry!*

The rattling dance begins to circle again, its orbit a little closer this time. I can pick up some of the words, though they're in one of the old languages that I don't understand. The dry, whispery sound of the gourd-rattle falls and rises, as if he's weaving back and forth.

Weaving and winding, in a weather-spell against rain? Snake-rattles. . . .

My concentration almost slips as I realize what he's doing. In the pure tradition Bloodhawk boasts of, Rattlesnake is linked to water. Bloodhawk is following the Rattlesnake Road through astral country, the Way that a shaman would normally "walk" to summon water, rain, the fertility of the Earth. But he's using it for the opposite purpose: to drive the waters away, dry and burn everything to sterility and death, make the whole land shed its skin like a snake. He's using the stored energy, the backlash, of all those generations—centuries, millennia—of earlier shamans' rain-prayers: the reaction generated from all those actions. It's the same theory as the Black Mass.

Bloodhawk is perverting the Path of the Rattlesnake. Any traditional shaman would be shocked speechless at the impiety.

I can't afford to let it shake me. Ignore the shocking perversion. Ignore the heat/thirst/pain. Concentrate. Reach. Sing in the skull. . . .

> *Thunder-winged, lightning-eyed,*
> *Come, oh, come. (Quickly!) Come, oh, come.*

Closer, coming I can feel the beat of his wings echoing in the muscles of my arms. The pressure of his vast, alien mind grows heavier.

But the heat is rising. I'm baking, dizzy with thirst. No, I don't dare stop to reach for my canteen, break my concentration by even that much, not now. If I do, the alien mind will lose me. Sing!

*Come and be welcome, be fed and be warm.*
*Come in thy physical, Earthly form.*

With a flourish of angry rattles, Bloodhawk closes the second circle.

The pressure squeezes down like a fist, crushing, burning. . . . Even my mental vision blacks out. I can't see/feel the contact anymore, have to trust that it's still there. I reach, sing, yell silently through it, concentrating on my lone hope. Don't think of how another circle of this will black me out, how the fourth circle will kill. . . . No. Only reach, call, sing, implore that blade-bright massive mind.

*Come, God-the-Hunter!*

A sudden battering of cool air shakes loose the grip of heat/pressure/pain, startles my eyes open as the sound of rattles, bells, footsteps, chanting falters.

He's here.

Behind me I can feel Bloodhawk gaping at the sight, and I don't blame him in the least. Even before I open my eyes, I can feel the halo of power like the breath from a blast furnace: bright, vast, ruthless, inhuman.

Iron-black claws touch down on the rocks, just outside my stone circle. The enormous wings—whose span would not shame a Piper Cub—flutter a last wind-spillage, and fold. Red eyes, as big as a bull's, roll at me. The dark-gold beak, the size of a powder horn, clacks once. The psychic power, almost visible, etches his feathers like St. Elmo's Fire.

In shape and color, he's a Golden Eagle. In size and power, he's beyond words.

From the ruffled crest of his bronze-feathered head, down to his dagger-sized claws, he stands at least seven feet tall.

Bloodhawk whispers an awed word in the old language, its meaning plain.

*Core of legends.*

Thunderbird twitches his huge bronze head back and forth, clearly wondering why these humans are here, which one Called him, and why. Eagles, of any kind, are not noted for their patience.

Remembering my task, I bend low and reach for the big metal bowl. The little sand-skink, awake now, darts out from under my leg and skitters frantically around the circle, looking for some escape. I wish I could spare the concentration to reassure him: The Eagle Does Not Hawk For Flies—nor Thunderbird for sand-skinks. Good thing I've practiced this maneuver, or I couldn't manage it now. Gods, all that power, that mind, pressing on me. . . .

No, don't falter. The bowl's heavy. Pull off the cover—carefully, don't startle him—lift up the bowl and offer it. Take care to stay directly under it, covered by its rim, hands safely out of reach. Eagles are not noted for delicate eating manners.

Thunderbird inspects the round, shiny object and sniffs at its contents. Pray to the gods I guessed right: that the Old People offered in bowls of gold, silver, or copper; that he's used to metal; that he likes what I've brought. Ten pounds of sliced calves' liver that I hauled up this mountain: pray that he finds it as rare a delicacy as his normal-sized brethren do.

I guessed right. The first peck nearly knocks me down. I can hear his huge beak clacking, less than a yard from my head, as he chops and swallows. I'm better braced for the second peck, and the third which follows faster, but my whole body feels the strain. Gods, but he's strong!

I struggle to maintain deep trance, hold up the welcoming images, but the effort is too much. All I can do is keep a thread of contact, the link of insight into that monstrous mind, a passive reading. I can feel static electricity lifting my hair, the merest fraction of his power.

Behind me, Bloodhawk begins to chant softly. His feather-decked hoop rustles. The heat/pressure rises again, slowly. This time, it's not centered on me.

He's trying to take control of the Thunderbird.

I can't begin to stop him. It's all I can do to hold up the bowl, maintain my worn shields against Bloodhawk's heavy-weighing circles, and keep contact. I'm out of the action.

Now it's all up to the Thunderbird.

Peck, peck, the blows fall heavier, almost hammering me flat. Through the contact, I can feel Thunderbird's irritation. He wants to finish his delectable meal, and someone is annoying him. The shaken hoop, the chanted words, the noticeable psychic pressure—he's aware of them, and not amused.

Right there, I see Bloodhawk's second mistake. All legends grow from a seed of truth; sometimes that truth is symbolic, metaphorical, but sometimes it isn't. In the traditions Bloodhawk studied so thoroughly, Thunderbird is worshiped as the storm-bringer. His ceremonies are largely symbolic, aimed at his image, his function—not the reality.

Bloodhawk uses those symbols now—the chanted prayers, the shaken feathers—just as he learned them. But they were meant for symbolic rain-making ceremonies, not for face-to-face meetings with the real thing.

This is the real thing.

A last ferocious peck dents the bottom of the bowl, driving my shoulders down to my knees. I struggle to keep the bowl upright, protecting my hands and body, and feel a sudden surge of fierce intent in that wordless mind. I realize he's finished the meat, and suddenly I know what he's going to do.

I try—truly, I try—to shout a warning to Bloodhawk. My throat's too parched to make a sound, but I try. I even risk lowering my shields to send him a mental warning, if he'll hear it.

*Bloodhawk, no! He's basically an eagle, and he takes it for a challenge—*

The great wings spread and slap the air with a blow like a thunderclap, slamming me to the ground. All I see is the blur of motion as his clawed feet leave the Earth. Brawling air beats me down as he rises.

I hear Bloodhawk's chant rise to a high, hard note. I feel him drop everything else and grab for mind-control.

And I feel that vast birdlike mind shrug off the thrust of power and its incomprehensible words, concentrating—as an eagle's ancient instinct must—on the strike.

I squeeze my eyes shut, not wanting to see it.

There's an instant of impossible pressure/heat/impact, shot through with astonishment and fury. Then comes a snap of psychic discharge, fierce as a bolt of lightning.

The walls of heat/pressure/power around me burst like a bubble.

I gulp air in blind relief, stay curled where I am, eyes closed, trying not to listen to the wet snapping sounds.

Is this the end of it? Did the weather-curse break with Bloodhawk's life?

I have to know. Thunderbird is hotly, happily, pre-occupied with food; he won't notice me, if I'm careful. I send a cautious probe of thought out into the dust-heavy sky, feeling for that cone of high-pressure air.

It's still there. Bloodhawk died before he could contact and renew it, and eventually it will weaken and fade, but the parched land can't wait for that. Gods, I'm going to have to go through with this. . . .

Wait until Thunderbird has finished eating. Wait until he's satiated and content. Then, perhaps, he'll feel kindly disposed toward my request. Wait, keep contact, make sure. Never interrupt a wild animal while it's feeding. That was Bloodhawk's mistake, and now he's the main course.

Thunderbird is a god only because people worship him, have worshiped him and his like for ages, built an arche-type—a psychic pattern—that he stepped into, put on like a robe: the mantle of godhood. Humans have done that, and history tells of the results.

But at the core, the living being is a Golden Eagle. He's a gigantic eagle, a pituitary giant just as one occasionally finds among humans; rarely born, still more rarely strong enough to reach maturity, rarest of all having enough intelligence and psychic talent to find sufficient prey and survive. Thunderbird is a brilliant psychic giant who stepped—or flew—into a pattern of godlike power that human worship made for him, but he's an eagle all the same.

You don't challenge an eagle for supremacy or territory, and you don't annoy him while he's eating—not unless you intend to fight him, and on an eagle's terms. Bloodhawk didn't think of that.

Forget that. Back to the work at hand.

Thunderbird pecks slower, gulps a last tender bit of organ-meat, stretches, shakes his neck and turns his attention to grooming his long bronze feathers. He's well content. The time is now, if ever.

The halo of power pulses around him. I could lose myself just by touching it. One thing to die, another thing entirely to lose my soul, spirit, mind. . . .

If I don't try, the land dies.

I reach.

Carefully, gently, I widen the contact. Touch all that power, very careful not to draw or absorb it. Caress his awareness, very gently, adoringly. Flatter him while he preens. Form the idea, the sensory image. Paint it in strokes of satisfaction, pleasure, good hunting, terms an eagle can understand. Implore, entice, seduce, appeal to his tastes. One can't command an eagle, but with care one might persuade him. That, too, Bloodhawk didn't understand.

One wrong move, or thought now, and I'll die as Bloodhawk did—at best.

Thunderbird ruffles his feathers, raises his head and glances in my direction.

I keep perfectly still, holding the image against the ever-flowing background of my song, displaying the pattern so simply that a bird can understand it. Imagine sweet cool winds, wisps of fog, the land below all green and sweet-scented. Imagine the abundance of food, sport, good hunting.

Now see how to make it happen. Do this: then the cool wind comes and all the rest follows. Do this thing: bring the rain.

*Break the walls of the standing air.*
*Bear the charge, to discharge it there.*
*Fly as only the eagles dare,*
*Soaring on Thunderbird Road.*

He shakes his wings, considering the idea. Full-fed, he'd rather rest than fly. Then again, this place is far from his home/nest, not overly comfortable, afflicted with the not-distant-enough smells/sounds/psychic feel of many humans. Yes, he would leave soon anyway. Yes, he will do this thing as he goes.

His wings spread, impossibly wide, rise and slap the air. On a buffet of dusty wind he rises, climbing in lazy circles. In a moment dust hides him from sight, but I follow him with the link of psychic contact. He feels the air thinning, cooling, growing cleaner as he soars.

Higher and higher still, and there—almost at the limit of his altitude—the apex of Bloodhawk's cone of power. There: the tip of the huge squat pyramid of high-pressure air, the focus, the keystone. The weak spot.

Thunderbird banks and turns, aiming toward the invisible peak, raising his own enormous power, picking up static charge as he swoops.

I pull everything out of my shields, draw all the psychic charge I can summon from Earth and sky and my own battered body—and pour all of it into Thunderbird. My help, my gift.

He flicks his tailfeathers in pleasure, enjoying the ripple of added power along his great wings, well acquainted with the forces of the air. He strokes into a long, high glide.

*Strike!*

Arrow-straight, he flies into the tip of that invisible cone.

*Discharge!*

SNAP.

To anyone on the ground, it would look like a flare of heat-lightning. To Thunderbird, it's a delicious tingle along his wide-spread feathers: an after-dinner treat. He gives a long screech of pleasure before banking and turning away, sailing off to the unguessed distant mountains of his secret home.

For me, it's the crack of a whip and the eye of a hurricane. The pressure change knocks me down again, ears ringing, nose starting to bleed, eyes blacked out. I don't need to probe for Bloodhawk's spell, even if I had the strength for that now. Every psychically talented creature for a hundred miles must have felt that wall go down. A long drumroll of thunder gallops across the sky.

The song of power rattles on in my skull, taking on a life of its own.

*Break that link, and let him go.*
*Come to ground as the wet winds blow. . . .*

Too drained to feel anything else, I grope blindly for my canteen. Find it, fumble off the cap, and drink the last of my water. I'll worry later about climbing back down the mountain. All I want now is sleep. . . .

A fat raindrop slaps my eyelid. Wet wind strokes my cheek. Tiny claws tickle as the sand-skink jumps off my chest and races for the shelter of the rocks. I wake to the first lazy drops of rain, raise my boulder-heavy head and look up at the sky. It's cloud-gray, pregnant with rain.

The last of the song is still ringing in my head.

*. . . Feel the rain falling cool and slow,*
*Down on Thunderbird Road—*
*Going home on Thunderbird Road.*

I groan, and the last of the tune echoes away, leaving me with silence, save for the wind.

I roll over and look out at the land below the mountain.

See a second horizon: a solid line of slate-blue clouds marching steadily over the land, tongues of lightning flickering under its edge. The long-delayed rains are coming at last, and the first of them will be a real cloudburst.

I manage to roll to my knees and watch for long minutes, too weary to feel more than a dull relief. I'm exhausted, aching, skin prickling with the promise of sunburn, and my head feels as if it's been stuffed with cotton. I've known psychic depletion before, but never like this. I can't feel/probe anything, can barely think, barely remember. I've drained myself to the bone.

With that understanding come the inevitable doubts. All right, Chantayna: how much of all that really happened?

Consider: I spent most of this afternoon sitting out in the sun, on a dry mountaintop, in the 110-degree heat, deep in trance-state, concentrating on a song—and most of that time with my eyes closed. Easy to imagine a dozen impossible things under those conditions.

Consider: I came to do a rain-making ceremony, and I seem to have succeeded in that. But then, the drought might have been ready to break anyway, despite predictions by the weather experts.

How much of the rest was psychological symbolism, wishful thinking, dreaming in the heat?

Was there really a Thunderbird or was that only my symbol for the rain-bearing winds? Was there really an evil sorcerer named Bloodhawk, or was that only my personified symbol for the deadly high-pressure zone? Did I really argue politics and magic with a super-psychic shaman, or was that just one more symbolic battle with my own unsteadily mixed heritage? It's too easy to confuse symbol and reality, working in the mental universe; that's the basic trap for all psychics, and I've fallen into it myself more than once.

If I were the traditional shaman Bloodhawk wanted to be, I'd never bother myself with such questions; I'd simply accept the fuzziness of the border between symbol and reality, inner and outer worlds. Perhaps I've learned too much, studied too many different traditions, can never completely trust any of them, must always doubt and analyze and question.

All right then, Teiner, the scientific rationalist: start at the top. Look around. Observe.

Item: a large, dented, metal bow—blood-smeared on the inside, smelling faintly of raw liver.

Deduction: I put out the food-offering, and some predator or predators unknown came to take it. Not necessarily a giant eagle, no: maybe just an ordinary Golden Eagle, maybe several coyotes, maybe even a desperately bold cougar. Nothing's proved yet.

Item: beyond my circle, two encompassing bands of colored sand poured over the rock.

Fact: I didn't bring any painting-sand with me.

Deduction: I wasn't the only person to come up here.

Oh, hell.

I really don't want to turn around and look, but I have to.

Maybe a dozen yards behind me lies what's left of Bloodhawk's body. Near it lie scattered copper bells, painted bone wands, a gourd rattle, and a broken feather-decked hoop.

I make myself get up and go there, gather the wide-strewn gear, try to arrange the corpse in some seemly fashion. It isn't easy.

Deduction: yes, Bloodhawk was real, and really here, and really was killed by a very large raptor-bird.

That's as far as I'll go. I can't swear to how big an eagle it really was. Thunderbird is a legend, an educated guess; a common or garden-variety Golden Eagle is quite capable of killing a grown man. And eating part of him afterward.

Gods, I can pity Bloodhawk now. Predators don't leave their meals in pretty shape.

I spread the opened medicine-bundle over the body, covering as much of the gaping abdominal cavity as I can. Add the bells, the hoop, the rattle, all the other gear. Open the last two unused sand-pouches and sprinkle their contents over the corpse. Gods, one of them really was powdered bone.

I wish I could think clearly enough to remember a good prayer. There's no dirt up here to bury him in; I build a rough cairn with my spell-circle's stones. Let his bones rest on top of Mazatzal Peak; maybe some future activist can use them as an excuse to claim the mountain as an ancestral burial-ground. Bloodhawk would like that.

I have no tools for carving a headstone, only a notebook and pen in my pack. I hope the ink is waterproof enough to survive the slowly thickening rain.

HERE LIE THE BONES OF CARL NATONHEY, CALLED BLOODHAWK, GREATEST MEDICINE-CHIEF OF THE SOUTHWEST—

No harm in flattering the dead. "Killed by an eagle" would be impressive enough, but it won't hurt to add the elaborations of poetry, or symbolism, or heat-fever dreams.

WHO DIED IN MAGICAL COMBAT WITH THE THUNDERBIRD.

There. Fold the paper and pin it under the topmost rock. Let the next climber of Mazatzal Peak make a discovery that will make him or her famous.

Enough for me that the drought is broken, and I'm still alive. That's all I'll claim, or believe. Let the rest become myth with no more help from me; I saw a Golden Eagle, and that's all.

Frankly, I'm scared witless of what I think I saw.

Enough. Time to get out of here. I turn to collect my bowl, canteen, and pack.

The wet wind stirs something on the ground ahead, something like a pine branch, up here where no branch has ever been or could be. I stop to look . . .

. . . And lose myself to legends.

It's a feather. A great bronze-colored feather. A Golden Eagle's feather—longer than my arm.

*There really is a Thunderbird Road in Phoenix, cutting across the north of the city from close-crowded high-rises to unchanged desert. Yes, I have seen rain ceremonies performed in the empty lands thereabouts, and have sung and played for a few as well. And yes, Arizona is one state where the Red Folk didn't lose; Native American art, religion, and politics pervade the culture down here in the Valley of the Sun, and it's wise to respect them. In fact, I originally wrote the song "Thunderbird Road" for use in a rain ceremony—which worked. The story evolved out of that experience.*

# OUR FATHER'S GOLD
### by Elisabeth Waters

Elisabeth Waters sold her first story to Marion Zimmer Bradley for *The Keeper's Price,* the first of the Darkover anthologies. She has sold short stories to a variety of anthologies. Her first novel, a fantasy called *Changing Fate,* was awarded the 1989 Gryphon Award, and was published by DAW in 1994. She is a member of the Science Fiction And Fantasy Writers of America and the Authors Guild. She has also worked as a supernumerary with the San Francisco Opera, where she has appeared in *La Gioconda, Manon Lescaut, Madama Butterfly, Khovanschina, Das Rheingold, Werther,* and *Idomeneo.*

"But, Father, I don't understand. Why are we here?" Toni waved a hand at the countryside around her. "There's so much dirt—and bugs! This is *not* my idea of how to celebrate my sixteenth birthday!"

Not that Toni thought her father cared how she wanted to celebrate her birthday. He had always treated her rather like some alien life-form he didn't quite trust. She wondered sometimes if things would have been different if she had been a boy—or if her mother had lived long enough for Toni to remember her.

Her father's laugh sounded forced. "There speaks a girl who's spent too much of her life in space." He swung the picnic basket in his left hand and grabbed her arm with his right. "Come along; there's something I have to show you."

Toni perforce accompanied him, looking dubiously about her. "You've been acting weird ever since Mr. Hagen came on board. Why is he chartering the *Loge's Fire* anyway? If all he wants is to stage an opera, he could rent part of one of the L5 stations."

She followed her father through a stand of trees and recoiled. "That's a river," she said, backing up a few steps. Her father stopped her by the simple expedient of dropping the picnic basket, moving to stand directly behind her, and gripping both shoulders.

"Yes, it's the River Rhine. Don't panic on me, Toni," he said reassuringly. "I know it's more water than you've ever seen in one place before, but it won't hurt you." He pushed her before him to the very edge of the river.

Toni looked down at the water rushing past her. Even here next to the riverbank the water was obviously over her head. She tried to back away from it, but her father held her firmly, and he was bigger and stronger than she. And she had the horrible feeling that he had lost his mind. "Father, you *do* remember that I don't know how to swim, don't you?" she asked in a quavering voice.

"Silly girl!" A woman's head popped out of the water about two meters away from the spot where they stood. "Of course you can swim!"

"No, I can't!" Toni recoiled, fighting what was threatening to become a full-scale panic attack. "What's going on here? Who are you, anyway?"

"I'm your Aunt Woglinde."

"My what?"

The head submerged briefly, then reappeared right next to the bank, accompanied by an arm which reached up to snag Toni's left ankle. "I'll have her back in a few hours—Captain." She gave a hard yank, and Toni slid out of her father's hands and into the river.

Toni choked back a scream and held her breath as long as she could, but she was being dragged rapidly downward, despite her frantic efforts to fight her way back up to the air. Whatever else this woman might be, she was certainly strong.

Pressure crushing against her chest and face soon

forced Toni to release the air in her lungs and try to breathe water, and she was amazed to discover that she could. The water didn't taste very good as it passed through her mouth, but at least her lungs stopped hurting as soon as they filled with it. She cautiously opened her eyes, which she had kept scrunched tightly shut, and looked around her.

Woglinde released the grip on her ankle and swam up to take her arm. She was completely naked, and looked like a normal human female, except for the fact that she could breathe underwater—and talk, too. "That's better, child. Life is much easier when you don't try to fight what you are."

*What am I?* Toni wondered. But she didn't feel up to trying to talk underwater quite yet, even if she *could* breathe.

Woglinde set Toni's hands on her bare shoulders and added, "Just hold on to me. We're running late, and there's a lot to discuss." She began to swim strongly upstream, towing Toni along with her. Toni was careful to keep her hands on Woglinde's shoulder blades; she didn't want to strangle her inadvertently—not before she found out what was going on and how to get back home again. Assuming, of course, that she wasn't asleep in her own bunk and dreaming like this because the gravity had cut out. "What are you?" she asked. "How can you breathe water?"

"I'm a Rhinemaiden," Woglinde replied swimming onward, "just like you."

"I'm not a Rhinemaiden!" Toni protested.

"If you're not," Woglinde asked, her voice teasing, "then why aren't you dead?"

"Maybe I am," Toni said hopefully. "And then I won't have to deal with the strange way that Father's been acting ever since Mr. Hagen chartered his ship to stage an opera."

Woglinde twisted briefly to look at her. "Hagen is on the ship?" She pronounced the name differently, and it obviously meant something to her.

"Mr. Hagen," Toni corrected her. "He's some sort of

impresario. He wants to stage an opera called *Das Rheingold* on the ship so that he can use the zero-G hold for the
scenes that are supposed to be underwater."

"It's *wyrd*," Woglinde said definitely. "We'll have to
tell the others."

The water was growing steadily grayer. Toni thought
they might be going deeper, but it was hard to tell. Then
there was an area of darkness ahead of and slightly
above them, and Woglinde dove straight into it. This time
Toni did scream.

"Nervous, isn't she?" The voice was lower-pitched than
Woglinde's and came from above them. Woglinde swam
upward, pried Toni loose, and set her on a flat rock. "Sit
there, child, while I find the others." Toni felt the disturbance in the water as Woglinde turned and swam back the
way they had come.

Toni clung to the rock where she had been placed,
noticing that her eyes were starting to adjust to the very
small amount of light available. She was in some sort of
underwater cave, and another naked woman—or, more
probably, Rhinemaiden—sat on a rock slightly above her.
She was playing with her long hair, twining it into loose
braids and then releasing it to float about her head again.
She looked at Toni's short hair and shook her head,
sighing.

"I'm your Aunt Flosshilde, child," she said. "What is
your name?"

"Antonia," Toni replied. "Is everyone here my aunt?"

Flosshilde laughed. "Most of us."

"My father told me my mother was dead?" It came out
as a question. Toni was coming to the sudden realization
that there was quite a lot her father hadn't told her. *No
wonder I always thought he was treating me like an alien,*
she thought, feeling stunned. *I am an alien.*

"In that, I fear he spoke the truth," Flosshilde said.
"Your mother was the youngest of us, and she was somewhat lacking in caution."

Toni had spent her entire life on a spaceship, where a
second's inattention to detail could kill you and a dozen
other people, and had heard death discussed like that

before. Judging from Flosshilde's tone, her mother's death had probably been stupid, messy, and totally unnecessary. But still Toni had to ask. "What happened to her?" she asked.

"She fell in love with your father."

There was a sudden turbulence in the water as Woglinde and six other Rhinemaidens swam in and took their places on the rocks.

"Is everyone here?" Flosshilde said.

"Yes." The reply came in chorus, a single harmonious chord.

"We are met here today," Flosshilde said, "to celebrate the continuation of our line. Today we welcome Antonia, our youngest-born."

"Welcome, Antonia," the chorus sang.

"Antonia?" someone said, *sotto voce,* "What kind of name is that for a Rhinemaiden?"

"I was named for Saint Anthony," Toni replied. "My grandmother said it was appropriate, because my father was so good at losing things that he'd need someone who was good at finding them." She looked at their uncomprehending faces. "Saint Anthony is the patron saint of things that are lost," she explained.

"I still say it's a strange name," the voice complained.

"No," Woglinde said, "it's *wyrd.*"

"Isn't that the same thing?" Toni asked.

"Not weird," Woglinde said impatiently, "*Wyrd.* Fate. Do I have to explain *everything* to *everyone* today?"

"You have to do better than you are doing, Woglinde," Flosshilde said. "So far you are making no sense at all."

"Hagen is on her father's ship," Woglinde said, "making preparations to stage *Das Rheingold.* So it seems to me that she's already begun the work of finding our missing gold."

"What missing gold?" Toni asked. "And what does Mr. Hagen have to do with anything?"

"Don't you know about the Rheingold?" eight scandalized voices asked. Toni shook her head.

"Listen carefully," Flosshilde said, "and remember what I am about to tell you." Toni looked up at Flosshilde and tried hard to concentrate. Obviously this material was going to be on the final exam—in whatever form that took.

"We are the daughters of Father Rhine," Flosshilde said.

"Granddaughter, in your case," Woglinde added helpfully. Flosshilde shot her a look and she shut her mouth.

"Our father created us to guard the Rheingold," Flosshilde continued, "which is a lump of magic gold. The reason it is necessary to guard it is that anyone willing to renounce love could make the gold into a ring which would make him master of the world. Now, you wouldn't think that *anyone* would be willing to do that— we certainly didn't think so—but there was one being who was. A dwarf named Alberich renounced love, stole the gold, and made the ring."

"So does he rule the world now?" Toni asked. "I've never heard of him."

"You would have if you had a decent classical education," someone snapped.

*I did have a decent classical education,* Toni thought indignantly. *I must have read nearly everything written from Homer's time to the present.*

"Wagner wrote four operas which tell the whole story," Flosshilde said.

*Oh, that explains it,* she realized. *That was the only thing that wasn't part of my education; Father never wanted me to study music.*

"*Das Rheingold* is the first opera," Flosshilde continued. "By the end of the story, we had the gold back, and most of the beings who had encountered it were dead. To make a very long story short, the ring was stolen from Alberich, and he put a curse on it. The curse was never removed, but as long as the ring is in the water here, it doesn't have any effect. And Rhinemaidens are immune to the curse in any case, so you can bring the ring back to us, where it belongs."

"But you just said that you had gotten it back," Toni protested.

"We did," Flosshilde sighed, "but recently it was stolen again."

"And you think Mr. Hagen is involved?"

"Hagen," Flosshilde informed her, "is Alberich's son."

"Oh," Toni said. Then something else occurred to her. "How long ago did all this happen?"

"About two weeks ago."

"No, the part with Alberich and the curse."

"Several centuries, at least," one Rhinemaiden replied.

"Actually," another one said, "I think it's been closer to three millennia."

"It hasn't been quite that long," Woglinde said firmly.

"Three thousand years?" Toni yelped. "Are you all that old?"

"Take a bottle of water from the Rhine to put the ring in when you get it," Flosshilde instructed, as everyone ignored Toni's outburst.

"How am I supposed to get it—assuming that Mr. Hagen *is* Hagen and that he has it?"

"That's easy," Woglinde said promptly, "just seduce him. His kind has always been vulnerable to us."

"Seduce?" Toni stared at her incredulously. "You mean, sex? I can't do that; fornication is a sin!"

"Did your grandmother raise you as a Christian or something?" Flosshilde asked disapprovingly.

"Yes," Toni said. "I'm a Christian."

"Of all the unsuitable things to do to a Rhinemaiden. . . ." Toni thought the voice was the one who had complained about her name, but she wasn't sure.

Woglinde sighed. "I have to take her back to her father now," she said. "It's time."

"Antonia," Flosshilde said sternly. "This is important. The curse on the ring kills people. The gold belongs here in the Rhine. Weigh that against your Christian 'sins.' "

"And nobody is saying you *have* to have sex with Hagen," Woglinde said. "It's certainly the easiest way, but there may be another way. Start by being nice to him; maybe that will be enough. Maybe he's lonely." She shrugged, then reached out to pluck Toni off the rock. "Come, it's time to take you back."

\* \* \*

When they surfaced at the spot where Toni's father waited for them, he had the picnic spread out. "We'll eat while you dry off, Toni," he said calmly. "Will you join us, Woglinde?"

"Not today," Woglinde replied.

The Captain smiled ironically at her. "Don't you want to talk about how you girls lost the Rheingold—again?"

Woglinde's answering smile could not have been called nice. "Talk to your daughter; she's the one who's going to get it back for us." She disappeared below the surface of the Rhine without another word.

Toni, who, between the unaccustomed exercise and the shock of the day's revelations, was starving, dug into the meal. Her father had apparently decided to wait for her to speak, so the meal was eaten in silence.

"Father," Toni said finally, after she had eaten nearly everything in sight, "there appear to be a few things about my life and family you haven't bothered to mention to me."

"Now, Toni, don't get hysterical on me; you know I hate that. I promised them that I would bring you back on your sixteenth birthday so that they could tell you about your heritage."

"Just what is my heritage?" Toni demanded. "What is a Rhinemaiden, anyway?"

"Something rather like a siren," he replied, looking embarrassed.

"Like in *The Odyssey*? Women who live underwater and sing and lure men to their deaths? Is that why you don't allow me to sing? Is that how you met my mother? *Am I losing my mind or have you lost yours? Or both?*

"It's not necessarily death," her father said; "it's more like their doom."

*"Wyrd?"*

"Yes, you could call it that." He stared into the river, lost in thought. "Your mother was the most beautiful creature I ever saw," he said softly.

"What happened to her?" Toni asked.

"She left the river when it was time for you to be born,

and your grandmother killed her right after she gave birth."

Toni gasped, trying to reconcile the mortal sin of murder with her memories of her strict Christian grandmother, who had made certain that their small ship had not only a chapel but also a full-time chaplin. Had she been trying to atone for her sin? "Why did she kill her?" she asked.

"She said that your mother was an inhuman monster."

Toni thought of Woglinde's casual attitudes about sex, deception, and theft. She shivered.

"My mother was convinced that I was bewitched." He fell silent, staring into the river for several minutes. "Perhaps she was right—about my being bewitched, not about your mother. Anyway, as soon as you were born, she took you straight to the ship and sent several female crew members down after me."

"Why didn't she kill me, too?" Toni asked.

"You're my daughter, Toni. That's why she waited until you were born, so you wouldn't be harmed."

"If I'm a Rhinemaiden, why did she care?"

"You're at least half human, Toni, so I don't think you're a true Rhinemaiden."

*Then what am I?* Toni wondered.

"They had to drag me away from the river by force," he continued. "I had taken your mother's body back and told her sisters what had happened to her. I think I hoped they would kill me, too. But they said that I had to take care of you and bring you back when the time came. And they made me promise that I wouldn't tell you anything that would prejudice you against them."

"And would the story of the Rheingold do that?" Toni inquired curiously.

"It might," her father replied. "When we get back to the ship, I'll give you the video and the score, and you can decide for yourself."

"Just how long is this story, anyway?" Toni asked.

"Approximately sixteen hours."

"Father, that's two whole duty shifts! What about my regular work?" Toni's job in engineering didn't leave her much spare time, especially after her required study time for home schooling was added in.

"I'll tell the Chief Engineer that I'm pulling you off regular duty and assigning you to be ship's liaison with Mr. Hagen. That should make it easy enough for you to get the ring from him. Then you can give it to me, and I'll put it in my safe. It will give you an excuse to study the operas and call it work."

"It doesn't exactly sound like play," Toni muttered. She drank the last of her fruit juice, rinsed the container in the river, and refilled it with Rhine water. *I'll take this back as a souvenir,* she thought, *and if it's gone when I wake up, I'll know I dreamed all this.* "I'm ready to go back any time you are, Captain."

Toni spent half the night reviewing the operas. She watched *Das Rheingold* in its entirety, both because it was the first and because it was the one Mr. Hagen/Hagen was producing. She skimmed through the written scores of the next two operas: *Die Walkure* and *Siegfried,* and read the last one, *Gotterdammerung,* very carefully. Hagen appeared in *Gotterdammerung.* Apparently he was the son of Alberich the Niblung and a woman from a human family. He was also devious and a murderer, even if it was at his father's behest.

On the other hand, the Rhinemaidens didn't exactly come across as guardians of truth, justice, and goodness. In *Das Rheingold* they were amoral teasing tramps, whose treatment of Alberich certainly explained why he was willing to renounce love. Toni watched the scene involving her Aunts Woglinde, Flosshilde, and Well-gunde and hoped that they had mellowed with age. She also hoped that no one would ever expect *her* to behave like that, although she had an uneasy feeling that Woglinde probably did.

Then she turned off the light, crawled into bed, and started wondering what it meant to be half-Rhinemaiden. Was this why her grandmother had strictly forbidden her to sing, telling her that she had a horrible voice that no one could stand to listen to? Did she have a human soul?

Was she going to live to be as old as her aunts? How long was "not quite" three thousand years? Two thousand nine hundred? How long could even a semi-intelligent being swim around in the Rhine without going utterly insane? Were the Rhinemaidens insane? Was her father? Was she? Had she hallucinated this entire day? She fell asleep hoping that she already was asleep and had been throughout.

But when she woke up the next morning, books and tapes of the Ring Cycle were still strewn all over her workspace, and the water from the Rhine still sat on her dresser. And as soon as she reported for duty, her father introduced her to Mr. Hagen, who readily accepted her as his production assistant, although something in the way he looked at her made Toni wonder whether he was also considering her possible hostage value. Or something. Her imagination seemed to be working overtime—or maybe sideways; she just couldn't seem to think straight. She had never felt so confused in her entire life.

"Shall we start with the zero-G set used in the first scene?" she asked Mr. Hagen respectfully. He was short, a few centimeters shorter than she was, but his build was stocky, so he was half again her size. "I believe that the rocks have been finished and bolted into place, but I imagine you'll want to inspect it before your singers try to use it."

He grunted, which Toni took for agreement as she led the way to the zero-G hold. "It's a good thing this scene requires only four singers. Do your singers have any zero-G experience?" She led the way into the air lock, checked to be sure that there was a breathable atmosphere in the hold, and started the cycle. Even with the same atmosphere on both sides of the lock, they always used it. Going through the air lock reminded people that something was likely to be different on the other side, whether atmosphere or gravity.

This time it was both gravity and air pressure. Most of the ship was maintained at a lower air pressure than Earth sea level normal, but, for the sake of the singers, who would need the extra oxygen, the hold was set at one standard atmosphere. Toni, accustomed to changes in pressure, cleared her ears without even thinking of it, until she saw that Mr. Hagen appeared to be in pain. "Try yawning," she advised him.

"My ears are fine," he snapped. "It's my stomach."

"Oh." Toni blinked in surprise, grabbed the nearest handhold and used it to push herself to the emergency first aid cabinet built into the wall. She grabbed an anti-nausea patch, bounced off the wall, caught her original handhold with her foot, slapped the patch behind Mr. Hagen's ear, and placed its wrapper carefully in a pocket of her jumpsuit to be put in the trash later. Anything dropped in a zero-G environment tended to float about until someone made the effort to retrieve it.

She set his hand on a grab bar next to the air lock. "Just stay here for a few minutes until your body adjusts." She paused and added diffidently, "I'm sorry. I should have asked if *you* had zero-G experience."

"Just underwater," he replied, "and there is a lot more difference than I expected there to be."

"I suppose there must be," Toni said, being careful not to give a hint of her own recent opportunity to compare the two. "Water is a lot thicker than air, although we've made the air here thicker than it is in the rest of the ship. That reminds me," she added, "I've been studying *Das Rheingold,* and there's something about the first scene that puzzles me. It takes place underwater, right?"

"Yes." Mr. Hagen seemed to be recovering; either the medication was taking effect or Toni was proving a sufficient distraction.

"It makes a certain amount of sense for the Rhine-maidens to be able to breathe and sing underwater," Toni pointed out, "but how come Alberich can? Aren't dwarves creatures of Earth rather than Water? Why doesn't he drown?"

"Alberich is not a simple dwarf," Mr. Hagen explained. "He is one of the lesser gods. Not like Wotan and his happy little family in Valhalla—" he grinned, and Toni, remembering all the bickering that went on among the gods in Valhalla, grinned back appreciatively, "—more like Loge."

"Oh, of course!" Toni said. "That's why Loge calls him brother."

"He also calls him *'Nacht-Alberich'*—do you know what that means?"

"Night, or maybe dark?" Toni asked.

"Precisely," Mr. Hagen said. "Loge is the other side of Alberich, Day-Alberich or Bright-Alberich—in short, Fire."

"And they seem to get along about as well as most siblings," Toni remarked. "I'm glad I'm an only child. Between Loge, and Wotan, and the Rhinemaidens—I don't blame Alberich for putting a curse on the ring. I'd have done the same thing." Then another thought occurred to her. "Is Alberich immortal?"

Mr. Hagen's lips compressed tightly together for an instant.

"No. Even the high gods were not immortal."

"Oh, yes," Toni remembered. "They all got killed when Valhalla burned up. But Alberich survived, and you and Loge and the Rhinemaidens lived through *Gotterdammerung,* and you're still alive now." *Oh, no!* she thought, aghast at her slip of the tongue. *I'm not supposed to know that he was alive then.*

But Hagen was too lost in memory to notice. "Not all of us," he said. "We don't die naturally, but we can be killed. Alberich is dead now."

"Poor soul," Toni said, discovering that she really meant it, and resolving that *this* time she wasn't going to ask how someone had died. "The ring should go to his son, then, shouldn't it?" She frowned. "But the way the curse is set up, it sounds as though it would work against even Alberich's son."

Mr. Hagen stared at her. "What do you mean?"

"I've been studying the opera," Toni pointed out, "and the curse *is* rather a central point. The curse says that the ring shall bring death to anyone who wears it, that no one shall find pleasure from it, that the master of the ring shall be its slave, 'until I hold in my hand what was stolen.' It says 'I' not 'I or my heirs.' So if he's dead, there's no way to end the curse, is there?"

Mr. Hagen stared at her. He was looking ill again, and Toni regarded him with concern. "Do you need another anti-nausea patch?"

"I don't think it would help," Mr. Hagen said slowly. "I need to lie down."

"Right," Toni said. She reached out and helped him gently into the air lock.

They cycled back through the air lock, and almost walked into Toni's father.

He looked at Toni searchingly, which did not make her feel any better. "How are things going?" he asked, as Mr. Hagen swerved to avoid him and staggered into the nearest wall.

Toni wrapped Mr. Hagen's unresisting arm about her shoulder and took a good portion of his weight. "Excuse us, please," she said. "Captain, I'll be in sick bay if you need me." She dragged Mr. Hagen down the hallway, wondering what was going on now.

Toni was glad when she got Mr. Hagen to sick bay; he was getting rather heavy. She was thankful to shove him onto the nearest diagnostic couch.

"How are you feeling?" she asked, leaning on the edge of the couch to catch her breath.

"Why was the Captain looking at us like that?" Mr. Hagen asked suspiciously. "And is he the one who named the ship *Loge's Fire?*"

Toni shrugged. "I don't know. Probably not. Somebody named Mr. Loge owns the ship, but he doesn't come here very often."

"And I thought the name was a *good* omen," Mr. Hagen said bitterly. "I should have realized that Loge would own it; it's just the sort of thing that would amuse him. Is he here now? Is your father kin to him?"

"Oh, Lord, I hope not," Toni said fervently. "As far as I know my father is a normal human being, but after the past week I wouldn't bet on *anything* about my family!"

"What happened this past week?"

Toni knew there was no reason why she should trust him, but she felt an odd sense of kinship with the little man. Besides, she had to tell *somebody;* this whole thing was just too crazy. She wanted to see how another person—one who didn't know her—would react to the story. "I turned sixteen, and my father took me on a picnic to the River Rhine, where I was promptly pulled underwater and informed that my mother had been a Rhinemaiden," Toni replied. "It was a bit of a shock to say the least, especially since I never even learned how to swim!"

Mr. Hagen reached out and gently patted her hand, which lay on the couch next to him. "Yes," he agreed reminiscently, "it *is* a shock to learn you're not simply human when you always thought you were. I still remember the day my father showed up to claim me—and that was centuries ago."

"Is Alberich really your father, then?" Toni asked. "They said he was."

"Your aunts?" Hagen demanded. "The Rhinemaidens?"

"Yes," Toni said nodding.

"Yes," Hagen said, "I'm Alberich's son."

*So either this whole thing is true,* Toni thought, *or else he's in on the joke. Well, I'll play along, but not their way. I'm not going to lie and deceive and connive and . . . I'm not going to behave the way* they *do!*

He looked at her consideringly. "You don't look like a Rhinemaiden—or act like one."

"I should hope not!" Toni retorted. "The ones in the opera weren't nice at all—and Aunt Woglinde told me to seduce you to get the ring back!"

Hagen looked amused. "Do I gather you don't plan to?"

"I'm sixteen years old, a virgin, and a Christian," Toni retorted. "Seduction isn't my style. I'm not like my aunts—at least I don't think I am. . . ."

She looked at him. *If he's half-and-half, too, maybe he knows*— "Hagen? Do I have a soul?"

Hagen sat up and put a comforting arm around her shoulders. "Poor child, you *have* had a bad week. Yes, you have a soul," he assured her. "I wondered the same thing about myself, but every priest I've ever met says that if you can formulate that question, you do have a soul. If you didn't, the question would never occur to you."

"Good," Toni sighed with relief. "I was hoping I did. I don't want to treat anyone the way my aunts treated your father. I think seduction is immoral and dishonest. I don't think Alberich deserved it, and I don't think you do, even if you *did* take that stupid ring."

"And by now, half the world must know I have it," Hagen remarked.

"Probably," Toni agreed. "Father was teasing Aunt Woglinde about having lost it again, so he must know."

"He must," Hagen said. "That's undoubtedly why he was hanging about in the corridor. It certainly appears that the curse is working." He frowned. "Did your father tell you to get the ring for him?"

Toni shook her head. "But if the curse is working, maybe you should put the ring back in the Rhine before something awful happens."

"I can't," Hagen said flatly.

"Maybe if we can break the curse, you can give it up," Toni said. "The inability to let go of it seems to be part of the curse—at least in the operas."

"So is getting killed because you have it," Hagen said grimly.

"Is Loge going to kill you for it if he finds you here?" Toni asked anxiously.

Hagen shook his head. "No, Loge is one of the few beings immune to the desire for it—Loge and the Rhine-maidens."

"That's good," Toni said in relief, "because he probably wouldn't care if he killed everyone on the ship getting the damned thing."

"Loge's immune," Hagen said slowly, "but your father isn't."

Toni stared at him in horror. "No," she whispered, "my father wouldn't—" She stopped, remembering. "He told me to give it to him to put in his safe when I got it from you. . . ."

"The curse is powerful," Hagen said grimly. "We'd better get out of here."

He slid down from the couch and together they headed toward the door. It slid open in front of them, but they both stopped at the sight before them: the Captain holding a gun. "Did you get the ring from him yet, Toni?" he asked intently.

Toni gasped in horror and hit the override control that closed and locked the sick bay door. "You're right," she said to Hagen. "We definitely have to get out of here." She crossed the room, pried the cover off the ventilation duct, and dragged him into it. "And I don't think the main hallways are the way to go."

Toni dragged Hagen to the closest shuttle, moving at a very fast, adrenaline-fueled crawl through spaces that would normally have triggered claustrophobia. But compared to the sight of her father pointing a gun at her, nothing could scare her. She kicked through the cover between the ventilation system and the shuttle bay, dragged Hagen into the nearest shuttle, and launched it as fast as her fingers could hit the controls.

The shuttle left the ship so fast that neither of them had time to strap in, so the first few minutes of the ride were chaotic, to say the least. Hagen, unfortunately, wasn't holding onto anything when they left the ship's gravity field, and Toni hadn't bothered with the proper alignment needed to hold the shuttle's passengers in their seats.

Hagen swore as the acceleration slammed him against the back wall and pinned him there until Toni got the shuttle on the proper course at a constant velocity and was free to retrieve him. She strapped him efficiently into the navigator's chair, and started to reach for the first aid kit. Then she realized that it had been less than two hours since she had put the patch on him in the zero-G hold.

"You don't need another anti-nausea patch, do you?" she asked.

Hagen looked at her blankly. "Anti-nausea patch?"

"The one behind your ear," Toni reminded him. "It's been less than two hours; it should still be working."

Hagen closed his eyes as if taking stock. "I think it's all

right," he said, "but I don't know if that's because it's still working or because I'm just too terrified to feel sick."

"Well, we have a little while now to come up with a plan," Toni said. "Father will undoubtedly follow us, but it will take him time—not much, probably, but some. And I'll crash us into the Rhine if I have to. You can breathe the water, can't you?"

"Why do you assume I can breathe water?" Hagen asked suspiciously.

"Because your father could, and because whoever took the ring would have to."

"Not necessarily," Hagen pointed out. "There's always scuba gear."

"The Rhinemaidens aren't deaf."

"All right, yes. I can breathe underwater. Can your father?"

"Not as far as I know." Toni frowned. "But I would really prefer not to crash-land in the Rhine. These shuttles are expensive, and I don't want to watch you and the Rhinemaidens fighting a battle for possession of the ring—you do have the damned thing on you, don't you?"

"It's not something one leaves lying about."

"No," Toni snapped. "I'll bet it's on a chain about your neck, lying next to your heart."

Hagen glared at her.

"There's *got* to be a way out of this," Toni said, thinking furiously. "When did your father die?"

Hagen gaped at her. "What do you care?" he asked.

"Please, Hagen, just answer the question. When did he die, and what happened to his body? Was it cremated?"

"Of course not!" Hagen said in horror. "He would have hated that. He's laid out properly in a nice underground cavern."

"How long has he been dead?"

"About two weeks. Why?"

"The curse says 'Until again I hold in my hand what was stolen'—it doesn't say he has to be alive."

"That's the craziest idea I've ever heard!" Hagen exclaimed.

"It can't be!" Toni said angrily. "I've heard a dozen

crazier things this week! My father pointing a gun at me is definitely crazy! All you have to do is put the ring in Alberich's hand—you can take it right back after you do. Surely you don't think he's going to magically arise from the dead and keep it!"

Hagen looked thoughtful. "Probably not," he admitted.

"And it's not as if we have much of a chance any other way," Toni pointed out. "If the curse isn't broken, we'll probably both die." She pointed to a screen on the panel between them. "My father is already following us. I only hope nobody else is with him."

Hagen shuddered. "On that we agree. But what stops *you* from taking the ring if I put it in my father's hand?"

Toni glared at him. "The same thing that stopped me from taking it when you were flailing about helplessly in the back of the cabin—I don't *want* the cursed thing!"

"Your aunts do."

"I'm not my aunts." Toni tapped the dot on screen impatiently. "Look! At least one person is after us already, and the longer you hang on to that accursed ring, the more people will want to kill us. Now where do I land?"

Hagen looked at her in bewilderment. "Why are you doing this? You could dump me anyplace and be out of this mess. You don't have to help me."

"I think it may be too late for that," Toni said. "As for why I'm helping you. . . ." She tried to find words for what she had felt from the moment she had realized who and what he was. "I guess it's because of what we have in common. We're both the children of people who tried to use us to fulfill their own goals, people who never expected us to think for ourselves, or even to *be* ourselves."

Hagen stared at her for a long moment, then called up a map on the navigator's screen. "Put us down here," he said, tapping a stubby finger on the screen.

They landed just outside the entrance to a cave. It appeared to be a rather large cave, but the area around it was so heavily wooded that there was barely room to land one shuttle. "Good," Toni muttered as they climbed out. "Father will have to find somewhere else to land."

"Hurry up," Hagen said, taking her arm and dragging her into the cave.

"Wait!" Toni said urgently. "I forgot to bring the hand light."

"We don't want it," Hagen said. "It would only make us easier to find. If your eyes can't adapt to the dark, I'll lead you—or you can stay behind."

"Lead the way," Toni said grimly. She hated small dark spaces, but she didn't want to see her father again until the curse was off the ring.

It seemed to her that they moved through near-darkness forever. Her eyes did adapt to what little light there was, but she had never considered rotting lichen an attractive light source. And the tunnels they were following kept getting smaller; they walked bent over and then had to crawl. It seemed like hours before Hagen stood up and pulled Toni to her feet. They were in a large cavern, and in the center of the cavern was a stone slab. The body on the slab was lit by pairs of torches at its head and feet.

"My father," Hagen sighed.

Toni looked down at the body. It was dressed in rich and very archaic clothing, and was still in an excellent state of preservation. The hands lay open and empty at its sides.

"Which hand?" Hagen whispered.

"Best to use both, I think," Toni whispered back. "The curse didn't specify which one."

She stood next to Alberich's head, reached out and placed her own hands under his, lifting them into a cupped position over his waist. They were cold and dry against her skin. "Put the ring in his hands," she said softly.

Hagen stared at her as he slowly removed a silver chain from around his neck. An ornate golden ring dangled from the chain. Slowly he lowered it into the cupped palms of the body before them.

Toni stared at the ring. "It's beautiful," she said in

wonder. "What incredible craftsmanship." She felt her
eyes fill with tears. "It's so sad that anyone capable of
creating so much beauty could ever feel any need to
renounce love." On an inexplicable impulse, she bent her
head and kissed Alberich's forehead. "For the great
wrong done to you by my kin," she said, looking down at
his face, "I am truly sorry. I wish that you could forgive
them, and all who wronged you."

Hagen's gasp brought her head back up. She followed
his gaze to the ring in Alberich's hands. It was melting.

As Hagen and Toni watched, the ring became a smooth
puddle of gold. Hagen lifted the chain out of it, and the
gold solidified into a lump.

"The Rheingold," Hagen said softly. "It reverted to its
original state." He looked at her. "You did it, Toni. You
broke the curse."

"No, you did," Toni said. "You're the one who put it in
his hands. I didn't realize that it would destroy the ring,"
she added, "but it should be easy enough to remake. All
you have to do is renounce love, and you'll know how."

Hagen shook his head. "I have no intention of
renouncing love," he said firmly. "I feel as if I have just
awakened from a horrible lifelong nightmare." He paused,
apparently searching for words. "I think I'm at peace."

He scooped up the gold and handed it to her. "Here,
take this back to your aunts, and tell them to guard it
better in the future."

Toni stared at the gold in her palm. "Are you sure?"

"Quite sure," Hagen replied. "Unless, of course, *you*
have ambitions to renounce love and rule the world."

"No," Toni said. "I just want to go home, and to have
my father be all right and still love me. Or at least tolerate me."

"Follow me," Hagen said, leading the way across the
cavern and down a short tunnel that led into water.
"That's the Rhine," he said. "Take the gold down there,
and I'm sure your aunts will find you."

"Farewell, Hagen," Toni said. "And thank you."

"Thank you," Hagen replied.

Toni secured the gold in one of her pockets and dove

into the river. She filled her lungs with water and let the current carry her. Soon she found herself near the cave where she had met Flosshilde and the others. She swam easily into the cave, and found Flosshilde still sitting on the same rock as before.

"You have the ring." It was not a question.

"Not exactly, Aunt." Toni opened her pocket and removed the gold. It caught what little light there was in the cave and magnified it tenfold. "I have the Rheingold."

Flosshilde stared at it for a long moment before pointing to a small depression in the top of the highest rock. "It belongs there," she said. Toni swam up and put the gold back into place. A ray of sunlight struck it and made the entire cavern glow golden.

Glowing water swirled all about the cavern as the rest of the Rhinemaidens arrived. "The Rheingold," they whispered in awe.

"What happened?" Woglinde demanded.

"Hagen and I broke the curse on it, and the ring melted," Toni said. "Then Hagen gave it to me and told me to return it to you and bid you guard it well."

"Alberich's son willingly gave up the Rheingold?" Flosshilde asked.

"Yes," Toni replied, looking around at the assembled Rhinemaidens. "After all, you never did anything to Hagen; it was Alberich you wronged."

"Wronged?" Woglinde said incredulously. "We were just playing a game with him."

"In the future," Toni said, "I would suggest that you not play that kind of game. Not everyone appreciates it." She slid smoothly off her rock. "If you have no objections, I'm going home." No one said anything or moved to stop her as she swam out of the cave and downstream to the spot where she and her father had picnicked only a week before. She surfaced cautiously in mid-stream and saw her father watching anxiously from the bank. His shuttle was parked behind him.

"Toni!" he exclaimed. "My poor child, are you all right?"

"I think so," Toni said cautiously, looking to see if he

still had his gun. "Are *you* all right? Do you still want the ring?"

"No," her father said, shaking his head in bewilderment. "I can't imagine why I ever thought I did want it. There's a spare jumpsuit in the shuttle. Why don't you come put on some dry clothes, and we'll go home."

"Sounds good to me." Toni climbed out of the river and went home with her father.

Two weeks later her father called her to his quarters. "This just came for you," he said, handing her a flat box. Toni opened it and gasped. To one who had seen the Rheingold, all other gold would forever be a pale imitation, but the craftsmanship on the jewelry in the box was breathtaking.

"It's beautiful," she said, looking at a necklace of gold strips interwoven in an intricate pattern. "Did you order this for me?"

"No," her father said. "Read the card." He shoved a small white envelope toward her. Inside was a square of plain white cardboard. "For Toni," it read. "Happy Belated Sixteenth Birthday—and many more." It was signed "Your Friend, Hagen."

*Many more,* Toni thought. *I wonder how many. Probably rather a lot. I expect I'll be glad to have Hagen as a friend.*

*This story came from a combination of things: my years as a supernumerary at the San Francisco Opera (I've been a dwarf in* Das Rheingold *twice, so I've seen first hand how difficult staging the parts in the River Rhine is); my experiences at the U.S. Space Academy, which taught me a bit about what variable gravity and weightlessness feel like; and something Anna Russell said in her justly famous talk on Wagner's Ring Cycle. She remarked that at the end of the four operas "you're right back where you started, sixteen hours ago" and wondered if the whole thing could start all over again. Well, most of the gods are dead, but there are some survivors . . . and the ring is still cursed. . . .*

# A SONG OF STRANGE REVENGE

## *by Josepha Sherman*

Josepha Sherman is a fantasy writer and folk-
lorist whose latest novels are *The Shattered
Oath* and its sequel, *Forging the Runes,* and
latest folklore book is *Trickerster Tales*.

We often sang together, my love and I, my own sweet
Yaromir. We sang together and loved and laughed
together. And we would have wed together—we whose
blood was of the oldest lines, then, when I was known as
Mlada. Our joining would have formed a sacred balance,
he the stallion, I the mare, he the fertile seed, I the waiting
earth. It would have made a rightful, joyous song against
the Dark that always seeks to overwhelm the Light—

When I was alive.

Now I—I sing alone, my voice a whisper on the wind,
unheard by Yaromir, and the balance we would have created has been upset, leaning ever more toward the Dark;
while he—akh, he is sought, weakened by mourning as he
is, by another, a living maid, Voislava the lovely, the
regal. Voislava, my cousin—

Voislava, my murderer.

I circle her, unseen by her, I see with my now-more-
than-mortal sight. She sings so sweetly, lovely young
Voislava, as sweetly as ever did I when I yet lived. But
her songs are tainted, as her mind and heart are tainted.
Tormented is young Voislava, tormented for love of
Yaromir, tormented into madness. She has spoken to
Darkness in her yearning, I feel it now, she has spoken to
an evil force, to Moreva. Was it that One who placed the
thought of murder in Voislava's mind? Was it Moreva

who pushed the balance toward the Dark in such a small, perilous way? Voislava's thoughts are tinged with red, lust-red, death-red, and it was surely no great thing for her to poison me.

And if she wins Yaromir . . . I tell myself it is the last faint touch of mortal jealousy that troubles me, no more than that, but I can no longer lie. Voislava is royal as was I, Yaromir is royal: the Darkness would be claiming two lands at once.

Akh, Yaromir is strong, I tell myself; Voislava's plans will come to nothing.

But she has begun to learn strange powers from her patron. Moreva, appearing like a dear old granny, full of charm and warmth, shows her how to blind the human will. And so, I come to realize, Voislava's father thinks only that an alliance between his and Yaromir's lines would be a good strong thing, never once remembering that I, too, was of his line. And so Voislava's father knows nothing, or thinks he knows nothing, of his daughter's ever-deepening descent into madness and the Dark.

And, thanks to those skills Voislava learns from foul Moreva, neither does Yaromir suspect—oh, Yaromir, my love, who sees only a charming young woman whom he does not love but does not wish to harm.

Voislava despairs. I see her unable to pierce Yaromir's shield of polite disinterest. The night is dark, but that is no barrier to she who sees with the eyes of Darkness. The night is dark, but that is no barrier to me, who sees with the eyes of the dead. So I follow her from her father's palace out into a wild barrenness of rock. I can feel no cold, but I shiver to hear Voislava call on her Dark mentor.

"Moreva." Her voice is wheedling, like that of a small girl begging a treat from her granny. "Moreva."

But when Moreva suddenly is there, it is not in the guise of a humble granny. The Dark may have its own terrible beauty by which it snares the unwary, and it is a beautiful woman who appears before Voislava—a woman of no earthly breeding, with eyes that look upon Eternity and find it empty.

"What would you, child?"

Oh, the music in that voice. Oh, the wondrous, horrifying songs it could sing! Voislava trembles, but her answer is bold enough: "You told me it would be easy to win Yaromir."

"Why, so it shall be!"

"How? When? I want him!" It is a spoiled child's wail. "He will not yield to me."

Moreva smiles. I cannot describe the coldness in that smile, not and still cling to the last of my humanity. "He shall," she purrs.

She tells Voislava of the festival to come, the joyous Feast of Kupalo of the Springtime. The feast, I think with a ghost's faint bitterness, at which Yaromir and I were to wed. Moreva tells Voislava of the dances she must dance with Yaromir, of the songs she must sing to him, of the words within those songs.

And as I listen, I all but scream my horror. I know, as only one no longer mortal can know, that these spell-songs will snare him, mind and will and soul. I know, too, now that Moreva has no intention of simply snaring the man for Darkness; oh, no, she means more than this one bit of petty malice. Her spell-songs, the truest perversion of music, will steal like the chill night mist into Yaromir's heart and soul, into the hearts and souls of all his followers, into all in both those lands. Hope will fade in that chill; joy and goodness will fade as well. Moreva will use this one mortal woman, this one mortal man, as the means to destroy all Light in two lands in one neat stroke of song.

Does Voislava know? Does she see what her patron means to do?

In my despair, I must have made some sound inaudible to mortal ears but perfectly clear to the Other. Morena's too perfectly sculptured head turns as sharply as that of a hunting wolf. "We are watched," she says, and I know she realizes who and what I am. I fly as swiftly as ever spirit flew, and though I have no mortal heart to pound in my

misty chest, the terror I feel is very real. Will Morena
catch me? Destroy me?

No. She has clearly decided that one small human ghost
is hardly worth the trouble of a hunt. After all, she must
surely be thinking, what can anyone as powerless as I do
to stop her?

What, indeed? If Voislava wins Yaromir's heart and
hand and soul—no, I vow, no, that shall not be.

But in my innermost self, the ageless, immortal self,
I know it is already too late for such dramatics. The balance has, with Morena's summoning, already tipped too
far. No simple rejection of Voislava's tainted love will
restore it.

And song comes to me without bidding, songs of
prayer. I have not remembered prayer since I entered this
not-living, not-dead state. But if living Voislava may call
upon demon Morena of the Dark, surely I, unliving
Mlada, may call upon the goddess Lada, Lady of the
Light.

Does she hear me, heed me? I cannot tell. But I speed
on to Yaromir. I speed to my sweet love where he sleeps
out under the stars like a man so troubled he can no longer
bear the crowded palace walls. And I plead with him as I
pleaded with Lada, "Hear me, heed me!"

I still linger, pleading helplessly, when Voislava returns
like a pale wraith herself, half-drained of her humanity.
She pauses to look down on sleeping Yaromir, and a
smile, the faintest chill echo of Morena's smile, plays on
her lips.

And I know in this one startling moment what I should
have known before: why I could not wake my love nor let
him hear me. Once again the balance is before me;
Voislava the Dark, I the Light, she the living, I the dead—
a tenuous, perilous balance. I am here and she is here, and
Yaromir wakes with a start, seeing Voislava standing over
him, yet knowing I, too, am there. I hear his quick little
indrawn gasp and know he loves me yet.

Voislava knows it, too. As I struggle to tell my tale, she
cries like a woman terrified, "A trick! A demon's trick!
Akh, akh, heed it not!"

Her living voice is far stronger than my ghostly whisper. Yaromir cannot hear me. But I, already seeing my love taken from the Light, do the only thing left to me and sing—sing of love and joy, sing of Lada, Lady of the Light. And this, Yaromir does hear.

"Sing!" he commands Voislava. "Sing praises of Lada with me."

Voislava cannot sing. Morena's Darkness fills her mind with a blood-red fog, and she cannot even speak Lada's name.

And I sing Truth into my song. I sing at last of my murder. I sing of the balance upset and the plans of Darkness. Yaromir whirls, falcon-swift as he ever was in battle, and I know he realizes that he dare not hesitate. I see his sword flash, I see Voislava fall, I see my murderer fall, and there is enough of the human left to me to glory in the sight.

But all is not ended. The balance is not returned. For Voislava, dying, cries not for forgiveness. Akh, no, she calls, "Morena! Morena! My blood the summons, my soul the seal. Here is no balance—let your Darkness reign!"

Her life flees. Her spirit swirls away into the endless night. Alone, I can no longer reach my love with words, let him see or hear or even sense me there. I cannot tell him, sick with my sudden horror, what he must do.

Yet he knows. The presence of Morena is all around us—feeding on him, drawn by his life, rejoicing with cold, cold delight in the Darkness yet to come.

And Yaromir says, as quietly as a man speaking of the weather, "No. You shall not have this. Most surely not through me. Hear me, all you gods: Mlada is innocent of Darkness, I am innocent of Darkness—and that Darkness shall not have our lands!"

He turns the sword in his hand. He lunges, and I sob to see the bright metal pierce him through. The link with Morena breaks, and sudden wild, bright moonlight pours down around us. The Darkness is banished.

But in this overwhelming moment, I don't care. In this moment I am nothing more than a human woman mourning for her love. I watch Yaromir sag slowly to the ground, and I hover over him, wishing I could weep.

But I hover over an empty husk. Yaromir is here beside me, and we cling to each other, spirit to spirit. Where will we go now? What will we do? That is still to be learned. All that matters now is us together, free of Darkness or despair. We are avenged, the balance is restored, and our lands will have their chance to live in peace. Singing as joyously as ever we did in life, we leave the living world behind us.

*This story was written to avenge a particularly disastrous Bolshoi production of Rimsky-Korsakov's opera, Mlada—the sort of production in which the director knows better than the composer what the music means! (In this case, it was a group of embarrassed-looking singers in burlap bags and bare feet!)*

# SONGCHILD
## by Robin Wayne Bailey

Robin Wayne Bailey is the author of numerous
short stories and novels, most recently *Shadowdance.* He lives in Kansas City, Missouri.

Alone upon her planet's highest pinnacle, Jilraen watched
the feeble sun rise. A chill passed through her, as it
always did at the sight. A bleak white ball that offered
neither warmth, nor adequate light, it crawled up from the
barren, featureless horizon through unrelenting darkness.

For long hours, she sat unmoving, doing penance
for her unspeakable crime. The sun passed zenith, slid
down the far side of the sky, and disappeared. Still, she
didn't move.

A handful of pitiful stars perforated the blackness. She
counted them accurately, one by one, and suddenly, her
rigid demeanor melted. Leaning her head upon her knees,
she wept quiet, grieving tears and remembered a time
when infinite stars had spangled the heavens.

A rare breeze rustled the graceful black quills that grew
long upon her head. Drying her eyes, she arched her neck
and inhaled, hoping for the hint of a flower's fragrance,
the smell of a raindrop, or the sweet tang of a distant
ocean come once more to surging life.

The sterile breeze teased her, kissed her upturned face,
then died away. She sighed with disappointment, a wistful
and lonely sound.

On the ground beside her lay a small harp. Bleached
white wood, worn smooth by her fingers, made its body,
and the slender silver strings gleamed like liquid strands.

She picked it up and hugged it to her body, rocking it like a precious child against her naked breasts.

Staring down from her high place, she gazed at the barren panorama that stretched before her. Even through the darkness, she saw the gentle roll and swell of rocky plains; the towering sweep of distant mountains; the empty, frozen seabeds of the world she called Yvala; and a pang stabbed her heart.

Raising her harp before her face, she gazed through the strings and tried to think of a song. If she sang her heart out, maybe she could make the sky weep with sorrow. Maybe she could make the rains fall and the oceans finally return.

A gust of wind shivered over the strings, raising a cascade of random notes. Jilraen stilled the sound immediately with her palm, frowning at the delicate cacophony. Capricious noise, she thought, without melody or pattern, without beauty or skill or feeling.

The wind rushed impatiently around her pinnacle; it rasped over the plain below, raising a veil of dust. If the night craved music, Jilraen could do better than these crude sounds. She closed her eyes and began to conjure with her three-fingered hands upon the silver strings.

The sounds of the ocean flowed suddenly from her harp as she unleashed the soft susurrus of surf and tide, the cries of gulls, the hushed murmur of lovers' voices on the sand in the night. Then from her throat poured a golden, textured richness of sound that soared beside the music her fingers made.

She sang her memories of the sea, of sparkling waves and Yvala's sun-drenched shores, of many-sailed ships gloriously skimming the waters. She sang a half-remembered story from her childhood, of a woman who fell in love with the sea, who strode naked into its burning depths, gave herself to it, and bore the sea's child.

Her voice broke, and she stopped, her song unfinished. A hideous, unbearable guilt swept over her, causing her to shiver uncontrollably.

Then, from behind came a ghostly laugh and a whispered chant.

*"Foolish, foolish
Child of magic!
Ocean-lover—
Very tragic!"*

Jilraen leaped up, wiping her tears with one hand as she whirled around, clutching her harp in the other. A deeper, angrier voice joined the first.

*"Helper, Healer,
Harper, Singer—
World killer,
Doombringer."*

At first, Jilraen saw nothing. Then the darkness overhead swirled, and pieces of the night coalesced into a pair of shapes. She caught her breath and took a step backward to the very edge of the precipice as she recognized the faces of her gods. "Tsharmirh!" she cried. "Kabahhh!"

Tsharmirh and Kabahhh turned two ethereal jumpropes made from starlight that stretched from one horizon to the other. A third figure, the goddess Mitiri, appeared suddenly between the strands, dancing on the black sky in that ancient game of skipping rope. As she skipped the ropes, she chanted in a mocking, childlike voice:

*"Poor Jilraen found a spell;
She didn't cast it very well.
Look and see what she has done—
Murdered, murdered everyone!"*

Jilraen's right hand curled into a fist. How dare they come to her in the forms of children? They were old gods, ancient creatures. They took these shapes only to taunt and hurt her!

"You shouldn't have interrupted me!" she shouted bitterly, shaking her harp at them. "I was close to succeeding that time! I was bringing the oceans back!"

Mitiri brushed one hand through her beautifully colored

quills and grinned as she skipped between the whirling ropes.

> *"Silly woman! It's so sad!*
> *How much longer till you go mad?*
> *One, two, three, four. . . ."*

"I can bring it back!" Jilraen screamed, a red rage fueled by their taunts building inside her. "I can bring it all back. The oceans were coming just now, but you scared them away when you interrupted!" She raised the harp high over her head as if to show them the returning waters reflected on the silver strings. "Leave me alone to do my work!"

Laughing, Mitiri danced out and took the ends of the ropes from Tsharmirh, whose turn it was to jump. Tsharmirh, a shy little boy with an unruly display of quills, wagged one of his three fingers at Jilraen as he skipped into the ropes. A vicious smile split his innocent-seeming face.

> *"Once came a lady with an evil plan*
> *To drink up all the magic in the land.*
> *First went the oceans, then went the sky,*
> *Then went the people in the wink of an eye!"*

Kabahhh and Mitiri laughed appreciatively, and Tsharmirh danced out to exchange places with Kabahhh.

"Go away!" Jilraen demanded, her voice taking on a lower, threatening tone. "This isn't the first time you've interrupted me." Her quills rose, standing nearly on end as a warning. "I won't tolerate your interference!"

Kabahhh ignored her. The most graceful of the deities, and a show-off besides, he jumped first on one leg, then the other.

> *"Good Jilraen found a spell*
> *To suit her purpose very well;*
> *Gathered all the magic for her own,*
> *And turned her world to a cold, cold stone!"*

"Don't you understand?" she said. "I can remake it! I have the power!" An unexpected rush of tears spilled from her eyes. She stepped backward, off the edge of the pinnacle, then took another step beyond, not falling. Instead she climbed, as if walking backward up an invisible stair.

If the three deities were impressed, they failed to show it. Kabahhh continued the game with a final bit of mockery.

> *"The gods jump rope with their own lifelines,*
> *But see? Jilraen has become divine!"*

"I didn't do it on purpose!" Jilraen cried. Her face darkened with anger. She raised her harp like a weapon now, and her hand poised over the harp strings. At the brush of her thumb, the darkness swirled around her like a maelstrom. She glared out from its center and issued a warning. "I can make you go away."

Mitiri glared back, her face no longer childlike. Ancient eyes, like mirrors, reflected the surface of the dead world below, and the images stabbed Jilraen's heart like daggers.

Tsharmirh, too, changed. Dropping his child's guise, he transformed into a beast with claws that cut swaths across the sky, making pale streaks like scars on the night, as he reached for Jilraen.

The child, the old woman, and the monster surrounded her, but Jilraen didn't cower back. "I've beaten you before," she said with weary dismay. "Why don't you help me instead?" She lifted her harp like a shield. The pathetically weak light from the sun caught the strings. For an instant, they gleamed brilliantly.

"You little fool," Mitiri hissed, as Jilraen's harp turned aside Tsharmirh's claws, "Even after all this time, you don't understand what you've done!"

With a shock, Jilraen felt the intensity of Mitiri's hatred, and recoiled from it. Staring through the strings of her harp, she turned toward the goddess. "Join me,

Mitiri!" she pleaded. "You were a goddess of love to my people!"

Mitiri's furious scream ripped a jagged canyon in the plain below the pinnacle, and the echo rolled across the face of dead Yvala. "Your people are dead! Love is dead. I'm only the ghost of Mitiri!"

"And you're dead, too, Jilraen," Kabahhh said accusingly in his hurt child's voice. "Where it counts—in your heart and soul."

"I can bring it all back," Jilraen insisted stubbornly. "I just need time. More time to find the music!"

"Fool!" Tsharmirh said. "There's nothing left. Come die with us."

Mitiri's voice softened. "More time has passed than you realize, Songchild," she said. "You've tried and failed. Some things cannot be undone."

"No!" Jilraen shouted, tears blurring her vision. "You're lying!" She struck a chord on the harp, and the notes shot forth like arrows. Mitiri screamed. Jilraen fired another chord, an octave higher than the first. Tsharmirth's claws shattered into burning fragments that, for a moment, hung in the night like reborn stars.

"I warned you!" Jilraen said, turning toward Kabahhh.

The child god backed slowly away, one protective arm around a cowering, blinded Mitiri, pulling her with him. Reaching out, he caught Tsharmirh's arm and dragged him closer, too, while the monster stared at his hands and wept in pain. Retreating into the heavens, the night folded around them, and they faded away.

"Wait!" Jilraen called suddenly, too late.

Alone again. She clutched her harp to her breasts and shivered. "Wait," she whispered, knowing no one would hear. Sadly, she gazed groundward and walked down the sky to stand once more upon her pinnacle.

"Lonely," she murmured to herself as she sank to her knees and laid the harp on the rocky soil. "I'm lonely," she repeated to the instrument. Without her touch, it offered no answer. Slowly, she lay down in despair and curled around the harp, numb, too tired to think, frightened that the deities had been right. Parting her quills, she drew them over her face.

She didn't know how many times the faded sun rose and set before she sat up again. She had not slept exactly. She didn't sleep anymore. She had simply withdrawn to some inner place of silence where no music played in her mind, and hidden there.

Or perhaps she had healed. Guilt weighed less upon her, a burden made lighter by new hope. She felt a potent determination, a special strength as she sat up. Looking around for the sun, she spied it, a milky spot perched on the eastern horizon. Morning, then. Today, she would set aside her usual penance. There was work to do, a world to recreate.

The breeze played over her nakedness as she rose and stretched. Mischievously, it tried to raise a chord from her harp strings as she picked up the instrument, but she stilled the chaotic splash of notes with her hand.

In her mind, she carefully constructed a melody. Seating herself on the pinnacle's edge, positioning the harp between her thighs, she gazed out over dry, dusty Yvala. She could bring it back, she told herself, remembering when her world was green and alive. She could bring it all back.

The melody in her head sprang to life on the silver strings. Her right hand played the tune; her left hand wove layers of harmony.

Hope surged in her breast. Jilraen rejoiced at the beauty of her composition. She knew she had found it this time, the right music! The notes swirled high into the air, lovelier than anything she had ever played, and exploded with a glimmering light.

Rain!

Jilraen screamed with happy delight. Placing the harp on her lap, she flung back her head and raised her arms to the shower. The cold wet touch on her skin thrilled her. Cupping her three-fingered hands, she caught some water in her palms and raised it to her lips. The sweet taste!

She screamed again, shivering with joy. She had forgotten the taste of water; now, to discover it again!

But the dead ground did not drink.

Jilraen's joy turned suddenly bitter. The dust at her feet remained dry. Yvala rejected the rain; it evaporated as quickly as it touched the soil. The dust rose contemptuously, and the wind laughed at her.

Biting her lip, she picked up the harp again and plucked a series of shimmering chords. This time she sang the melody, filling the air with a raw sentimentality, and the notes of her voice transformed into tiny, fluttering birds. For an instant, the night sparkled with golden plumage.

The birds faded as swiftly as the notes of which they were made.

Disappointed, Jilraen did not lose hope. She felt the magic strong within her now, stronger than ever. But she had sat too long upon her pinnacle, too high above the land, too far from Yvala's heart. Walking the world below, she would find inspiration for a still greater song.

Rain and birds had come at her calling. When she called again, they would stay.

Clutching her harp, she rose and stepped beyond the pinnacle's edge. Walking on the very molecules of air, she descended, brushing her harp strings as she went, singing to awaken the world.

The air stirred with the wings of hummingbirds, the buzz of bees. Flowers crept up shyly, cracking the rocky soil to burst into colored bloom. The sun ignited, and from far beyond the mountains came a breeze bearing the salt tang of returning oceans and the sound of waves slamming on majestic rocks.

Heart brimming with pride, Jilraen took the last step to the ground. She remembered this plain, these low rolling hills. She had danced here and gathered herbs on those rare nights when three full moons hung opulently in the sky.

Here, in her younger years, she had met Yvala's Feyfolk. They taught her much about healing and the natural magic that suffused their world.

Then, almost by accident, Jilraen found the Ranerok—the One Spell. She swallowed, remembering, and her fingers stumbled briefly on the harp strings.

The Feys had been the first to fade away.

She touched the strings anew and sang the fairy songs she recalled from that long-ago time. Let the hills hear those songs again, and let the land remember with her. "Come, Fey children!" she sang. "Dance with me, and call down the moons. Yvala lives again!" She tried to recall their names. They would answer if she spoke their names.

But memory failed her—too much time had gone by. Undaunted, she sang, calling to them, filling her music with Power, building a bridge to hasten their return as she strode through their hills.

An old riverbed ambled down out of the hills, and she stopped on its wind-eroded bank. She remembered the river, even its name. "Letye!" she sang, stroking her harp. "Come!" The sound that poured from her harp was the sound of water tinkling gently over smooth stones between shaded banks.

She followed the river down the plain to the bed of Great Mother Ocean. The beach glittered like black, broken glass. As Jilraen walked out upon it, she stopped singing, and her fingers froze. An enormous, smothering fear enwrapped her.

Where once great waves had lapped the sand, there was no sound at all, no surf, no soothing susurrus of tides, no whisper of curling seafoam. The utter stillness and desolation paralyzed her.

She had bathed in this ocean, played and laughed here. Where was the sound of girlish laughter now? Where was the rush of wind and water?

Clutching her heart, she stared out at the empty sea, striving to remember sparkling water and a salt perfume that tickled the nose. She squeezed her eyes shut, forcing the memories until she almost heard the soft booming of waves again.

Tears leaked from beneath her lids. Jilraen bent forward to let them fall into the once-sea. Feeble atonement, such small drops of moisture, for the abundance she had unwittingly destroyed.

As she wept into the dry bed, she played once more

upon her harp. A low song filled with anguish and regret flowed from her throat. Sinking down upon the harsh shore, she sang all the chanties, all the sea-ballads, all the ship-songs she could remember. The music that rose from her strings were sounds of wind and foam and breakers, guy-wires and ships' rigging, creaking wharves, gulls.

She sang as she had never sung, her heart full of longing for what was lost, voice full of yearning for its return. "Come back," she sang.

But when Jilraen opened her eyes, she saw that nothing had truly changed. As far as she could see with her magical sight, Yvala was still dead. She had hung a pretty shroud over it, no more. She stopped singing, stopped playing, and all that she had striven to create disappeared as the last note quavered away.

The harp fell from her numbed hands. A crash of disharmony wailed upward, and that, too, faded. Then a single silver string plinked and separated into two curling pieces. With a cry of despair, Jilraen swept up the harp and wept over it.

All hope left her. Turning away from the dead sea, she fled back to her lonely pinnacle. It waited like a stone beacon, hard and jutting, her place of penance.

She sang no more, nor did she play. Yvala turned uncounted times, and the pale sun rose and fell without her notice, and two more stars vanished from the heavens. She held her harp gingerly and wept sometimes over the broken string, and deliberately avoided looking upon her world, for she could no longer bear the sight or the guilt.

"Songchild."

Jilraen started at the voice, but didn't bother to look up. It was only Tsharmirh or Mitiri or Kabahhh come to torment her. She stared instead at the broken string, and with one arm she swept her quills forward to conceal her face. Everything she touched, she destroyed.

"Songchild," the voice spoke again. Strangely gentle, it dared to intrude upon her misery and self-pity. "What have you done?"

"I broke my harp," Jilraen whispered with a child's

hurt. Meekly, she held the instrument up to show the broken string.

In that moment, wiping away tears, she gazed skyward. Surprised, she discovered a new presence, a deity that had not visited her before. It wore an aura of weakness and frailty. This god, too, neared the end of its existence.

Jilraen blamed herself. "I'm sorry," she said, hanging her head.

"What have you done?" the voice repeated curiously. There was no anger in the question, no hatred, no accusation. Instead, there was warmth, caring.

Jilraen crumbled. "I found the Ranerok—the One Spell!" she wept, covering her eyes. "I cast it! I killed my people, my entire world. I killed the gods, and I've killed you, too. Forgive me!"

"You didn't know," the voice said. "You didn't understand."

"I didn't understand!" Jilraen echoed. "I was a healer with only a small magic. My music comforted the sick. Sometimes it even made them better. But with the Raneork I could gather the world's magic to myself, become a goddess, and really help my people. That's all the One Spell was supposed to do—give me the power to help others." She banged her fists on her bare breasts and wailed. "So I searched the world for it, and—curse me!— with the help of the Feys, I found it!"

"Then your mind was only mortal," the new presence said. "How could a mortal understand such an age-old thing as the Ranerok?"

Jilraen continued without hearing, pouring out the guilt she had fostered for so long. "It leached magic from every source and poured it into me." Slowly, she rose, went to stand at the edge of the pinnacle, and wept tears that plummeted through the darkness to the dead land below.

"First the Fey disappeared," she said. "Then the fantastic beasts. Then healers, the witches, and sorcerers. The Ranerok sucked away the magic that gave them life." She hugged her harp against her body, rocking it. "And it still didn't stop. How was I to know," she asked, "that *all* life is magical?" She swallowed hard, forcing herself to remember. "The trees and flowers faded. Rivers and oceans, and the life they spawned, dried up. The sun itself died, and the stars, too. My people. . . ."

She choked suddenly, her throat dry and constricted with emotion. She forced the words out. "Their very souls, the divine spark inside each of them. . . ." She hid her face in the palm of one hand and let go a terrible sob. "The Ranerok fed even that to me!"

"I am too weak to help you," the Presence said regretfully.

"All the magic on Yvala," Jilraen sighed. Turning her gaze down again into the darkness surrounding her pinnacle, she balanced on the very edge. If the stone under her feet suddenly crumbled, she might allow herself to fall. "I would die to give it all back."

Despite its obvious weakness, the Presence spoke with waves of soothing power. "You cannot die, Songchild. You have raised yourself beyond mortality."

"You're not mortal either!" Jilraen shouted bitterly. "But you're dying. The Ranerok is killing you as we talk, draining your divinity and pushing you toward oblivion!"

The night sky above the pinnacle churned suddenly, and a shape took form—an infant's shape with gentle eyes and a smile of infinite tolerance.

"I am weak," the young god said, "because I am small and new. Not because my time is ending, but because it just begins."

Jilraen turned a wide-eyed gaze upon the infant. It was no mere image, not a disguise, as Tsharmirh and Mitiri and Kabahhh had used to taunt her. A shock trembled through her as she peered into strangely shimmering eyes and saw in them something of the ocean's half-remembered blue. She saw something else there, too—something of herself.

"Songmother," the Presence whispered, nodding.

Jilraen pressed a hand to her lips and squeezed her eyes shut. This was a dream. Or madness had finally claimed her, as Mitiri had warned.

"Look toward the ocean, Songmother," the Presence instructed. "See what you have made."

Jilraen dared to open her eyes. Turning, she stared seaward, defying distance, to the place on the shattered beach where she had sung her sea-songs.

Right where she had dropped the harp, where the edge of the tide might once have reached, grew a handful of flowers, weird flowers like none she had ever seen. Heart-shaped blossoms, so deeply scarlet that the color hurt her eyes, swayed on long yellow stalks. A small spring bubbled up from the black ground to feed them, and tiny streams of water trickled down among the rocks into the seabed.

Shutting her eyes again, she wept for joy, filled with a sudden new insight. A jarring chord had risen from her broken harp—music not of her making, beyond her control.

All her careful compositions!

What an arrogant fool she had been!

She had tried to remake the world exactly as she had known it, with carefully constructed melodies, according to her memories. She had plucked so delicately at her strings and sung her magic with a composer's deliberation, note by note.

So many times the random wind had blown across her harp, and she had stifled the strings, smothered the sounds. But for her pride, she might have learned. There, too, Mitiri had warned her. *Some things cannot be undone.* . . .

How could she remake a world she had never completely experienced? How could she rebuild from a few flawed and fragmented memories that were mostly the flashes of a young girl's mortal mind? She knew the Fey and flowers and the ocean. She knew things. She had healed small injuries and sicknesses. But what did she know of true misery and suffering? For that matter, of passion and love? All the myriad intangible things that made a world?

How could she, for all her power, remake Yvala when she knew so little of it? As well try to sing without a voice, or play without her harp.

"Some things cannot be undone," the infant god said as

if it had been the shape of her thoughts, "but new things can arise from the songs of the old." The infant smiled down at her. "You understand now, Songmother."

Jilraen nodded as she held up her harp. She could make Yvala live again, but she would not work with a crippled instrument, would not allow the disharmony of a missing string. The new Yvala must be bright and beautiful, as music was to her. For that, she needed a whole harp.

Bending down upon her knees, she set the harp aside and plucked the longest quill from her head. As the infant god looked on, she chewed and chewed it, softening it, making it pliable with teeth and saliva. She stripped it on a rock, thinning it, and then she chewed it some more.

At last, with a prayer of hope, she kissed it and fixed a new black string in place of the broken silver one.

"What will you play, Songmother?" the infant asked. "What will you sing?"

"Nothing," Jilraen answered. Cradling her instrument, she stepped from the pinnacle and walked down the night to the plain. The infant followed, watching over her shoulder with palpable anticipation.

"Let Yvala play its own music," Jilraen said softly. She raised the harp above her head, and the breeze quivered the strings. A strange vibration rose, and she smiled. It wasn't music to her, the wind in the strings, but it was a kind of music. She poured power into the harp.

The notes turned into a swarm of small, jewel-colored insects, whose fluttering wings made flames in the air.

Jilraen's faint smile blossomed into amazement. "I would never have thought of insects," she said.

Close to her ear, the infant god whispered. "Run, Songmother," he urged. "Run, and never stop!"

Jilraen laughed. Holding the harp high, she ran across the plain, up the hills and down, into the river valleys. The faster she ran, the more the wind poured through her strings. And as the music soared, wonders transpired.

Silver-leaved trees broke suddenly through Yvala's dead crust. Thick carpets of grass spread across the land. The sun burned a bright golden, and the sky turned sapphire blue. Rains fell, filling rivers. Great Mother Ocean surged against new shorelines.

Only once did Jilraen stop as a little girl's laugh touched her ears.

A brown-skinned child climbing on the branch of a tree, reached toward a bird's nest. Her quills were white as seafoam, thin and fine and wavy, not really quills at all, and her hands had five fingers instead of three. But she was beautiful, and there was music in her laughter.

Jilraen ran joyously on, lifting her harp higher. The sun rose and set, rose and set, and she ran.

"Run, Songmother!" the infant called after her. His voice was stronger now, and she could feel his presence with her always, no matter where she ran. "Run—creation is flowing through your harp."

Jilraen laughed without slackening her pace. "When shall I rest?" she asked, though she had no intention of ever resting. She twisted her head over her shoulder, watching wonders spring up in her path.

"When another well-meaning soul discovers the Rane-rok," the infant whispered, unexpectedly grim.

Quietly then, a wrong note slipped from the single black string among all the silver ones. But even if the Songchild heard through her laughter, it was too late to do anything about it.

*This might have been a different story. When Annie sent me a note about the anthology, she scrawled in the margin, "Don't make it too gross, Bailey." Of course, I took it as a playful challenge and wrote a tale of the blues and Bourbon Street and aliens and a serial killer on a quest for the ultimate lyric. However, as I prepared to send it, it occurred to me that scrawl might have been, not a challenge, but a plea. So I prepared "Songchild," instead, a quite different kind of tale, whose roots lie in a recurrent dream I have and a secret I know—that the universe was created, not by God, nor in grand and cosmic explosion, but in a song—a soft bit of music.*

# SASKIA
## By Charles de Lint

Charles de Lint is a full-time author and musician who lives in Ottawa, Canada with his wife
MaryAnn Harris, an artist and musician. His
most recent books are a collection of Newford
stories, *The Ivory and the Horn,* and a novel,
*Memory and Dream.* His new novel, *Trader,* will
be published early in 1997.

> *The music in my heart I bore*
> *Long after it was heard no more.*
> —WORDSWORTH

### 1

I envy the music lovers here.

I see them walking hand in hand, standing close to each
other in a lineup at a theater or subway station, heads
touching while they sit on a park bench, and I ache to hear
the song that plays between them: The stirring chords of
romance's first bloom, the stately airs that whisper
between a couple long in love. You can see it in the way
they look at each other, the shared glances, the touch of a
hand on an elbow, the smile that can only be so sweet for
the one you love. You can almost hear it, if you listen
closely. Almost, but not quite, because the music belongs
to them and all you can have of it is a vague echo that
rises up from the bittersweet murmur and shuffle of your
own memories, ragged shadows stirring restlessly, called
to mind by some forgotten incident, remembered only in

the late night, the early morning. Or in the happiness of
others.

My own happinesses have been few and short-lived,
through no choice of my own. That lack of a lasting
relationship is the only thing I share with my brother
besides a childhood neither of us cares to dwell upon. We
always seem to fall in love with women that circumstance
steals from us; we chase after ghosts and spirits and are
left holding only memories and dreams. It's not that we
want what we can't have; it's that we've held all we could
want and then had to watch it slip away.

2

"The only thing exotic about Saskia," Aaran tells me,
"is her name."

But there's more going on behind those sea-blue eyes
of hers than he can see. What no one seems to realize is
that she's always paying attention. She's listens to you
when you talk instead of waiting impatiently for her own
turn to hold forth. She sees what's going on at the
periphery of things, the whispers and shadows and pale
might-bes that most of us only come upon in dreams.

The first time I see her, I can't look away from her.

The first time I see her, she won't even look at me—
probably because of the company I'm keeping. I stand at
the far end of the club, wineglass in hand, no longer
paying attention to the retro-Beat standing on the stage
declaiming her verses in a voice that's suddenly strident
where earlier I thought it was bold. I'm not the only one
Saskia distracts from the reading. She's pretty and blonde
with a figure that holds your gaze even when you're
trying to be polite and look away.

"Silicone," Jenny informs me. "Even her lips. And
besides, her forehead's way too high. Or maybe it's just
that her head's too long."

Aaran nods in agreement.

Nobody seems to like her. Men look at her, but they
keep their distance. Women arch their eyebrows cattily
and smile behind their hands as they whisper to each other

about her. No one engages her in conversation. They treat
her so strangely that I find myself studying her even more
closely, wondering what it is that I'm missing. She seems
so normal. Attractive, yes, but then there are any number
of attractive women in the room and none of them are
being ostracized. If she's had implants, she's not the first
to do so, and neither that nor the size of her forehead—
which I don't think is too large at all—seems to have any
bearing on the reaction she seems to garner.

"She's a poseur," Aaran tries to explain. "A pretender."

"Of what?" I ask.

"Of everything. Nothing about her is the way it seems.
She's supposed to be a poet. Supposed to be published,
but have you ever heard of her?"

I shake my head, but what Aaran is saying doesn't
mean much in this context. There are any number of fine
writers that I've never heard of, and—judging from what I
know of Aaran's actual reading habits—the figure is even
more dramatic for him.

"And then there's the way she leads you on," he goes
on. "Leaning close like you're the most important person
in the world, but turning a cold shoulder the moment any
sort of intimacy arises."

So she turned you down? I want to ask, but I keep the
question to myself, waiting for him to explain what he
means.

"She's just so full of herself," Jenny says when Aaran
falls silent. "The way she dresses, the way she looks down
at everybody."

Saskia is wearing faded jeans, black combat boots, a
short white cotton blouse that leaves a few inches of her
midriff bare and a plaid vest. Her only jewelry is a small
silver Celtic cross that hangs from a chain at the base of
her throat. I look at my companions, both of them over-
dressed in comparison. Jenny in silk blouse and skirt,
heels, a clutch purse, hair piled up at the back of her head
in a loose bun. Nose ring, bracelets, two earings per ear, a
ring for almost every finger. Aaran in chinos and a dark
sports jacket over a white shirt, goatee, hair short on top
and sides, pulled into a tiny ponytail in back. One ear

double-pierced like Jenny's, the other virgin. Pinky ring on each hand.

I didn't come with either of them. Aaran's the book editor for *The Daily Journal* and Jenny's a feature writer for *In the City,* Newford's little too-cool-to-not-be-hip weekly arts and entertainment paper. They have many of the personality traits they attribute to Saskia, and the only reason I'm standing here with them is that it's impolitic for a writer to make enemies with the press. I don't seek out their company—frankly, I don't care at all for their company—but I try to make nice when it's unavoidable. It drives my brother Geordie crazy that I can do this. But maybe that's why I can make a comfortable living, following my muse, while all too often he still has to busk on the streets to make his rent. It's not that I don't have convictions, or that I won't defend them. I save my battles for things that have meaning instead of tilting at every mild irritation that comes my way. You can fritter away your whole life with those kinds of windmills.

"So no one likes her?" I ask my companions.

"Why should they?" Jenny replies. "I mean, beyond the obvious, and that's got to wear thin once she opens her mouth."

I don't know what to reply to that, so I say, "I wonder why she comes around, then."

"Why don't you ask her yourself?" Aaran says with the same little smirk I see in too many of his reviews.

I'm thinking of doing just that, but when I look back across the club, she's no longer there. So I return my attention to the woman on the stage. She's onto a new poem now, one in which she dreams about a butcher's shop, and I'm not sure if she really does or if it's supposed to be a metaphor. Truth is, I'm not really listening to her anymore. Instead I'm thinking of Saskia and the way Aaran and Jenny have been sneering at her—physically and verbally—from the moment she walked in. I'm thinking that anyone who can call up such animosity from these two has got to have something going for her.

The poet on stage dreams of cleavers and government-approved steaks. That night I dream of Saskia, and when I wake up in the morning the events of last night's reading in the club and my dream are all mixed up together. It takes the first coffee of the morning for me to sort them all out.

### 3

I have a friend who owns a bookstore just outside of the city and knows everything you'd ever want to know about literature, highbrow and low. She's the one who first turned me onto Michael Hannon and Jeanette Winterson. The first time I read Barry Lopez was because Holly sent me a copy of *River Notes*. We don't get together as much as either of us would like, but we've been corresponding for years and talk on the phone at least once a week. She's in love with books, and knows how to share that love so that when she's tells you about a certain writer or a book's merit, you immediately want to read it for yourself. More importantly, she's usually dead on the money. Holly's the only reason I still look at the Saturday book pages in *The Daily Journal* since Aaran took them over.

With her expertise in mind, I call Holly up after breakfast to see if she knows anything about Saskia and her poetry.

"What's her last name?" Holly asks.

I can picture her sitting at the big old rolltop desk that doubles as a sales counter in her store, a small figure in jeans and a sweater, long, dark red hair pulled back from her forehead with a pair of bobby pins, hazel eyes always bright with interest. You could come in looking for *Les Misérables* or a nurse romance and she'd treat you with the same courtesy and respect. The store is crammed with books, literally, floor to ceiling. They gather like driftwood in tall stacks at the ends of bookcases, all around and upon her desk, in boxes and bags, filling the front window display except for the small cleared area where her Jack Russell terrier Snippet lies watching the street when she's not ensconced on Holly's lap. The sign painted onto the window, Gothic lettering, paint flaking, simply reads, *Holly Rue, Used Books*.

I think about what she's just asked me and realize I don't know.

"Well, Saskia's unusual enough," Holly tells me. "Hang on while I go on-line."

Holly and some friends have been creating this huge database they call the Wordwood somewhere out in the Net, assuring themselves that the Information Highway will remember the old technologies—books and printing presses were marvels of technological import in their day, after all—at the same time as it embraces the new. I don't know how many of them are involved in the project, but they've been working on it for years. The Net connects them from every part of the world, each participant adding book titles, authors, bios, publishing histories, reviews, cross-references, and whatever else they might think is pertinent to this amazing forest of information they've cultivated.

I tried logging on once when I was out visiting Holly and lost an afternoon glued to the screen, following some arcane trail that started with a short story by Sherman Alexie that I was trying to track down and ended up in a thicket of dissertations on Shakespeare's identity. Holly laughed at me when I finally came up for air. "The Wordwood's like that," she tells me. "One of these days I'm going to go in there and forget to come back." The way she talks about the place it's as though she actually visits it.

"Got something," she tells me. "Her last name's Madding, but she only uses her given name for a byline. We've got three titles listed—hey, wait a minute. I think I have one of these." I hear her get up from her chair and go looking for it, roam-phone in hand, because she's still talking to me. "Yeah, here it is. It's called *Mirrors* and it's her, let me see, second collection." More shuffling noises as she makes her way back to the desk and looks through the book. "You want me to read one to you? They're all pretty short."

"Sure."

"Okay. Here, I'll just do the first one, 'Tarot.' "

*What she said:*
*You turn from me*
*as I turn*
    *from the cards*
*refusing to face*
*what we see.*


Holly's got this amazing speaking voice, rough and resonant, like it's been strained through years of whiskey and cigarettes, though she doesn't smoke or drink. It gives the poem an edge that I'm not sure would be there if I'd just taken the words from the page.

"Nice," I say. "It sneaks up on you, doesn't it?"

"Mmm. There's a lot of sadness in those few lines. Oh, this is cool."

The word's just come back in fashion, but Holly never gave it up. She's been known to say "far out" as well.

"What's that?" I ask.

"I was looking back at the Wordwood and I see she's involved with *Street Times*. She does some editorial work for them."

That is interesting. *Street Times* is a thin little paper produced for street people to sell in lieu of asking for spare change. You see them selling it on half the corners downtown. The vendors pay something like fifty cents an issue and whatever you give them above that is what they earn. Most of the material is produced by the street people themselves—little articles, cartoons, photographs, free classifieds. Every issue they run a profile of one of the vendors, seriously heartbreaking stories. Jilly and some of her friends do free art for it occasionally, and I remember Geordie played at a benefit to raise the money to set the whole thing up a couple of years ago.

"I wonder who entered this stuff on her," Holly asks.

The question's rhetorical. Considering how many people are involved in building and maintaining the Wordwood, it could be anybody.

"So you want me to keep this book for you?" she goes on.

"Sure."

I'm too intrigued to even ask the price.

"Should I put it in the mail or are you actually going to visit me for a change? It's been months."

"Five weeks, if you're counting," I say.

"Who's counting?"

"I'll be by later today if I can catch a ride with someone."

"There are buses that come out this far," she says with a smile in her voice.

"If you don't mind walking the last couple of miles."

"That's right, I forgot. You're an artiste and need to be chauffeured. So is she cute?"

Sometimes Holly's abrupt changes of topic throw me. You'd think I'd get used to it, hanging around with Jilly who can be worse, but I never do. Conversations between her and Holly are bewildering for common folk to follow.

"What do you mean, cute?" I ask.

"Oh, come on. You're calling up, looking for books by someone whose last name you don't even know, and then—and this is the real giveaway—you don't even ask how much the book is. She's got to be cute."

"Maybe I'm just stimulated by her, intellectually."

I can almost see her shake her head. "Uh-uh. It's a guy thing, Christy. I know I've called you an honorary woman in the past, but you're still a guy. A single guy, yet."

So I tell her about last night.

4

It starts with a heartbeat, rhythm laid down, *one*-two, *one*-two, deep in your chest. It's not the pulse of everyday life but something that runs more profound, a dreaming cadence, a secret drumming that you can't share at first, not with anyone and especially not with her. The melody and chordal patterns might come later, when you've first made contact, when you discover that you haven't made an utter fool of yourself and she might actually reciprocate what you feel, adding her own harmonies to the score tattooed across your heart.

For now, all you can do is repeat her name like a mantra.

*Saskia Madding. Saskia Madding. Saskia. . . .*

For now, it's all unrequited. New age washes of sound when you think of her, great swelling chords if you happen to catch her going about her business. There, across the street, walking briskly in a light rain, skin glistening, hair feathered with moisture. There, squeezing melons at a fruit vendor's stall, laughing at something the man's said, standing with one hip jutted out, leaning over the front of the stall. There, leafing through a magazine in a smoke shop, a brief glimpse of her on the other side of the glass before you force yourself to walk by.

The music thunders in your chest. Nothing with structure. Nothing that can be transcribed or scored. But it leaves you helpless before its tumultuous presence, desperate to breathe.

5

I've read *Mirrors* a half-dozen times since Sue drove me by Holly's to pick it up. I've got Holly doing book searches for the other two collections. I've been by Angel's walk-in on Grasso Street and gone through her back issues of *Street Times*. I've even got my own modem hooked up—the one the professor gave me that's been languishing unused in a drawer of my desk for the past few months—entering the Wordwood myself to see if I can find some trace of her that Holly might have missed. A bio. A review. Anything.

In short, I've become obsessed with Saskia Madding.

I couldn't meet her now if I wanted to because I've become too desperate and there's nothing quite so pathetic or off-putting as the scent of desperation. It clings to you like a second skin, a nimbus of melancholy and pathos that, contrary to the Romantics with their marble skin and pining eyes, adds nothing to your attractiveness. You might as well have "Avoid me, I'm so hopeless" stenciled on your brow.

"The problem," Holly tells me the next time we're

talking on the phone, "is that you're treating her no better than Aaran or Jenny do. No, hear me out," she says when I try to protest. "They've got their misconceptions concerning her and you're blithely creating your own."

"Not so blithely," I say.

"But still."

"But still what?"

"Don't you think it's time you stopped acting like some half-assed teenager, tripping over his own tongue, and just talked to her?"

"And say what?" I ask. "The last time I saw her was at that launch for Wendy's new book, but before I could think of something to say to her, Aaran showed up at my elbow and might as well have been surgically implanted he stayed so close to me. She probably thinks we're friends and I told you how he feels about her. I don't doubt that she knows, too, so what's she going to think of me?"

"You don't have to put up with him," Holly says.

"I know. He was on about her half the night again until I finally told him to just shut up."

"Good for you."

"Yeah, Geordie'd be proud, too. Wait'll Aaran reviews my next book."

"Does that bother you?" Holly asked.

"Not really. What bothers me is that I can't get her out of my head, but I can't even find the few ounces of courage I need to go up to her. Instead I just keep seeing her everywhere I go. I feel like I'm being haunted, except I'm the one playing the stalker and I'm not even doing it on purpose. She's probably seen me as often as I've seen her and thinks I'm seriously twisted."

"A dozen pieces of advice come to mind," Holly says, "but they'd all sound trite."

"Try one on me anyway. I need all the help I can get."

Sitting there in my apartment, receiver cradled against my ear, I can picture Holly at her desk in the bookshop. The image is so clear I can almost see her shrug.

"Just go up to her," Holly tells me. "Ask her if she

wants to go for a coffee or something. The worst she can do is say no."

## 6

I love the poems in *Mirrors*. They're as simple as haiku and just as resonant. No easy task, I know. Every so often I turn from prose to verse, but under my direction the words stumble and flail about on the page and never really sing. I sit there and stare at them and I can't fix them. Give me a pageful of the crappiest prose and some time and I can whip it into shape, no problem. But I don't know where to begin with poetry. I know when it doesn't work. I even know what makes it work in someone else's lines. But I'm hopeless when it comes to trying to write it myself.

Saskia's poems are filled with love and sadness, explorations of social consciousness, profound declarations and simple lyric delights. The same small verse can make me smile and weep, all at the same time. But the one that haunts me the most, the one I return to, again and again, is "Puppet."

> *The puppet thinks:*
> *It's not so much*
> *what they make me do*
> *as their hands inside me.*

In what shadows did those words grow? And why wasn't I there to help her?

That makes me laugh. I can't even get up the nerve to approach her, and I expect to protect her from the dangers of the world?

## 7

In the end it's my brother Geordie, of all people, who introduces her to me. We're sitting on the patio of The Rusty Lion on a Sunday afternoon, trying to do the familial thing that neither of us are much good at, but at least we try. Jilly always says the family we choose for ourselves is more important than the one we were born into; that people have to earn our respect and trust, not have it handed to them simply because of genetics. Well, blood ties aside, I'd still want Geordie as my brother, and I think he'd want me, but we've got so much weird history between us that our good intentions don't always play out the way we'd like them to. Every time we get together I tell myself I'm not going to rag him, I'm not going to be the know-it-all big brother, I'm not going to tell him how to live his life, or even suggest that I know better. Trouble is, we know each other too well, know exactly which buttons to push to get under each other's skin and we can't seem to stop doing so. Bad habits are the hardest to break.

We immediately start off on a bad foot when he orders a beer and I hear myself asking if he doesn't think a few minutes past noon is a little early for alcohol. So he orders a whiskey on the side, just to spite me, and says, "If you're going to have a cigarette, could you at least not blow the smoke in my face?" We're sitting there glowering at each other and that's when Saskia comes walking by, looking like she stepped out of an Alma-Tadema painting for all that she's wearing jeans and a baggy blue sweater that perfectly matches her eyes.

Geordie's face brightens. "Hey, Sass," he says. "How's it going?"

I've had this mantra going through my head for weeks now—*Saskia Madding, Saskia Madding*—and all of a sudden I have to readjust my thinking. Her friends call her "Sass"? And how'd Geordie become one of them?

She smiles back at my brother. "Taking the day off?" she asks.

I have to give Geordie this: he works hard. He may play in a half-dozen bands and meet his rent and utilities by busking on street corners, but lazy he's not. Suddenly I want to tell him how I blew Aaran off the other night and didn't care what it might mean about how I'd get reviewed in the *Journal* in the future. I want to know if he's ever talked to Saskia about me, and if he has, what he's said. I want to ask Saskia about "Puppet" and a half-dozen other poems from *Mirrors*. Instead, I sit there like a lump with a foolish grin. Words are my stock-in-trade, but they've all been swallowed by the dust that fills my throat. I find myself wiping the back of my hand across my brow, trying to erase the "Avoid me" I know is written there.

Meanwhile, Geordie's completely at his ease, joking with her, asking her if she wants to join us. I wonder what their relationship is and this insane feeling of jealousy rears up inside me. Then Saskia's on the patio, joining us. Geordie's introducing us. My throat's still full of dust and I wish I'd ordered a beer as well instead of my caffé latte.

"So that's who you are," Saskia says as she sits down in the chair between Geordie's and my own. "I keep seeing you around the neighborhood."

"He's the original bad penny," Geordie says.

A part of me feels as though I should be angry with him for saying that. I wonder does he really mean it, have we drifted that far apart? But another part of me feels this sudden absurd affection for him for being here to introduce Saskia and me to each other. Against the rhythm of my pulse, I hear the first strains of melody, and in that instant, everything is right with the world. The desperate feeling in my chest vanishes. My throat's still dry, but the dust is gone. My features feel a little stiff, but my smile is natural.

"I've seen you, too," I find myself saying. "I've been wanting to meet you ever since I read *Mirrors*."

Her eyebrows arch with curiosity. "You've actually read it?" she asks.

"A number of times. I've tried to find your other two collections, but so far I haven't had any luck."

Saskia laughs. "I don't believe this. Newford's own Jan Harold Brunvand not only knows my work, but likes it, too?"

It never occurred to me that she might have read any of my books.

"Okay," Geordie says. "Now that we've got the mutual admirations out of the way, let's just try to enjoy the afternoon without getting into a book-by-book rundown of everything the two of you have written."

He seems as relaxed as I am, but I'm not surprised. We always do better in other people's company. It's not that we feel as though we have to put on good behavior. For some reason we simply don't pick at each other when anybody else is around. He also reads voraciously and loves to talk about books—that's probably the one thing we really have in common beyond the accident of our birth—so I know he's kidding us. I wish we could always be this comfortable with each other.

We both love books, only I'm the one that writes them. We both love music, only he's the musician. That makes us something of a rarity in our family. It wasn't that our parents didn't care for culture; it's just that they didn't have time for it. Didn't have time for us either. I'm not sure why they had children in the first place and I really don't know why they had three of us. You'd think they'd have realized that they weren't cut out to be parents after our older brother Paddy was born.

The only thing they asked of us was that we be invisible which was like an invitation to get in trouble because we soon learned it was the only way we'd get any attention. None of us did well in school. We all had "attitude problems" which expanded into more serious run-ins with authority outside of school. The police were forever bringing us home for everything from shoplifting (Geordie) and spray-painting obscenities on an underpass (me) to the more serious trouble that Paddy got in which eventually resulted in him pulling ten-to-fifteen in a federal pen.

None of us talked to each other, so I don't know for sure why it was that Paddy hung himself in his cell after serving a couple of years of hard time. But I can guess. It's hard to be alone, but that's all we ever knew how to be. Walled off from each other and anybody else who might come into our lives. Geordie and I made a real effort to straighten ourselves out after what happened to Paddy, and tried to find the kind of connection with other people that we couldn't get at home. Geordie does better than me. He makes friends pretty easily, but I don't know how deep most of those friendships go. Sometimes I think it's just another kind of wall. Not as old or tall as the one that stands between us, but it's there all the same.

8

Holly looks up in surprise when I walk into her shop the next day.

"What?" she asks. "Two visits in the same month? You sure you haven't gotten me mixed up with a certain blonde poet?"

"Who?" I reply innocently. "You mean Wendy?"

"You should be so lucky."

She accepts the coffee and poppyseed muffin I picked up for her on my walk from the bus stop, and graciously makes room for me on her visitor's chair by the simple expediency of sweeping all the books piled up on it into her arms and stacking them in a tottery pile beside the chair. Naturally they fall over as soon as I sit down.

"You know the rules," she says. "If you can't treat the merchandise with respect—"

"I'm not buying them," I tell her. "I don't care how damaged they are."

Holly pops the lid from her coffee and takes an appreciative sip before starting in on the muffin. She no sooner unwraps it, than Snippet is on her lap, looking mournfully at every bite until I take a doggie bone out of my pocket and bribe her back onto the floor with it. I know enough to come prepared.

Holly doesn't ask what I'm doing here and for a long time I don't get into it. We finish our muffins, we drink our coffee. Snippet finishes her bone, then returns to Holly's lap to look for muffin crumbs. Time goes by, a comfortable passage of minutes, silence that's filled with companionship, a quiet space of time untouched by a need to braid words into a conversation. We've done this before. There've been times we've spent the whole afternoon together and not needed to talk or even react to each other's presence. Sometimes just being with a friend is enough. I've never been able to tell Holly how much I appreciate her being a part of my life, but I think she knows all the same.

After a while I tell her about finally meeting Saskia yesterday, how Geordie introduced us, how I'm going to be seeing her tonight.

"So you're deliriously happy," Holly says, "and you've come by to rub it in on a poor woman who hasn't had a date in two months."

Holly smiles, but I don't need to be told she's teasing me.

"Something like that," I say.

She nods. "So what's the real reason you're here?"

"I logged onto the Wordwood last night and something really weird happened to me," I tell her. "I wasn't really thinking about what I was doing and started to type a question to myself—the way I do when I'm writing and I don't want to stop and check a fact—and the program answered me."

Holly makes an encouraging noise in the back of her throat to let me know she's paying attention, but that's it. I can't believe she's being this blasé and figure she hasn't really understood me.

"Holly," I say. "I didn't type something like 'Go Emily Carr' and wait for the program to take me to whatever references it has on her. I entered a question—misspelled a couple of words, too—and before I had a chance to go on, the answer appeared on my screen."

She shrugs. "That kind of thing happens all the time in the Wordwood."

"What? There's somebody sitting at their keyboard somewhere, scanning whoever else happens to be on-line and responding to their questions?"

Holly shakes her head. "The program wasn't set up for two-way dialogues between users. It's just a database."

"So who answered me?"

"I don't know." I hear a nervousness in the laugh she offers me. "It just happens."

"And you're not the least curious about it?"

"It's hard to explain," Holly says. "It's like the program's gone AI, kind of taken on a life of its own, and none of us quite knows how to deal with it, so we've sort of been ignoring it."

"But this has got to be a real technological break-through."

"I suppose."

I can't figure out why she's not as excited about it as I am. I don't keep up on all the scientific journals, but I've read enough to know that no one's managed to produce a real artificial intelligence program yet—something indistinguishable from a real person, except it hasn't got a body, it's just living out there in the Net somewhere.

"There's something you're not telling me," I say.

Holly gives me a reluctant nod. "None of us has been entering data into the program for months," she admits.

"What are you saying?"

"I'm saying it's getting the information on its own. The Wordwood's so comprehensive now that we couldn't have entered all the information it now holds even if each of us had spent all our time keying it in, twenty-four hours a day, seven days a week."

I give her a blank look, still not understanding why she's not excited about this, why she hasn't trumpeted their accomplishment to the world.

"The Wordwood's everything we hoped it would be and more," she explains when I ask. "It's efficient beyond anything we could have hoped for."

"And?"

"And we're afraid of screwing around with it, or talking it up, for fear that it'll go away."

"It."

I suddenly find myself reduced to one-word responses and I don't know why.

"The program," Holly says. "The entity that's taken up residence in the Wordwood, whatever it is. It's like a piece of magic, our own guardian angel of books and literature. Nobody wants to take the chance of losing it—not now. It's become indispensable."

"Holly—"

"Did you recognize its voice?" she asks.

I shake my head.

"Some of the others using the program recognize its speech patterns, the cadences of its language, as belonging to people they once knew—or still know, but rarely see anymore."

I finally manage a whole sentence. "You mean it's mimicking these people?"

"No. It's more like it really is these people—or at least it is them when you happen to be talking to it. When I'm on-line with the Wordwood, I hear my grandmother's voice in the way it responds to me. Sometimes. . . ." She hesitates, then goes on. "Sometimes it's like I'm actually sitting in a forest somewhere with Gran, talking about books."

I love a good mystery and this has all the makings of the best kind of urban myth.

"How long has this been going on?" I ask.

"About two years."

It's not until much later that I realize this is the around the same time that Saskia first arrived in Newford.

9

Spirits and ghosts.

My last serious relationship was with a woman who wasn't so much flesh and blood as a spirit borrowing her cloak of humanity. Her name was Tally. Tallulah. The essence of the city, made manifest for the nights we stole from its darker corners, the hours in which we made light between us when everything else lay in shadows. She left because she had to be hard, she had to be tough to survive, the way the city is now. Loving me, she couldn't meet the spite and meanness with like intent. She couldn't survive.

She's out there still. Somewhere. I don't see her, but I can still feel her presence sometimes. On certain nights.

The last time Geordie got serious about a woman, she turned into a ghost.

My therapist would have a heyday with this material, but I've never come right out and told her about any of it. I couch the truths I give her with the same thin veneer of plausibility that I slip onto the facts of some of my stories. I know how weird that sounds, considering what I write, but I've seen things that are real—that I know are true—but they're so outrageous, the only way I can write about them is to start with "Once upon a time." Truth masquerading as lies, but then it's all artifice, isn't it? Language, conversation, stories. All of it. Since Babel fell, words can no longer convey our intent. Not the way that music can.

And the music I hear now. . . .

I can't get enough of it. Long slow chords that resonate deep in my chest for hours after Saskia and I have been together, tempered only by the fear that she's too deeply cloaked in mystery and that, like Tally, that mystery will one day take her away.

I don't mean the mystery that we are to each other, small islands of flesh and bone that are yet great with thought, lumbering like behemoths through dark waters, occasionally interacting with one another, but rarely understanding the encounter. No, I sense that Saskia is part of a deeper mystery, the kind that catwalks over the marrow of our spines, the kind that wakes awe deep in our chests and makes our ribs reverberate with their sacred tones. The kind that we may experience, but only briefly. The kind that resonates so deeply because of its brevity. Because our mortal frailty was not meant to hold such music for more than a whisper of time. A few days. A few weeks at most.

In short, I imagine Saskia as Geordie's ghost, as my Tallying spirit, a mystery that will hold me for a brief time, fill me with her inescapable music, then leave me holding only memories, chasing echoes.

I try to tell Geordie about it one day, but all he says is that I'm merely exaggerating what all new lovers feel, blowing my insecurities way out of proportion.

"Like you're suddenly an expert," I say, frustrated. "When was the last time you were even on a date?"

I regret the words as soon as they're out of my mouth—long before the hurt look comes into my brother's eyes. It was a cheap shot. Neither of us has to be reminded of our deficiencies, least of all by each other.

"I'm sorry," I tell him.

He knows it's true. He knows I mean it. But it doesn't change the fact that we're walking wounded, both of us, we've always been walking wounded, we've just learned how to hide it better than most. It's not simply the ghosts and spirits; it's the emotional baggage we've had to carry around with us ever since we were kids. Don't feel sorry for us. But don't pretend you understand either.

"I know you miss Tally," Geordie says to me. "But—"

"Saskia's not Tally," I say.

Geordie nods.

"So what are you trying to tell me?" I have to ask.

"Just remember that," he says. "Take people as they are instead of always trying to second guess them. Have some faith in her."

He smiles as he uses the word. We both know all about faith, how belief in something is a commodity that requires a coin that we usually find too dear to pay.

"What about music?" I ask suddenly, changing the subject as abruptly as Jilly or Holly might, but it doesn't faze Geordie. He and Jilly see so much of each other that he's obviously used to it by now.

"What about it?" he says.

"Where does it come from?"

Now he gives me a blank look.

"I mean, where does it originate for you?" I say. "When you write a tune, how do you hear it? Where does it come from?"

Geordie taps his ear. "I just hear them. Faintly at first. There's always music going on in my ear, but every once in a while a tune becomes insistent and won't go away until I work it out or write it down."

"So you have like a soundtrack going on inside your head all the time?"

"No," he says. "It's not like that. I guess the tunes are always there, a kind of background to whatever else I'm doing, but I have to pay attention to them to bring one of them out from the rest. And it's not as though I can't ignore them. I can. But if I do ignore them for too long, they just go away. Like when I don't play my fiddle or whistle for a while. The music kind of dries up inside me, and all I know is that I'm missing something, but I don't always know what. That's why I can't do the regular nine-to-five—I'm away from the music too long, and I end up carrying around this desert inside. I'd rather be broke but with a forest of tunes in my head."

I can't remember the last time Geordie talked to me like this, exposing such a private piece of himself at such length.

"For me it's like a soundtrack," I tell him. "I can't write a tune, but I hear this music all the time, especially when I'm with somebody."

Geordie smiles. "So what do you hear when you're with me?"

"Sad tunes," I tell him. "Adagios. A bittersweet music on bowed cellos and piano that seems to hold a great promise that never quite has the chance to break through."

Geordie's smile falters. He wants to think I'm kidding him, but he can tell I've given him an honest answer. One thing we've never been able to do is lie to each other. To ourselves, yes, but never to each other.

"I guess we should try harder," he says.

"We do try, Geordie. Look at us, we're here, talking to each other, aren't we? Have been for years. When was the last time you saw anybody else in our family? Our problem isn't a lack of trying, it's getting past all the crap we've let get in the way."

He doesn't say anything for a long time, but his gaze holds mine for longer than I can ever remember him doing.

"And Saskia?" he asks finally.

"I can't even begin to describe that music," I tell him.

## 10

Until I met Saskia, the most curious person I knew was Jilly. Everything interests Jilly—no object, no event, no person is exempt—but she's particularly taken by the unusual, as am I. I know the reason I started chasing down urban legends and the like was because it was a way for me to escape from what was happening in my home life at the time, a chance for me to feel like I was a part of something. I don't know what her excuse is. She and Geordie have exchanged war stories, but conversations between Jilly and me invariably center around the latest curiosity we've happened to stumble across.

Saskia's inquisitiveness is more like Jilly's than mine—only multiplied a hundredfold. She wants to see and hear and taste everything. Whenever we eat out, it has to be at a different ethnic restaurant from the one before. I've seen her try every kind of coffee in a café, every kind of beer in a tavern, every kind of pastry in a bakery—not all in one day, of course. She simply keeps going back until she's had the chance to sample them all.

She's entranced with music and while she has very definite likes (opera, hip-hop and flamenco) and dislikes (anything by Chopin—go figure), she approaches it in the same way she does food and drink: she wants to sample it all. Ditto live theater, films, TV, how and where we make love—everything except for books. The odd thing is that while she's incredibly knowledgeable with the background of just about everything she experiences, she savors each experience as though coming upon it for the first time. It can be disconcerting, this juxtaposing of familiarity and ignorance, but I like it. It's like being in the company of a friend with a particularly up-to-date edition of *Brewer's Phrase and Fable* in the back of her head.

What's less easy to accept is the negative reaction she garners from most people. Even complete strangers seem to go out of their way to be rude or impolite to her. Needless to say, it infuriates me, though it doesn't seem to bother Saskia at all. Or at least not so she ever lets on. Who knows how she really feels about it? It's not exactly the kind of question I feel comfortable bringing up this early in our relationship. What if she's never noticed it?

I ask Holly about it when I drop by the store, almost a month to the day from when I made my last visit. This time I come bearing fresh slices of banana bread with the usual coffees and doggie bone for Snippet.

"So now you've met her," I say. Saskia and I ran into Holly at the opening for a new show by Sophie last night and went for drinks afterward. "What do you think?"

Holly takes a sip of coffee to wash down the last of her banana bread and smiles. "I think she's lovely."

"Me, too." I pause for a moment, then ask, "Did you notice anything unusual about her?"

Holly hesitates. "Well, she seems to know an awful lot about brandies for someone who says she's never had one before."

"Besides that."

Holly shakes her head.

"The way other people reacted to her in the bar?" I prompt.

Holly strokes the fur on Snippet's shoulders—the dog, having hopped up on Holly's lap when she finished her own treat, is now looking for possible holdouts in the folds of Holly's skirt. Holly glances at her computer screen. I recognize the Wordwood menu.

"A lot of people feel uncomfortable around magic," she says finally. "You must've noticed this by now. The way some people will review your work, going into it with a negative attitude simply because of its content. Or the way they start to fidget and look uneasy if the conversation turns to the inexplicable."

"Of course," I say. "But I'm not sure I'm getting your point."

"It's Saskia," Holly says. "She's magic."

"Magic." I'm back to one-word echoes again.

Holly nods. "Her being magic is what antagonizes them. They recognize it in her, but they don't want to believe it, they can't believe it, so they lash out at her in defense. Humanity's whole unfortunate history is one long account of how we attack what we don't understand, what's strange to us. And what's stranger than magic?"

"How is she magic?" I want to know.

"It's like . . . well, does she remind you of anyone? Not the way she looks, though that seems familiar, too, but the way she talks. The cadence of her voice."

I shake my head.

"Well, she reminds me of Gran."

I'm starting to get a bad feeling about this as I realize that after one brief meeting, Holly's picked up on something that I should have seen from the start.

"Your grandmother," I say.

"Mm-hmm."

This time I'm the one who glances at the Wordwood menu on her computer screen. I turn back to Holly, but she won't quite meet my gaze.

"What exactly are you saying?" I ask.

"Maybe you should ask her about the Wordwood," Holly says.

That's when I realize that Saskia does remind me of someone—not in what she's saying, but in how she says it. She reminds me of Tally.

## 11

I feel like the person in the folktale who calls the cat by its true name which makes it leave. Like the shoemaker putting out clothes for the brownies. Like the seventh bride with Bluebeard's key in hand, approaching the forbidden door.

I can hear, in the joyful music that arcs between Saskia and myself, the first faint strains of sadness, a bittersweet whisper of strings, a foreshadowing of the lament to come. If this were a film, I'm at the point where I'd want to shout up at the screen, "Don't screw it up! Leave well enough alone." But I can't stop myself. I have to know. Even understanding the price one must pay when unmasking faerie, I have to know.

So heart in throat, I ask Saskia that night, where did she live before she moved to Newford; where is she from, expecting I'm not sure what, but not that a merry laugh would start in her eyes and spread across her face. Not that she'd put her hand tenderly against my cheek, look long into my eyes and then lean forward to kiss my mouth. I can taste the good humor on her lips.

"I thought you knew," she says. "I lived in the forest."

"The Wordwood."

She nods. "A forest of words and names and stories. I love it there, but I had to know more. I had to experience firsthand what I could only read about in the forest. I knew what the sun was supposed to feel like. I knew about rain and how it must feel against your face. Imagine what food tasted like and drink and music and love. But reading about something's not the same as doing it, is it?"

I shake my head.

"So I chose a shape from a magazine picture that I thought would be pleasing and came across to be here."

How? I want to ask, but I realize it's irrelevant. Mysteries are what they are. If they could be explained, they would lose their resonance.

"Do you miss it at all?" I end up asking.

Saskia shakes her head. "No. I. . . ." She hesitates, looking for a way to explain herself clearly. "Part of me's still there," she settles on. "That's why I—" she laughs again "—seem to know so much. I just 'look' it up in the forest."

"When I put it all together," I tell her, "I didn't know what to think. I guess I still don't know."

"You think I'm going to leave you," she says. "You think I'm going back and when I do, I'll leave you behind."

I don't trust myself to speak. All I can do is nod. I can feel a deep chord welling up in my chest, building, building, to a crescendo. A tsunami of swelling, thrumming sound.

The merriment flees her eyes and she leans close to me again, so close I'm breathing her breathing. She looks so serious. The deep sea blue of her eyes starts to swallow me.

"The only way I'll leave you," she says, "is if you send me away."

The tsunami breaks over me as I hold her close.

## 12

Geordie doesn't usually come over to where I live unless it's to help me move, which I seem to do about once a year. So he gets to see the old place twice, the new place once, until I move again. The image he carries in his head of where I live must consist of empty apartments, bare walls and rugless floors, the furniture in odd arrangements, preparing to leave or having just arrived. And then there're all the boxes of books and papers and what-have-yous. Sometimes *I* think I just live out of boxes.

But we're in my study this evening and I'm not in the middle of a move, neither coming nor going, although there still are a half-dozen boxes of books in one corner, left over from the previous move. Geordie's standing by my desk, reading a poem called "Arabesque" that's taped to the wall beside my computer.

*The artist closed her book,*
*returning it to the shelf*
*that stored the other*
*stories of her life.*
*When she looked up,*
*there were no riddles*
    *in her gaze;*
*only knowing.*

*Don't make of us*
*more than what we are,*
*she said.*
*We hold no great secret*
*except this:*
*We know that*
*all endeavor is art*
*when rendered*
*with conviction.*

*The simple beauty*
    *of the everyday*
*strikes chords*

> *as stirring as*
> *oil on canvas,*
> *finger on string,*
> *the bourée in*
> *perfect demi-pointe.*
>
> *The difference is*
> *we consider it art.*
>
> *The difference is*
> *we consider*
> *art.*
>
> *When it consumes us,*
> *what consumes us,*
> *is art:*
> *an invisible city*
> *we visit with our dreams.*
>
> *Returning,*
> *we are laden down with*
> *the baggage of*
> *our journeys,*
> *and somewhere,*
> *in a steamer trunk*
> *or a carry-on,*
> *we carry souvenirs:*
> *signposts,*
> *guidebooks,*
> *messages from beyond.*
>
> *Some are merely*
> *more opaque*
> *than others.*

Geordie stands there, whiskey in hand, and reads it through a couple times, before coming back to join me on the other side of the room. I have two club chairs there with a reading lamp and a table set between them. Geordie places his whiskey glass on the table and sits down.

"Did you write that?" he asks.

I shake my head. "No, it's one of Saskia's. I couldn't write a piece of verse if my life depended on it."

I've got a roast in the oven, with potatoes baking in a circle around it. Saskia was making a salad, but she ran out to the market to get some lemons just before Geordie arrived.

"I like it," Geordie says. "Especially that bit about art being like an invisible city from which we bring things back. It reminds me of Sophie's serial dreams."

Saskia moved in a couple of months ago, setting up her own study in what was my spare bedroom. It's a bright, airy room, with a thick Oriental carpet on the floor, tons of pillows, a shelf filled with knickknacks running along one wall and all sorts of artwork on the others. She writes at a small mahogany desk by the window that stands so short it won't take a chair. She sits on one of the pillows when she writes at it. There aren't any books in the room, but then she doesn't need them. She's got her own reference library in her head, or wherever it is that she connects with the Wordwood.

Now that I know, about that forest of words, how she grew up in the shelter of its storied trees, she doesn't remind me of Tally anymore. I can't remember how she ever did, though Holly still hears her Gran, and I suppose other people hear who they expect to hear.

"You guys seem pretty happy," Geordie says.

I smile. "We are. Who'd have though I'd ever settle down."

Ever since Saskia moved in, we've had Geordie over for dinner at least once every couple of weeks. But this is the first time we've been alone in the apartment.

"You know," I say. "There are things we never talk about. About back when."

I don't have to explain back when to him. Back when we lived at home. Back when Paddy was still alive. Back when we hid from each other as much as from our parents. Back when we shut each other out because that was the only way we knew how to deal with people, the only way we knew to relate to anybody. Stand back. Give me room.

"You don't have to say anything," Geordie tells me.

"But I do," I say. "I want to explain something. You know how sometimes you want something so bad, all you can do is drive it away? You keep looking for the weak link so that you can point at it and say, there it is. I knew this couldn't work out. I knew this was too good to be true."

He looks a little confused. "You're talking about what you went through with Saskia now, aren't you?"

"I went through that with Saskia," I agree. "But she was patient and waited me out instead of walking away."

"What's that got to do with us?" Geordie wants to know.

"I just want you to know that I'm not simply going through the motions here. That it's not only Saskia who wants to see you. I want to see you, too. I should have been there for you when we were kids. I was your older brother. I shouldn't have let you grow up alone the way I did."

"But we *were* just kids."

I nod. "But you had to resent me or not being the big brother you needed. I know I sure as hell resented Paddy. It's taken me a long time to work through that, but now that I finally have, it's way too late to tell him. I don't want the same thing to lie there between us."

"I never hated you," Geordie says. "I just didn't understand why things had to be the way they were."

"I know. But we've had that lying between us for all these years, the knowing that we weren't there for each other then and maybe we won't be there for each other in the future, some time when it really matters. It's the same self-fulfilling prophecy. You don't trust something to be true, so you push it to the point when it isn't true."

"That'll never happen," Geordie says, but I can see it's something he wants to believe, not something he really believes.

"We can't let it happen," I say. "So that's why I'm

telling you now what Saskia said to me: The only way I'll leave you, is if you send me away."

## 13

I don't envy the music others hear anymore; I'm too filled with my own now, the strains that connect me to Saskia and my brother and the other people I love in my life. I'm not saying my world's suddenly become perfect. I've still got my ups and downs. You should see the review that *The Daily Journal* gave my last book—Aaran Block at his vitriolic worst. But whenever things get bad, all I do is slow down. I stop and listen to the music and then I can't help but appreciate what I do have.

It's funny what a difference a positive attitude can have. When you go out of your way to be nice to people, or do something positive for those who can't always help themselves the way Saskia does with her editorial work on *Street Times,* it comes back to you. I don't mean you gain something personally. It's just that the world becomes a little bit of a better place, the music becomes a little more upbeat, and how can you not gain something from that?

See, when you get down to the basics of it, everything's just molecules vibrating. Which is what music is, what sound is—vibrations in the air. So we're all part of that music and the worthier it is, the more voices we can add to it, the better off we all are.

Sure beats the silence that's threatening to swallow us otherwise.

## 14

"Tell me a story," Saskia says that night after Geordie's gone home.

I turn my face toward her and she snuggles close so that my mouth is right beside her ear.

"Once upon a time," I say, "there was a boy who lost his ability to sing and the only person who could find it for him lived in a forest of words, but he didn't meet her until he was much, much older. . . ."

*"Saskia" comes from the same place that most of my stories do: a collision between the central conceit of the anthology I've been invited to contribute to and the handful of themes that permeate my work in one form or another. "Saskia" touches on a number of these, but primarily I wanted to explore the music that underlies our lives and play it against the difficulty of maintaining a good relationship, particularly when trust has been breached at one point or another. A good relationship—be it between friends, lovers, or family—is like a garden, and requires time, care, and nurturing to maintain. When we put up walls, we not only keep others out, but we lock ourselves in.*

# CALLING THEM HOME
## by Jody Lynn Nye

Jody Lynn Nye is the author of numerous science fiction and fantasy books, including *The Ship Errant, The Magic Touch,* and *Mythology 101.* She has also coauthored four books with Anne McCaffrey: *Crisis on Doona, Treaty at Doona, The Death of Sleep,* and *The Ship Who Won,* and cowrote *The Dragonlover's Guide to Pern.* She lives in a northwest suburb of Chicago with her husband, Bill Fawcett, and their two cats.

The relief operator met them on the other side of the air lock with unconcealed impatience. Margette saw that he was already in his shipsuit and his duffel stood ready on the floor.

"Your mail is queued up," he said. "I've done a final check on the equipment—everything's fine—and I cleared out all the waste tanks. Twice," he finished, almost breathlessly.

"You really should have brought something with you to do, you know," Margette said, grinning at him mischievously. "I know you were sent the briefing. . . ."

He interrupted her. "I don't know how you stand it," he said.

The relief zipped up his suit, grabbed his bag, and shouldered past her into the transport ship with a worried backward glance lest Margette grab him for some last-minute, unfinished task. The transport captain exchanged amused glances with her and gave her a thumbs up.

"Hope you enjoyed your holiday," the captain said.

Margette's musical laugh filled the small control room. "Glad to get away," she said, "but always, always glad to get back. Thank you."

She swung her guitar case onto one of the two swivel couches, and the captain dropped her other two bags near the air lock. He gave her a respectful half salute, and the air lock sealed behind him, leaving her alone in her beloved place once again. She threw out her arms as if to embrace the whole beacon, and let out a sigh of joy.

The needle indicators on the wall of gauges jumped and twitched behind their glass panel. Margette suddenly realized she couldn't hear anything except the low burble and clatter of ventilation and life support. She rushed to the control panel and flung all the potentiometers to high. The speakers on the wall blared forth a cacophony which her trained ear immediately began to sort into individual phrases. She slid into the couch-chair in front of the panel, and just listened.

"Eh-oh, ha-oh, ma-ne, ah-oh," rumbled the song from Beacon 17, out toward Alpha Centauri, sounding like a North American native chant. Margette had sent a message to Van Blake a good year ago. Idly, she scrolled through the mail drop to see if he'd ever responded. Van was a good-looking guy, but a slow correspondent. "Ho-ah! la-la, be-ne-*eh*-eh-ma," a liturgical-sounding phrase. Another friend, on Beacon Five. She smiled, letting that thread drop, and isolated another. "*Ba,* ba-ba, ba-*ba,* ba-ba ba," came the cha-cha rhythm from Beacon Eight, as close to next door as anything in deep space could be.

One by one she greeted the other beacons' call signs, humming them to herself in her calm, pure soprano. At last she came to her own, Beacon Nine. She lowered the other pots and listened to it alone, a sound she knew like her own heartbeat.

"He-me-oh, om-oh-ah-he," the beacon repeated, a sweet, hopeful sound.

"All is well, now that I'm home," Margette sang to its tune, a little sheepishly, knowing she was greeting a machine. It was more than that, though. It was a guardian and a friend.

That's what one of the hauler captains had told her once. His navicomp had gone out on a long approach to Sol System, and all he had had was the beacon, with Margette's music program broadcasting on the two main sidebands, to guide him back. Those seven notes formed the rope he'd hauled himself in on, until he was close enough for Earth itself to guide him into a safe orbit. To show her how much it had meant to him that she'd saved his life and those of his crew, he'd bought Margette a real-steak dinner and a huge jeweled ring. Margette had protested she hadn't done anything except her job. She kept the beacon running, and played music to entertain anybody near enough to pick up the transmission of the main signal.

Other spacers were equally as devoted as the hauler captain, although not so extravagant. She got plenty of e-mail and real-mail, praising her choice of music and her low, smooth voice—which many called sexy—but mostly thanking her just for being there, the presence on which they could count. She was their last hope in the darkness of space, their last chance of getting home if all else failed. Margette had never before thought of herself as anything much more than an animated tape-player, the spanner that kept the machinery from breaking down, but not any more. Now she had a calling.

Margette's wide mouth twitched in a grin as she leaned over the microphone and flicked it on.

"Ladies and gentlemen and all the ships in space," she said. "This is Margette Olberg. I'm just back from holiday, and I have thousands of new tunes for you to hear. My replacement—" she had to think for a moment to remember his name, "—Bef Blanchard, asked me to tell you all farewell and good flying."

She knew Blanchard had not been thinking any such thing when he left, and knew, too, that the transport ship's radio would be turned to her frequency. The man was probably telling them right now how dull it had been, stuck out in a lonely metal ball for three months straight, and then he would hear his name. Well, Blanchard was ill-fitted for the job. She knew his type. He probably thought it was soft duty, three months of slacking, volunteered for it, and then forgot to bring anything with him to do. The transport crew wouldn't give him a lot of sympathy.

Margette reached for her canvas bag with a toe, pulling it toward her so she didn't have to move away from the microphone. Fumbling around in the bottom, she pulled out a chip at random.

"Let me start things off with a recording I picked up in a pub on Marsbase two months ago. You'll love the way they played with the dome acoustics. I think they have real promise, and you ought to go hear them if you're out that way. This is Final Countdown."

She poked the chip into the reader bed, and slid the mike pot down to zero. A soft thrum of guitar and harp strings swept out of the speaker, weaving a silk tapestry that enveloped her in mystery and color. Six months, she thought with a sigh, as she sat back with her hands behind her head. Six beautiful months ahead of her to do nothing but play music, and write music, and sing.

The beacon signal kept cycling in the background. Margette hummed its seven notes, then opened her mouth to let the round tones roll out.

"I am here, Calling them home," she sang. "Hear my song, Calling them home." Her voice resonated, deep enough not to compete with the ventilation sounds, and high enough so that the endless square-wave tone the machines emitted didn't drown it out. She had a hundred lyrics she'd set to the seven notes, but that one was her favorite. A soft glissando issued from the Final Countdown chip, and she smiled. The indicator said the side had thirty-two minutes to run. Plenty of time for her to unpack, change, and make a pot of tea.

Later, she sat in front of the control console sorting out her newest haul of chips. She gloated over a live concert recording from Europa. There had been no way she could have gotten tickets to that one even if she hadn't been on duty at that time, but here it was in her hand, in all its true fidelity and forty-eight tracks of audio, and free of charge.

Beacon operators, stationed at system's edge or in deep space for six months on and three months off, were endlessly interesting to the recording companies. There were men and women whose job it was to drop off new chips to each of the beacons, with offers of bonuses for playing them.

Margette liked the gifts but they never swayed her much. She wouldn't play anything she didn't like. She usually sampled the chips while she was doing other things. If she could sing along or dance to the music, she'd give it a whirl on the air. If not, not. Four years on this job had made her immune to the threats by recording agents whose job it was to lean, but they couldn't lean too hard. She was, after all, a government employee, and no matter how big the corporations were, Big Brother was bigger.

The agents hadn't been blind to seeking out new talent either. Fully six of the albums in her playlist were her own music.

The bored Mr. Blanchard had indeed left the place shipshape. Margette couldn't see a spot or a mote anywhere. She was glad. She hated housecleaning. Running an eye over the chips she'd already sorted out, she chose a short one to follow the first long recording, and cued it up. Mentally, Margette composed a playlist for the next couple of hours, selecting chips from her old collection, and interspersing public service announcements. She wanted time to go through her mail.

Ex-system e-mail came with a line in the address that strung together all the beacons through which the message had passed on its way to its final destination. Margette listened, humming along, to a long train of call signs, until the music finished with her own seven-note benison and her name and code number, spoken aloud. It delighted her to be able to identify its source and path without referring to the computer address.

"Hi, Rommy," she said with a grin, even before her brother's face appeared on the screen.

The use of music as beacon call signs had been propounded by a scientist some fifty years before. His logic ran that a recited string of numbers was prone to confusion during emergency conditions. Visual signs were out for the same reason; that a crew in distress wouldn't have time to stare at a graphic, and how would you judge signal strength? Patterns of monotone beeps were not particularly descriptive, hence the failure of Morse code as a means of identifying location. But human beings have excellent memories for specific sounds, especially music. The scientist studied documentary evidence collected by radio stations during the late twentieth and early twenty-first centuries which determined that constant listeners could accurately name a song out of thousands, after hearing a sample of only one to four notes. It would be a century before there would be a thousand beacons. An audio signal was as close to being foolproof as anything, and it was the simplest transmission to maintain and to track.

Using government funds, he commissioned a composer to write a hundred distinctive short pieces of two to four bars each, like jingles, and began the testing. The experiment was a notable success. The scientist and composer were given medals and plenty of news exposure, but most important, the songs were to be used on the first hundred beacons built. A suitable form of immortality, in Margette's opinion.

The original composer had died twenty years ago, but her successor had already had to devise seventy-four tunes so far. Judging by Margette's mail, he ought to keep writing. Humankind was reaching out farther and farther, and it would need more beacons soon.

The assigned operators made up a fraternity, a web which wove the worlds together. She liked that. It sounded like a lyric.

Each beacon did have its own numeric code, but after the first experiment with musical notes, it was seldom used except on official documents and in the call sign to ship navicomputers. The only places Margette saw Beacon Nine's address was on the manual of emergency procedures and on her paycheck.

She reached for the recording button to reply to her

brother's message, when she noticed a flashing LED on the communications link. A live call! Excited, Margette hit the answer button.

"Hey, Margy," said the man on the screen. His face was a weathered red, in contrast to his pale neck and hands. A cluster of men and women stood behind him. Space miners, she guessed. "Welcome back."

"Thank you," she said, leaning in toward her microphone. "I'm happy to be here." She observed a ten-second delay on the yellow wall chronometer before the miner nodded his head, showing he'd heard her reply.

"Yeah," the man said. "Didn't much like your replacement. Played the same, real long stuff all the time, and had lots of dead air in between. Bo-oh-oh-*ring!*" The others murmured agreement, and some of them chuckled. "Hell of it is," the man continued, "now you're back, we're on our way out-system. We just wanted to say we liked you and the stuff you play, and hope we'll be assigned back here some time."

"Thank you!" Margette beamed. "Safe going."

"Thanks, Margy. Give us something good to cross out on."

"You bet," she said, running her finger down the playlist and pulling a short, peppy, traditional reel out of the queue. "What's your ship's name?" The time delay between them was already stretching to fifteen seconds.

"*Guppy's Luck.* I'm Guppy. Thanks, Margy."

The whole crew waved to her as the screen darkened. Margette waved back until the link broke, then cued up the chip. As the last cut ended, she leaned over the microphone again.

"That was Devil's Ranger, and their symphony on the letter M. This next one is Mezzo, for the crew of *Guppy's Luck,* with all the best. Enjoy, folks." She closed off the mike, and let the music roll. The light on the communication link came on again within minutes, a pair of mining school students taking a ride out from Neptune Station who wanted to hear a love song. Margette found one among her chips before the seven-minute delay brought her their next reply.

"Aren't you lonely up there all by yourself?" her mother had asked her on one of Margette's rare visits home.

"By myself?" she had laughed. "I'm not alone. I'm never alone. There's always somebody who wants to chatter. And I have my music."

The students' call was all but interrupted by a signal from David Caputo, a Space Patrol officer whose duty area ran between Saturn and system's edge. For the last few years, the ringed planet had been creeping toward perigee with her beacon, bringing David into closer contact, a situation she liked very much.

"Hey, welcome back!" he said. His handsome, square face with its wide hazel eyes and cap of brown curls beamed out at her from the screen.

"Hello, yourself," Margette said. She waved a handful of chips. "Lots of new music. Come up and hear a concert some time."

"I'd love to," he said, with a grin that said the visit meant more to both of them than just listening to recordings. "Say, have you watched the weather report yet?"

"No."

"Ion storm, two degrees counterclockwise. Make sure everything's bolted down."

Margette sat up in alarm. "It's not coming through me, is it?"

"Shouldn't be," David said. His head tilted down, and the screen changed to show Saturn's great back, and the tiny dot that represented her beacon. Filling the space between them was a swath of sparkling gray. "Here's the projected map. It ought to sweep right past you, but keep an eye out. You can ride out the periphery, but be prepared to abandon ship if necessary."

She frowned, knowing he knew how she felt about keeping station. He must indeed be serious. "I'll watch out," she said.

"That's all I ask," he said. "See you soon." The screen blanked.

Margette took the time out to answer her mail. Chelle on Beacon Four had sent her a pretty air on keyboard in exchange for one Margette had written her before her holiday. Chelle used Margette's theme as the harmony to her melody. Neat stuff. Margette grabbed her guitar and strummed along on the second playthrough. *Very* neat stuff, with almost a syncopated cadence and a complicated change of key Margette had to strain to work out. At once she sent a message to Chelle asking if she could put it on the playlist.

Funny how many musicians ended up as lighthouse keepers, but where else would you get paid for sitting by yourself for six months at a time?

On the professional side, she received dozens of music requests. Some of them had been waiting in the mailbox for months, from way out in space. Ships returning liked their requests timed to be played as they came within earshot. Margette looked at the date of one, glanced up at the yellow characters of the wall chronometer, did a little calculation, and realized that she'd just about have time to put it on the air before the arriving ship crossed the heliopause.

"Here's one going out to Vanessa from Captain Marion," she said. "Love to both of you, and welcome home."

Margette hit the play button right on the mark, and sat back with satisfaction. She didn't want to do anything else all her life.

The job almost maintained itself. The system had triple backups. If the power dropped, the feed automatically shifted to battery power. If the first battery failed, there was another. Fixing it took little to no time at all. Margette's previous employment had been in a solar-reactor power company, where things were always breaking down. The triple redundancy of the beacon system was like a permanent vacation to her. She would wake up at the beginning of shift always happy to be there. Sooner or later the miracle had to wear off, but it hadn't in four years.

At least one of the small packages in her heap of real-mail was more samples. The rep from DRC had been due just before she got back, on his way out to the beacons between here and Alpha.

In the middle of the next long selection, Margette turned on the video repeater station off Neptune.

"*This* is GNN." The stentorian voice over the simple graphic gave way to a shot of a neatly suited woman with red hair reading the weather report.

"In the headlines: the ion storm we are tracking through the edge of Sol System." The woman vanished, to be replaced by a starmap. "The storm, measuring 500,000 kilometers by 7 million kilometers is due to pass the outer orbit of Uranus in the next five days. It's moving very fast. All ships in the area are advised to avoid it."

Margette excerpted the weather report, and worked it into her show at intervals. The information was available on direct beam to ships coming within range, but it didn't hurt to repeat vital data like that.

With a niggle at the back of her memory, she pulled up her e-mail again. One of the mining ships was coming back to Saturn while the storm was likely to be in the area. She stopped the scroll of messages at a note from the *Broadway*. Yes. Their projected flight plan would take them within a few hundred thousand klicks. Depending on which side of her beacon they flew, they'd avoid the storm, or sail right into its heart. Margette sent a message to the *Broadway*, letting them know. She was a lighthouse, but an interactive lighthouse, playing music against the darkness.

Over the next few days, the idea for a song about lighthouses started coming to her in bits and bytes. She hummed it over her tea and in the shower, and while she was setting up playlists. The beacon's song would sound well as a chant in the background.

A message came back from the *Broadway*, thanking her for her vigilance.

"We'll keep well clockwise of your signal," said the captain, a woman in her fifties. "See you soon."

Margette stored the message, then glanced up at the wall chronometer. It showed her position on all three axes from Sol's center. All read normal. In the next long cut, she checked the station-keeping jets, and the weather report. All was well. The storm, though a wild one, looked as if it would miss her. The beacon's song chanted thanksgiving.

She had relaxed too soon. In the middle of her dark shift a hard thump kicked Margette right out of her bunk. She was awake before she hit the deck. Margette scrambled to her feet, feeling for the light. It didn't go on, and the switch felt hot. She dropped to her knees, looking for the emergency lights, then leaped back onto the bunk as blue fire raced through the chamber, climbing up the metal edges of the cabinet, the door frame, the computer table, where two tendrils of power met with a terrifying crackle. Margette ducked as her computer screen burst outward in flame and smoke. The storm had lashed the beacon!

Margette flailed a hand under the edge of her bunk for her slippers, ignoring the pain where a burst of St. Elmo's fire slapped her wrist. She had to get out and make certain the beacon was all right. Another tremendous burst of power swept through the room, going the opposite way, like a wave rushing back out to sea. Margette held onto the cloth cover of the mattress, trying to keep from being thrown off again. The station bucked underneath her, jets roaring against the wave of force, but she held on. The blue fire vanished, leaving her in darkness and silence. Fearfully, she climbed off the bunk. Nothing touched her. It was over. Thank goodness, no radiation alarm.

Where were the emergency lights? Margette thought, as she padded out into the hallway with one hand on the wall for guidance. Suddenly the beacon, her home for four years, felt eerily unfamiliar. Except for the compressors, all was silent. For the first time in four years, she felt terror.

The pale, gray emergency lights and the loudspeakers went on all at once as she burst into the control room. She fought her way through the cacophony, turning down the pots one by one. At that moment, Margette felt her heart rise in her chest, choking her. Something was terribly, tragically wrong.

Her beacon was silent. Probably the storm had shorted the power. Never mind. She twisted the switch for the backup battery system.

Nothing happened. Margette sat in her chair, clutching the edge of the console in flat astonishment. She clicked the switch over to the second power setting. *Still* nothing. Now what should she do? The *Broadway* was coming, would be here within hours. It needed the beacon. It needed her. She had to get the beacon up and running again. She glanced up at where the chronometer should be, and saw only empty gray wall. The smell of burning silicon and plastic was proof, if she needed more, that much of the equipment had been damaged by the passing storm. Under the wan lights she opened one panel after another, exclaiming over the destruction behind them. It looked as though every capacitor had burst, and half the boards were smears of solder and gold wash. She'd been lucky not to have burned to death. At least life support was okay. The station held on its axes.

Margette almost cried out in relief when she opened the transmitter cabinet. Everything seemed to be intact, except that the power cable had snapped. Donning rubber gauntlets, Margette climbed under the console and ran a new cable, and was rewarded by a low thrum that grew in strength.

The VU meters lit as soon as the transmitter power came on, but their needles were fixed at zero. Margette stabbed at the button on the signal generator, waiting to hear the sweet seven-note call. It was dead. When she pried off the faceplate, she knew it was pointless to try again. That meant the computer hail was dead, too.

She had to get some kind of signal out over the air. With every minute Margette felt agitation grow until it threatened to overwhelm her thoughts. She *must* keep her head clear. What about patching in the chip-players? No, every piece of recording equipment was dead, and so was her personal unit. Then what was left?

"Isn't there anything on this beacon that can make

noise?" she demanded of the darkness, then smiled. "Me."
*If* she could make it work.

She grabbed her microphone and cable off the console
and hurried with it to the patch board on the front of the
transmitter. She jury-rigged the panel so impedance
didn't feed back, making her efforts useless. The signal
must be recognizable. It must. Time was running away.
How much was left before the *Broadway* blundered past
her into the storm's heart?

The cable was too short to let her go far. She'd have to
sit right in front of the transmitter. One more moment,
and she opened up the cabinet to find the emergency
radio, miraculously intact. She sent a message to David,
asking for help, praying he wasn't far away. One more
moment, feeling guilty for every second's delay, and she
ran to the gallery for a pitcher of water, a lidded pot and a
towel. It'd be enough for personal matters.

Seating herself with her guitar in front of the transmitter, she began strumming. The soft sound was almost
the only noise in the cabin. Her heart rate slowed.

Margette had to get the pitch and the rhythm exactly
spot on. But it was a part of her, after four years. She
knew it as well as her own heartbeat. Or did she? She
sang the phrase through once. In her panic, her voice
squeezed the seven notes until they were riding three
tones too high. Relax, she told herself. Take a deep
breath. Bring it from the diaphragm. Remember your
training. This is only a coffee shop, and the audience
loves you. You're on. When she opened her mouth this
time, the sweet, round tones came out.

"Hear my song, calling you home. See the path, safely
you go." She paused for a moment, her fingers on the
guitar strings. Her mind went blank, trying to fit more
words into the melody. She sang the same two lines over
and over again, hoping she hadn't been off the air too
long. Her song was her prayer. She longed for the safe
passage of the ships, wondering how far the storm had
progressed between her and Saturn, and where David was.
Could he scramble a repair crew and some equipment
before she ran out of voice?

"Hear my song, calling them home. Ships who sail, the darkest sea/Hear my song! Avoid the storm! Help me now, Beacon Nine's down! Greatest power, preserve their lives. Let not dark, obscure their way."

Margette sang and sang and sang. Her eyes followed the VU needle jumping and twitching in hypnotic rhythm. On the guitar, she played counterpoint to her own voice, varying fingering and harmony to keep the task interesting. At first she was anxious, wondering if her pitch was true, if the ship hadn't passed her during the storm, if indeed the transmitter was working at all. Then the exercise became achingly dull.

One hundred, one hundred and one, one hundred and two times through. . . . Four hundred and fifty, four hundred and fifty one. . . .

Margette caught herself with a jerk as her head drifted down toward her chest. She was beginning to fall asleep. Her fingers fumbled over the strings, and she had to put the guitar down for a while, letting her voice carry the song. Margette counted on her long training to hold the notes correctly. She sang them and sang them and sang them until they were a pulse in her body. Margette was the beacon, the lighthouse in the void, and the song was her heartbeat.

One thousand and one, one thousand and two, one thousand and three. . . . Five thousand and one. . . .

Hours passed. She glanced at the music chips scattered on the floor, and longed to play them, to hear something other than her monotonous chant. Wouldn't it be great to hear that chorale from Earth's Petrillo Band Shell? Sixty voices and acoustic instruments, without a single amplifier. Or that musical comedy she'd seen. The cast album was just there, that blue chip. She wanted to hear anything but her own voice. Her black jumpsuit stank of sweat, and her rear was numb. Why was she doing this? She was quitting this damned job as soon as a replacement could be found.

The music faltered, and her heart jumped into her throat. No! Her mouth dried, and she swallowed. Forget selfish considerations. Of all things she must not allow her own mind to fight her. The beacon must continue! If she didn't discipline herself, people would die. She thrust the beacon's phrase out of her belly again, stronger than before.

"Now I am, Sick of this place," she sang, with a bitter edge to her voice. "Come and help, quick to this place. Beacon's down, I'm singing now. How can I, sing on all day?" She wished for a working chronometer, wondering how long she'd been acting as a drone, doing a job that could be handled by a clock-chip and a windup music box.

At once she was ashamed of herself. She loved her job, and what it stood for. Her mind recalled the soft phrases, proof against the darkness, and the grateful face of the ship's captain. The hundred lines she'd thought up over the years began to come back to her.

"Hear my song. . . ." Nine thousand one, nine thousand two. . . .

The crackle of the emergency radio was the most welcome thing in the universe to her.

"Margette, can you hear me?" David's voice shouted. "Saturn's screaming about an interrupted signal on top of all the storm damage. Every craft in the area's blazing about it, wondering if the radiation got you, too. Then I got your message. What happened? Respond, please. Over!"

Still keeping in rhythm, Margette reached for the microphone and pulled it around to her mouth.

"Keeping on, as best I can," she sang. "Help me now, can't go too long. Ion storm, turned out the lights. Wrecked the place, all machines gone!"

David's voice was amused and concerned at the same time. "Just keep it going, baby. I'll be there ASAP."

Umpty-thousand and what? Margette had at long last lost count. She was almost falling asleep over the guitar when the contact alarm roused her. Limp as a rag, she reached for the receiver.

"Who is there, at Beacon Nine?" The hoarse croak that came out when she opened her mouth alarmed her. She tried for more voice, swallowed water in the intervals between lines, but it wasn't dryness. There was simply nothing left. Margette brought the guitar close to the transmitter, played the seven notes with ridged and bleeding fingers, kept on whispering the words behind it.

". . . Calling them home. Hear my song, calling them home. Hear my song, calling them. . . ."

Behind her the radio was jubilant.

"Ahoy, Margette! This is the *Broadway*. We're close to you. We've been in touch with space patrol, and we're shuttling over our stereo equipment and a deck recorder to you right now. We owe you, lady. We'd have gone right past you into that storm. We'll help you now. You kept going long enough. We're safe."

Margette felt a surge of joy. Her voice came back just for a second, strong and clear. Her prayers were answered, and her song had been heard.

*I've worked as a control room techie in both radio and television. During the television stations' early days, we showed music videos. A technical operator, like a radio DJ, frequently works alone, and while each segment was playing I had plenty of time on my hands. Working out the day's playlist took up only a small fraction of it. When I tried to think of a place for someone in space whose job and passion were music, I thought of those lonely control rooms, and the human touch of the announcer's voice in between cuts.*

# BIRD IN THE HAND
## by Anne McCaffrey

Anne McCaffrey is regarded as one of the best-selling science-fiction writers in the world. Her *Doona, Pern,* and *Rowan* series have all won worldwide acclaim. A winner of both the Hugo and Nebula awards, her recent novels include *Freedom's Landing* and *Power Play.* She lives in Ireland.

I am absolutely no one's idea of a detective—which is probably why I've been so successful in my particular line of work. I am small, dumpy—if you're being kind—and middle-aged. I am, by vocation, a choral singer and because of my particular vocal abilities, I usually sing descants as I can be heard above full orchestra and choir—synthetic or live—and I'm never late, never sick, and never off-key. I'm not sure which is the most valuable in my daily work.

My detecting is something else again. I hear sound very well indeed and can identify (as they do with handwriting) voices, even if they are badly distorted. It's a trick of the mind, I suppose, for someone who has been trained as a singer and a musician, and while I'm not called that often by the Law Enforcement Agencies to use that ability, I've had some very interesting professional engagements which have nothing to do with the stage.

There was that business with the serial killer over on Space Station 84, one of the hub transfer points. They had to close down all traffic which—since space stations rely heavily on a constant supply of food, water, and air—caused major problems. Three big liners had been docked,

each with well over a thousand passengers who were
severely annoyed at being laid over. But until the murderer had been identified and apprehended, no one could
leave.

My task was not easy, since I had to listen to hundreds
of voices—usually rather querulous, which didn't help
my task because I had to identify the murderer on the similarity of a voice recording he had made to the Station's
Peace Guards. I don't understand, myself, why criminals
have to be *sure* everyone *knows* why they're doing this.
It's psychological, but it's also very grisly. This person
thoroughly enjoyed relating the steps by which he
selected his victim and planned the torture and then
method of secreting the body. On a space station which
has to recycle so much, this was particularly gross.

I know they called me in as a last gasp (the air was getting rather stale on the Station by that time) and I know
that the LEO Officer didn't *believe* in my ability. I mean,
you don't expect someone of my undistinguished appearance to be effective.

I had to listen over and over to the details, catching the
nuances of speech, the cadence, and the use of certain key
words. That's what people don't realize. They aren't very
inventive, verbally, and constantly reuse the same
phrases. Well, musicians do it, too. It's called a reprise.

So I immersed myself in these awfully repetitive
sounds until I could almost "sing" his words. A tenor-
range voice. Yes, it was a man, and the victims were of
both sexes and five species, too. He wasn't *that* choosy.
The Station Guards had long since decided his victims
were chosen on a random basis and had advised everyone
to have two or three companions with them if they moved
about the station rings. With just one other companion,
one might very well have also picked the killer.

The Peace Guards couldn't say whether he was a resi-
dent of the Station who had gone spacey or a transient,
but the fact that the awful disappearances continued, and
evidence which "surfaced," (you should forgive my
expression, please) indicated that he was still on the Station. So, perforce, all outgoing vessels had to stay put,

and no incoming ones could give the serial killer the opportunity to escape.

Once I had his voice and verbal patterns firmly in mind, then I had to stroll—with several discreet cover agents always tracking me—through the various function and meeting rooms, through the various liner lounges, trying to isolate the wicked speaker. It took me three weeks and, unfortunately, two more murders, but I finally pinpointed him.

The moment he was arrested, he broke down. No, not in remorse for his crimes, but to elucidate, once more, every single moment of every single victim's final agonies. He was an environmental specialist, so, of course, he had known the many ways of disposing of what remained. And he had gone spacey. I suppose his legal advisers will use that as his defense, but personally I don't think it's valid. They really have to tighten up the psychological testing for Station workers.

However, the most unusual case I ever had to solve was more sensitive than that one. I had to find the birds!

Now that space explorations are discovering more and more diverse sentient races, new precautions have to be taken: sometimes sentience is hard to establish. And, with each new habitable planet producing wonders and beauties that the acquisitive *must* have, a new sort of evil has developed: smuggling in these desirable objects, including some of the new species.

Cats have always been space-goers: useful in their ways at keeping vermin down, independent in their activities and, of course, affectionate pets. Birds, their natural prey, are also space-goers and for the same reason that canaries accompanied miners into the deep pits: they would detect minute quantities of lethal gases. Of course, they'd be dead, but at least the cessation of their singing gave the miners a fair chance at escaping a similar demise.

So cats and birds followed humans, and similar creatures for our alien neighbors went with them into space. Most Space Stations had to limit the population of birds and cats, but they were there and, I must say, working cats did not attempt to eat working birds . . . as if they recognized fellow professionals.

However, there are birds, and then there are other birds. And some of the "other birds" were not only singers but sentient. New laws had to be promulgated, and strictly enforced, to keep the desirous from smuggling off their world and enslaving the Birdfolk of Antares IV. These are perhaps the most beautiful of avians, their feathers ranging from vivid purple to the palest of blues and yellows, with incredible pinions, marked with individual geometric designs of great beauty. The males tend to oblique shapes while the females sport circular ones. They grow to great size over their long life spans, so to speak, and outgrow their juvenile stupidities—like any one of many other species including our own.

At first, when Antares IV was explored, it was the frivolous young, trying their wings and increasing their awareness of Life around them, who were noted. The more mature birds, having had their youthful flings, settled down to agriculture or architecture, examples of which gave the best indications of their intelligence. Using a variety of building materials, for when a life-form has a ten-foot wingspan, it can lift heavy objects and deposit them in pleasing geometric patterns, mature Antareans built replicas of their own wing patterns into the design of their permanent abode: the female wing having hers as separate from the male wing for they mated for life, although not until their fifth or sixth decades.

One of the first things the exploring team noticed was that the avians copied their words, somewhat like a parrot from old Terra would. But the copy was not a slightly distorted repetition of meaningless sounds, but an *exact* copy of tone, cadence, and syllable. Whatever the sentence was, the line was repeated by the Antarean and then embellished with cadenza, arpeggios of sound, concerti and symphonies on a single word. For a musician, like myself, listening to Antarean bird song was dessert in the best gourmet dinner in the galaxy. I had several recordings and wished that I could afford a ticket to one of their all-too-infrequent concerts.

However, during the initial stages of contact with the Antareans, the xenologist, also a musician (a cellist, I believe) looked beyond that singsong repetition to discover it an early attempt to communicate. This was substantiated by the appearance of the adult avians who made full sentences out of words and phrases used by the team. At first, a lot of scatological words punctuated comments, but always where such words would be added. Once the Antareans realized what these words were, such were quickly discarded as the useless sounds they are . . . for most swear words don't "sing" well. Such deletions, of course, proved the intelligence of the species and its nicety of expression.

But the innocent nestlings became easy targets for an illicit trade. Caged Antareans never developed adult wingspans nor adult intelligence but their singing speech, human or the beautiful soaring sounds with which they communicated to each other, made them a commodity that was desirable to rich collectors.

Of course, they had to be kept in a soundproof enclosure and the magnificent songs restricted to those who the owner of the avian was certain would keep the matter a secret, for possession of an Antarean juvenile was punishable by deportation to Antares IV. And no government asked what happened to the offenders once they arrived at that destination.

Despite that, there were sufficient covetous and despicable types who wished to possess, however briefly, the nestlings—as much because it *was* illegal and that was in itself a thrill, as to enjoy the performances so that there was a lucrative market for any juvenile Antareans who could be smuggled off-planet. The fact that they died within a few months of their incarceration only increased the trade.

One did have to be careful about accusing anyone of owning an illegal anything. Especially an Antarean juvenile whose neck could be wrung quite easily, since it was caged, and the evidence disposed of irretrievably—

especially since waste disposal was now quite an art in itself. Some red-faced LEO folks "apprehended" the owner of a not-at-all-illegal recording of juvenile Antareans in one of their ritual concerts. So one had to be very careful.

I was approached by Verdi Grisson, head of the criminal branch of Station Administration. Operatives had been following a suspect whose ship was sighted leaving one of the main continents on Antares IV. He had been under covert surveillance for a long time and was known to be a smuggler. His ship was docked at Space Station Prime, undergoing repairs for an unfortunate collision with space debris. Ignatius Brisket (ostensibly a purveyor of fine furs) had arrived with only his pilot compartment containing atmosphere. His manifested cargo didn't suffer from lack of oxygen, being dead already, and the most stringent examination of that same cargo did not uncover a single inadmissible pelt though he had some rare exotic capes.

"He seemed far too pleased with himself, Simona Xing said in her report," Verdi told me as he slid across a fax of the perp. He looked like an Ignatius to me—skinny, with a nose the size of a parrot's beak—and a receding chin. He was dressed in a shipsuit that looked four or five times too large for his frame. Perhaps it had been the first one handy when he realized that he was losing air from his hulled ship. His expression was undeniably smug.

"Smug is not admissible evidence," I replied, although I knew such hunches were the stuff top-notch Security folks never ignored. The statistics of how many hunches materialized into solid fact is a fascinating document.

"Very true, but it makes him suspect, especially when Simona also says there's been incoming traffic of some very particular types." He winked slowly. He named a very well-known Name who had expensive hobbies and esoteric tastes.

"Have they been tagged?"

Verdi grinned. "Not so's they'd notice."

As well they shouldn't, I thought privately. There could be severe ructions if someone was tagged, discovered the

tag, and raised all sorts of trouble. Tagging was an invasion of privacy and people could get upset about such
invasions: generally just the people who needed to be
tagged, of course, which didn't make LEO's job any
easier.

"You've improved the mechanism?"

"Constantly," Verdi answered with a slightly sour twist
to his lips.

I had always liked Verdi. He was a grandfather and a
very pleasant man off-duty. He frequented concerts by the
chorale society that employed me so he had good taste as
well. I'd even given him, his wife, and members of his
extended family free tickets now and then when there was
a concert of ancient music that I knew he'd enjoy and
which wouldn't have that much of an audience anyway.

"We've tagged nineteen," he added and I regarded him
with great surprise.

"And they all think they're going to be delighted with
their . . . ah . . . upcoming acquisitions."

"That's just it, Armana," he said with a twist of chagrin
to his broad shoulders. He doesn't look or act like a
grandfather. "They're all pretending they're here on some
convention. . . ."

"Illegal Possessors of the world, unite! We have
nothing to lose but our clandestine belongings?"

"It's a legally registered convention. That's the problem," and he sighed again. "I know there're Antarean
juveniles involved. The Antarean government has even
sent the geometrics of the missing nestlings . . . that's
where our new tag comes from: they're taking direct
action against such invasions."

"Really?" I was dying to know the parameters of the
improvement, but I also knew better than to ask.

"It'd be easier for us if they had off-planet tracers, too,
but these are geared only for Antarean ears. They know
what's been taken but not where the birdlings are right
now."

"Oh. But you said Ignatius arrived in a damaged ship,
with only the pilot compartment airtight. How could
Antarean juveniles survive without oxygen?"

"Yes, precisely. It may be why he's so smug. He's figured out a way. We've had the most acute listening
devices attached to his hull to detect the least chirp but we
haven't heard a sound . . . or rather, not the sound we're
listening for."

"And you think I can do better?"

Verdi pointed his stylus at me. "I think he's got the
birds secreted somewhere on the Station. They may still
be unconscious because that's about the one thing that
shuts up an Antarean juvenile. But he's got to revive them
soon or they'll be dead and worthless feathers. Which
lose their color the moment their host is dead, you know."

"Hmmm." I hadn't, but one learns something new
every day. "Unless . . ." I know it was an outrageously
whimsical thought . . . "he's found a way to shut their
mouths for them."

Verdi blinked at me, did a double take and then stared
at me in wide-eyed surprise.

"They have to open their mouths, you know, to sing.
They can't hum." I embroidered on that theme by saying,
"And if he had also dyed their feathers with one of those
wash-out preparations, without their feathers, you'd never
give them a second look. They're just birds . . . and, if
they're real nestlings and have never flown, they're not
much bigger than Station canaries."

"Oh, my God, he might have hidden them right out in
the open!" Grisson fumbled for his contact button and ini-
tiated a link with his on-Station contact. I suspected that
Station Prime was in the middle of a three-ringed
scramble. "Yes, you heard what I said. Check all the
canaries on the Station to see if they can sing. If one can't,
wash its feathers. . . . No, it's not an invasion of privacy if
you suspect there's a virulent disease that's killing down-
side canaries and may have been transported, innocently
of course, to the Station. . . . Yes, I have a good idea how
many canaries are on the Station. . . . First check the guest
facilities of any of those we had tagged. . . . So they'll
scream 'invasion.' Do they really want to infect every
bird on the Station? And those who scream the loudest are
doubly suspect. . . . Yes, I can do that." He covered the

speaker and grinned at me. "Can you double as a songbird specialist?"

"I don't see why not, but I'd best have a briefing on legitimate symptoms and stuff."

Verdi uncovered his speaker. "I'll have experts up to you as soon as we can arrange transport."

"Just how many Antarean juveniles were snatched?" I had thought in terms of eleven or maybe an even dozen.

"Twenty. That's two-oh," Verdi replied and it was my turn to stare at him bug-eyed.

"No wonder!"

I went up to the Station in the company of a baker's dozen of genuine ornithologists who gave me the buzz-words I needed—like feather mold, and mites, and decayed claw, and raddled beak, and other such things. I was told where to locate the tags the adult Antareans had placed on their nestlings . . . cleverly attached to the wing in the armpit: not an easy place to access when dealing with an active avian. The "disease" we were supposed to identify required stretching the pinions and discovering a body rash which was the first manifestation. Lack of appetite was another, so that if we offered tidbits to the bird and it didn't open its beak to scoff it right down, we knew that it was either sick with this fictitious disease and could be confiscated, or it had its beak glued shut so it couldn't sing and give itself away.

I was given a set of gloves with extra padding which might protect me from an irate junior birdperson but would also make examination a little difficult. Fortunately the shuttle had its own—legitimate—canary and so I was allowed to practice opening wings and inspecting bird armpits. The canary submitted gracefully but grew short-tempered about repetitions and I was grateful for the extra padding.

But twenty juveniles! And on a station as large as Prime.

As I mentioned at the outset, I don't look at all like a detective, and so I was assigned with one of the legitimate ornithologists. They had all been appalled at the kidnapping of Antarean juveniles and quite willing to help. Dr.

Zozi Tuma, my partner, specialized in predators: owls, eagles, falcons, and such. They were being assiduously protected so that actually the populations had been increasing back on Earth. He was as unlikely a detective as myself, for we were of the same build and size.

During the course of our lengthy investigations, I heard one of the local Station personnel refer to us as Tweedle dee and Tweedle dum; but I'm used to such nonsense. It did upset Zozi, though, and I don't blame him.

However, it was amazing to me just how many canaries there were on Station Prime—one in every cubicle it seemed—and how many actually had some of the diseases I had been instructed in. I got so I was as proficient as Zozi in diagnosing both the ailment and specifying the cure. Some people shouldn't have the care of any living creature, even a canary.

I digress. The three five-star spotels featured the inclusion of a canary in every one of their suites as an extra added precaution. We hit paydirt, as it were, in the first suite we entered. As each of the eleven suspects were having their birds spontaneously inspected at the same time, we were able to surprise and arrest the offenders. Naturally, they protested their innocence: the birds had been supplied by the management; how were they to know that the avians were kidnapped Antareans. (Proof was supplied by large credit transactions from nine of the eleven to a numbered account which would be investigated by the local Fraud squad.)

So we got nine in the first go-'round and the illegal possessors were privately whipped off the Station in the same shuttle that had brought us up. That left eleven to be located. And fast, time was running out. The birds had to eat soon, and they had to have their beaks unglued in order to partake of the necessary refreshment.

Ignatius Brisket was under close surveillance and, from his idle ramblings around the Station, it was obvious he knew he was. So where were the remaining birds?

By that time I had met Simona Xing, head of Station Security. She had made all the arrests of the notables. ("The least courtesy I can do them under the circumstances," she'd told me with a grin. She looked no more like the crackerjack security officer she was than I did, being a tall, willowy brunette with a Eurasian cast of countenance . . . (inscrutability was of paramount importance in her job.) . . . and seen them off, incommunicado (even to their legal advisers who were back on Earth anyway).

"Look, some of those men and women will get off, I'm sure of it," I said, knowing all too well how such matters were contrived. Only the "little" ones would be fed to the Antareans, as it were. (And maybe it was. I never inquired for details though they deserved everything they got.)

Simona laughed. "That's up to the Antareans, of course, but they'll pay up to do so since the Antareans are busy upgrading their internal administrative systems and that's one way of financing it."

I stared at her, hearing what she wasn't saying out loud. "You mean, they may have connived in . . ."

Simona gave me a bright smile, the kind a teacher would give a student who had finally got the answer to a troublesome ethical problem.

"I hear you singing, Armana," she said, wiggling her fingers at me to indicate I should not pursue that line of inquiry.

"Of course," and I salved my twinging conscience with this, "it's the notion that any other species would enslave another that's appalling and must be curtailed." I considered. Well, to catch such perverts one did have to bait the trap, didn't one? Poor brave birdlings. I only hoped we found the remaining victims.

"Since the others were, so to speak, in plain sight," Simona said as she led me down the service alleys of Station Prime, "we might consider that's Brisket's modus operandi. I'm sure he didn't put all his eggs in one basket, as it were, so let's try the next most obvious place."

So she led me to the Station Aviary, a huge enclosure housing those birds circulated to Station personnel, both permanent and transient. In between work assignments, the birds were set free in the huge facility, to fly or mate, if they wished. There were trees and vines and all sorts of bird places, including delightful bird baths and feeding stations.

When we arrived, we found the aviarian near one of the feeding stations, trying to revive a lump of feathers that had fallen to the ground. It had been seriously pecked. Which is what birds do to a nonconformist. I ran to help.

"Is it an Antarean?" Simona yelled after me.

When releasing the caged juveniles in the guest quarters, I had been supplied with a solvent for the glue used to keep their beaks closed. Pushing my way to the floored bird, I fumbled for the solution in my pocket, forgetting in my haste to reglove my hand as I dribbled drops on the beak's edges. The bird was limp in my hands as I also felt for the tabs which would proclaim its true identity.

"Here's another one," I cried triumphantly just as Simona . . . and Zozi who had been called by the aviary keeper to attend to the fallen bird, reached me.

Zozi, with trembling and careful hands, felt its breast for life signs. He was shaking his head ruefully when all of a sudden the bird roused and gave me a savage bite on the finger.

"Hey, I've been rescuing you, you . . . you . . ."

The angry bird was notably unimpressed by my complaint and I let Zozi tend to it, allowing it a few drops of water after its long dry period, and then a few carefully soaked pieces of nutritive feed.

I stood on the sidelines, sucking my injured finger. It had quite a peck for a juvenile.

"And that poor bedraggled thing is an Antarean?" the astonished keeper asked me.

"I think we better check any other birds that have been pecked or aren't eating," I said, rousing to a sense of duty.

We found four others, one so badly injured that it died shortly after we found it. That only made finding the rest of the birds more urgent. They had reached the end of their internal resources, and would have to be fed and watered or die. A half dozen more.

Three were traced by records showing who had rented birds for private use. Two of these folks had noticed their birds were not eating and had managed to release their beaks. They hadn't thought to wash the creatures and discover their true plumage, but at least they'd tended them. That left three. And time was running out for them.

Then Simona had a call from the surveillance team: Ignatius had given them the slip in the public toilet on the Mall.

"And you fell for that worn-out ploy?" she cried, not a thing inscrutable about her dismay and opprobrium for the erring agents who had let him slip. She had a fine command of curses, too.

"Look, he's probably got to release the others, wherever he had them stashed," I said.

"And we've got to catch him in possession because we have no other proof of his complicity in this mass kidnapping."

"You don't?"

She stared at me as the teacher to the dense child. "No, we don't. No one has connected him with their theft or their delivery. The recipients of the birds are unanimous that they had no contact with the purveyor. They received anonymous messages that they would find a surprise in their spotel suites. And they did."

"But they'd paid credits. . . ."

"To an anonymous account and just prior to coming here to that convention of theirs. Nothing to connect Brisket with them."

"So, we have to catch him with a bird in hand, so to speak."

"Got it in one, Armana. Of course, the return of the juveniles is very important, too, and we've rescued them."

"All but the one pecked to death." That sad bunch of drab feathers was going to haunt me. Then I had a sudden thought. "If the others have to be fed and watered, they'll also have their mouths free to sing with, won't they?"

"Yes," Simona said but failed to immediately grasp my intent. When she did, she shook her head. "You would never be able to cover the Station."

"But don't you have an audio override? Can't you

access, at least as a listener, every facility on the Station?"

"Yes, we can—but only in emergency situations."

"Well, this is one. Life and death of an Antarean juvenile . . . if he hasn't decided to wring their necks." I went over to the immense comunit that covered one whole wall of her office space. "Open up all channels."

"All?" She stared down at me as if I'd lost my senses.

"All!"

Her hand hesitated over the appropriate bank of switches. "If that's what you want. . . ."

The cacophony that resulted was, indeed, overwhelming, but my ears had been trained for just such inundations of sound. And over all the many voices and noises, I heard the ones I was listening for, faint and certainly buried in the torrent of noise, but audible.

"They're free!"

She rolled her eyes. "However can you tell?"

"I can. Look, can you turn off areas one at a time . . . then I can isolate the song."

"You can?" She did not believe me. But she did as I asked.

I heard the thread of song, barely discernible, but audible to my finely trained ear. I lost it on the nineteenth of the twenty switches on the board.

"That's storage area," she said, staring at the legend. "How did he get them in there?"

"Maybe." Simona was not the only one to have hunches. Mine came on seeing the outsized garb Brisket still wore. He had had the freedom of the Mall: he could have purchased clothing that fit. Instead he still wore his baggy shipsuit, the blouse overlapping his belt, the sleeves and trouser legs appropriate for a man three times his weight. "He hasn't been physically searched, has he?" I asked her. As her eyes widened in astonishment, she nodded. "He's had them on him all the time."

"Good God!"

She closed other switches on that massive board. "I've closed all the security hatches in that sector. We'll have him . . . feather-handed," and she grinned at me.

She spoke brief commands to those in the duty room and gestured for me to follow her. We took the service ways, a full patrol of security guards with us. As I have said, I may be dumpy but I'm fit, and I prided myself that I was only a bit out of breath when we reached the storage area where we had trapped our "bird." Even those with me could hear the faint sound of Antarean juveniles, in chorus.

Oh, but it was a lovely sound. I stopped, not only to catch my breath which was nearly taken away by the beauty of the singing but to enjoy it. Suddenly, one voice was silenced.

"Quickly," I cried, leaping forward and then not sure where to go.

Simona knew and we were through the secured access door at the flick of fingers on the numberpad.

"Oh, quickly, quickly," I cried, not wanting another heap of feathers on my conscience.

The mellifluous song had taken on a shrill, helpless tone now. But we were in an anteroom, doors all around us. Which one? The sounds were muffled now. I put my ear to first one door then another . . . and at the third I gestured wildly for the security guards to break it.

And there he was, in the process of glueing a beak shut again while the other two birds fluttered from the tethers with which he had secured them to the perches where he had fed and watered them.

Flashes from behind me indicated that he was being photographed with bird in hand. And two on the perch. I shot Simona a glance of pure triumph as she slapped restrainers on his legs and arms, and then carefully removed the Antarean juvenile from his possession.

I took the nestling from her and applied the glue dissolver at which point it broke into a paean of exultant gratitude.

I'm not what you would expect a detective to be nor even a singer. Singers haven't been dumpy since metabolisms were programmable. But I liked being different and I really think my guts provided me with the mass to

produce the sounds I could. Not sounds such as adult
Antareans can produce.

But very few people in this century have been given an
individual concert by the foremost Antarean singers. And
no one else was ever asked to sing a descant with them!

*Although I was certainly delighted to be co-editor with
Elizabeth Ann Scarborough, I wasn't so sure I could think
of what to write myself—especially as I read more and
more high-caliber submissions.*

*Then, one morning on the BBC, there was a report on
the smuggling of exotic birds into England. They were
drugged and rolled up in mailing tubes and sent via post
from their natural habitat to England and the bird
fanciers. Many, of course, did not survive such man-
handling. But I suddenly thought of an immediate way to
tell the story of tracking fowl smugglers in an sf context.
And put in a little of my past glory, too. Some stories are
more fun to write than others. This was one of those!*